The Black Lily

BELLA HABIB

E-mail: bellahabibwriter@gmail.com
Instagram: bellahabibofficial

ISBN: 978-1-9192575-0-1

Publishing services provided by Bookbow Publishers Ltd.
Edited by Sajida Sanusi of Bookbow Publishers Ltd.
E-mail: editor@bookbow.com
Website: www.bookbow.com

Cover design by Haleemah M.

1.

The Hertworth's union was by all standards what every young girl could wish for in a marriage.

Miss Marianne Blaby had met Mr Edmund Hertworth shortly after he had returned from one of his leisurely expeditions. He was the exemplary personification of everything her heart had always desired in the man she wished to marry. His physical attributes may not have been particularly in vogue, but Marianne had been enraptured from the moment she laid her eyes upon him. He was elegantly built, and despite all his travels, he possessed a very fine, fair complexion. His sharp, dazzling eyes were dramatically imposing. As for his hair, though it often looked quite unkempt, he wore his luscious raven curls in accordance with the high fashion of the time. However, as he seemed to find it rather an inconvenience, he would often resort to a ribbon or some other fitting to keep them in place. To add to her luck, he also happened to be the first born son, and would eventually succeed his father as Lord of the Hertworth Estate.

Edmund and Marianne's sudden marriage had caught many people by surprise, including Edmund's highly opinionated mother. But this mother was clever enough to condescend to her son's union with a mere daughter of a clergyman, as the highly reprehensible degradation of the alternative could have stirred such a disgrace, she would not fathom to even speak of it within her own mind, let alone discuss it with any of her many acquaintances.

Edmund's mother, the current Dowager Lady Priscilla Hertworth, had given birth to two sons, but she happily indulged her first born, as Edmund was by far her favourite out of the two.

He had been the exemplary child any mother could wish for, and as he grew, she would often disclose, to whomever would take care to listen, how her son had indeed been born for some superior distinction in one field or the other.

He thrived in his education and had great excellence in his understanding and principles. He was capable of great passions for whatever topic aroused his attention, while being quite talented at governing his feelings. She always believed politics would do quite well for him, as worldly affairs seemed to interest him very much. However, she would also often observe how she despised the common mothers who tried to influence their children according to their wishes. So, whatever Edmund chose for himself would have been just fine by her, as her beloved son was by far without any faults!

That was, of course, until his mother's heart was dealt a blow when her dear Edmund returned from his excursion from the south of the continent of the negros. The oddness of his fancy was indeed a step too far, even for someone as indulgent as she considered herself to be. Therefore, better having a respectable English woman, no matter how lowly connected she may be, as the future mistress of Hertworth Manor, rather than her precious son possibly considering.... well, the unspeakable!

It had been five years since the mother had been forced to accept Edmund's marriage to Marianne, however, the couple were still yet to produce an heir.

But, by the grace of God, the desired outcome started unfolding after Marianne's third miscarriage...

2.

"What good are you to me if you cannot help me give my husband a child!"

Inside her private chamber at Hertworth Manor, Lady Marianne was rebuking the family doctor. It had been a few days into the familiar bleeding, and all her hopes had been dashed – yet again.

"I refuse to believe all those years you spent with your head immersed in those books avail me for nothing!"

"You mustn't despair so! Indeed, you are still very young, and it is my conviction you are more than capable to bring a child amongst us," Dr Hashford offered.

"How, Henry? How! I have failed him once again!" She cried in anguish. "He must now think of me as nothing but barren. And his mother… oh, Henry! You cannot begin to comprehend my desperation! None of you can!"

"W-well, Marianne... I-I suppose it is my duty as the caretaker of your health to discuss some findings with you...," he appeared visibly uncomfortable with the conversation he was about to engage in.

"What findings?"

"I... uhm, I have examined you time and time again, and as the person whom you have made responsible for your hopes, I had taken the liberty of extracting samples from your previous losses...," he confessed.

"You did what?!"

"I... please, Marianne, allow me to explain," he pleaded. "Well... having done so, I then discussed my diagnosis with a man whom I highly esteem, and I am happy to say that he is of a similar opinion as me... however," he then hesitated, "we just do not agree on the proceedings in order to provide you with a solution!"

Dr Henry Hashford had been a part of Marianne's childhood. They had grown up together, and as far as Henry thought, planned their future together.

From quite an early age, he had proven himself capable of distinction for his scientific thirst and talent, and as he went away, he had supposed her supportive of his aspirations in furthering his knowledge.

Naively, he led himself to believe Marianne's loving countenance was enough reassurance to suppose she would wait for him. Until one day, he received a letter informing him of her sudden marriage to the future Lord Edmund Hertworth!

Henry was uncommonly young for a doctor who had managed to achieve the notoriety the local papers were eager to write about. He was also quite a handsome man as far as the general beauty standards went. He indeed possessed the fairness in his features so popular amongst many of the local girls. His eyes, in particular, were of such a blue shade, you would be forgiven to feel you were losing yourself in the depth of a storm in the ocean every time you looked at him.

By the time Marianne had met Edmund, she had already stacked a considerable number of articles from the local papers, each lauding Henry as a man of science. And so, when Marianne heard Henry had returned to their local village as Dr Hashford, instead of choosing to head off towards further glory, the most natural course of action was to recommend her dear, long-time friend to her illustrious husband as the family doctor.

"What solution?! I beg you Henry, stop talking in riddles and tell me if there's a way to end this endless agony!" Marianne cried, pulling Henry out of his own thoughts.

"Very well, Marianne, I will make myself plainly clear to you. I… I am of the opinion you are perfectly capable to conceive and birth a healthy child, and lately it has become my conviction that perhaps the reason for your troubles could be connected to a... a repairable malfunction of your internal physiology!"

Marianne stared at him blankly for a moment before replying, "Are you saying, Henry, that I am perfectly capable of birthing a child, however due to some faults inside of me, I cannot?"

"Perfectly so, Marianne!"

"I have never heard of such notions! And pray, how do you suppose this revelation to bring me any comfort?!" She turned away from him. She would have risen from her chair and walked away, if she could. "You have done nothing but add to my shame! I will never be able to fulfil my obligation to this family, and soon enough he will be rid of me!"

"But this news should bring you comfort, Marianne!" Henry urged. "I told you there is a remedy! This man I told you about... he is considered a genius! He has conjugated a concoction which he claims, and he has proven it too, if taken correctly and consistently throughout one's pregnancy, would result in a perfectly healthy child in the end, Marianne!"

Marianne could not believe her ears; she turned her gaze back to him expectantly.

"I must add, however, that men such as your father may not approve of such ways. This method is purely a scientific procedure, and some men of conscience may deem it possibly heretical. Also... there are concerns about the potential adverse and possibly long-term effects of such a medication–"

"–Henry," Marianne did not let him conclude, "I am sure you have assessed all the risks. You would not have come to me with such information had you not already done so! Lily dear, please help me out of this bed!" she then said, calling her companion to her.

"Now, tell me, where is this doctor of yours? You must bring him to me immediately!"

"That is part of the current predicament too... Marianne; he is all the way in the East Indies."

"Well then you must persuade him to come here!"

"That is not possible unfortunately; for I know he cannot be persuaded to come to us."

"Offer him whatever he pleases; price is not a concern, as you know very well."

"He is not that sort of man, Marianne."

"I have never heard of a man who does not have a price! Tell him of my name, surely he must have heard of the Hertworth's influence!"

"Well, Marianne, I can guarantee you he will not agree to leave his beloved India for anyone! I believe you must make your way to him instead."

"Well... in that case, Lily dear, what do you say to Henry's ideas?"

"I would not know...," the companion responded. "But may I suggest you seek his lordship's council before you make a decision?"

"We certainly cannot involve Edmund in any of this!" cried Marianne most resolute, "he must have no awareness of it all!"

"Perhaps you may request a change of scenery?" Henry suggested. "It is not uncommon for a wife, in times of indisposition, to require such considerations." He straightened slightly before he proceeded, "and if you wish, it will be my pleasure to come along with you. I could personally escort you during your visits to Dr Bathia, Marianne. Your husband need not be bothered at all."

"I suppose a change of scenery will do me some good," Marianne agreed. "What do you say to that, Lily dear?"

"I am afraid I really cannot envisage his lordship consenting to journeying all the way to India for a mere change of scenery," the companion felt compelled to say.

"But, my dear," Marianne stretched out her arm towards her, "You have also been looking rather forlorn lately, and Edmund does care a great deal about your wellbeing too. I am certain if you were to suggest it, he may be more inclined to consent to my wishes after all."

Lily moved closer to her ladyship and readily took her hand, "Will he not think it rather mundane, Marianne? Considering the pain and suffering your body must be enduring at present?"

"Hence why you, my dear, must be the one who ought to be in need of it!" Marianne concluded with a smile.

*

British East India, Mumbai, November 1876

The home where Lord and Lady Hertworth had taken residency was situated in one of the most distinguished neighbourhoods of the city.

The glamorous residence offered all that was to be expected from the finest of Indian abodes. The owner of this home was himself another notable Englishman who had been stationed here to command one of the many British troops of her Majesty the Queen.

Though not lacking in fortune himself, how could the General decline the large sum Lord Hertworth's steward had offered him; better still, in advance!

The letting of the house came with its own entourage of local servants. Most probably, the General did not wish to risk the welfare of the precious artefacts displayed all over the three-storied house.

These artefacts were relics quite varied in their origin and nature. Some seemed to have been locally obtained, while others had come from faraway places. Judging by their appearance, the General must have paid quite a good sum to come in possession of them; and the result of such a collection was that each corner of the house seemed like a gallery, with each gallery evoking a different theme.

The upper floor of the house, dedicated to the masters quarters, showcased what the general regarded as the most precious pieces amongst his relics. Every wall on this floor was lined with head trophies of wild animals the General had hunted himself.

The General also spared no expense for the comfort of the society he must have liked to entertain around him.

At the back of the house, a large balcony led to an extensive park surrounded by a graceful row of wide-leaved trees. These trees created pleasant gardens ideal for refreshing assemblies but, for now, only a selection of exotic animals the general enjoyed keeping as his own pets wandered freely in his gardens.

Though the Hertworth's acknowledged their polite gratitude for the many local servants left at their service, the couple were always sure to be followed by their own entourage of devoted personnel in every journey they undertook.

Such personnel were Edmund's personal valet, alongside Mr and Mrs Jenkins; a stern-looking steward and his good-hearted wife.

In addition to these English personnel, there was also the presence of Marianne's companion, Miss Lily.

As presentations were made, it was not very clear if the local servants were too pleased to welcome the extra hands. In particular, the butler and housekeeper seemed rather wary of the companion who was standing next to Lady Hertworth almost as if she were her equal. After the expected introductions of Lord and Lady Hertworth, she was the first person to be introduced to them by Mr Jenkins, who also felt it necessary to add that she would be occupying the guest room right across from Lady Hertworth.

On the second day after their arrival, the Indian housekeeper seemed quite determined to restore some kind of balance in the world as she expected it to be!

She could not deny Lord Hertworth's importance in society since her own master felt obligated to vacate his own home for him. However, how could this noble Englishman compel his own white servants to treat such a woman with the deference and respect they all seemed to be offering to her?

In the evening of that second day, shortly after dinner, Mrs Jenkins had informed Lady Hertworth and Lily they would each be procured with their own washbasin; however, Lady Hertworth had long been done with her washbasin and retired for bed, while Lily was still waiting for hers.

In the later hours of the night, Lily, who could not get herself to sleep without refreshing herself, made her way down to the kitchens to find Mrs Jenkins.

Mrs Jenkins surprisingly asked, "Lily dear, what are you doing down here at this hour?! You could have rung the bell for any of the servants to come up to you!"

"I came for the washbasin–"

"–Ah, well, I reckon you're done with it now, then?" Mrs Jenkins interrupted, "I'll send the manservant and have it removed from your room straightaway. You certainly did not need to trouble yourself in coming down here for such a frivolous task," she added, offering Lily a warm smile.

"I thank you, Mrs Jenkins, but I still have not used it. I simply presumed everyone to be busy with their chores."

"Do you mean to tell me they still have not brought the bath up for you?!" Mrs Jenkins gasped, her hands flying to her hips.

"She can use the basin the houseboys have just brought down from Madam's room," the Indian housekeeper suddenly appeared in the kitchen.

"They still have not emptied the water from it, so she needn't bother herself by bringing the water from the well either."

*

Lily knew not what occurred between Mrs Jenkins and the housekeeper, but a very short while after she had sternly been sent back to her room, she did get a fresh bath brought up to her in the end.

3.

It had been three days since the Hertworth's had been tolerably settled despite the intolerable weather.

However, Marianne's anxiety was growing in intensity each passing day.

"I must find a way to keep Edmund engaged out of the house! No matter what I suggest, he seems determined to keep himself indoors!"

"Do not concern yourself so easily, Marianne, I am sure he only needs a little getting used to the weather," Lily offered.

"Didn't he always like to be outdoors?! I really cannot comprehend what he finds so interesting about the library in this house! It's only one to ten in size compared to the library he has back at the Manor!" Marianne continued as she paced the floor of her own chamber, conjecturing all the possible ways she could resort to in order to keep her engagements out of Edmund's knowledge.

At this remark, Lily noticed the offended smirk on the Indian housekeeper's face.

"I am sure there are plenty of good reads to be found in the library here too, Marianne; some of the books downstairs are indeed quite a rarity to be found." Seeing the housekeeper's smirk change into a smile, Lily wished to consolidate it further.

"I had quite given up on finding the book I read to you last night! I will let you know; I went to three different bookshops last time we were in London, but to no avail!"

"Oh please!" Marianne exclaimed, throwing herself back on the beautifully ornamented sofa, right beside Lily. "I am quite convinced I will never understand what you both find in your discourses! If it were up to you, the only occupation worthy of consideration for any respectable person is to sit idly in a library and read all day about some new law or other!

And Edmund is of the same disposition, as you know!" Marianne appeared to find the coincidence rather diverting; however, Lily could not be as amused as her friend.

"You could suggest he goes to seek the society of some of his compatriots from England," Lily proposed. "I am sure you could easily find some familiar names to recommend to him from the many calling cards Mr Jenkins has been receiving since your arrival."

"Upon my word Lily, that is precisely one of the first suggestions I presented to him! But can you guess what he did instead?" And without waiting for Lily to take her guess, she proceeded, "he sent for them to call on him instead! You cannot have missed all those peacock-looking gentlemen who have been marching in and out of the house since yesterday! Some of them, I must say, look so drearily obsequious! Oh, I wish you could have seen them! You would not be faulted to assume they thought they were coming to pay their respects to none other than her majesty the Queen!"

Despite the relief Lily was feeling at the innocuous turn of their conversation; she was again made to feel agitated by the prickled reaction of the attentive housekeeper, so, once more, she felt compelled to reign in Marianne's disregard for such formalities.

"But, Marianne, indeed you cannot fault the same countrymen for their want of propriety and deference wherever they see due distinction. Sir Hertworth may not be the Queen;

he is, however, an excellent connection to procure for anybody fortunate enough to be acquainted with the family name."

This reminder, though it did serve its intended purpose with the housekeeper, also had the unhappy consequence of returning Marianne to her gloomy state of anxiety, and so it fell upon Lily to add, "Talking of propriety, Marianne, should you not be downstairs doing the entertaining alongside his lordship...?"

"I am really not in the mood at present," Marianne responded, offering a look ominous enough for Lily to comprehend the trail Marianne's thoughts had taken.

"Do not lose heart so quickly; you have indeed come this far, Marianne, and one way or the other, I know you will find a way to pay your visit to Dr Hashford's associate."

"I cannot help but despair! Just last night there was this lady amongst the callers, and she was intentionally trying to discredit me in front of Edmund. She was shamelessly excited to 'share the excellent news of the next Sir Hertworth being on his way'!"

"Who is she to possess such news?!"

"She is some wife of an important admiral, I understand."

"I see... but why should her opinion matter to you?"

"Oh, do not let her husband's position mislead you," Marianne sighed heavily, "unlike him, she is young, and quite beautiful I should add, and worst of all she is a distant cousin of Elisabeth!"

The Elisabeth in question was the wife of Edmund's younger brother, Mr Edward Hertworth. Edward had been quite eager to betroth himself and was promptly married soon after Marianne's second miscarriage. His Mrs had already granted the Hertworth's lineage not one, but two grandchildren. However, their idyllic accomplishment did have a dent in it, as both children were females.

"I can quite possibly see her having a boy this time!"

"Come, Marianne, you cannot dishearten yourself so soon! Mrs Edward Hertworth may want to try and credit her own self with a prosperous childbearing; however, you cannot fall prey to her boasting and allow it to affect your own path. After all, you have the advantage of being the one and only Lady Hertworth.

"And you must consider, Marianne, should you fail to perform your expected hosting duties, you would only be allowing Mrs Edward Hertworth to relish her glory even further. And perhaps, just like news of her are being delivered to you, just as so, your exertions, or lack of them, may very well be delivered to her."

"But I really cannot fathom the idea of entertaining anyone in this mood," Marianne sighed, gazing at her own sorry reflection in the mirror.

A mischievous glint entered the companion's eyes, "Well, you could keep yourself outdoors in the gardens and enjoy the company of the real peacocks, while looking like you are leisurely appreciating the company of the pretentious ones indoors!"

A small smile appeared on Marianne's lips, "Very well, but only if you consent to accompany me this time."

"I really should not...," Lily hesitated.

"Whyever not? Am I not the lady of the house? Am I not to decide whom I choose to accompany myself with?!"

"Yes, of course you are, but you must understand this may have a negative repercussion on your own acceptance amongst your society while you are to sojourn here."

"Nonsense! I wish you beside me and that is the end of it!" Marianne declared. "But Lily, I absolutely hate this hairstyle! Change it! These maids understand nothing! I want something grander; do what you do best with me!"

Lily obliged her, and as she applied herself on the hair, Marianne appeared struck by a new thought.

"She has her eyes set on Edmund, you know."

"Who?"

"That Mrs Pembroke!"

"But what of her husband?"

"He is an old man!"

"Well… he may not be as young as her, but he is not too old, I am sure."

"Oh, Lily, do not be so naïve! I know what I see, and I fear I ought to worry this time."

Lily said nothing, only focusing on the final touches of Marianne's toiletry. When Lily had finished and stepped back, Marianne studied herself in the mirror.

"Well?" she then said, "I knew you would make me look the part of a fine, presentable Lady Hertworth."

"You do not need any help, Marianne; you know very well how beautiful you are," Lily offered.

Marianne acknowledged the compliment with a smile, then came to take Lily by the hand; and together, they made their way to face the peacocks and hyenas alongside her husband.

*

"How kind of you, my lord!" Mrs Pembroke was saying to Lord Hertworth as she caught sight of Marianne walking in their direction. "My cousin tells me Lady Hertworth is most fortunate to have you so attentive in alleviating her spirits in spite of her unfortunate failures…," requiring her husband's intervention, she continued, "you certainly would not set sail all the way across the Empire simply to oblige a mere whim of mine!"

"But, my dear, only the very rich can afford such indulgences, and as you know there is nothing to compare with their excellence and wealth," the admiral offered apologetically to his wife.

"But, forgive me, my lord, you have not always been this fortunate, have you? Pray tell me, what dealings has your family ventured in to secure such a standing with the Crown?" the wife pressed, echoing her husband's commendation.

"Ah, but it was our predecessor, Arthur Hertworth!" Marianne stepped forward to answer before her husband could speak. "He was a simple captain at the time, but I am told he single handedly led a valiant force in one of those holy wars, and since then our family has had nothing but gratitude from both Church and Crown."

"You are so well informed, my dear," Mrs Pembroke conceded. "It must be such a joy to have one's own husband spending so much of his wealth on you," she said, succeeding in catching Lord Hertworth's eyes. "Indeed, my lord, your wife's superior elegance is proof of your distinguished generosity... and yet, I must confess, I find it rather curious why a family of your standing would concern themselves with matters of trade as you do?"

"But you must know, our family is not alone in such ventures, I assure you," Marianne interjected once again. "Though I am proud to say the Hertworth's were amongst the very first to trade across all the seas."

"But, my dear lady, even you must admit selling to the French is hardly a patriotic pursuit!"

"Ah, but trade knows no borders, Madam," Edmund obliged, coming to his wife's rescue. "And one might argue that by securing such alliances, we only further the strength of our Empire and highlight the superiority of all that is English, which you must agree is a matter of no small importance, especially in our time."

"Capital! Quite right, Sir, very well put!" the admiral intervened.

"But the admiral tells me you concern yourself with the commercial side of things yourself my Lord," the wife pressed on. "Surely you cannot be lacking in men whom you can trust... I am sure there must be better things to engage your time–"

"–but my husband takes great pleasure in keeping himself engaged beyond the confines of the house," Marianne offered. "He would far sooner busy himself with matters of consequence than spend his days in idleness."

"I see… you must be quite right, my lady. A man must find himself new distractions once the old ones begin to lose their charm."

*

From a short distance away, Dr Hashford observed the exchange.

"I despise not the man, but myself...," he said, his voice low, but loud enough for Lily to hear him.

Dr Hashford had been amongst the evening's attendees, and as Lily had descended with her mistress, he had called her to him.

"You know, I could not understand how Marianne could have chosen him. His manners were so conceited even when I first met him... though in time I came to understand her," he conceded. "You know that frock alone must have cost him hundreds of pounds! And as for the rest of her ornaments, I confess I have no idea."

"But Marianne is happy with her choice," Lily could not help but remind him. "And I understand that to be valuable to you, is it not, Sir?"

"You are quite right, Miss Lily," he admitted, offering her a small but sincere smile, "thank you." He sighed, his expression softening as he watched Marianne. "She does look satisfied with her environment… and her happiness is all that matters! And so, we must secure the heir, must we not, Miss Lily? We have our work cut out for us, you know. I cannot imagine how Marianne is to persuade him to meet Dr Bathia, but she must; and I suspect she will require your assistance, as she so often does."

"Indeed!" Lily exclaimed, before lowering her voice. "I have read a little about it, but I confess, I am entirely ignorant of such things, I scarcely understood a word!"

"You are far too modest, Miss Lily! I knew you would not sit still! So, tell me, what have you read?"

"But it is true, Sir!" Lily protested earnestly. "I understand very little of what is to be done."

Before Dr Hashford could reply, Mrs Pembroke's voice cut through the hum of conversation.

"Ah! That over there must be the peculiar companion we have heard so much about; how exotic of you! But, pray tell me, is she as learned as I hear? And does she give you no cause for concern?"

"Oh yes, she is the best thing my Edmund could have gifted to me!"

"Indeed...?! And so, she has his lordship's approval too!" Mrs Pembroke turned her attention to Edmund, who had become engaged in a conversation with another guest.

"Oh yes, he dotes on her too! I see Elisabeth must have failed to inform you about all matters pertaining to our affairs."

"Yes, quite... and what of the man beside her, he is handsome to be sure! Is he a gentleman?"

"He is our family's doctor, Dr Hashford; and I should tell you, he and I are quite inseparable!"

4.

Fortunately for Marianne, her husband was not one amongst the genteel kind averse to exerting himself. Pretty soon, his lordship was regularly going out of the comforting coolness of the study to brace himself in the stickiness of the testing weather much more often than he would have desired.

So, it was not long before Edmund became occupied with overlooking the commercial books of the Hertworth Fleet, which presented quite a few irregularities against the records periodically sent to the family back in England.

Lady Hertworth was then free to enact the scheme she and Dr Hashford had meticulously agreed upon before their departure from England.

On the Monday of their second week in these parts of the world, Lord Hertworth left the house particularly early in the morning and, expecting his return rather late in the afternoon, Lady Hertworth made her long-awaited visit to the renowned doctor.

In the secrecy of an unmarked carriage, they rode along winding narrow lanes for quite a while, moving further and further from the pretentious glamour of their quarters. There was decay all around them as their vehicle navigated the streets, but as it took its final turns, the scene before them began to transform. The cramped, meagre homes gradually gave way to sturdier, more dignified buildings, some of them freshly decorated with new paint. And the last road they turned into opened into a vast expanse, offering Marianne and her entourage an ample view of an elegant square stretching out before them.

At last, the journey came to an end as their carriage halted beside the most presentable structure around.

Inside the premises, a sense of busyness was all around them, but shortly after their arrival, Henry secured the attention of a nurse who appeared to have been waiting for them.

She was a little woman, with a rather dark brown complexion, very obliging in her ways as she promptly escorted them to the renowned doctor.

Once in his presence, Dr Hashim Bathia was everything Marianne had imagined him to be. He was a severe looking Indian man, quite advanced in his years. Unsurprisingly, his English was as impeccable as the rest of him. There was a certain affability about him, however Marianne was soon to discover such affability was accompanied by a very stern determination of principles.

Marianne's initial meeting with him did not go as she had hoped, and she ended up leaving Dr Bathia's presence with very little hope for her dire prospects.

Though the man stressed how he understood her current plight, the doctor and her ladyship could not get to agree on a clause which, to her, was quite inconsequential, but to the doctor, was certainly vital for the process at hand.

The expected procedure of Dr Bathia's practicum required the active participation of both male and female subjects in order for him to prepare the concoction needed for their ailments. And everyone who knew Dr Bathia knew he was not one to compromise his subject's safety by cutting corners in his modem operandi. Therefore, unless both parties were willingly present, he would not hear of dealing with Marianne on her own.

For Marianne, the ride back to their residency was nothing like their ride to Dr Bathia. All the joy and expectations she had carried with her had now been overtaken by a renewed sadness and hopelessness.

After dropping Marianne and her companion at their residence, back at his own lease not too far from the Hertworth's, that whole night Henry contemplated upon an idea which he had hoped he would not need to consider. However, should Marianne agree to his proposal, this could also prove an excellent opportunity for him as a doctor, as he would finally have the opportunity to observe the acumen of a man who had caused such a stir amongst so many men of intellect back in England.

*

The next morning, in the breakfast room, Henry found Marianne in the same poor dejection he had left her the day before; and her husband was right beside her.

"Dr Hashford, I am rather pleased to see you with us this morning! I am sure Lady Hertworth would greatly benefit if you were to give her something to alleviate her spirits," encouraged Lord Hertworth.

"Gladly, and if Lady Hertworth would not mind having a private doctorly meeting with me, I could perhaps, uhm… convey a solution to her current trouble, which I am sure will lift her spirits up again!"

Those words were more than enough to make Marianne jump out of her chair and almost scream: "Oh, Henry, I knew you would!" but remembering her husband's presence, she calmly said, "please, follow me to the library."

"Dr Hashford, I understand Marianne is very fond of your long-time friendship," Lord Hertworth admonished," and I have no doubt your medical expertise has been of great comfort to her."

Marianne rose up and made her way to the library expecting Henry to follow her, when she realised Edmund was following her too.

"My dear, please do not trouble yourself with keeping me company. We will be leaving for England soon and I am sure you still have plenty of duties you may wish to attend to with your clerk before our departure."

Though Marianne endeavoured to maintain an air of composure, the anxiety depicted on her face betrayed her efforts.

It is certainly true, people are more likely to disclose their dearest secrets while overtaken by their emotions, and, unknown to Marianne, she had finally exposed a glimpse of her mission to her husband.

Edmund did not doubt his wife's loyalty to him in any way.

He understood Marianne well enough to know she had never glanced at another man the way she looked at him from the first day he met her by the cliffs.

However, since their departure from England, Marianne appeared to be possessed by a certain new passion, and such ways may inadvertently risk encouraging another man, a man already in love with her, to take more liberties than he should.

"Am I permitted to at least say goodbye to my wife?" remarked the husband.

Marianne could not fail to sense the tint of annoyance in his voice, but then he proceeded to give her a parting kiss. The kiss lasted much longer than it ought to and felt much more intense than any kiss Edmund had bestowed on Marianne's lips.

As he freed Marianne from his embrace, so lost was he in his thoughts he did not notice his wife's companion walking in his direction on her way to keep Marianne company during the meeting with Dr Hashford.

Edmund and the companion bumped into one another.

To the outside eye, the collision between the two would not have looked of much consequence. The fleeting contact merely resulted in his lordship's arm brushing lightly against her covered chest; a touch so slight it would hardly warrant notice. Yet, judging by their reactions, one might have assumed the impact had been far more ruinous than it seemed.

"I beg your forgiveness, my lord! I really should have been more careful and watched where I was going…" Miss Lily's voice faltered. She wished to say much more to deepen her apology, however, as she looked up at Lord Hertworth's face and saw his expression, she decided against it and kept quiet.

A brief silence followed, during which everyone present expected Lord Hertworth to politely acknowledge the companion's apology, however the sense of discomfort between the two was such, Marianne decided to intervene.

"Lily, I am positive his lordship is not troubled by your clumsiness, is that not right, Edmund dear?"

However, without much of a reply to his wife, he offered Miss Lily a quick bow of his head before he proceeded out of the room.

*

Edmund did not head to the port to meet his clerk as Marianne had suggested, instead he strode towards the study on the other side of the house.

Once inside, he poured himself a generous glass of his strongest wine, downing a good portion, before grabbing a cigar too; and only then, he felt comfortable enough to throw himself on his chair and gather his thoughts.

He remained in such a state for quite a while, and by the time he roused himself from his drowsiness, the air in the room had grown thick with smoke.

Had Lily seen him kiss Marianne in the manner in which he did? This thought was all his mind kept pondering since he had the pleasure of colliding with her.

*

While Edmund was thus preoccupied, Dr Hashford was relaying his ideas in the library.

"Marianne, I have known Dr Bathia and his work for a while, and as you were able to ascertain yourself, he is not the kind of person who can easily be persuaded."

"But, Henry, I assumed you would make him fully aware of the situation, and you would guarantee to him he would receive whatever price his discretion would cost!"

"This is not about discretion for him; men like him like to be dictated by their morals rather than money!"

"By coming all the way here, I have inconvenienced my husband much more than he can suppose! The least he can do is offer me his discretion," countered Marianne fretfully.

"Dr Hashford, please forgive my intrusion, but you alluded to a possible solution earlier...," Lily intervened.

"Indeed, you did, Henry! You would not have come so early unless you had happy news for me!" retorted Marianne, while directing a grateful smile towards Lily.

"Yes, indeed I did. Well... uhm, there may be something Dr Bathia is known for appreciating, I would say." Henry was evidently struggling to put his ideas into words.

"For heaven's sake, Henry, this is not the time for you to start mincing your words! Tell me what it is, and I will be sure to provide him with whatever he appreciates!"

"You see... I have often heard amongst some colleagues of ours that – mind you though, I am quite positive that many of them may be led by jealousy when they accuse a man such as him with these sorts of contentious behaviours – but I do not, and many other colleagues in fact! We believe he must have simply been inspired by his genius mind; I really cannot imagine a kind-hearted man such as him…," Henry was simply blabbering words both Marianne and Lily were struggling to follow.

He had been pacing up and down all along, and deciding to come to his aid, Lily offered him a seat. As he sat, she put a glass in his hand.

Marianne could not contain her nerves as Lily attended to Henry.

"Do you truly have anything to offer other than how much you admire the man's genius?"

"Well… I do," he continued, recollecting his thoughts. "What I am trying to say is that, yes, it is indeed close to impossible to have the man agree to cut corners in his mode of protocol. However, I have heard of a very poorly kept secret amongst many men of science. You see, there are some who speculate Dr Bathia may have a thirst for experimenting… uhm, I would say… yes, that's the idea! I happen to know he has been quite scarce in subjects… uhm, I suppose, subjects like our good Miss Lily here… and I suppose she could very well prove to be a rather appealing inducement for what he does."

"I beg your pardon, Dr Hashford, but may I ask what such subjects would be required to do?" Lily queried in her attempt at understanding this new turn of events.

"Unfortunately, I am not privy to that sort of specific information. To be quite frank with you, I have some vague ideas, but I am unsure about the specifics," Henry wryly explained.

Lily turned to look at her mistress.

"Lily will do it, of course!" Marianne let out, surprising both Lily and Dr Hashford.

"Will I?!"

"Dearest Lily, will you not do this for me? Will you not help in fulfilling my obligations to Edmund…?" Marianne probed.

"I-I... uhm... as you please, Marianne."

*

But unfortunately for Marianne, no matter how tempting a young, healthy, negro in the prime of her life was, Dr Bathia could not be persuaded to enlist Miss Lily as one of his experimental subjects.

"You surprise me, Dr Hashford," Dr Bathia began in his rejection to the three people sitting in front of him, "I assumed you better capable in your judgement of me!"

The Indian doctor then turned his focus directly to Miss Lily.

"Do you have any idea what you may be subjecting yourself to if I was to accept your offer?" There was a certain affability in his address to her.

"My dear friend is indeed very well aware," Marianne responded on Lily's behalf. "In fact, you will find not only is she rather uncommonly exceptional for her kind, she is above all most loyal to me!"

"Indeed, I find myself in agreement with you, Lady Hertworth! She does appear singularly favoured in her current position...," observed the doctor, as his gaze remained fixed on Lily.

"Quite right you are! She does indeed have my favour," Marianne added.

"What about the favour of his lordship?" Dr Bathia countered, surprising everyone in the room.

"I fail to comprehend how my husband is to have anything to do with our point of discussion!" Marianne exclaimed, appearing rather disturbed by the query.

"I beg your pardon, milady; of course, I didn't mean to imply anything untoward in your personal affairs, but you must understand, I cannot risk any adverse consequence from someone in the position of Lord Hertworth."

"I assure you, Dr Bathia, I am here out of my own wish," Lily intervened at last.

"Oh, what a surprise! You do have a tongue of your own, I see!" Dr Bathia teased. "However, I regret to inform you all, it will not suffice. There is only one way to secure my services! Bring the man along with you next time you come to see me, or you can stop wasting your and my time! And now, I must be allowed to excuse myself, as I have real patients to attend to!" he concluded, dismissing them all from his presence.

5.

It had now been two days since Lord Hertworth had his wife and her companion followed.

Something about Dr Hashford's doctorly conduct had begun to make him feel quite uneasy. The report given to him stated Marianne and Miss Lily had been visiting a local physician in the company of Dr Hashford. He was made to understand the neighbourhood where this building was situated was a place where he would certainly not like his own women to be around.

"What in God's name would you be doing in this part of town?!" Edmund's voice rang sharp as he came upon his wife from the intersection of the alleyway. "How could you expose yourselves to this sort of danger! Around here people are not accustomed to women such as you two," he continued, as his gaze turned to pierce his wife's companion. "You cannot begin to imagine what sort of situations you could possibly put yourself in!"

He then caught sight of Dr Hashford returning with the carriage.

"Hashford, I should have known you were behind this! Only a desperate man such as yourself could possibly tempt them to venture into this squalor! You must know this part of the city is where kidnapping women such as her is a favourite sport for the locals!" he yelled, pointing to Miss Lily.

Edmund would have happily carried on lashing out at Dr Hashford, but his attention was caught by the sudden appearance of a man from within the building.

"I am the person your wife has been coming to see," Dr Bathia informed. "You are directing your reproach in the wrong direction... my lord!"

"And who might you be?!" Edmund retorted, turning to Dr Bathia.

"I do not believe here is the appropriate setting for the explanations you require. As you can see, you have attracted enough attention towards your ladies."

The scene unfolding at the entrance of Dr Bathia's premises had gathered quite a few local spectators. Many of the bystanders seemed quite engrossed with Miss Lily's presence amongst people who visibly resembled the emblem of British nobility at its best.

"Take her back to the carriage, now!" Edmund then ordered his wife.

"But... what will you do?!"

"You do not need to worry about what I will do for now; do as I said, now!"

He then turned to address Dr Bathia, "Listen my good man," Edmund began, "I must say I am rather impressed by your manners, and as I understand, my wife has been visiting you more frequently than I would have liked, therefore you, or whatever you do, must mean something to her. I will gladly forget about your inexcusable behaviour and not take it up with the authorities if you would be very quick in relating to me whatever it is you have to do with my wife!"

"You are more than welcome to report whatever you wish to whomever you desire. In fact, I suggest you leave my premises and get your answers from your wife yourself!" Dr

Bathia countered. "Now, if you would excuse me, my lord, I would like to bring our meeting to an end!"

It was not common for Dr Bathia to lose his calm, but he was possessed by a very strong dislike towards anything which highlighted his countrymen's servitude to the few, but highly snobbish Englishmen representing Her Majesty's authority.

Perhaps he was wrong to mirror his feelings about the British empire on this man; he did not know much of him after all. But this man's arrogance did emblem the British way at its best.

*

"Only in such a squalor amongst these people could Hashford have found a person to give credit to any of his preposterous ideas!"

Inside the carriage, Edmund was the first to break the silence, "I knew you were up to some kind of mischief; but this is certainly a new low, even for you, Marianne!"

"Edmund... I confess, all I want is to give you a child!"

"For the love of God, Marianne!" He stared at his wife and her companion for several moments, incredulous at what his ears had heard. "How could you have been so damn reckless to drag us all the way across the other side of the world believing anything but God can give a child!

"What sort of witchcraft has your doctor been feeding into your head?!"

"It is not witchcraft, Edmund, I assure you! That man... he has his ways... I-I wish I could explain it to you myself, but I do not quite understand the science behind it, but he can give us a child!" Marianne insisted. "If only you would listen! Lily, you must tell him, Lily believes it too!"

"Do not waste your breath, Marianne; there is nothing anyone can say to persuade me against what I have personally witnessed! Besides, what can she have to say against any

31

outrageous speculations I can only presume you must be referring to! This is indeed what is bound to happen when half-breeds of obscure understanding try to elevate themselves to the practice of our sciences. No reputable man of science back in England would ever suggest such notions. Indeed, they better leave such matters to our kind!"

"Edmund, I know you cannot mean that," his wife felt compelled to respond. "I have never heard you attribute obscure understanding to Lily; and we all know how much you value her mental accomplishments!"

"What does she have to do with any of this?! It goes without saying, she is not included in my observation of them!"

"But whyever not? If as you say, Dr Bathia's opinion is to be disregarded because of his nature, then surely anyone else who is not from our kind cannot be worthy of having a worthwhile opinion!"

"I am quite at loss at what you might be implying here Marianne, but all I will say to you for now is, I never should have consented to come to this blasted, god-forsaken place!"

"Lily herself has convinced me knowledge is to be appreciated whenever one may find it," Marianne pressed on, "and… besides, you ought to know she too agrees with Dr Hashford's suggestion."

"Are you still talking of Hashford to me?! I could not care two straws for what your precious Hashford and the likes of him may think of these heretical ways; they are all made of the same essence as far as I am concerned! I am not surprised their reasoning is as dark and filthy as their appearance!"

"Edmund!" Marianne exclaimed, "you have made your thoughts quite clear enough for today!" she then ventured to hold Lily's hand in hers.

Lily, for her part, had been diligently sitting beside Marianne, and though she was very well versed in appearing as if she may not be there; she could not help suddenly looking up at Lord Hertworth. And his lordship managed to catch a glimpse of the offence his words had caused to her before she quickly resumed her blank expression and returned her gaze upon her own feet.

Silence had fallen back in the carriage as each occupant became absorbed in their own considerations, and when the carriage arrived at the residence, Marianne was the first out of the trio to descend from it.

It appeared Marianne supposed her husband would follow suit, but contrary to her supposition, Edmund did not follow her into the house. Instead, he remained quietly sat in the same manner since his eyes had locked with the offence he had caused to Lily.

'Look at me...,' he was mentally imploring her, 'look back at me and I will make it right!'

However, not only had Lily masterfully hidden the hurt he had caused with his words, but her face had now reacquired the very familiar unaffected composure she was very good at presenting to the world.

6.

The first meeting between Edmund and Miss Lily had occurred several years prior, when Mr Hertworth had been the one to rescue her from her previous employer after he happened to witness the villainous conditions she was expected to work in.

Much like his father before him, Edmund took great pride in their Englishness and did not hide his beliefs in the superiority of the English above all subjects of the Empire. Yet, in one crucial respect, he differed from the late Lord Hertworth: Edmund could not, in all conscience, agree with the vogue of the time and suppose the rest of humankind should not be granted the decorum and politeness owed to all of God's creation.

Lily, who was not always referred to by this name, had been employed at the residency of one of the prominent Dutch families stationed at her beloved Cape Town.

When she was a few years of age, her mother had begged the lady of the house to offer her daughter employment too. Though Lily could remember the lady's disdainful stares, she eventually succumbed to her mother's request, and Lily worked as a scullery maid in the kitchen under the protective skirts of her mother.

"Now my child, be good, do not be seen by any of the masters, and do not make our lady regret her charity to us."

Such words would be her mother's usual counsel whenever Lily would wander off.

Life under the Von Hisen's was tough, but Lily was happy. During the day, they worked for the masters, but at night Lily and her mother would return to their hut in the neighbourhood her people were confined in; here, she was free to be the spirited child her mother encouraged her to be.

Growing up, Lily always seemed to have just a little bit more comfort than her peers. She could not quite understand why their neighbours would very often tell the other children not to mingle with her. She would often hear some of the women in the neighbourhood refer to her mother with derogatory terms and they would frequently shout their abusive remarks towards her too, but her mother would always shield her and tell her lovely stories of faraway lands they would journey to together and start a new life.

Lily was peculiarly bright for her age and sex. However, girls like her were only destined to serve the masters; no matter how clever they may be.

But her mother would encourage her to dream of the day they would board a ship together and journey to the New Land, where their kind were now free to dress, speak and indeed read like the master's daughters.

Her mother could not read or write herself; however, after she had caught her daughter imitating the learning ways of the children of the masters, Lily would very often find a generous supply of books in their hut.

These books would always appear the morning after some of the white masters visited her mother at night. Her mother had decided she would do anything she was capable of in order for her daughter to receive an education and be learned like the children of the masters.

Sadly however, Lily's education came to an untimely halt.

One of fevers brought by the sailors who would usually visit their hut had made her mother severely ill, and one fateful night, the only love she had known in her entire life was gone.

By the time the fever had taken her mother away, Lily was at the prime age of seven-and-ten; and by then she was quite familiar with the kind of visits her mother was entertaining.

One of the last night visitors who called upon her mother had been none other than the master Von Hisen, and he had even been attentive enough to take care of her mother's burial.

Lily, for her part, tried her best to keep herself away from him; like her mother had always warned her. However, though it was only for very brief moments, Lily could very well grasp the meaning inscribed in the looks he directed at her.

Lily carried on serving at master Von Hisen's residency following her mother's passing. Lady Von Hisen was a stern looking woman whose eagle eye seemed to overshadow the entire house. There was a butler and a housekeeper who were quite capable of fulfilling the strenuous duty of watching over the servants, but this lady seemed pretty determined to watch over them herself... especially the servants, male and female alike, who would approach the master's quarters of the house.

This worked very well in Lily's favour, as master Von Hisen was constantly lurking around. Lily had managed to avert his attempts many-a-time before Edmund finally rescued her…

7.

The Odyssea had been anchored in the Cape for close to a week.

At four-and-twenty, Mr Edmund Hertworth revelled in the prime of his youth, savouring all the pleasures life could offer to a young nobleman without any care in the world.

His father, Lord William Hertworth, though quite advanced in age, still oversaw the management of the family estate, so Edmund had been left free to indulge himself in the mundane affairs easily accessible to someone with his wealth, name and intriguing dark looks.

Edmund, alongside two long-time travelling mates, had already done so much exploring around this part of the world to fill their hearts' content, and as such, their attention could now be turned to exploring the good local society.

"I can honestly vouch for the man's exquisite taste," one of his friends was saying. "I strongly believe the inducement could very well be worth the inconvenience."

This first companion was his friend, Mr Frederick Galloway, whom he had known since their early days during their formal education at Eton.

Freddie, as his friends would informally refer to him, though well-bred himself, did not equal Edmund Hertworth in rank or wealth, but he certainly had a vast amount of thirst for what the world had to offer to unattached, carefree, young, noble Englishmen. It was this easy-going nature of his which made Edmund feel prone to venture to some of their daring excursions, which Edmund would otherwise be more inclined to stay away from by nature.

"He insists this one is by far the best amongst his chattel," Freddie was eagerly pressing on with his persuasion. "Gentlemen, he literally said: 'if you are unsatisfied by the end of it, I will not only return the money to you, but I will double the initial payment for the inconvenience upon your time.' If this is not the epitome of confidence, then I truly do not know what confidence is!"

"Get to it with all our blessings! I am quite content to take my pleasure from our own kind," retorted the second friend, Mr William Bormer.

"You must come and see her at the very least!" Freddie insisted. "He told me to spread the word that an encounter with her is bound to shake our distaste of the negro flesh."

And this friend would not desist until both companions would at last capitulate and agree to accept the invitation of a renowned Dutch settler; a Mr Von Hisen.

*

Once they arrived at the Von Hisen manor, the three gentlemen were escorted to the music room where the family were expecting them.

Each member of the family was absorbed in a leisurely task, offering a picturesque view of nobility at its finest.

"We are very pleased you were able to visit us this morning," said Madam Von Hisen as she stood up from her needling to personally welcome the gentlemen. Edmund was the first to be offered her gloved hand.

"When my husband told us that gentlemen such as yourselves had arrived in our town, we could not contain our excitement, right girls?" She turned to look at the two young, elegantly dressed women also present in the room; she then proceeded to introduce her daughters to them.

After the mother had finished the intricate presentation of her two daughters, it was the turn of Von Hisen to rise from his seat and welcome his guests himself.

The three gentlemen remained in such company for what felt quite a prolonged stay in Edmund's mind; surely, if something spectacular was supposed to appear, it should have appeared by now.

He could not deny, however, their hosts had indeed been very kind with their display of impeccable hospitality. Many different courses of refreshments had already been served.

"Johanna, why don't you entertain our dear guests with the pianoforte," the mother prompted her eldest daughter.

"I would be delighted, Mama," and offering a most gracious smile in Edmund's direction, the daughter added, "I may need some assistance with turning the pages however…"

"But of course, my lady, please allow me to assist you," interjected William. "Edmund seems pretty raptured by your refreshments," teased the friend, coming to Edmund's rescue. "Judging by the way you are stuffing your mouth my friend; you may lead our kind hosts to assume you do not have any provisions on your own ship!"

Johanna had indeed managed to prickle the interest of at least one of the Englishmen.

It was quite evident the Von Hisen's had done their due diligence and looked into the family histories of their three guests. Mr Bormer was the least well-connected out of the trio, and this lack of connection seemed to be the cause of the frown clearly visible on Johanna's face as William accompanied her to the pianoforte.

Meanwhile, while the eldest Miss Von Hisen was struggling to contain her displeasure at failing to secure Mr Hertworth's attention, the second Miss Von Hisen seemed rather pleased to receive Freddie's flattering praises of her drawings.

The gentlemen had been in the company of this society long enough to ascertain that while one believed herself gifted at the pianoforte, the second daughter did truly possess a natural talent with her drawings and paintings. As such, Edmund could easily presume Freddie's task proved to be more sincere than their other compatriot.

This young lady's paintings were quite varied in their themes, but her talent appeared to thrive best at conveying different emotions when she depicted people.

"Though you may mistakenly attribute my impartiality to my motherly feelings, Clara's art is indeed renowned amongst many in our society."

Mrs Von Hisen had taken the liberty of accosting Freddie in his walk along the walls to admire some of the drawings which had been flamboyantly framed all over this enormous room.

Edmund too had joined in the admiration of Miss Clara Von Hisen's art. Upon closer inspection, Edmund supposed this young lady to be particularly drawn to depicting facial expressions, and in this regard, she seemed to prefer depicting eyes above anything else.

He would later come to understand that the pair of eyes which regularly appeared in these drawings belonged to the same person.

In each frame, feelings of joy, sadness or curiosity were all beautifully illustrated. And every single feeling being portrayed seemed to be acutely felt by the possessor of those expressions.

The guests must have appeared to be marvelling at those eyes much longer than Mrs Von Hisen considered it appropriate, as she suddenly turned to her youngest daughter to suggest, "Clara, why don't you show our gentlemen the portrait you have just finished of your sister!"

She then solicited the attention of the guests away from the drawings and attempted to justify her daughter, "Clara can get a bit liberal with the servants," and glancing towards her husband, she warily added, "her father seems to encourage some of her eccentric ways; however, she has now stopped giving her considerations to nonsense such as these scribbles."

Many native people at the service of Mr Von Hisen had entered and exited the room, each bringing a new replenishment. However, none of them had been exhibited as having any particular relevance to the purpose of their visit.

"Miss Von Hisen, your fingers are indeed remarkable, you seem able to bring the pianoforte to life," William was complimenting.

"Well, I thank you, but I am positive you have heard much pleasanter music than mine back in England. We hear the Hertworth's dinner parties are renowned for securing only the best performers; Mama says that even some of the artists from the continent found their debut due to your family's patronage." Miss Johanna Von Hisen seemed quite eager to carry on singing more acclamations for the pleasure of Edmund's ears, when her target's attention became thus interrupted by the butler:

"I am sorry to interrupt, the concertmaster which we were expecting tomorrow has just arrived. Jansen is experiencing some difficulty in finalising the list with him and solicits your approval, Madam."

With such duty at hand, the mother, followed by her two daughters were required to leave the room.

"Thank you indeed for your kind hospitality, Madam; you truly made us reminisce about our homes back in England. Should you ever venture back to our parts of the world, I would be truly honoured if you would do my family the honour of visiting us," Edmund obliged.

41

"I am sure my mother will be more than happy to make your acquaintance. And," turning his attention to Miss Johanna, "I would personally arrange for a memorable orchestra in honour of Miss Von Hisen!"

These encouraging words were the least Edmund could offer to a mother and daughter who had taken all the trouble to impress him.

"My dear gentlemen, it was indeed our pleasure to receive your visit," and turning towards her husband, added, "My lord, please ensure to inform your esteemed guests of our annual costume event taking place next week. Though we may not compare to the magnificence they may be used to–" she found herself hastily interrupted.

"–Do not worry yourself my dear, I will see to it!" the husband said, appearing rather eager to see her out. "I assure you; our gentlemen will be present at your event."

After shutting the door behind him, he then proclaimed: "Now gents, let me show you what you have come for!"

Master Von Hisen had been oddly quiet for most of their visit, leaving the entertaining to the women of his household.

Now, however, he seemed to have been blessed with new life.

He then proceeded to the other end of the room and, to the astonishment of his visitors, purposely knocked over the table near one of the south-facing windows. In doing so, he spilled most of the abundance his Madam had eagerly exhibited.

"Jacob, proceed in escorting her here... be quick man!" Shouted the master to his butler who had now reappeared.

A few moments later, the same butler re-entered the room followed by one native woman.

As far as appearances went, the woman had been called to put the room back in order. However, the master of the house had purposely chosen that table. The table in question was in the furthest part of the room, ensuring that the walk the woman took from the entrance to reach it was long enough for the three spectators to fully appreciate the veracity of the man's promise.

"Indeed, I cannot fathom how we have allowed Freddie to drag us into this circus," whispered Edmund to William.

"You are right! How many times has he seen negros of the female sex? How can he even tell the difference from one to the next?" Added the friend.

William had lost most of his interest in this affair after Miss Von Hisen had left the room, so his feelings about the scene in front of them were not very different from Edmund's.

When suddenly, William remarked, "Oh MY...!" his attention directed at the newcomer, "I certainly was not expecting this!"

Edmund felt compelled to follow his friend's gaze.

The woman had reached the upturned table and was bent on the ground to remove the mess into a basin.

Though it took her a while, the woman began to sense the strong gazes coming in her direction. She then stood back up.

The next thing she did caught all the men by surprise.

Coming face to face with the butler, she cast the dirty contents of the basin onto the man and stormed out of the room.

8.

The three companions hastily took their leave shortly after the acclaimed woman had left their presence.

Edmund suggested they walk back to their ship, instead of using the carriage he had hired since they anchored at the shores.

The two friends were quite accustomed to living off Edmund's generous hospitality, therefore, they always politely accepted Edmund's solicitations at dwelling on any of his ships while they amused themselves from one place to the next.

As the friends were merrily on their way, Edmund began jesting with Freddie.

"You seem to have enjoyed our leisurely afternoon very much."

"Oh, yes, you can be very sure of that!" Von Hisen had certainly lived up to Freddie's expectations. "You two did not?!" Looking at his two companions, Freddie appeared surprised to see his friends did not seem to share his current feelings.

"I found the whole experience a tedious spectacle," Edmund responded, and then recollecting the music he had to put up with, he emphasised, "especially the women! I cannot in all honesty decide who I found more unpleasant between the mother and the daughter!"

He was referring to the eldest daughter, as he could not find much to reproach Miss Clara Von Hisen for. The younger daughter had been rather quiet throughout their stay, and she only offered some obliging remarks to the genuine compliments she received for her captivating drawings.

"I was indeed struggling to contain myself when your sweetheart genuinely thought she could impress us with her mediocre performances!" Edmund was again addressing his observation at William.

"Well, I will concede her charms may not be in her musical accomplishments, but I certainly thought her rather pretty... in spite of her red hair," replied William defensively.

"Come, William, no need to fret over her. I can guarantee you will, sooner than you may think, find your next conquest in our first ball back in England and forget all about Miss Von Hisen!" And suddenly remembering another fault of the woman, added, "What about her freckles?"

"I certainly do not remember noticing any freckles on her glowing skin!" retorted William defensively. "You are purposely confusing her with her fat sister! Miss Clara is the one who had freckles all over!"

"Forget the Von Hisen girls, you two!" Freddie interjected. "You must admit the man has good taste in his choices amongst his stock! How could you not notice that negro's appeal?! I haven't been able to stop myself from imagining all the possibilities a man can enjoy with a thing shaped such as that!"

"I would personally find it much more exciting if any conquest of mine is willing to reciprocate me during any sort of intimate liaison I am to have with her!" interrupted Edmund. "I would find that to be much more rewarding to one's own self-worth."

Edmund did not mind offering his spirited friend his own views on the visit; "Though this may make me sound unexciting to your ears, I was not made to feel any incentive in acquitting my current tastes, and I am still of the opinion that I can be very well satisfied with the respectable beauties I am accustomed to amongst our equals."

"You cannot think me a simple nitwit to imagine I am basing my infatuation with her purely on her body!" Freddie retorted. "I cannot, in all honesty, recollect a woman from amongst our kind, or the other kinds, who has aroused my interest as much as what we have just seen. And you know, I can boast of a very good record at that!

"I grant you; she could pass as coming quite close to some of the other negros around Von Hisen, and yet, there is more to her than what her flesh leads you to imagine!

"What makes her all the more appetising is her total lack of awareness of the power her body can have on a man's senses. She has a certain sense of grandiose pride in her manner of conduct; a man cannot help but feel the need to exert his dominion over such a fascinating conquest!"

"Are you seriously talking of grandeurs and conquests?!" exclaimed Edmund. "You are now being simply too ridiculous! How about we recommend her for the next presentation at court!"

Though he offered no opinion on the woman being described, Edmund could not help his humour as Freddie seemed determined to single out this latest passion of his above the many other amorous encounters Edmund could very well recall.

It was quite common for Freddie to become easily enraptured by women in general, therefore Edmund could not give this latest infatuation the seriousness it required; an unfortunate oversight he would later come to regret!

"William, I did not have much hope in Edmund, but you must agree with me, you certainly must!"

"Her curves do certainly have their appeal, but that is rather common for her kind, is it not?"

Freddie was not going to give up, "Let's put everything else aside, what about the fire in her countenance? You cannot have missed the power coming out of her eyes! Such a defined face with those piercing eyes is simply too delightful for you both to belittle it as unworthy of a man's attention! The moment I saw her eyes, I understood straight away it was these eyes Miss Von Hisen kept on depicting in her paintings!" exclaimed Freddie. "So, you see, even her own sex sees the magic in her!"

"For heaven's sake! She is a negro!"

"From the moment I looked into her captivating face, I have been contemplating if God was to ever create a black angel, surely such an angel would indeed resemble her!" Freddie carried on, totally ignoring Edmund's remark.

"You may choose to see an angel in her, but I only saw fire coming out of her! She certainly knew how to put that poor butler in his place," Edmund mocked.

9.

The Von Hisen family were hosting one of the usual lavish ceremonies which they normally gave at this time of the year. Amongst the esteemed guests were the future heir to the Hertworth Eastern Company and his friends.

Edmund was quite uninterested in partaking in the festivities; the entertainment currently on offer was not particularly enticing his prudish tastes.

"Your friend here claims you are not particularly fond of dancing," Miss Johanna Von Hisen brazenly said to Edmund.

The three Englishmen had been at the ball for a while, and William had frequently offered himself as the man to escort Miss Von Hisen onto the ballroom; however, she seemed determined to secure Edmund's request for a dance this time.

"I beg your pardon for my negligence; I have been lost in admiring... uhm, shall we say the exotic performances," Edmund responded.

"It is fascinating, is it not? Mama takes personal care of the performance of these negros for this particular event! Clara and I would not normally be allowed to be present when our kind joins in, but as you can see, today only the negros are the ones performing on one another."

Miss Johanna was proudly enlightening her foreign visitors on the pastime the Dutch nobility liked to compete in. "Though, if I may say so myself, the Von Hisen events are by far the most authentic ones." She then resorted to whispering, "I heard that in previous years, even some of our kind have joined in and made the negros perform on them!"

"If I may be so bold," William started, "I do not quite understand the point of wearing a mask. I mean, since only the native people are the ones having all the fun with one another, then why did we need to come wearing a mask?" William was simply trying to jest with his darling, but her prickly reply was not the response he had hoped to receive.

"It is a preventative measure of course! Some of us may accidentally feel prone to lose control over our own superior judgement!"

She then turned her attention to her own prey, and at last she managed to secure a dance from him.

Mr Hertworth had truly tried his best to fulfil his social obligation and forced himself to dance with as many English and Dutch ladies as possible, however he had eagerly been looking forward to the hour it would be acceptable for him to pay his respects to Lord Von Hisen and make himself scarce.

"Where is Freddie? I have lost sight of him since I last saw him conversing with Von Hisen," Edmund enquired of William.

However, William had decided to disappear again with his sweetheart and enjoy a new performance which involved a group of men and a single woman.

Edmund could no longer partake in such amusements, and as he recognised the same butler he saw during his last visit, he decided it was time to make his escape.

"Where can I find Von Hisen?"

"The master is currently entertaining a small group of guests in the summer house," acknowledged the butler, and noticing that the gentleman seemed quite at a loss about the activities taking place in the summer house, he then added, "if you would like to follow me this way, Sir, I will escort you to them."

It was now quite deep into the night, and the music being played by the orchestra in the ballroom began to dim in Edmund's ears. The lights coming from the house faded away into the emptiness of the gardens, and he could hear the insects in the trees now playing their own night sounds.

The debaucheries taking place right behind him were now sounding oddly in contrast with the soothing calmness of the night.

He felt pleased to be breathing in the distinct fragrance of the distant ocean.

Though the sea was where Edmund truly found his solace, he had missed home.

It had now been almost a year since he set sail from Exeter; this journey had been his longest absence from England, and at present, he was looking forward to returning home to grant his mother's wish of having the family's heir finally settled and taking charge of their estate.

While lost in these pleasant reminiscences, Edmund heard brassy, piercing screams coming from the direction they were headed. He looked up at the butler only to notice a smirk on the man's face.

He hoped for some kind of explanation; however, the closer they came to the source of the sound, the more the butler seemed to be enjoying it.

"Is there a beastly creature around here?"

"It is not an animal, my lord," the butler remarked, "though she certainly bites like one! In fact, milord, this is all part of the entertainment the master has reserved for his esteemed guests this evening, and I thought you would be one of them."

The summer house was still out of sight, but Edmund realised he had come close enough when he could clearly distinguish the nature of the sounds.

It was the cry of a woman pleading to be let go! The pleas were mixed with threats; she sounded desperate and angry, almost as if she thought herself capable of self-salvation.

His natural instincts urged him to run and offer his assistance to whomever it was that sounded in great need of it. However, the strange expression on the butler's face engaged his rational mind with one possible dilemma.

Was there some sort of torture taking place in the summer house?

And, if Von Hisen was involved, then would it be right for a foreigner such as him to involve himself without the prior knowledge of the local authority? The last thing he wanted was to cause trouble for himself in another nobleman's private territory, while on the verge of returning home.

He was about to address the butler once again, when another plea came his way. This time, however, there was despair in the voice. The screams and cries had now turned into implorations.

Edmund, with the butler in tow, finally had a clear vision of the summer house. It appeared rather small from the outside, purposely built in a very remote area of the vast garden, surrounded by very tall trees. And as these trees were no longer tampering with the voices coming his way, Edmund could distinctly hear other voices overpowering the voice of the imploring woman. He was surprised to hear laughter and merriment from the house; the few men inside it were evidently at their utmost leisure.

When Edmund burst the door open, the macabre scene in front of him reminded him of images he had seen depicted by navy men returning from the Americas.

The single room he had marched in had a group of at least five men, some fully and some partially undressed, and one of these men was none other than Freddie!

All of them were blindly hoarding around a woman on the wall. He could not see the face of the poor soul, as her body was turned, and her arms were forcibly held against the wall.

Imbali's eyes were on their last stroke of life; but they were open just enough to catch a glimpse of some form of light which emanated into the room when Edmund entered. Instead of callous hands, she felt the breeze of the night against her body, and just then her mind gave her leave to finally let go.

Though she had no idea how long it took, she did regain her consciousness, and as she did, she caught glimpses of the interactions between the person who had covered her nakedness and master Von Hisen.

10.

"Are you hurt?

"–Would you like me to take you to the authorities?

"–What is your name?" Were some of the many questions Edmund had been asking the woman he just rescued. They had been journeying throughout the night and were finally far away from the Von Hisen property.

Edmund had instructed his coachman to keep to the road close to the harbour. Though he did not regret his prompt assistance to this poor soul, he certainly did not wish to find himself caught up in any kind of trouble with foreign authorities so far away from home; the sooner he returned to the safety of his ship, the better it would be for his peace of mind.

As they neared the port, sunlight penetrated Mr Hertworth's carriage, offering him a better view of the woman sitting lifelessly in the furthest corner of the carriage, her expression marked by a resolute but sombre silence.

Her attire was no better looking than her frail, exhausted frame. He had offered her his coat, but it was barely providing a sense of propriety in her appearance.

If he was to take her to his ship with him, he certainly could not risk having her around his subordinates in her current state.

"Stop the carriage," he ordered.

He got off the carriage and turned to one of his footmen, "I need you to promptly run back to the town we have just passed and find a physician."

The footman hesitated, "Shall I summon the physician from the white townsfolk, Sir?"

"No, certainly not! Take care to find one from amongst the villagers."

Edmund then turned to a second man, and after depositing a good sum of silver coins in the man's hand, he instructed, "I will need you to head to the village too and purchase appropriate clothing for the lady."

The man nodded, but as he turned to depart, he paused and asked, "I beg your pardon, Sir, would you like me to purchase clothes fit for a lady or a negro?"

It was highly probable the poor man meant no offence; however, these words stirred a rage Edmund had been brewing since the previous evening, and the reaction his man received was such a rarity for any of the men at his service to witness.

"Be gone with you!" Edmund commanded, shoving him away, "Don't let me see you ever again!"

From the carriage, a movement caught Edmund's attention away from his employee. When he looked up, he found himself facing her on the road, no longer lifeless, but now directing her eyes at him.

"Please excuse my men for their poor manners...," he offered, sounding more apologetic than he ought to be.

She did not respond.

He then decided to remind her of her poor physical state, "Unless you would not mind my personal physician attending to you on my ship, I don't know where else I can find the assistance I am sure you require at the moment."

Still, she remained silent, but her eyes never left his.

"Alternatively, I can escort you to whichever part of this town you will direct my men to," he then offered, as he was beginning to find her silence rather unnerving. "Are you able to understand what I am saying to you?"

"My mother named me Imbali...," she finally said.

"Oh, so you do understand me, thank heavens!" he exclaimed, relieved to hear her speak. However, in his moment of relief, he failed to grasp what her name was. "Your name is... what?!"

"Imbali," she repeated.

Edmund was aware of the custom prevalent amongst Dutch families of assigning European names to their subjects, however, the woman in front of him was proudly introducing herself with her native name.

"Do you have any other name?" he asked.

"No."

"I see... and does your name have something to do with flowers…?" he pressed on.

"It does…," she countered, as a hint of surprise softened her severe features.

It really seemed fate had intended for him to meet this woman, Edmund considered.

Earlier that morning, as he and his mates started on their quotidian excursion, Edmund's attention was caught by a crippled old woman. She was selling some type of merchandise, and none of her stock looked remotely appealing. However, something in him could not help but take pity on the woman, so he offered a few coins to her.

Though her words were incomprehensible to them, the woman did not seem pleased to receive such a form of charity as she kept encouraging the trio to take something from her merchandise in return for the monies. In the end, she extracted a pile of flowers from her stock and offered them to Edmund. There was nothing extraordinary about the flowers, and the native words uttered by the elderly negro seemed totally inconsequential at the time, however as Imbali introduced her name, he suddenly recollected the one word he vaguely grasped the meaning of.

Interesting the young woman standing in front of him should possess such a name.

"I must say your name sounds quite suitable for the moment," Edmund could not help but remark as his eyes moved away from her to the marvellous field they were surrounded by.

The road they had been riding along cut straight through a field covered by a multitude of lively flowers. And as she introduced him to her name, he suddenly took notice of the numerous flowers around them.

The scene was truly enchanting, quite picturesque, Edmund thought. It was as though a grand arena had been arranged where blooms of every kind and colour vied with one another in splendour.

In the depths of this colourful arena, one particular type of flower caught Edmund's eye. These flowers looked like lilies. He had seen many kinds of lilies in a variety of different colours before, however, he was yet to come across lilies of the intense dark shades such as the ones in front of him. One could simplify the colour by merely assuming it black, however, these lilies were not a mere black. The darkness in their colour had a brightness to it, making all the surrounding flowers pale in their conventional colours, which only served to make these dark lilies even more exquisite.

"I am grateful to you for your assistance," Imbali started, once Mr Hertworth's eyes ceased contemplating upon the field of flowers and were upon her once again. "I wish I had a mode of repayment; however, as I do not, I can only express my eternal gratitude and pray that God will bless you with the same generosity you bestowed upon me."

Edmund could not help but look at her intrigued. He was quite open to the idea of this woman's singularity, but he certainly did not expect her to sound like she had been plucked from one of the finest finishing seminaries in London!

"I am Edmund Hertworth, madam, at your service," he obliged, as he presented to her one of his most refined bows, "pleased to make your acquaintance, Miss flower."

Her lips made a sudden twitch; however, it disappeared again so quickly, he was not sure if he had simply imagined it.

"I thank you, Mr Hertworth, but you and your men do not need to concern yourself with me any longer, I have troubled you enough."

"Very well then," he conceded. "But, I must insist you allow one of my men to escort you to anywhere you may like to go, at the very least,"

"There is no need, Sir. I am not very far from where I need to be," she countered. She then reached to remove the gentleman's coat and pass it over to him, when she recalled the state of her attire under his coat and looked back at him.

"You may keep it, madam!" he offered.

She seemed rather uncomfortable with his offer, but she must have capitulated to it, as a moment later she simply turned towards the opposite direction of his carriage and began to walk away, wearing his coat.

*

Imbali could not return to her mother's place, for that would be the first place Von Hisen and his men would look for her, so in truth she had nowhere, and no one, to go to. However, one thing she did have was a high dose of pride which would not allow her to be at the mercy of anyone, even a person who she had seen pay a large sum of money for her, and demand nothing in return. And she certainly did not trust his sex enough to want to risk him demanding anything in return, therefore, the sooner she put a distance between them, the safer she would feel.

She had been walking unsteadily on the muddy road for quite a while, deeply immersed in her woes, when unexpectedly, a thorn from a nearby shrub injured her foot.

"It was only a matter of time before your bare feet would add more wounds to your other injuries," a voice startled her from behind.

She then looked up to find Mr Hertworth offering her a hand to help her get up from the ground.

She refused the hand and instead raised herself up.

"I told you to go away... why are you following me?!"

It was not too difficult to guess the cause of the woman's distrust towards him or any member of the male sex, however, Edmund could not help but become irritated at her himself.

"You misunderstand me completely; I had no intention of following you, of course! I found something which belongs to you in my carriage, and assuming it had some type of value to you, I had a mind of returning it to you personally when I happened to see you stumbling on the road," he explained. He then opened his hand and presented her with her mother's chain.

"I... thank you for returning it to me, Sir," she said hesitantly, taking the seemingly insignificant looking object off his hand.

He made his way back to his carriage angry with her. What kind of man did she think him to be?! Surely, after all the troubles he had gone through because of her, she could not possibly imagine him interested in her!

And to think that he had actually felt quite proud of his benevolence!

The sum he paid Von Hisen was indeed of no consequence to him, and though he did not expect her to profess rapturous undying gratitude to him, such disrespect was indeed uncalled for!

"You mentioned a ship, Sir," she called to him.

"Aye, I did..."

"You also mentioned you are Sir Hertworth, proprietor of the Hertworth Fleet?"

"Well, I am indeed a Hertworth, however, my honourable father is Sir Hertworth; I simply have the privilege to be one of his sons."

Imbali vividly recalled a spirited conversation she overheard the two Miss Von Hisen's having on one of those days the master was trying to display her to one or other of his guests. That whole day, Johanna seemed beyond herself with the news of a Sir Hertworth from England who would marry her and sweep her off to the best corners of civilisation, saving her from rotting away in these horrible parts of the world amongst 'half-bred human beings!'

"May I enquire about the direction your ship is headed?"

"I am on my way home to England…," replied a surprised Edmund.

Squeezing tightly to her mother's necklace, a sudden impetuous idea overtook Imbali.

Was her beloved mother guiding her to take the journey she had so dearly hoped for them to make?

This man was not going to the Americas for sure, but getting to England would certainly give her better chances of finding respectable work, and then she could save enough monies to seek straight passage to the land of her mother's dreams.

"Would it be too much of an inconvenience for me to seek employment on this ship of yours, Sir? I work very well in the kitchen... I can also clean; you could trust me to take on the cleaning of your entire ship!"

"You wish to leave here with me...?" Edmund responded pensively. He had no serious reason to deny her wish, he considered. "Well... my staff will certainly not mind a change of hands in the kitchen! All our current cook seems capable of putting together is mashed or dried fish! So, the role is yours, should you wish to take it."

His eyes then descended upon her current state of attire, and after a brief pause, he felt compelled to add, "however, I must warn you, there are not many women on board my ship... and the few aboard are travelling in the safety of a male companion. I will of course ensure to properly introduce you to my shipmaster, but I cannot help in feeling obliged to inform you of, I would say, some risks that may arise with some of the men.

"What I mean to say is that many of my men have been at sea for months and as you can imagine, have not seen or had, uhm, female company..." he found himself thus interrupted:

"I thank you, Sir, for what I wish to assume as a kind consideration for my wellbeing, however, I can assure you that I indeed do not intentionally prompt men to direct their most unwanted attentions towards me!"

As these words were said, Edmund could not help notice the trembling which had overtaken the poor woman.

He could easily understand her anger at his inopportune words, but in truth, all he was trying to do was find the appropriate way to offer to get her some proper clothing without incurring another refusal from her seemingly proud head.

Should she appear on board wearing his coat as the prime source of shelter for her nakedness, he could very well imagine how many members amongst his crew could easily feel a sense of entitlement in soliciting certain types of demands from her.

He tried to explain himself, however, Imbali would not let him speak as she had raised her hand and continued, "if you mean to imply I may intentionally disturb the order on your ship, I thank you once again for offering your assistance, however, I must suggest we part ways from here!"

Fortunately, she then looked up at his face and saw some form of embarrassment written all over him.

"If," she then added, "if, however you would be so kind as to ensure your men stay away from me, I will ensure to keep myself away from everyone."

There was not much for him to say after this, so he silently proceeded towards the carriage with his unexpected protectee in tow.

Upon arriving at the harbour, Edmund summoned the shipmaster to him.

"We set sail at first light," he instructed, and then introduced Imbali as the new assistant cook of their ship.

Though the majority of the staff were composed of men, once below deck, Imbali was quite pleased to see a couple of black women around too. She tried to direct pleasing smiles their way, but she was met with scorn by one of them, and the second one simply ignored her.

"Edmund, is that not the negro from the Von Hisen's?" William asked.

"You have finally managed to surprise me, I must say! You got her all for yourself?! You certainly gave no inclinations of having such preferences!" William failed to realise he was the only amused one out of the two. "I thought we agreed to sail off this forthcoming Sunday," he then rejoined. "Is Freddie aware we are taking off much sooner than you originally intended?

"As a matter of fact, I have not seen him return from the Von Hisen's, and unless you have already informed him of your decision... or, has something happened? Wait... are you leaving him behind?!" William exclaimed at last.

Without negating or confirming his friend's queries, Edmund simply turned to the shipmaster to reiterate, "as I said, we leave at the first morning light." As he walked off, he turned to his friend and added, "all expected passengers are already accounted for."

Within an hour of Edmund's command, the ship set sail back north; and by the looking glass in the kitchen, Imbali stood for a prolonged time, watching the golden plains of her beloved land fade away from sight.

11.

Back in British East India, Mumbai.

Edmund and Lily had been sitting alone in the carriage, opposite one another, for quite a while now.

Edmund was recalling the many times, before this occasion, where he had stared into this woman's bewitching eyes struggling to retain his state of mind.

Thankfully, over the years, he had gone through such a substantial transformation whereby he had learnt to master his composure around her, without the need to usher her out of his sight before losing control over his actions.

Besides, it was such a rarity for him to get her all to himself like this, so much so that he could not care what mood she was in; he was simply too grateful to be in her proximity.

"Propriety demands you need to leave first!" Lily commanded.

"I am quite comfortable here to be honest," and leaning closer to her side of the carriage, he playfully added, "but I would be even more comfortable if you were to occupy the seat my dear wife has just vacated."

He finally managed to get her to look back at him, and what a look he got.

"You really do not need to resort to such antics! It will suffice if you would simply allow me to leave the carriage and assist her ladyship!"

"Imbali, you do realise I did not mean to include you in what I said to Marianne, don't you?!" He wished she would let him hold her hand. But he knew enough of this woman and her principles to know such a liberty would not be afforded to him.

"Why would it matter what I understand from your words, milord?" She responded calmly. "You are indeed at liberty to express any opinions you may have about anyone, let alone the dark and filthy people around you."

"You are being rather unfair to me! You surely must be able to make excuses for me!"

"So, you expect me to make concessions for what you openly profess, simply because you consider me privy to some inner beliefs of yours?! Is this excuse enough for you, milord?"

"Yes, indeed it is. At least with you it must be!"

"Do you feel the need to excuse yourself with the coachman, or Mr Ranjey over there?" Her gaze went to the Indian butler who was obsequiously waiting by the front door of the house. Without affording him any chance for a reply, she carried on, "I assure you, milord, you owe no apology to me! In fact, it is rather assuring to hear you speak so!"

"How so?"

"You simply pointed out my place in the world, and for that I can do nothing but congratulate you! My only hope is you will finally come to terms with it too!"

She could no longer keep herself in his presence.

She realised this situation had indeed provided Mr Ranjey with enough ingredients for the succulent gossip he was sure to take to the rest of the servants in the house. And if such rumours reached Marianne's ears, she would not be able to forgive herself.

Casting propriety aside, she rose from her corner and exited the carriage without waiting for Sir Hertworth to leave first.

As Lily rushed into her own chamber, she hoped she would at last be granted some solitude for the day. But upon entering her room, she found Marianne eagerly waiting for her.

"It's all been in vain!" cried Marianne. "I will never succeed in giving Edmund a child!"

"Come now, Marianne, I am sure not all is lost," Lily offered, as she sat beside Marianne, who placed her head upon Lily's lap.

"In truth, how can I fault Edmund for his mistrust! What was I thinking believing the gibberish you and Henry have been putting in my head?!" Marianne lamented. "Perhaps I would be much better off accepting my fate and let the Lady Mother bring forth whatever she has been speculating behind my back!" By the end of this remark, Marianne's words were only faintly audible amidst all the sobbing.

"Of course, I will not claim to possess much understanding of this sort of science, but I honestly do not believe these methods to be gibberish," offered Lily reassuringly.

"What makes you so sure?! If I remember correctly, you yourself weren't too keen on this expedition at first!"

"Well, Marianne, I suppose I might not have been in favour of you concealing it from your husband; but I was never averse to Dr Hashford's claims. I simply did not consider myself informed enough at first."

"And...? What has changed now?!" probed Marianne, sitting upright.

"Well, I have come to know Dr Hashford is not alone in his convictions of the credibility of Dr Bathia's methods," Lily offered. "Long before we sailed off, I started reading all the articles in the journals Dr Hashford had brought to you since he first mentioned Dr Bathia."

"What journals?" Marianne frowned.

"You were still quite indisposed from your... recent loss, and so I would certainly not fault you if you may not recollect the event," said Lily, smiling at her mistress.

"But on the day Dr Hashford first brought the idea forward, he also came with a copy of the Royal Society Journal, and in there we first saw these new ways being mentioned. There was one particular article Dr Hashford tried to bring to your attention; do you recollect it?" enquired Lily, fairly confident Marianne would not.

"I do not," Marianne responded.

"You see, that particular article had been written by a notorious Dr Watson, does that ring a bell?"

And after another negative response, Lily went further with her explanations.

"I knew Dr Watson could claim some type of acquaintance with Sir Hertworth; he and your husband moved in similar circles during their days at Oxford. They were within different fields of course, but I had heard Sir Hertworth mention his name quite favourably a few times, when he would come across his name in the morning papers."

"Do you truly suppose me capable of remembering all of Edmund's morning conversations?!" interjected Marianne.

"That would certainly provide you with more topics of conversation between the two of you!" Lily replied. "But no Marianne; I do not expect you to remember all of them.

"I bring this up because I understood Sir Hertworth to highly value this man's mind; hence, I suggested we write to the man to enquire further ourselves."

"Did we write to him...?" Marianne appeared rather confused.

"Well, since you would not, I took the liberty of corresponding with Dr Watson on your behalf and... well, Marianne, let me get you his letters! You can see for yourself! There is one particular letter of his which left me in no doubt about the sincerity of Dr Hashford's convictions!" Lily said as she went to her trunk to retrieve the letters.

"Oh, Lily, you did this for me?!" Marianne exclaimed, appearing much more cheerful than when she first entered Lily's room.

"Marianne, I will always attempt to do anything in my power to ensure your happiness," Lily offered to her mistress.

"Why are you so good to me?!"

"Well... how about my eternal gratitude for your prompt rescue from the Dowager Lady Hertworth?" laughed Lily, glad to be able to bring a smile back to her mistress's face.

At this recollection, both ladies spent a good time laughing over the early days of their acquaintance.

"You did not need my rescuing, you know! For a while, I honestly believed you when you insisted on claiming I rescued you from her! But in time, I have come to understand you were doing an excellent job keeping her at bay all on your own!"

Lily studied Marianne curiously, "how have you understood so?"

"I am not too sure to tell you the truth! To be quite frank with you, I still do not fully understand why she hates you so fervently. It cannot be simply because of your skin. I have seen her around the other negros in the Manor, and she does treat them with tolerable civility... has she ever given you any inkling as to the reason for her particular disdain for you?" At this question, Marianne's eyes pierced Lily's intently, but Lily's face suddenly turned gloomy.

Understanding she was not to receive an answer, Marianne then carried on, "Have I ever told you how I tried to ask her several times, after she was done with her usual scolding of you, but she would simply dismiss me and encourage me to be rid of you instead!"

The conversation had taken a dangerous turn, and the sooner they moved away from it, the sooner Lily would be able to regain her composure.

"Marianne, I did inform you of Dr Watson, do you not recall the conversation we had about how you were supposed to correspond with him instead of me? There was a picture of him in the journals."

"Oh yes, I remember now! The old white bearded fellow whose eyes were barely visible through his ugly spectacles?" exclaimed Marianne, recollecting the face depicted in the journals. "I really could not get myself to correspond with such a bore!"

Taking her fair share in Marianne's humour, Lily had a mind to correct Marianne's views on Dr Watson's appearance; she returned to the same trunks and retrieved a portrait of the man himself.

"The first drawing we saw of him was indeed quite far from the truth. He is older than Dr Hashford to be sure, but he is not too far off from Lord Hertworth in age," informed Lily.

"How did you manage to have a portrait of the man?!"

"Oh, it is truly nothing, Marianne! He sent it to me himself, as a mere token of appreciation for keeping up my correspondence with him."

"Does he know what you are?! I mean, you ought to make him aware of where Edmund brought you from."

"I believe he came to his own conclusions on the nature of my origins, Marianne," offered Lily.

"Then whyever would he want to keep up the correspondence if he knows you are not his equal?!"

"I cannot tell you; but I am of the opinion he lives quite a secluded life, and he may not count more than five people altogether in his society. I am even more positive that the people who take the time to correspond with him are even less than his personal acquaintants! So, I think it is quite possible he has come to see our correspondence as a leisurely diversion for him."

Alongside the pocket-sized frame, Lily had also taken out some of the letters she had been exchanging with him for the past few months.

"In that case, I cannot thank you enough for taking such a boring task upon yourself!" was all Marianne could acknowledge after this explanation.

"You certainly do not need to thank me, Marianne. All in all, I do not consider my correspondence with him a bore at all! I have become quite accustomed to the thorough scholarly detailing he likes to write about in his letters. In fact, I quite look forward to them!"

"Would you read his letters to me?" asked Marianne.

"You may not be interested in them all, Marianne, but there is one; I believe it may interest you very much," said Lily. She then proceeded to read the letter in her hand:

"17th June, 1872.

Dear Madam,
Please do not feel the need to be obsequious in your tone with me, as I have received and read your letter with pleasant surprise at first, but ended it in full gratitude.

I think it admirable that you have been able to elevate yourself out of the confines society has created for an intelligent woman such as yourself simply because of a particular colour of your skin.

You say my answers have satisfied your enquiries concerning the aforementioned methods. I am indeed relieved to know I was able to be of service to you in obliging your mistress.

I will also add, not only is Dr Bathia onto something with his work, but there are many in our circles who envy the man for having such acumen, and the freedom to practice his brilliance. None of us could dream of accomplishing his results.

But then I suppose even if any of us had intended to pursue such speculations, our society is such at present, we may be deemed sceptical of God's ways. We have certainly come a long way from the days of being called heretical; but nonetheless, it is my belief England is still quite lacking in its acceptance of the marvellous ways nature can offer to aid us in our progression as a human race—"

"—Please Lily, I beg you, spare me his words any further! Anything but a bookish man who thinks himself above everyone else's opinion!" Marianne interrupted, appearing rather annoyed. "So… you are telling me this prestigious doctor claims Dr Bathia is to be trusted and I should pursue my intent? But even so, how am I to sway Edmund to do my bidding?! You have seen how categorical he was in his refusal!"

Then, a sudden recollection of the manner in which her husband had conducted himself in the carriage earlier seemed to have given Marianne a new idea.

"Now that I come to think of it, there is something else you could assist me with!" She faced her companion with a newfound eagerness. "Do you suppose Edmund may become more inclined towards Dr Bathia's procedure if he was to see these letters?"

"I, uhm, I-I w-would not know," said Lily quite apprehensively.

"Oh, my dearest friend, how about you be the one to show these letters to him?! I have often observed how he seems quite predisposed to listen to whatever notion you choose to bring forward to him!"

"No, Marianne, he does not!" exclaimed Lily with more passion than she intended. "Where do you get such silly notions from?"

"I do not mean to imply you walk around flogging him with ideas, Lily! No need to take offence, my dear! I just meant to say that he, and to be quite honest I cannot fault him for it, seems to esteem your superior mind. We both know quite well I owe my very presence here to you. Despite my many pleas, was it not your intervention which led him to finally agree to coming here?"

"N-no Marianne, you are indeed quite mistaken!" said Lily defensively.

"I remember the last conversation between the two of you quite well, and you were the one who decided to involve me in it. I simply nodded to Sir Hertworth's query when he enquired whether I thought the weather would be favourable at this time of year in India!"

"You may believe it to be so my dear, but the truth is only you could have convinced him to sail all the way here on the pretence of a favourable change of weather!" Marianne remarked more firmly than she had intended.

"I am sure there must be something you could say or perhaps do to sway his lordship to change his mind towards Dr Bathia's methods," Lily insisted.

"Lily, you know I truly cherish your companionship, even though we both know I could easily find better suited companionship elsewhere," Marianne now acquired a more sombre tone in her speech.

"But truly, my dearest, I take you everywhere with me as I happen to value the manner in which you support my wants and wishes when it comes to my husband," Marianne was quite careful to emphasise her last words. "However, if you are no longer able to assist me, then what use do I have of you?

"Besides, my dear, it is quite unfair of you to think only of your own comfort! And if, as you say, you will not convince Edmund, then it is all a lost cause now!" she pressed on, "will you please show him these letters?" she concluded, taking hold of Lily's hands.

"You are more than welcome to take this letter with you, Marianne…," Lily offered, unsure of herself. "There is not much in it that I would not want to share with you. You could read its contents to his lordship yourself."

"How about these other letters?" enquired Marianne.

"Well...," Lily appeared slightly nervous, "you are more than welcome to them yourself, Marianne, but it may be that his lordship may lose interest in your scope, if you divert his attention with more letters than one. I know the content of this letter to be more than satisfactory to subdue his doubts."

"No, Lily, it must be you!" Marianne exclaimed. "I will go to him now and see what state he is in, and you must follow along too!"

And without allowing her friend any time to formulate a coherent response, she ran out of the room and headed to her husband's study.

12.

"I beg your pardon, milord, Dr Hashford is here and is requesting a private audience with you."

Marianne, passing near the study, paused as she overheard the Indian butler delivering the message to her husband.

"Oh? What a surprise! For once he is not here to have an audience with my wife, is he? Please, do let him in! We do not want our miraculous doctor to be kept waiting; he may lose his magical intellectual powers!"

By the time Dr Hashford was admitted into the study, Lord Hertworth was visibly inebriated, and though reason dictated he steered clear of Marianne's marital affairs, Henry could not help but throw all precaution aside. He simply could not let Marianne deal with her husband on her own, especially since he supposed he could resort to the aid of science to make the man comprehend the facts.

"You have been looking for any pretence to drag Marianne unto you," Edmund scorned, swirling the dark liquid in his glass. "I honestly pity you; I can only imagine how torturous it must be for you to see her with me; the way she comes to me… What did you imagine she would do?" Edmund continued, "you certainly lack in your understanding of Marianne's character if you suppose she could ever be persuaded to abandon all that she possesses with me for a man such as you!"

"You may think of me as you please," responded Henry at last. "I will not mock your intellect and deny what I have respectfully concealed from Marianne," and then correcting himself, proceeded, "from Lady Hertworth, and the rest of the world.

"I am not here to cause alarm; I have simply taken the liberty of coming to you to appeal to your superior understanding," Henry had decided to head directly to his point. "I have known your wife for as long as I can remember, and in all my acquaintance with her, I have never seen her as determined as she is to birth your heir, and my regard for Lady Hertworth has always been such that I would do anything in my power to grant her wishes. So, you can rest assured when I tell you that I did not act on my desires, regardless of my internal struggles, when I took the liberty of liaising with the man you have recently met, to try and grant Marianne her wish!"

Unknown to the men, Marianne had been listening by the door to their interactions.

She did not catch the full length of Edmund's accusations; however, she had been there long enough to hear most of Henry's retaliation.

Marianne did, at times, eavesdrop on her husband's conversations, and now she could not believe her own ears!

How could Henry do this to her? What was he supposing to obtain out of exposing his romantic feelings for her to Edmund?

She expected him to deny it, and yet, as the conversation progressed, Henry did not deny her husband's accusations. Instead, so diligently, almost with a pedagogical touch, Henry carried on elaborating their plan, as if dismissing from his mind who the man in front of him was.

"I became of the opinion that it is very plausible her ladyship's complications may quite possibly arise from a mere internal malfunction between her eggs and your fluids," Henry pressed on.

Edmund for his part met Henry's address with strange silence, and this was encouragement enough to proceed.

"It is all quite simple really... in order for Dr Bathia to be able to prepare a possible remedy for her ladyship, he will need to retrieve some eggs from her, which is extraordinary, but fear not as I have seen him do it with my own eyes; and you... may then be required to provide him with–" however Dr Hashford never had the chance to complete his explanations.

"–There is no need for you to continue. It is all quite clear to me now," Edmund said, turning to pierce Hashford with a most ferocious stare. "I must say your lecture is quite enlightening. I often wondered if you would ever be brave enough to act upon your ill-conceived feelings! I did imagine a few tricks you could possibly resort to, but I must confess, you have managed to surprise me beyond my wildest imagination with this!

"However, you must understand, you fail to impress me, but I can only deduce this is the same tale you must have offered to Marianne and her company."

As he faced the doctor, Edmund perceived little else besides his own reoccurring thoughts: 'What must Imbali think of him?!'

"I will not keep tolerating such insolent affronts at the state of my personal affairs by you and whomever likes to give themselves doctorly airs!" he then rejoined. "I do indeed find your clever touch of the ominous picture you tried to paint quite fascinating, but I think this masquerade has gone far enough!

"You were useful to my father once upon a time, and in honour of my father's memory, I will not pursue this insult any further with you; but I shall warn you, should I ever find you in my presence or within this household, I will not stop until I have ensured you have been condemned in prison for the rest of your life!"

There was nothing else Dr Hashford could add after being dismissed in such a manner, so, ignoring propriety, he simply turned around and exited the door.

Marianne had withdrawn herself in time from the door, as such, she had been spared witnessing the mortification Henry was wearing on his face as he left the study. She did, however, keep herself around the lower grounds of the house, and she saw Henry's exit. She considered whether she ought to run after Henry or intrude upon her husband's solitude.

*

As his study was again his, Edmund resumed indulging himself in the intoxicating refuge of his drink and cigar. He could not bring to a halt the thoughts going through his mind; did Imbali think him less of a man because of these men's insinuations?!

Had she allowed him, at least once, to show her with what a passion he was capable of loving her, he would not have these agonising doubts going through his mind!

A sudden knock on his door awakened him from elaborating upon such thoughts.

"Oh, my dear breaker of hearts! Please, do come in!"

Marianne had decided to intrude upon his solitude and regretted it instantly.

"You ought to have warned me of your impending visit," he continued, rising unsteadily from his chair. "I would have been sure to keep your admirer behind. Or better yet, perhaps the two of you might have treated me to a charming display of, how shall I put it... perhaps your child-making talents?"

"You are obviously out of your mind, Edmund! Forgive me; I see now that I have come at an inopportune time." She took an instinctive step backward, but by then, he had managed to steady himself and stumble toward her.

"You are not to go anywhere," he countered, his voice low and commanding, "until I have reminded you of how you are to behave yourself!" He then motioned for her to sit down, and did not speak again until she had. "I do not care two straws about Hashford or any other conceited fool who may want to hang himself over you!"

"E-Edmund, this is quite enough," Marianne interjected, seeking to escape from the oppressive weight of his presence towering above her.

"I am not done yet!" he yelled. "You have made your choices along with me; I am bearing it all, and I expect you to do the same.

"I have never interfered with any of your caprices," he continued, when just then his gaze drifted from her eyes, descending upon the delicate jewels adorning her throat. "Those are very fine stones, Marianne... are they new?" he scorned, "how much of my wealth have you squandered on this?!"

She did not answer, merely turning her face away.

"All your indulgences, and any other whim you like to entertain may all come to an end if you were to decide, my dear wife, the sacrifice may not be worth the price... as always, the choice is entirely yours!"

With that he then proceeded to leave the study and headed towards the private quarters in the upper part of the house.

*

By now, most of the servants of the house, including the Jenkins', were well aware of the mood the lord of the house was in.

Mr Jenkins had stationed himself quite promptly by the foot of the staircase, where he tried to restrict Lord Hertworth's access to the stairs, but Edmund abruptly ushered him away from his sight.

Mrs Jenkins, on the other hand, had placed herself in a strange proximity to Lily's room.

"Sir, I have prepared your coffee mixture. Please allow me to show you the way to your quarters, and I am sure we can make you better in no time!" Mrs Jenkins tried to solicit her employer to head towards his room and deviate from his current course. However, the glance Edmund threw her way had such an intimidating expression, in spite of her generous bodily constitution, she felt powerless in stopping him from barging into Lily's room.

13.

Left alone in Edmund's study, Marianne caught a glimpse of her own reflection in the window. The rubies encircling her neck gleamed against the light. She stared at them feeling mocked by the same stones burning against her skin.

She tore the necklace away, and as the jewels scattered onto the floor, tears began to stream down her cheeks; and yet in spite of the mist clouding her eyes, something outside of the window caught her attention. "Henry!" she gasped.

Without another thought, she fled the room, burst through the front doors and ran towards the coach waiting in the distance.

She opened the door and climbed inside.

"Marianne!" he exclaimed, startled by her appearance.

"You're still here…," she murmured, her chest still heaving from the exertion.

"I... I was just about to leave," he responded hesitantly.

"Oh, Henry! Why would you tell him of your true feelings when you could never confess them to me?!"

"You knew?!"

"I have always suspected it, but you would not talk to me directly!"

"Then why; why have you never given me any hope?! Is it because I was not good enough for you, Marianne, is that it?!"

"No, of course not; but you left and–"

"–You always had dreams of grandeur, Marianne! You always spoke of things I knew I could never afford to provide you with; but I supposed if I went away and exerted myself you may grow to consider me…"

She had been sitting across from him, but as she spoke again, she placed herself right beside him and took his hand, "I may have done this all wrong Henry… I have been an immense fool all these years! For all it is worth, I am truly sorry."

Marianne had come alarmingly close to him, and he did not pull away.

Heat rose up Henry's face as her gaze locked with his deep blue eyes.

"I wronged us both Henry; he never loved me…," her breath was warm against his skin.

And Henry needed no further encouragement.

*

As the events in the carriage were in full swing, Edmund had succeeded in securing the lock behind Lily's door.

"Milord, is there any particular request you have of me?"

She was still sitting in the same manner Marianne had left her in, going through Dr Watson's letters again; contemplating and dreading what was expected to come next.

"You certainly did not need to take the trouble of coming all the way here, milord," she continued, "you could have simply sent for me, and I would have reported to you."

All the while, as she spoke, Edmund had been walking towards her. There was a menace in his approach which made her wary.

"So, this is the consideration you have of me?!"

"I beg your pardon, milord?"

"Are you of the same opinion as them?" he hissed.

"I am not sure about who you may be referring to, milord; but I can see you have been intoxicating yourself again. Allow me to get Mr Jenkins to assist you." With the firm resolve of getting out of his way, Lily deposited Dr Watson's letters on her bed. She then turned back around, only to find herself an inch away from him. "Milord, please excuse me so that I may find assistance for your predicament."

"I asked you if you think me incapable of pleasing of you!" He barked at her.

"Milord, I have asked you to let me go," she slowly, but firmly barked back.

"I expected many things from you, but not this! Is this all I am worth in your eyes?!"

Lily remained silent. This man was not the same Edmund she had left in the carriage earlier. Earlier, though he was overtaken by rage, he could still be reasoned with; but now, he had turned himself into a beast.

"It was all your doing; not Marianne's! Did you purposefully make me sail across half of the world so that you could make a spectacle of me, is that it?! I suppose you got what you came for! Are you satisfied at last?!"

"Milord...," she stuttered. "You must understand this journey was not meant to be about you, milord. Her ladyship was suffering, she is suffering! If you had witnessed her despair as I have, you would not be talking so!"

"At what price?!" Edmund mocked. "And you had to make yourself her accomplice, is that so?!"

In an instant, she found herself thrown on her bed, pinned down by the arms.

"What of my despair!?" he cried into her ears, eager to act in accordance with his inebriated sense.

His mind was not his, and reason was not to be evoked at present. But this side of Edmund was not unknown to her.

She had experienced incidents such as this several times in their common past.

Though no other man had ever come close to her since the providential day Edmund had rescued her from that wretched summer house; Lily had developed a certain familiarity with the outbursts of a married man she knew to be wretchedly in love with her. Such manifestations had lessened since his marriage to Marianne, and in time, Lily no longer dreaded such encounters; in fact, she had grown quite familiar with them.

"You are hurting me, Edmund," she found the strength to say at last.

Her words seemed to have an effect on his reasoning.

Visibly in possession of his wits once again, he stared adoringly into Lily's piercing eyes.

At last, after they both did not know how long, he finally slid his body off of hers. But as he was getting up, he knocked Dr Watson's pile of letters off the bed.

Picking them up from the ground, he took the liberty of inspecting who this correspondent may be.

"What do we have here?!" He roared, after his inspection was over.

The distance she put between them while he was busy with the letters availed her of no advantage, as before she could even grasp the meaning of his enquiry, he was back on her, restraining her body against the wall this time.

"So, this is the type of attention you crave! I am not bookish enough for you, is that it? And here I was, believing your character to be only equal to God's angels! But all along you are just like the rest of us! You seem very pleased to be receiving this man's attentions!"

When he had nothing left to accuse, he started to rip the letters in half, one by one.

"Edmund, you need to stop this nonsense and leave my room this instant! You have been in here long enough already!"

"I was so certain you would never allow anybody but me to be close to you! But I now realise I have foolishly misled myself! Did you concede to Watson what you persistently refused me?" he yelled, tossing the ripped papers aside.

Lily pushed him away with all the strength she could gather in her body; but Edmund was stronger and seemed more determined than any other past occasion to have his way with her.

In his desperate attempt at restraint, he grabbed the back of her chemise and inadvertently ripped it apart.

She froze as a sudden breeze touched her flesh, sending a shiver through her.

The sight of her back seemed to be precisely what Edmund needed in order to regain some sort of mental composure.

Lily held on to the front of her mutilated garment; she would not turn around and grant him the satisfaction of seeing the tears welling in her eyes.

Had she turned around however, she would have witnessed the agonising battle Edmund had barely managed to overcome with his own demons.

His heart had loved this woman long enough for him to be fully able to recall that should he choose to surrender to his temporary carnal gratification, no matter how blissfully satisfying the encounter may be, he would forever lose the timeless tranquillity her nearness provided to his soul.

And, after a period of time which felt like an eternity to them both, Lily felt him walk past her, heard him leave the room, and shut the door behind him.

*

Outside Lily's room, Edmund was not surprised to find Mrs Jenkins positioned in the corridor.

"Where is my wife?" He enquired.

"Her ladyship has retired in her quarters, Sir."

"See that we are not disturbed!"

The loyal servant seemed quite relieved to see her employer finally retire in his marital chambers; she then granted herself leave to return to her own duties.

"Am I disturbing, wife?" Edmund remarked, as he entered the room.

Marianne had returned only recently herself, and upon her return, was relieved to find the usual cloths and basin placed by her bedside table.

She had just concluded cleansing herself from the surreal liaison she had just consummated with Henry when Edmund arrived.

"N-no..., Edmund, please, do come in! What may I do for you?"

"Turn off the lights," he requested, as he came to avail himself of his marital rights.

14.

The sun had slowly begun to rise in the horizon, when the Indian housekeeper, having made her way upstairs to extinguish the lanterns, saw Lord Hertworth come out of his wife's room and head back into the negro's room once again.

Closing the door behind him, Edmund was surprised to find the bed empty. His eyes swept the room and there she lay, exactly where he had last seen her standing, fast asleep on the floor.

He walked towards her cocooned figure and gently took her up in his arms, carrying her sleeping body to the bed.

Had there been any spectators at that particular moment, they would not be wrong in assuming the fragile bundle who was being carefully tucked into bed was indeed as precious as a dearly beloved woman could be to an adoring lover.

Once the source of all his anguish had resumed the rhythm of her soft and peaceful breathing, he eased into the chair beside her. There he blissfully lost himself watching over her for he knew not how long.

The hand resting closest to him caught his attention and he gently took hold of it.

His recent intimacy with Marianne reminded him he could never quench the thirst only Lily was a remedy for.

Will he ever be permitted to touch her; feel her as he had allowed himself many years ago?

As his mind became lost in his memories of her, he almost failed to notice a sudden alteration in her breathing. Reluctantly he released her hand from his hold and rose from his seat.

She stirred awake moments later; by then, he had placed himself by the cooling hearth on the far side of the room, occupied with the very same letters he had torn apart the night before; only this time he appeared intent at trying his best to undo the mess those letters had become.

From across the room, Lily observed him in silence, but as he felt her gaze, he turned to meet her eyes.

He had always understood her eyes best. Once, at the start of their acquaintance, they had brought so much agony to him; and yet, despite her many attempts to shield her emotions from him, her eyes had evolved into an addiction his very existence depended on.

This particular morning, as their eyes locked, Edmund noticed a slight change in the resignation she would usually display after his customary outbursts.

Though it may sound prideful in its expectation, he had become quite accustomed to her generous acceptance and forgiveness towards him after a display such as the night before.

"I see you are finally awake," he casually remarked as he walked back towards the same chair he had occupied as she slept. As he approached her, he realised he had not imagined the change in her usual forbearing countenance, and the closer he got to her, the more fearful he became of what she may say to him on this occasion.

Her eyes appeared quite red and swollen, from what he could only assume to be the consequence of crying herself to sleep.

As he was about to reach for the chair, she retreated under her covers and asked, "What time is it, milord?"

"It will be morning soon," he obliged. "I have instructed Mrs Jenkins to delay breakfast until you are ready to come down, but if you prefer, I can have a plate brought up to you."

"I do not need you to worry about my breakfast... How would you expect me to explain your presence in my room should anybody come in at this moment?"

"Is this what worries you?!" he exclaimed, letting out a sigh of relief that bordered on amusement. "Well, we are far from home! I could understand your considerations had you been in the Manor, but seriously Imbali, we are indeed on the other side of the world at present. I suppose this could become one positive outcome I could thank Marianne for!"

He appeared evidently grateful to see her main distress concerned her want of propriety. She may not reproach him for his wild conduct from the previous evening after all!

He then ventured to return to the casual ways Lily would sometimes allow him to converse with her.

He talked about the weather and how irritated his skin had been since their arrival.

He talked of politics.

He talked of his business by the port.

He talked of the irregularities he had found in the books he forced the local clerk to hand over to him.

He talked of everything and anything except their own selves.

Lily remained totally silent. But he seemed not to mind the silence; it was indeed much more welcomed than the words her steely eyes were communicating.

He at last recollected Dr Hashford and his feelings for Marianne, and he would have disclosed it all to her; but she seemed to have found her tongue at last.

"Edmund, I need you to understand, I truly care for Marianne, and I would not be able to forgive myself if she was to be exposed to this foolishness! We might not be in England, but we are right beside your lawful wife who has no knowledge of...," she was about to say 'us' but she wisely refrained from using such a dangerous word. "You reassured me you would love and respect her!" Lily found her words again. "I am honouring my part, but all you seem to be offering is your disregard to her wishes and to her as your wife!"

"I never said I would love her!" interjected Edmund. "I told you I would respect and honour my wedding vows; as per your wishes, but I would never claim to you or anyone that I will love another woman! I must ask you not to insult me by attributing to me feelings which are decidedly against myself! I have tried, and you too know how I desperately tried! But it is of no use! I have now come to learn to live with these arrangements; all I have asked of you is to accept this fate along with me!"

The air between them grew thick with an unbearable tension, as though the weight of years of unspoken pain and yearning was pressing upon them both.

She needed distance from him. She stood from the bed, wrapped herself with the blanket and walked to the window where the bright light of dawn peeked through the curtains.

"How long will this insanity carry on unnoticed?" she then murmured, almost as if speaking to herself, and not him.

"I grant you, what occurred last night was unforgivable, but I was not myself! I assure you it will not happen again!" he pleaded. "Surely, you must find the allowance for my temperament of yesterday! Even you cannot expect me to remain impassive to the shocking allegations that so-called doctor was alluding to!"

"Edmund," she began, turning to face him, "you must allow yourself the possibility of opening your heart to your wife. And I have been thinking... rather, hoping, that if you and Marianne were to finally have a child, perhaps you could begin to develop a meaningful attachment to her. I understand your aversion to Dr Bathia's methods, but I truly believe them to be credible–"

"–You stay out of this!" he interrupted.

"But I would not have seconded Marianne in this endeavour had I believed it to be unworthy of consideration," she countered, refusing to oblige his order. "Those letters you see there are the results of a couple of months of my intent at trying to understand more of Dr Bathia's unconventional methods," she pointed at the letters resting on the mantelpiece. "I first wrote to Dr Watson one morning after you had spent a good ten minutes praising the man from your days together at Oxford."

"All that the man does in those letters is grace himself onto you! How could you allow him to address you in such liberal terms? Are there any other letters from him apart from those ones?" At these words, Edmund stood up and went back to the mantelpiece to grab one of the hated letters and read out its contents:

"*I can no longer conceal from you how much you intrigue my curiosity, dear Miss Lily.*

Responding to your queries has long ceased to be my main inducement at keeping my correspondence with you.

Your elevated curiosity can be nothing but a testament to your superior opinions, and these I must confess have indeed aroused my otherwise dormant interest in life.

You say you are pleased with your occupation under your current tutelage, but I sense there may be more to it than you reveal to me.

I would not aspire to equal the offerings of a family such as the Hertworths, but I cannot help sense your dissatisfaction in your current engagements–"

"–How do you explain these words?!" he questioned, interrupting his reading. "I had full faith in you!"

"You misunderstand the man!" she defended.

"What is there to misunderstand?!" he shot back at her. "I've read all of his letters! The tone, the phrasing; it's all there! You cannot deny his obvious interest in you! But it matters no longer. You are not to correspond with him again. Do I make myself clear?!"

"Edmund, there is nothing to deny here! Dr Watson was simply obliging my enquiries-"

His expression darkened as he cut her off mid-sentence. "Never once did I think I would come to doubt the constancy of your regard for me, and I do not intend to begin doubting it now! How could you allow him to use such liberal terms in his address to you?!"

Edmund had turned her into the guilty one as his heavy words hung in the air, his mind clinging obsessively to the implications of the letters. Each phrase he had read seemed, in his eyes, a betrayal of the tacit understanding between the two of them.

Lily had dealt with enough of him to know there was not much for her to say any longer.

They both spoke nothing; his gaze pierced hers until, at last, her eyes granted him a silent assent to his latest command.

She crossed the room and climbed back into her bed, drawing the covers around herself. She turned her back to him, dismissing him.

But he lingered above her, his fists clenching and unclenching at his sides, as though grasping for control. At length, however, he turned on his heels, and left the room to her, the door closing behind him with a soft, mournful click.

15.

Marianne had woken shortly after Edmund left her side, her mind immediately overtaken by the mess she had dragged herself into.

Fortunately for her, during her escapade, it appeared no one within the household had taken note of the events unfolding within the confines of a public coach. Surely, were Edmund aware of her misconduct, he would not have come to her.

She derived immense happiness in having Edmund come to her bed voluntarily; an event which had been occurring less and less as the years went by. He had been more passionate than he had been in a very long time, almost as passionate as Henry, she then recollected.

At the thought of Henry, she could not help but ponder upon how different the consequences of her actions would feel at present; how different her life might have been had she married him instead of Edmund. Would she have been happier as Mrs Henry Hashford, would her life be more fulfilling, less burdened with the pressures and expectations she now felt as Lady Hertworth?

As Marianne brooded over her plight and the uncertain prospects before her, her thoughts inevitably turned to her companion. Lily's counsel was sure to alleviate her spirits.

She came out of her chamber just as Edmund was closing Lily's door behind him.

"Edmund!" she exclaimed, surprised to find her husband still lingering on the upper floor. "Is anything the matter with Lily?"

Edmund did not answer. He silently stood across from her, his eyes fixed on her with an unsettling intensity. She did not feel strong enough to sustain his penetrating gaze this morning, and as she turned her eyes away from his, she noticed the letters clutched tightly in his hand.

"Those letters Edmund... did Lily show you the letters from her Dr Watson?! Oh, I so knew she would!" she exclaimed.

But her husband could not respond to her, as Marianne's voice must have carried into Lily's chamber, for moments later, Lily emerged to greet her mistress and join them for their usual morning meal. So, the three of them silently made their way to the breakfast room.

*

As Lily sat in her usual place, right beside Marianne, Edmund began speaking.

"Dr Hashford is not to step foot into this house, and as soon as we return to England, he shall be replaced by someone else."

Marianne's fingers tightened around her fork, but she managed to keep her eyes on her plate, summoning a calmness she did not feel.

Edmund appeared to be expecting some response from her.

"Edmund...," she then hesitated, "I-I had hoped we might stay a little longer; at least until I can be certain of the... well, of the outcome of your visit last night."

At these words, Edmund's gaze shot upward and he caught the swift, subconscious glance Lily cast toward him before she quickly returned to the contents of her plate.

"I do not think this is the proper time or place to discuss such matters," he countered.

"But, Edmund, I hold no secrets from Lily!" Marianne protested. "How could I, when I consider her the very reason for us coming together?" She placed her hand gently over Lily's. "Do you think me as inopportune as Edmund would have me believe, Lily dear?"

"N-no, Marianne," Lily stammered, catching herself immediately after. "Of course, you are at liberty to discuss whatever you wish."

"See, Edmund!" Marianne exclaimed triumphantly. "You were very passionate last night… I am sure I will be with child once again," she continued, coming to place her hand upon his.

"But, Lily dear… is something the matter with you?" she queried with a note of concern in her tone. "I cannot be certain; it is rather hard to tell with a complexion such as yours, but you have been looking rather pale lately."

"I am well, Marianne… thank you," Lily replied softly.

Lily kept her gaze averted from his, and Edmund felt at liberty to look at her at will. She did indeed seem unwell, but how could she not, following the night she must have had to endure because of him.

"I see nothing particularly unusual about her," he muttered, turning his attention back on his breakfast.

"But, Edmund, I must insist, for Lily's sake; and as you know, we have no other connections, other than... Dr Hashford."

"I have said nothing is the matter with her!" he snapped. "And no man of such profession is to see or correspond with either of you! Have I made myself clear?!" he yelled as he pushed back his chair and stood abruptly. Moments later, the sound of the front door slamming echoed through the house, reverberating long after he had stormed out.

*

With Edmund out of sight, Marianne spent the rest of the day by the windows at the front of the house, watching the streets below, her thoughts fixed on Henry.

She found herself waiting, expecting he would come to see her directly, but as the day came to a close her hopes were to remain unanswered.

The following morning, she rose again holding the same expectations. She refused Lily's company, declaring she was rather taken by the embroidery she meant to complete before the end of the afternoon, and as such wished to be quite alone. She sat beside the same windows at the front of the house; but this day too came to a close to Marianne's disappointment.

*

Marianne began to grow fastidious at Henry's silence. Perhaps he lacked courage, she then considered. But, if he had been so brave to declare his affection for her in front of her husband, how could he now be intimidated by Edmund and not come to see her again; was that not the least he could do, considering what had taken place between them?

But even as the first few days went by, in spite of his impolitic lack of consideration towards her, she still presumed she could positively confide in his secrecy; but by the seventh day of his absence, she thought it best to ensure it from him directly, so she ventured to send a letter to the address where she knew him to be staying.

*

Every single morning, for the next three consecutive days, Marianne would personally inspect the post herself.

However, not only did Henry never appear before her, but on the same day she was able to ascertain she was with child again, the letter she had sent him was returned alongside a note he had left for her.

> '*My dearest Marianne,*
>
> *I must urge you not to consider me nor my present actions cowardly.*
>
> *My strongest wish, in writing this, is for you to allow me the concession of your understanding, and subsequently your forbearance.*
>
> *I will not enumerate my own considerations of what has transpired between us, in fear this missive may fall in the wrong hands; but one detail I will allow myself to disclose to you.*
>
> *I am now a changed man. You have offered me purpose.*
>
> *I must run... but not for my own sake. I do so purely with you, and our future, in mind.*
>
> *I will leave this place, and please know my biggest regret is to leave you behind in it; but I do so with the hope that I may one day be able to take you along with me.*
>
> *I will not disclose to you my destination, but be sure I will write to you again, and when I do it will be my biggest wish to be able to pose to you the offer my own weaknesses had rendered me incapable to pose so long ago.*
>
> *Yours faithfully,*
> *Henry.*'

Marianne's eyes flared as she reached the end of the note, "What a coward!"

*

While Marianne fumed over the new predicament caused by Henry's note, elsewhere by the port, Edmund was engaged in his own heated exchange with his loyal Mr Jenkins.

"I'm sorry, Sir, truly I am, but I need more time! Believe me, Sir, I can't stand these streets any more than you do! Blimey, the stink in the air, like rot and filth; it turns my stomach!"

"I would have left time ago had it not been for you!" Edmund shot back. "Where is this man you spoke of?!"

"I-I haven't found him yet, Sir," Jenkins admitted reluctantly. "I curse my own stupid head! I had him right in my grip! I should have never let him go!"

"For the love of God, Jenkins! As I recall, you took him for an impostor!"

"Aye, that I did! Couldn't let him slander your good name, Sir! But then Dr Hashford vanishes just like that; and so I started thinking… something didn't sit right, Sir."

"I have grown tired of waiting," Edmund countered. "As far as I am concerned, you have nothing to prove your claim!"

16.

"My dear Marianne, you cannot be leaving us so soon! Please, tell me it is not true!" cried Mrs Pembroke as she swept into the tearoom, the admiral following close behind.

"I so dearly hoped you and his lordship would not refuse to join us for our humble gathering! I specifically had it all arranged with you in mind, my dear! Indeed, I would have arranged it much sooner had you not misinformed me! I was even ready to welcome your negro along with you...," she added as her eyes glanced over Marianne's shoulders and caught sight of Lily coming beside her mistress.

"I beg your pardon," Marianne countered, "but I cannot presume to comprehend the nature of your information."

"Are you not expected to be leaving us before the end of the week?! Believe me when I tell you, company such as yours is hard to come by amongst our small circle so far away from home! But I suppose that is not to be had! As you suppose to deprive us of it! Of course, I can do nothing but speculate on your motives!" the lady continued, appearing offended by Marianne.

"But, my dear Mrs Pembroke," Marianne interjected during the brief pause as the lady caught her breath, "we have made no definite plans for our return just yet."

"Are you quite certain?" she said, frowning. "How peculiar! My sources never fail me, and it was the admiral himself who brought me this news!" She then turned ever so slightly toward her husband, "Did you not say, earlier today at the Royal Navy's quarters, Lord Hertworth's man was granted leave to set sail for England in two days' time?"

"Ah, yes! I did say so," the admiral obliged, clearing his throat. "It was brought to my attention this morning; Lord Hertworth's affairs, it seems, have concluded sooner than expected."

"It must be true if the admiral himself says so," Marianne countered, accepting the cup of tea Lily poured for her. "But I am as surprised as you are; you must believe me when I tell you, I was quite truthful with the information I gave you when I last saw you... but now that I come to think of it, I can only suppose my new state may have induced him to change his plans," she continued, setting down her teacup with deliberate grace. "I believe I shall very soon be able to announce the good news to our family once more."

"Oh, how wonderful!" Mrs Pembroke exclaimed. "But... will you be able to succeed this time? I really hope you do; I so dearly wish it for your own sake!"

Marianne smiled at the lady, though with very little warmth in it, "I believe I shall, and my dearest Edmund believes it too! He shows me nothing but the best consideration!"

"Good Lord!" the lady exclaimed, a sudden thought coming to her mind. "Why would Dr Hashford be gone away from you?! Surely you must need him beside you, now more than ever! I must confess I heard many great things about him! You were indeed quite fortunate to have him at your personal bidding!"

"Yes! Marianne was indeed very fortunate with him!" a familiar voice interjected.

Lord Hertworth entered the room, drawing all eyes upon him.

"My good lord, how good to see you!" Mrs Pembroke cried, extending a hand which Edmund dutifully accepted. "I was just reproaching your wife for depriving us of your company!"

He gave a polite nod to the compliment, his gaze wondering about the room. He hesitated only a moment before deciding to sit beside Lily, just as she rose to refill everyone's tea.

"Must she be the one to serve us the tea?" the lady remarked. "My dear Marianne, I do not know how you bear her presence; she stands close to you, too close, for my liking!"

"But I cannot quite do without her!" Marianne countered in defence of her friend. "Come, Lily, sit beside me."

"He is no longer under your services, is he then?" Mrs Pembroke turned their conversation to Dr Hashford once again.

"N-no, he is... I mean to say, yes, he is no longer under our services," Marianne responded.

"Oh, very well; but I wonder, with our countryman gone, I ought to recommend a most distinguished physician, he is Indian; but he is all the rage at present. What was his name? Ah, yes, Dr Bathia!" she answered herself immediately after. "You should have him attend you while you are here."

"Where did you say Dr Hashford has gone off to?" she turned to her husband, seeking his input.

"I was surprised at his peculiar choice, my lord," the admiral remarked, addressing Edmund directly. "These are uncertain times, I tell you! There are rumours of unrest across the Mediterranean waters, and here he is gone off to Anatolia out of all places!"

"Oh, I long to visit Greece!" his wife proclaimed, unwilling to be cut out from the conversation any longer.

"The admiral has promised to take me several times, but alas our duty to the Crown needs us here a little longer."

"This place is a bit down south on the map, my dear," the husband corrected.

"Oh, I see...," she stumbled for a moment. "I remember all about it now! This must be lands it is said where all the Gods ever known to humanity had decided to manifest themselves to us! A most wonderful place, full of tales of intrigues and... such seductions!"

"That may have been so in the past, my dear," the admiral countered, "but the Ottoman empire is a hotbed of unrest at present! The Turks no longer hold the Arabs under their grip! A war could possibly break out in the nearest future."

"You cannot expect us women to understand politics as you may do, indeed I cannot help but find this whole conversation most romantic indeed!" the wife countered. "Do you not think so, milord?" Her eyes fixed on Edmund. "Indeed, I long for adventures! I am growing quite bored of this post of yours, I must tell you!" she then said to her husband.

"I know my dear, but you know very well it cannot be helped," the husband offered apologetically.

"She does look rather fastidious I daresay... you must find her rebellious, I am sure!" the lady then remarked as her eyes came to settle on Lily once more. "At least these Indians are quite accepting of our superiority; but her kind," she continued, her gaze lingering on Lily, "seem resolute in maintaining their stubbornness by not giving up their rejection of it!"

"On the contrary! Lily is far from rebellious!"

"Indeed?! It seems you have tamed her well then."

"She is tamed alright, but she does not fare well around strangers," Edmund cut in, rising from his seat. "Your tales of our good doctor and his new pursuits are very diverting I must say, Madam, but I fear we have taken enough of the admiral's time today."

"Quite so indeed! It seems Dr Hashford's departure has inspired quite the discussion; but I can only assume he had his reasons to go to such a place, and I dare say they are his own to keep," the admiral obliged, rising from his seat himself and coming to shake hands with his counterpart.

"I wager upon my life; she will write to Elisabeth the moment she steps through her front doors!" Marianne cried as she found herself alone with Lily.

"Elisabeth can do nothing but rejoice for you; but is it true? Are you truly expecting? Please allow me to congratulate you on your happy news–"

"–Why do you sound surprised?!" Marianne snapped. "Indeed, I am expecting again; Edmund cannot keep himself away from my bed! But it is still too soon for me to rejoice; so, you can keep your congratulations to yourself for now!"

"Please forgive me... I–"

Marianne sighed, her irritation fading as quickly as it had flared.

"–No need for such antics between us, you know too well I cannot remain angry with you my dearest Lily; are we not the best of friends?!"

"What an odious woman! I hope you haven't taken offence at her words," she then scoffed with a roll of her eyes.

"I have no reason to," Lily responded timidly. "Besides, it is only your opinion I care about."

"Good, I am glad to hear it! But what good will expecting once again do for me if I cannot secure the child inside of me!" Marianne grumbled. "You heard about Henry... how am I to secure Bathia's assistance without him?!"

"I cannot believe what we heard about Dr Hashford, it is all so strange–"

"–Do not speak his name to me again!" Marianne interjected. "He must have run there, wherever that is, as to leave no trace behind! All the better for me, as I have no wish to see or speak to him again!"

"Are we to return to England without Dr Hashford?"

"What do you mean return to England?! Do you also concur with Edmund?!"

"N-no, of course not," Lily stammered apologetically. "I only meant–"

"–You only meant to remind me of what I already know!" Marianne interrupted. "Mark my words, the moment Elisabeth hears of my state, I will lose this child too! And what have you done to help me? Nothing! Not a single thing!" she cried storming out of the tearoom.

As she made her way up the staircase, Marianne saw Edmund striding towards his own chamber. She decided to follow him.

"So, you are with child again…," his words greeted her as she stepped inside his room. His tone was distant, and as Marianne observed his face more closely, she noticed his gaze betray the trace of an emotion she could not quite make out. Perhaps he had simply grown weary of raising his hopes, only to have them dashed time and again, she reasoned; surely, it could not be anything else.

"I expected to hear of it differently," he continued, "... since when have you known?"

"Of course, you are right, Edmund, I would have told you properly in the evening, but that odious woman was so fastidious about her pretensions, and so I just had to put her in her place!

"It is still quite early…," she drew a breath, choosing her next words carefully. "Edmund, please, you must allow me to hope all shall conclude well this time. And for that, I must see that Indian doctor, at least once. You heard Mrs Pembroke, even she knows how good he is in these matters!"

His expression did not soften at her plea, "My stance remains unchanged Marianne. We return to England this Saturday," he responded, turning away from her and beginning to loosen his cravat. "You got what you came for on your own; I see no reason why you still require the services of such a charlatan."

She stepped closer to him, reaching up to untie the rest of his cravat. Her fingers brushed against the coarse line of his beard before trailing to his cheek. "Leave Bathia aside for a moment," she murmured, "should I really be traveling in my condition? Surely, being at sea in my delicate state should be out of the question..."

"And why not?!" He scoffed as he withdrew from her touch. "Throughout my travels I have seen plenty of expecting women at sea; in fact, my own mother spent most of her time on a ship while she was expecting me! And the journey back to England will not require more than two weeks altogether."

"But, Edmund, surely you cannot be so unfeeling to my situation, to our situation! I need to ensure I will fare well this time!"

"My word is final, Marianne; believe me I have been delayed long enough!" and with that, he turned and left his room to her.

*

He made his way to the study, but as he entered, he was startled to find Lily standing in the dimly lit room.

"What are you doing in here?!"

"My lord... I wish for you to persuade Dr Bathia to attend to Marianne," she said.

"I see!" he exclaimed. "Three entire weeks, close to four, I should say; you have avoided me, and now, you choose to break your silence, to plead for her?" He reached out, catching her arm and moving her closer to him.

"Milord, let go of my arm," she said, unfazed by his imposing presence, "and I was not avoiding you. I simply had nothing to say to you."

"If you are angry with me, then you ought to know I went to her that night after I left your room… I was furious; I-I desired you more than ever–"

"–You did well," she cut in, her expression betraying nothing of what she felt, "and Marianne is rightfully bearing the fruits of it. Please allow me to offer my congratulations, milord."

"Do not speak to me so coldly; I beg of you!" His grip on her loosened, at last letting go, "You have condemned us to being strangers under the same roof; the least you can do is spare me the torment of your contempt!"

"You are mistaken if you suppose me contrary to your intimacy with your wife," she met his gaze. "In fact, it is my biggest hope for your wife to succeed this time; and in this regard, she has done her part. But in spite of her pleas, you are resolute in denying her a very reasonable wish, and so I find myself compelled to speak on her behalf."

"She is with child already! What else do you expect that charlatan to do for her?!"

"We cannot ignore what has gone wrong before… I do not know exactly what else he can do for her, but I do know that she will find comfort in having him with her nonetheless!"

"And I suppose her comfort will bring you happiness...?"

She said nothing, but her eyes answered for her.

A bitter smile played on his lips, "Even if I were to consent to your wish, I will not let you step foot anywhere near that squalor!"

"Then make him come to her!"

"How am I to persuade him to come here?!"

"Every man has a price... as you know very well, milord. Find his price and offer it to him."

17.

Not only did the Hertworths remain in India, Dr Bathia had been appointed Marianne's new personal physician, and to Lily's contentment, Marianne was very pleased with this new arrangement.

For the next several weeks, the doctor would regularly come to their residence to personally attend to Marianne.

Marianne's interesting state had noticeably advanced to the furthest stage she had ever come so far. If all continued as Dr Bathia predicted, she would hold her child before the end of the next rainy season; within five months at most.

And yet, despite the joyful prospect, Marianne could not bring herself to rejoice, as who had fathered this child of hers was a poignant dilemma she could not ignore; no matter how ardently she wished it out of her mind.

Would this child bear the distinguished features of her husband or would it inherit the angelic traits of Henry?

In the heat of that eventful evening, it had felt highly gratifying to hear of Henry's feelings for her, but in truth, Marianne was no romantic. She had now come to regard her amorous liaison with Henry as a complete, foolish misjudgement on her part.

Henry understood her well.

She truly valued prestige and position in society above all else; and she had a mind of stopping at nothing to earn and secure such privileges.

*

"You are as good as people claimed you to be, but I cannot help wonder what might have been offered to induce you to come to me so diligently," Marianne said as Dr Bathia conducted his routine examination of her. "Not that I mind of course, whatever it is you are giving me seems to be working rather well; but Dr Hashford supposed it impossible to persuade you to do anything against your principles, and I can tell my husband is certainly not a favourite of yours."

The doctor smiled, though his touch remained methodical as he continued to press along her stomach. "Dr Hashford was quite right about my sentiments… but I suppose there are some inducements even I cannot resist."

"If I remember correctly, my companion was of particular allure to you, but I shall warn you, you can forget about her!"

"Miss Lily is indeed an interesting girl, but your empire is vast; it holds much to be seen, and many more people to discover."

"And my husband promised you these discoveries?!"

"Not quite… at least not for the present," he admitted, before fixing a smile towards her.

"But you must allow me to tell you how pleased I am to see you two did not require the assistance of our heretic ways after all; what do you say to that, milady?"

Marianne frowned at him, "I fail to comprehend your meaning."

"I don't imply much, milady," he obliged. "I am simply pleased to see that providence will always find its way to overpower the mind and logic of us mortals.

"And you coming this far with your pregnancy, which you have managed to secure all quite naturally, without any intervention from me, is indeed an excellent demonstration of that!"

"I'm sorry to intrude, milady, but we need him immediately!" Mrs Jenkins burst into Marianne's chamber; her voice overtaken with urgency.

"What is the matter with you?!"

"It's Miss Lily!"

"What of her?"

"She's become unwell, milady; and now she-she's began to shake all over!" Mrs Jenkins cried, wringing her hands on her apron as she struggled to piece together an explanation. "And he," she glanced anxiously toward Dr Bathia, "he is said to understand these things. He must come now, please!"

Dr Bathia rose immediately, and Marianne followed him close behind. The once quiet corridor now buzzed with frantic upheaval as servants darted up and down the stairs, all converging towards Edmund's chamber.

They followed the procession and as Marianne entered the room she saw her own husband already there, kneeling right beside his own bed, wholly absorbed in the task of wiping a cloth all over Lily's face.

Lily, however, seemed totally unaware of the spectacle Edmund was presenting to the entire household. She lay on the bed, pale and drenched in a pool of sweat; and though her eyes were firmly shut, her body was overtaken by some strange convulsions all over.

"What has happened to her?!" Marianne gasped.

Edmund barely registered her presence. His focus never wavered from his meticulous task of drying each of the beads of sweat which continuously reappeared as soon as he was done wiping them.

At last, he spoke, but not to Marianne. He looked up to Mrs Jenkins and commanded, "Get her out of here. Now!"

"What has happened to her?!" Marianne insisted, though she allowed Mrs Jenkins to escort her back to her own chamber.

"It's them wretched ones who brought her to this state! But would she ever listen to me? No, why would she?!" Mrs Jenkins wailed.

"I do not follow, Mrs Jenkins, pray explain it properly!"

Mrs Jenkins took a steadying breath, attempting to compose herself, "Begging your pardon, milady," she obliged. "As you know, she has the best of hearts our Miss Lily! Too kind for her own good! She insisted on caring for those poor, forsaken children herself!"

"But I would see her going into the kitchens; I assumed she was busy helping you!" Marianne countered.

"In the kitchens she would come for sure! But to gather the leftover food, and she would insist on personally taking it herself to them! Every day without fail she would walk to them! And... I-I should have stopped her! I should have told Mr Jenkins everything!"

"Why are you not the one attending to her? Surely you can be of much better assistance to her than my own husband!" Marianne cried. "And for heaven's sake, how did she end up on his bed?!"

"You are quite right, milady... but his lordship was the one who found her struggling on the streets just outside–"

"–I must go inside and get him away from her!" she rejoined, attempting to turn back the way she came.

"It's the lordship's orders…," Mrs Jenkins countered. "Maybe he is thinking of the babe. We still don't know if what she has is catchy, milady! It is better for you to stay away."

*

To Edmund, Dr Bathia's inspection of Lily felt interminable, but in truth it lasted only a few moments before he reached his verdict.

"Her symptoms do suggest malaria... but her condition is precarious–"

"–can you treat it?!"

"I might have been able to had it been caught earlier," the doctor said grimly. "But I fear the disease may have spread too severely into her body. I may be able to help a little with the discomfort but... unfortunately, these convulsions are not a good sign–"

"–they said you could save her!" Edmund interjected, his voice rising with uncontained fury. "This is not the time for you to seek your revenge on me!"

"Two others have come before you, and they presumed the same damn thing as you just did!"

"But you sent them away!" Bathia countered, "So, what do you want with me?!"

"Because the last one said you are best equipped in understanding her physiology and what to do for it!" Edmund's voice wavered, anger giving way to desperation, "I never believed in you, that is true; but she did, she sent me to you! Please... I beg you; save her, and you can ask anything you ever wish of me!"

For a long moment, Bathia said nothing, his gaze wandering between Lily's fragile, now motionless form, and the nobleman pleading to him. If the doctor felt any oddity in the current desperation Lord Hertworth was displaying for the negro, he wisely chose to keep his thoughts to himself.

*

Dr Bathia acquiesced to assemble a team of physicians to attend to Miss Lily thereon, though Lord Hertworth became resolute at having him as the lead physician. As the days passed, the Indian doctor found himself running tirelessly around the clock, attending to the needs of his lordship's wife, and ensuring that Miss Lily regained her full health and strength.

18.

Lily's sickness came to be regarded contagious by most of the servants in the house; therefore, everyone seemed quite relieved to abide by the strict protocol Lord Hertworth had put in place around the negro.

The only other people he would allow in the room along with him were Mr and Mrs Jenkins, and the handpicked physicians whom he expected to pay their daily visits at least once in the morning and a second time in the evening.

For over a fortnight, Edmund had confined himself in his room with Lily.

As the days passed Lily seemed to be slowly improving; she even had a few spates of lucid consciousness.

Marianne too had been banished from Edmund's quarters, and therefore she found herself forcefully obliged to refrain from questioning her husband about any part of his behaviour around her companion.

Up until this point in their lives, she had grown skilfully accustomed to her husband's magnanimous impartiality towards her companion, but never had she expected him to display it quite so publicly!

Deciding to force her way into his room, she became visibly disturbed by the sight of her husband fully tucked under his covers, holding her companion's body tightly against his own.

"What are you doing under there with her?!"

"What did you come in here for?!" he shot back. "Have you come to admire your accomplishment?!"

"You clearly have no idea what you are saying!" she countered. "Please Edmund, you must stop this madness at once! You are offering too much for everyone to speculate upon! I beg you to allow Mrs Jenkins to take care of her! It cannot be you!"

"Never again will I allow anyone else to take care of her!"

The air inside the room was oppressive, thick with the bitter smell of sickness and medicine, and Marianne could not ignore it.

"Edmund! You must see your state! She is fully drenched in God knows what! And you, I am sure, will soon catch the disease off of her!"

"And you suppose that to be of any concern to me, do you?!" he retorted. "It did not matter to me then, and it certainly does not matter now! Where is the ice? What's causing this delay?!" he then shouted out to Mrs Jenkins.

"Milord..., you have already used all the ice stored in the house," Mrs Jenkins stepped in to remind him.

"I said I do not care where you get ice from, Jenkins must spare no expense! Tell him to run to every single house in this wretched land and buy all the ice there is to be found! She is boiling all over again! And tell them to fill up the bath again with fresh water!"

Minutes later, as the servants hauled in the bathtub and filled it with fresh water Edmund carried Lily's limp body in his arms, and, to Marianne's shock, he was wearing only his drawers, and nothing else!

He began bathing her; so tender in his attention it appeared as though he had cradled her the same other times in his past.

"You will not leave me. You will rally, just as you did that night at sea. I know you can hear me... come back to me and I promise you, I will make this right by you."

"Edmund, this is quite enough!" Marianne exclaimed, attempting to reclaim some authority in her own home. "Mrs Jenkins can handle this much more efficiently than you!"

Edmund did not so much as glance in her direction. His focus remained entirely on Lily, his hands working steadily to cool her fevered skin.

Frustrated, and desperate to put an end to the spectacle her husband, and by extension her own self, had become, Marianne moved toward him, reaching out to take hold of his hand. But before she could, Edmund startled her by coming to meet her gaze, his eyes darker than ever before. "I personally hold you responsible, Marianne! You have done this to her!"

"B-but, Edmund, I am with child!" she stammered; her hands pressed against the swell of her stomach. "Must I remind you; I too need you!"

Edmund laughed a bitter laugh, "Fear not, Marianne," he said coldly, "once you birth this child, I intend to proceed with an intent of divorce in order to release you from your duty." His ominous words hung in the air, silencing Marianne.

"Divorce?!" she found her voice. "You intend to divorce me! For her?!"

"Yes, for her!" he said solemnly. "Mrs Jenkins don't just stand there; she's letting draft come in; shut the door!" he then commanded.

"Come, milady... this is not good for you either, let's take you back to your chamber," Mrs. Jenkins offered.

*

As the door latched behind Marianne, silence folded over the room.

From the silence he heard Lily whisper to him, "Edmund… that night at sea… finish it."

"I'm here my love," he offered, "she's gone; don't strain yourself, I'm here with you."

"I cannot bear to see you surrounded by them... so beautiful and elegant," her voice trembled as she spoke again, more fervently this time. "And that Mrs Pembroke! She should not have you; you are mine alone!"

A thin smile played on Edmund's lips, "Jealous of another?" he teased. "You only speak so because of the fever. In your senses, you would never–"

"–I have never felt clearer!" she cut in. Her eyes flew open, two dark embers catching the firelight. "Yes, Edmund, I too have a heart and it pleads to you."

She rose from the tub in a single, fluid movement. Water ran down her skin, each droplet glinting like molten copper. The flames painted her reflection in the mirror, her body luminous against the shadows.

"W-what are you doing?" he stuttered.

Her gaze fixed upon his with such an intensity he should have looked away, but he could not.

She slid the wet chemise from her shoulders, the linen clinging to her palms for a moment before falling soundlessly to the floor. Steam rose from her body in the cold air, turning her into something unearthly.

"I am burning, Edmund," she said softly, stepping toward him, her arms outstretched. "Every part of me burns for you."

He swallowed hard; his throat had grown dry. "I… I shouldn't. You must stop–" But his protest faltered as her fingers hovered inches from his face.

At her first touch his breath caught, his resolve crumbling, "Do not tempt me so, Imbali…," his words were rough and low. " I cannot resist you… even in your state you are reducing my will to ashes." He turned his face aside, as though the very nearness of her hand burnt him more fiercely than the fire in the hearth. His jaw tightened, yet his body betrayed him, leaning toward her warmth.

"You'll catch a chill," he muttered hoarsely, "I should not... Mrs Jenkins should–"

"–I am not cold…," her tone dropped, almost a plea, "Do not turn from me, Edmund."

Slowly, as if drawn by a power he could no longer resist, his gaze returned to her. The flickers from the hearth danced across her skin, each glimmer and shadow drawing him nearer.

The struggle within him was fierce, but brief. Alas, reason gave way beneath the weight of feelings long restrained. His lips spoke in silence before he finally accepted her hand; "forgive me in the days to come," he breathed, "but not tonight."

*

Morning seeped into the chamber, the light dim and colourless against the heavy curtains. Edmund slept beside Lily; his body lying half-curved around hers.

When the door opened, Dr Bathia entered with his usual measured calmness. He did not remark upon the sight of the nobleman lying entangled with his patient, instead he remained impassive until his presence was noticed.

"How was she last night, milord?" Dr Bathia sounded unfeeling, almost detached.

Edmund tightened his hold on Lily before answering, "She was very fine," he responded drowsily. Then, unsettled by the stretch of silence that followed, he added, "I mean… she seemed well. She spoke... she answered me; she was her old self."

The doctor bent closer, studying the rise and fall of Lily's chest, the fragile flutter beneath her eyelids. His brow furrowed.

"I do not believe she was as responsive as you imagined, milord. The laudanum can stir strange illusions… hallucinations, perhaps."

Edmund's head snapped up, "Why are you so gloomy, man? I told you she was fine!" He sat upright; his voice growing louder, "What is happening to her?!"

"She has grown weaker, milord. Weaker than yesterday."

"You are wrong!" Edmund's cry echoed through the chamber. "Give her more of your syrup, summon your leeches," his words half a plea, half a command. "Take my blood and pour it into her veins but she must come around!"

Dr Bathia remained silent, his expression a mask of professional restraint.

Then unable to bear the stillness of Lily's body, Edmund tore himself from the bed and stormed out, the door slamming behind him.

*

In the corridor, Marianne was waiting. When she saw her husband emerge from his room, she rushed to him, her face incredibly pale from a sleepless night.

"Edmund," she began, "I heard you shouting. What did he say of her?"

Edmund's chest rose and fell with the force of his anger; anger directed at himself this time.

"He says she is weaker...," he brought himself to respond, "weaker than before–"

"–Edmund I could not sleep all night," Marianne interrupted, reaching for his sleeve, her temper rising. "I am expecting your child Edmund! How could you threaten me so?!"

"My threats needn't have been of any consequence had you carried on acting the role you were supposed to play in the façade of our lives!"

"What of your role then? How is it going to be with you and her?"

"The only behaviour you needed to worry about was your own!"

"So, you expected me to publicly display my consent to you in spite of the humiliation you have subjected me to in front of everyone who has happened to stumble upon our lives over the past days?

"How can you choose her over me! She is inferior to me in every way! She is a negro, Edmund! You must be out of your senses; there cannot be any other explanation!"

"You are at liberty to assume whatever you may choose regarding my attachment to her," he countered, "but never forget Marianne; everything you have become you owe it to her!

She chose to be a friend to you since day one! And she has been most constant in her service to you, in her loyalty to you; yet all you can see is the inferior woman you dare to address a negro!"

"She was no friend to me! She has deceived me all along!"

"You are also at liberty to see yourself as the injured party here, but I clearly informed you of my terms when I proposed to you.

"You knew perfectly well I was granting you all your wishes of grandeur for as long as you remained steadfast in your positive connection with her!"

"How can you be so cruel to me, Edmund! You can reproach me for many things, but you cannot castigate me for the one thing I strived for in all my time with you! I have cared for nothing but you and your happiness! You know it too! You have seen what agonies I have suffered whenever I failed in my endeavours to give you a child!" she sobbed. "Do not walk away from me, Edmund; I cannot bear to see you running to her!" Marianne yelled as she watched him vanish once again into the darkened chamber.

117

She stomped away, her footsteps carrying her instinctively to Lily's now empty quarters. She paused at the threshold before stepping inside. The room lay in silence, abandoned yet strangely alive with the ghost of its owner.

The neatly folded shawl upon the chair, the books aligned with careful precision; and the faint smell of Lily's scent clinging to the air.

Her eyes drifted and a glint of leather beneath the bed caught her attention. Kneeling, she reached beneath the frame, retrieving the hidden object, and turned it over in her hands.

A diary, Lily's diary.

It was a volume bound in dark, supple leather, its cover too fine, too elegant for Lily's modest allowance. Quite naturally, Marianne could do nothing but speculate Edmund himself must have bestowed it upon her.

Marianne had long prided herself in the knowledge she knew everything about her companion, even all the secrets Lily and Edmund believed hidden from her.

But never once did Lily mention keeping a diary, nor had Marianne ever seen her writing in it.

She opened it, and with these chronicles laid in front of her, Marianne was taken back to a time when it all began.

The first page in this diary was dated October 1871.

Lily and Marianne had not yet met.

The next several anecdotes elaborated some sinister scenes around Lily's native village, which Marianne found quite unremarkable, but as she turned the page, she came across Edmund's name.

The accounts unfolded into rather captivating entries narrating some particular events at sea.

End of Part One

19.

Atlantic Ocean, 8th October, 1871

It had been two days since the Odyssea had de-anchored off the port of the Capes and was calmly sailing upwards, across the Atlantic.

Edmund had enough experience with his employees to know they relaxed much better when he was not amongst them; so, after most chores were completed, he left them to entertain one another on the top deck with their marine experiences.

Most nights, he was content enough to earwig on their merry stories in the quietness of his own study but, as this particular night progressed, he started to find the noise a bit too discomforting, and William was not of much good company.

"So, how's your precious protectee doing?" William remarked.

Edmund did not respond.

"I suppose we owe the positive change in our meals to her, do we not?" the friend continued.

"You are quite well-informed on her doings yourself," Edmund offered at last.

"You know, I still cannot fathom you left Freddie behind!"

"Fredrick incurred the consequences of his own actions."

"For God's sake, Edmund! How can a little inconsequential escapade warrant such a consequence?!"

"I suppose you and I are not to agree on what we deem acceptable gentlemanly behaviour!"

"I may be inclined to agree with you, Edmund; but she is a mere negro! Do you not suppose you may have overreacted?! You have known him for a long time after all! Surely you ought to have a little more understanding towards such a friendship!"

"You are more than welcome to retain such friendship, as for me, I would rather pass."

"But how is he to make his way home?" William insisted.

"That is no longer a concern of mine." Edmund cut in rather abruptly, "you can keep this room to yourself, I think I would rather retire for this evening."

He proceeded towards the secluded cabin at the farthest end of his ship; the sanctuary he had deliberately designated as his own library.

Over the years he had amassed an enviable collection made up of some rare, exotic or simply different editions of books, which he had purchased in one corner of the world or other during his excursions.

He did not expect, when he opened the door, to see a faint light coming from a lantern deposited a bit too close to his precious books. Whoever had ventured into the privacy of his library had certainly no idea of the dangers he was putting his books, and the entire ship in.

"You there!" he called out to the figure who appeared warmly cloaked by the night shadows.

As Edmund inched closer to the intruder, it became evident the person had not heard his attempts at rebuke. The figure kept himself timelessly still, and whomsoever he was, he appeared eagerly immersed in a small-sized book.

The lantern had been set down with alarming precariousness upon the very edge of the shelf where the text had been removed, and Edmund observed the figure leaning against that same shelf, positioned in a way as to catch every possible gleam of the lantern's modest light.

He had now come close to the lantern, and at this proximity, his attention was caught by the peculiarity of the scene before him.

A sudden chuckle moved his attention to her face.

She was so blissfully engrossed in her reading; he saw her smiling at the words in front of her.

His shadow must have startled her, and his fears came to pass as she knocked the lantern off the shelf; but he had the promptness to grab it before it hit the ground.

"What are you doing in here?" Edmund enquired.

"I beg your forgiveness, my lord, but I was done with my chores in the kitchen," she started to burble. "The shipmaster said everybody was free to be at their own leisure tonight–"

"–So, you presumed you could allow yourself to my books?!" he interrupted.

She looked horrified, "U-uhm... the shipmaster did not include this room in the list of places I was not to venture into when I first came on board," she stuttered.

With the lantern in his hand, Edmund leaned closer, "the shipmaster must have failed to consider you may be interested in the contents of this room. Not many members of my crew would be easily entertained as you just were by... Rumi," he replied, inspecting the small manuscript he had picked up from the floor.

Admittedly, he was quite annoyed at her.

Did she have any idea how precious such a copy was? He had indeed paid quite a fortune to secure it just recently from a merchant in Persia. Not only did she endanger his ship by being so reckless with the lamp, she also allowed herself to carelessly drop such a precious artefact.

Or perhaps she did know its value, he then considered. He could easily recall the delicate manner with which her hands had been handling the copy. These hands looked nothing like what he had seen in the carriage. Her fingernails had been meticulously cleaned, and he could not but notice their slender grace as she turned the pages.

Edmund realised too late he must have had some residue of his earlier ire imprinted on his brow, for she curled herself into the smallest size her body would allow and seemed to be waiting for him to do something to her.

"Do not be afraid!"

Edmund lowered the lantern quite close to the ball she had now become, and sinking down to her level, he could not hide his alarm at her reaction.

"I will not hit you, if that is what you fear."

"You mean to say you are not angry…?" she enquired wearily, after quite a prolonged silence where she appeared to be weighing the credibility of his words.

"Well, I will admit I was not too pleased to see somebody jeopardising the safety of my books, and the entire ship as a matter of fact, with this," he said, pointing at the lantern. "But no harm done!" And straightening himself back up, he tried to offer her his hand for her to do the same.

However, she did not take his hand and, raising her own self up, she said, "Thank you, my lord, for your kindness once more. I can assure you I will never venture into this room again."

And as soon as these words were uttered, she ran out of the cabin.

Edmund was then left alone in his sanctuary to contemplate upon the oddity this woman was indeed turning out to be. Enjoying Rumi out of all the poets she could have chosen from his diverse selection?!

While still lost in such contemplations, a sudden recollection crossed his mind.

Was he right in noticing his coat had been turned into a gown?

He was quite unsure, as she had walked so fast out of his sight; but nonetheless, he did catch the familiarity of her attire just before she shut the door behind her.

*

As Edmund made his way back to his room, he began to wonder, with a mixture of curiosity and disbelief, whether she had, in fact, fashioned his coat into a gown.

And if indeed she wore his coat as her sole attire, he could not help but surmise that she was scarcely dressed to withstand the frigid conditions they were sailing through.

The weather back in England was expected to be relatively pleasurable as they arrived, but here, in the south of the world, it was very cold at this time of the year.

Edmund had been quite clear with the shipmaster that he was to provide her with whatever charitable assistance she may require; therefore, if she had no other garments to wear, then surely, the crew would provide her with one.

What would be the need to turn his coat into a garment if she had been provided with the appropriate clothing?

But even if she had nothing else to clothe herself with, surely, she must have been provided with a blanket, which he was certain all his crew members were given. So why would she be roaming about the cold corridors of the ship without it? With such thoughts running through his mind, he came across the shipmaster's attendant.

"What is your name, man?"

"Jenkins, at your service, Sir!" was the obliging answer he received.

"Pray tell me, how thick are the blankets available to the crew?" Edmund enquired.

"Which blankets, Sir?"

"The blankets you are each provided with when you travel on board my ship!" he retorted with a hint of annoyance.

"We don't have blankets, Sir."

"What do you mean you do not have blankets?!"

Edmund truly prided himself in striving to ensure that anyone at his service would be provided with the necessities required for them to offer their service to him diligently. This way, if he ever had a need to reproach any of them, he could not be at fault for their failings.

"Do not answer me," Edmund interrupted, "I will personally take that up with Mr Evans.

"Now, I want you to promptly run after the woman who recently joined us and see that she is provided with some appropriate garments and a blanket!"

"Where am I to get them from, Sir?"

With his frustration mounting, Edmund was on the verge of instructing Jenkins further, but anticipating yet another possible annoying remark, he quickly restrained himself. Instead, he gave a curt command for the man to follow him directly.

Once inside his quarters, Edmund grabbed a couple of the thickest blankets he had scattered about the room. He was about to hand them over, when he decided to add a coat to the pile.

"Now, go and give these to her," he thrust the pile in Jenkins' hands, "and come to inform me once you are done!"

Edmund prepared himself to retire for the night. He wondered a few times whether the shipmaster's attendant had perhaps not heard his last words, as it had been a while, and the man had not returned with an update. He considered having a word with his crew master about this Jenkins; he came across rather too insubordinate for Edmund's liking.

As these thoughts ran through his mind, he was startled by a loud and insistent banging upon his door.

"I finally found her, but I don't think she'll make it, Sir!" Jenkins was standing by his door, holding a shivering Imbali in his arms. "Where am I to take her, Sir? I asked the women, but nobody knows where she sleeps, Sir!"

"Come inside and put her on my bed," Edmund immediately offered. "Run and get the doctor, now! Have the people in the kitchen boil lots of water for the doctor's use."

He then turned to where he expected his bathtub to be, "Oh good, the bath is still here. Fill it up with all the hot water you can gather! Quick man!"

Jenkins ran out of his room to execute the instructions Mr Hertworth had given to him.

*

Edmund thought, while waiting for the doctor to arrive, he surely could not watch this poor girl shiver to her death! He put his hand on her forehead and alarmingly, though her thin garment was drenched in sweat, her body felt extremely cold.

Being the gentleman that he was, he ran out of the cabin to call for female assistance. However, nobody, females or males, seemed to be anywhere around his quarters tonight.

So, at last, he resorted to removing the useless garment himself. He then quickly clothed her with one of his thick shirts and a pair of his breeches. Subsequently, he wrapped her body around the blanket he was going to wrap himself with before the sudden interruption by Jenkins.

Deciding to forego his bed to her, he finally tucked her under another blanket, hoping he had provided her body with enough heat, at least until the doctor arrived. Persuaded there was not much else left for him to do, he made himself comfortable in the seat beside his bed.

After what seemed an interminable wait to Edmund, Jenkins finally stormed back into his room. "The doctor did not re-embark, Sir!"

"Whatever do you mean he did not re-embark?! What nonsense are you saying?!"

"Yes, Sir, he is not on board! I looked in his room first, and then I looked in many other rooms. And then when I asked for his whereabouts, they said he had not been told of your change of mind, and did not make it back for our departure. So, you see, Sir, you left him behind!"

Ignoring this last comment, Edmund simply enquired, "Did you ask them to boil the water?"

"Yes, Sir, I did! I told them to bring it to your room directly, since you don't mind her being in your bed!

"You know, Sir, this poor soul does not have a bed! It's not the shipmaster's fault though! He told the negros in the kitchen to provide for her amongst them; but Lucy has just told me none of them wanted her around." Jenkins seemed quite eager to report back on his discovery, but when he noticed the sudden change of expression on Mr Hertworth's face, he promptly informed him, "It's not Lucy's fault either, Sir! You see, Sir, Lucy is such a nice girl! She even told this girl to share her bed! She don't mind that she's negro!"

As far as Jenkins was concerned, Lucy's heart had no boundaries when it came to benevolence. With such well-timed praises, it was no surprise Lucy was promptly summoned to the master's cabin.

Once Mr Hertworth's personal bathtub had been finally filled with hot water, Edmund asked Lucy if she felt competent enough to manage this sickly girl on her own.

After receiving a passionate, affirmative reply, Edmund instructed Lucy to undress Imbali, deposit her in the hot water and leave her there until the temperature came down.

And so, Lucy was left all alone in the master's cabin to attend to Imbali.

As Edmund paced restlessly up and down the corridor, he heard something crack under his foot.

He bent down to inspect what it was that his foot had accidentally broken, and for the second time, he found himself holding Imbali's precious necklace in his hand.

He could not prevent his thoughts from wandering off to the recent interaction he had with this girl in his library.

Perhaps, had he left her unbothered where she seemed so blissfully content, he would not at present be this preoccupied with the survival of a young soul to whom he had guaranteed safety.

While thus absorbed in these gloomy considerations, Lucy opened the door of his cabin to inform him the girl's temperature had finally come down considerably, however she required assistance in taking her out of the bathtub.

Without giving it much thought, Edmund placed the broken necklace in his pocket and rushed back inside.

Jenkins, who had been highly cooperative since he first brought Imbali into the cabin, was strangely keeping himself out of the room. For reasons quite beyond Edmund's current understanding, Jenkins seemed eager to demonstrate some form of propriety around Lucy, so Edmund was left to volunteer himself in nursing Imbali alongside her.

The temperature did come down, as Lucy informed him. The shivers too, which Imbali's body had been engulfed with when she was first brought to his room, had started to subdue. Edmund then handed Lucy his own clothing to dress the girl.

In spite of Lucy's offer, Imbali was at last gently tucked back into Edmund's own bed.

Edmund was wise enough to understand depriving any of his workers of their own resting place would have a much higher impact on their comfort compared to his; especially considering he had a very comfortable chair he could sleep on for the night. Lucy had also offered to stay behind to carry on nursing Imbali, and following this kind proposal, Jenkins was then eager to offer his assistance too.

However, no matter how big-hearted Lucy was, Edmund could not bring himself to deprive them of a much-deserved rest for the night.

After reassuring them he really could not foresee any serious complications, he sent them both on their way.

If Jenkins or Lucy thought anything reprehensible about the circumstances they were leaving behind inside the cabin, they both did an excellent job at concealing it from their employer.

20.

The first half of the night passed by without anything worth noticing. Imbali had remained fast asleep on his bed, and though Edmund felt compelled to raise himself from his chair to adjust the blankets a couple of times, she truly seemed to be rallying her strength.

Eventually, he was able to find a comfortable position in his seat and he, at last, found some sleep.

However, the latter part of the night commenced with a series of distressing cries which startled Edmund awake. It was quite impossible for him to comprehend whatever it was Imbali was fighting in her nightmare, but he felt he ought to do something.

Gently, he removed the first layer of the blankets and was finally able to see for himself that her eyes, though widened by the terror which must have awakened her, were not living in the presence of his room, but rather in the distant realm of her nightmare.

Though her cries would come and go, the tremors which seized her body returned with a relentless persistence.

Without much consideration, Edmund found himself placing his own body right next to hers, as a shield for whatever she was combatting.

"Shush, shush, shush, it is only a bad dream," he murmured gently into her ear. While he tried to soothe her mind with his words, his hands then moved to soothe her flesh.

He was quite determined to retain as much propriety as the unexpected circumstances would allow, as such, he strove to ensure his hands avoided the inappropriate parts of this body he had heard quite enough about.

His motions seemed to be having an effect on her, as sooner than he expected, her shivers began to lessen.

But his words did not have the same success as his hands; her eyes were still lost in that distant place.

"Am I dreaming now...?" she asked.

"You are safe now," was Edmund's gentle reply. Her eyes were radiating such a power, he felt his own eyes losing themselves in their light.

Unlike the apprehensive glances she had cast upon him during their brief encounters, there was no fear in her expression this time.

"I knew your eyes would not deceive me," she continued, "you could not have her eyes for nothing; Mama must have chosen you to come to me! Have you come to take me to her?"

Not only had her expression acquired a sudden worrying merriment, her thoughts had strayed into believing him to have come to end her worldly trials!

Edmund could not help but feel a growing concern for where the spirits of his patient had wandered off to.

Her forehead felt deadly cold. He decided to remove the next two layers she had been tucked under, with the intent of passing more of his body heat to her.

He embraced her tightly, and soon enough, her body no longer felt as icy as it initially did.

Quite unexpectedly however, she embraced him in return.

She was still addressing him, believing him to be a celestial being with her mother's eyes, but her words were more relaxed, and to Edmund this was soothing enough for his anxious nerves.

He carried on stroking her arms. Though her mind was far away, her body relaxed at his touch. As the minutes went by, he started to become convinced he was not imagining the subtle heat emanating from the parts of her body he was caressing. Edmund contemplated whether he ought to remove a layer of the shirts Lucy had dressed her with. He had to deprive her of his embrace in order for him to remove it, but this change in their physical arrangements did not seem too pleasing to her, as she began to murmur words of disagreement.

He then quickly resumed his place beside her, and with his body closely wrapped around her again, her words returned to disclosing contentment at his nearness.

Upon his return, he realised his embrace no longer had the harmless feel it initially possessed.

Perhaps he ought to return to the chair.

She looked and felt out of any immediate danger. However, against reason, he did not return to the safety of his chair.

As the minutes ticked away, his arms had stopped being the only part of his anatomy providing her with heat. His entire body was intent at contributing to it.

No sounds could be heard from the world outside of them, not even the crashing waves of the ocean on his ship. And from within the cabin, the regular ticking of the clock mounted on the wall had been overtaken by the accelerating beat of their synchronised hearts.

Though his body was too far gone for an awakening, his mind seemed still quite capable of reason after all. He could not help but admit to himself how his behaviour at present was not much different from the misuse he had recently rescued her from. Surely, he ought to stop this compromising entanglement and leave the bed to her… yet, his carnal instincts were overpowering his ability to do what was proper. To make matters worse, he unexpectedly started recollecting those marvellous black lilies he saw in the field where she first spoke to him, and his thoughts evolved into wondering what it would feel like to deflower a flower such as hers.

Perhaps, had he felt himself to be the only one this inebriated, he would have rallied any ounce of scruple available to him and vacated the bed; however, she too, was highly receptive of the sensations his nearness was awakening in her!

Her eyes had been closed for a while, but her physical response to him was more than enough to supplement what her eyes could have conveyed.

*

While his thoughts were dangerously evolving, sudden tremorous changes in her countenance forced him to recompose himself.

She was once again repossessed by spates of the cold shivers from earlier.

"For the love of God! What has gotten into me!" he then realised.

Promptly, he commanded his body to distance itself from her, and grabbing the blankets which had fallen on the floor, he covered her as best as he could before running out of his own cabin.

Once in the corridor, he did not pause to congratulate himself for being able to walk away with his dignity intact. His fast-beating heart was still too evident a proof of the strong desire his entire being had been captivated by.

He continued towards the upper deck, where the sweet scent of the ocean enveloped him.

The symphony from the early risers amongst the sea creatures was a well-needed substitute for the humming of their synchronised hearts still replaying in his mind.

He earnestly hoped this familiar concert of the sea would grant him the essential composure his body, as well as his mind, were in dire need of.

When Lucy, followed by Jenkins, came to find him, Mr Hertworth appeared intently engrossed in the open scenery of the ocean.

"We came to inform you we removed the poor girl from your bed, Sir," Lucy began obsequiously. "I also changed all the bedding and brought your room back to its previous order. If you please, Sir, you now have your cabin all to yourself once again."

"There is only one of your blankets still missing from your room, Sir," added Jenkins. "I took the liberty of carrying her in it this morning when we brought her out of your room."

"Where did you move her to? I thought you said she had no bed!"

At this abrupt remark, the crew master decided to make his presence known, "Sir, I instructed the other two negros in the kitchen to find her a bed with them. But I have just discovered that no such thing was done.

"When I asked them about it this morning, after Jenkins told me what had happened last night, they said that they would rather be without a bed than to sleep alongside a loose skirt such as her, Sir."

"What do you mean 'loose skirt'?!"

"I truly beg your pardon for the insinuation, Sir; but they are convinced you brought her on board for one particular reason...," the crew master could not bring himself to spell out the insinuation.

Almost everyone on board assumed Imbali to be not only a practised courtesan; but they supposed Mr Hertworth had brought her along exclusively for him to fulfil his unusual, exotic partialities.

The impending rage which overtook Mr Hertworth's features was visible for all to see.

However, a swift recollection of what had almost occurred between himself and that poor girl, whom he knew to be as innocent as the innocence in her eyes, restrained him from lashing out.

He could still vividly recollect Von Hisen's despicable remarks when he finally agreed to hand Imbali over to him.

'You must think me a fool if you think I will accept anything less than double your current offer. You cannot have any idea of the struggles she has made me, and these gentlemen, go through to finally get a taste of her!'

The so-called gentlemen he was referring to included Freddie, his old-time companion.

'I am sure you can understand my reasons simply by looking at her. But, fear not; you can rest assured no man has touched her until tonight. And since you mean to deprive us of our enjoyment," Von Hisen continued with a grin, "I must solicit you to increase your offer. After all, you will take her along with the full knowledge you will be the first to enjoy her superb attributes all to yourself!'

To think he had almost behaved as the swine Von Hisen expected him to be!

To make matters worse, he had almost been responsible for the malicious rumours becoming a reality for the poor girl.

And the knowledge of such rumours was indeed a much-needed reproach from reality. He certainly had a lot to be grateful for this morning.

He should have been able to foresee how the circumstances of their encounter would certainly give rise to such vicious speculations amongst his employees.

After ensuring that she would have her own bed somewhere on his vessel, he decided he would be better off forgetting all about any recollection from the previous night. He could certainly find more agreeable thoughts to contemplate upon. Indeed, he had a lot to look forward to, now that he was finally returning to England.

*

Two days passed, yet he still could not fathom how he allowed himself to be in such a compromising situation with a woman, especially the kind of woman, that she was.

As the sun dipped below the ocean, and the day was coming to a close, Edmund stood, engaged with his shipmaster. But from the corner of his eye, he caught sight of Jenkins making his way to him.

"I came to return your blanket from the other morning, Sir."

Assuming Mr Hertworth's intense stare towards the blanket to be a look of disdain, Jenkins proceeded to add, "Lucy washed it with her own hands, Sir."

"Why did you take it back from her?" Mr Hertworth retorted.

"We didn't, Sir! She thinks the blanket to be Lucy's. She don't remember she was in your room that night; she thinks she was in Lucy's bed, Sir! I wanted to tell her it was you she should thank, Sir, but Lucy didn't let me. She thinks the girl would feel even worse if she knew you gave her your bed."

To Jenkins, this information was totally inconsequential, but to the receiver of the news, this shed a whole new light on how to behave with Imbali.

"How is she faring?"

"She's improved a lot, Sir! And I think it's all thanks to Lucy! We told her to stay in bed one more day, but she didn't listen to us, and this morning she went back into the kitchen." Jenkins paused before adding, "One more thing, Sir... Lucy gave her one of her garments, but she said it didn't fit on the negro, so she is still walking around in the thing she made out of that coat of yours, Sir!"

And so, Imbali was promptly summoned to appear in front of Mr Hertworth.

*

She did appear as recovered as Jenkins had claimed. Her brown complexion had reacquired the same golden tint he first noticed that morning by the flowery field.

During that night, her delirious state was such it was highly probable she would not have much recollection of the events which occurred in his bed. And if that was the case, he could be spared the trouble of having to explain his actions to her.

Indeed, it would be better off for everyone if he never spoke a word of it to her, and more importantly, he needed to forget all about that night himself.

But Edmund supposed he ought to assess her recollection of those fateful events for himself. She could very well be putting up pretences... but it was quite possible she was not, too.

As soon as she arrived in his presence, he stood up, but she kept her eyes down and Edmund was deprived of the opportunity of addressing her personally, as the shipmaster took it upon himself to speak on Edmund's behalf. And so, after enquiring after her health, he informed her she was to take an extra day away from the kitchen in order for her to regain more of her strength.

She then presented her gratitude for the kind offer, but firmly declined it, insisting she was more than ready to resume her duties alongside everyone else.

She did, however, agree to accept a replacement for her current attire, which the resourceful shipmaster had conveniently found somewhere from his stock.

She did not gaze in the direction of Mr Hertworth even once. As such, she walked away without him determining if she too was as tormented by their night together.

She certainly appeared to be entirely unaffected by him. He then recalled she believed her gratitude was due to Lucy and Jenkins alone, so he could not fault her for appearing this unaffected.

Or perhaps she really was a master at concealing her emotions? His pride could simply not accept he was the only one to be thus affected by their experience together.

Either way, he finally decided, this response of hers was indeed a positive outcome for him. He could now cease blaming himself for the inopportune reaction he had, which must have been provoked by his concern for her sickly state.

He gave himself leave to busy his mind with looking forward to enjoying the company of the many young women he knew his mother would be ecstatic to introduce to him.

And directing his attention to the women from the same society as him was certainly much more appropriate than concerning himself over a girl who, though quite noteworthy, was still a negro after all.

21.

And then quite suddenly, while trying her best not to look up at him, Imbali had a terrible flashback of all that occurred between her body and the body of the man who was strangely staring down at her. Their physical interaction had taken place inside a cabin that looked nothing like any other cabin she had been in.

A second recollection followed as her mind was busy dismissing what must be a terrible hallucination; her mother had been there too.

Surely, whatever feverish images her mind was tricking her with, they could not have taken place in the presence of her mother; as such, she could calmly erase the image involving the man standing above her as Mr Evans carried on with his elaborations of her duties.

She could not recall very well how she had come to be under Lucy's care, and yet the providential Lucy had been so genuinely attentive to her, she was certain it was to her she owed her entire gratitude, and the kind Mr Jenkins.

There was no way this mighty master could have had anything to do with her recovery, but then, she suddenly thought, why was he showing a sudden interest in her convalescence?

At last, she was finally able to recede from the penetrating gaze of Mr Hertworth, and Imbali returned to Lucy's quarters.

Upon entering, she found that a new bed had been added beside Lucy's. The women's resting quarters, though comfortable in its way, was rather cramped, for Lucy shared it with several other women. Some slept in bunks, others in hammocks; but very few enjoyed the luxury of a bed all to themselves.

She could not help but wonder whether this bed had been intended for her. But immediately after, her thoughts turned to the places where she had seen the other Africans sleep, and as such she concluded that it was most improbable they would permit her to join the white personnel in their private quarters.

It was best, she then decided, to leave the matter where it was and think no more of it.

She was quite content to keep herself in the coal room, where she found warmth and enough light to carry on indulging in her only leisurely concession. She was hopeful one day she would have enough money to be able to procure herself some real writing paper, instead of the pieces of scrap she had been gathering from around the ship.

Deciding to leave the bed to the concern of others, she headed directly towards the kitchen to resume her chores.

Unfortunately for her however, she was met with the disgust of her fellow *negros* the moment she entered.

"I said it from the moment she came amongst us! It is the likes of you that make all of us look bad in the eyes of the masters." It was the younger one who had refused any cordiality towards her since the day she boarded the ship. "You came to us with your innocent face and a very touching story; and you thought we would just stand by and watch you engorge yourself in the bed of none other than the big master!"

The words were being so vehemently spat she found herself immobilised.

"And you still have the audacity to walk around in his coat! Surely you can make him give you something more to parade under our noses. They say that he has not been himself since the night you spent in his bed!" the woman continued.

"You know, Miss Lucy's sweetheart was barely able to disperse a group of at least six men who were all betting on how long the master would keep you all to himself before they could get you in their beds next! I must say though, I really expected a bit more brains from you; surely you could have made him get you out of the kitchen by now!"

The fury coming from this woman was so passionate it transcended words, and it was not long before Imbali found herself trying to protect the makeshift gown from the hands of the woman who was determined to rip it off her.

"That is quite enough!"

Lucy's duties did not require her presence in the kitchen, but the commotion coming out of the place was so loud anyone who was not even in close proximity to it could hear all the racket.

"Come, my dear," said Lucy, grabbing Imbali by the hand and escorting her out of the kitchen. "You are quite a stubborn one, are you not? Were you not told to stay out of the kitchen and keep in bed for today?"

Lucy received no reply as they walked.

"What is she talking about, Miss Lucy?" Imbali queried hesitantly when they entered Lucy's cabin.

"Are you seriously going to pay any attention to anything that has come out of that witch's mouth?! Don't you know she has had her eyes on your rather lovely gown since the morning you converted it from a coat into a dress!" Lucy chuckled, "I must say I quite like it myself, but fortunately for you, I am twice your size, therefore I give you leave to keep it; otherwise, I would have asked you for it as the price you owe me for keeping me out of my bed that night," Lucy offered. "I see they have finally brought a bed for you. Have you tried it?" and then looking about the cabin, she added, "It's got a bit cramped in here, but I am sure that can only do us good. The more we are, the warmer we can be, eh?!"

Imbali could not partake in Lucy's conversation as the accusations thrown at her in the kitchen had been the only slander she promised herself to never accept from anyone.

"She accused me of spending the night in the master's bed... but here you are telling me otherwise! Please, Miss Lucy, I beg you to tell me the truth; did I not spend the entire night usurping you out of your own bed?"

Lucy, like most of the personnel on board, had become familiar with the story of how Mr Hertworth had come to rescue this wretched creature, and she truly could not get herself to add more agony to her misery. About a good ten years older than Imbali, Lucy had certainly seen enough unkindness passed around.

Watching the torment in Imbali's inquisitive eyes, she could not help but feel a positive inclination towards her, negro or not.

And so, instead of responding to Imbali's enquiry, she startled herself by exclaiming:

"My dear, you really seem determined to waste my precious time on silly questions! If you have no care to try your bed, then I suggest you accompany me to the shipmaster's quarters where I am expected to help Jack carry some books and papers and whatnot to the accounting room."

Lucy paused for a very brief moment and corrected herself, "I mean to say, I am expected to help Mr Jenkins! I am already very late; I would hate to cause him any trouble!"

As she was about to leave, she turned to Imbali and cheerfully added, "come along, you, I am sure we can find you something better to do than to listen to all that nonsense down in the kitchen!"

Lucy was indeed late. She assumed Jack must have gotten tired of waiting and decided to go on without her.

"He must have made his way to Mr Evans all on his own!" Lucy then considered, "quick girl, make haste, let's help him!"

On their way to the upper deck, they saw Jack carrying many notes and some very heavy looking ledgers; Lucy and Imbali were presented with an almost comical sight of Jenkins on the stairs, trying to manage more than he could comfortably carry.

Jenkins could not see much in front of him. His view was almost entirely covered by the piles of books and papers which he had precariously stacked together.

As he was on his last step, he heard Lucy calling him, "Jack, be careful, you will certainly trip and cause havoc by the way you are going about!"

He turned to look back at her, but as he did, he stumbled over his own foot, scattering the contents he was carrying down the stairs and across the upper deck.

If only Lucy had not been so hasty to aid him.

Jenkins and Lucy stood still; their eyes wandering back and forth between their petrified expressions and the mess all around them.

How could they make amends for this?!

A countless list of dramatic thoughts was going through their minds.

Jenkins appeared overcome by a sense of anxiety, which, considering the mess around him, seemed quite justified to anyone who saw him or heard his anxious mumblings.

"How am I going to keep my job after this? I bet you anything, he will think I am meddling with something by trying to fluff around with his numbers! He's the one who got his figures wrong; but now I have definitely given him the perfect reason to put all the blame on me!"

Lucy's emotions, on the other hand, were transitioning from anxiety to utter hopelessness.

Jack Jenkins would never look at her the same, which could only mean she had just lost the only chance she felt she ever had of having someone care for her. Recently, she had even begun to entertain the faintest hope that perhaps, he may like her just enough to want to marry her.

These considerations were so gravely preoccupying Lucy's mind, she failed to notice that not only the mess around them was gone, but by the time she roused herself, Jenkins was already holding half of the contents back in his arms, and Imbali was calling her name with the intention of handing her the other half. Consequently, without much explanation, Imbali encouraged them not to waste time much longer, and make haste in taking the ledgers to the shipmaster.

Once in the presence of Mr Evans, Lucy waited for Jenkins to carefully deposit his load before she did the same. And as soon as her arms were free of their cargo, she took her leave and rushed back outside, away from Jenkins.

That evening, within the confines of their now shared accommodation, Lucy found herself unable to dispel her anxiety and would often repeat to Lily, "I am very afraid. Do you think they will allow him to stay aboard?"

The more time passed, the more anxious she became, "Oh my dear, imagine if they drop him off in one of the countries along the way! I will never see him again!"

"I am sure the situation is not as bad as you presume it to be, Miss Lucy," Imbali offered reassuringly.

"I so wish you could be right; but I can't help feeling this heavy burden upon my heart!

"It's all my fault! He will never look at me the same way. What am I to do?!"

"I am afraid there is really not much anybody can do for the time being; but what do you say you get some sleep for tonight, so that we may start afresh tomorrow?"

The evening progressed into the late hours of night. Most of the women who shared their accommodation had retired for the night. Several of those who hadn't ostensibly showed their dislike at the prospect of having to share the same space with a negro. However, to Imbali's surprise, they said little directly to her, apart from the disgruntled word or two.

*

Unfortunately for everyone, as the night progressed, Lucy could not be dissuaded from voicing her own fears for Mr Jenkins' state of affairs with the shipmaster.

"I really would not be able to stand it if Mr Evans was to tell him off because of my stupidity. He is a proud man you know! And now he will be in trouble all because of me! I am so worried, I fear my brains will burst any minute now!"

Lucy was rather loud in her speech, and so it seemed this already long night would drag on until the next morning, leaving little hope for any of them to find any rest.

"You really ought to give yourself some respite," Imbali whispered towards her, afraid of bothering the women closest to them. "In fact, if you insist on being this severe upon yourself, how do you suppose you can be of any good to Mr Jenkins should he need you tomorrow?"

"I know I won't be able to sleep," Lucy rejoined. "But you ought to try. How could I forget about your state! Silly me! Please, don't think me ungrateful to you, my dear! You certainly must have done Mr Jenkins some good, I am sure. Surely, if we haven't heard anything until now, it must mean he is safe... right?" And then Lucy studied her interlocutor curiously, "I wonder my dear... are you as learned as you sound?"

"I have done nothing Mr Jenkins could not do himself, I assure you," offered Imbali.

"I really don't want you to think me untrusting or ungrateful for the way you put those books together of course; but I really cannot help fearing you might have put something out of place. After all, you only had but a few moments to... well, I don't know, do whatever it was you did with those books!" Following this exclamation, Lucy untucked herself out of her bed and immediately after, without permission, moved into Imbali's bed.

Imbali's initial amazement was not hers alone, for the women in the immediate vicinity shared her surprise. Yet, while theirs lingered, Imbali's soon subsided, and she found herself tenderly stroking Lucy's silken hair. In turn, Lucy nestled herself into Imbali's arms, where she found a warmth and comfort she couldn't find before.

"Jenkins truly loves being at sea, and he's been doing so well lately. Even the Sir has noticed him." Lucy continued.

"When will you shut it?!" A woman interrupted her, "we are trying to get some sleep here!"

"Easy for you to speak! You don't know what I suffer!" Lucy responded angrily, and turning to Imbali, she cried, "if only my mind would give me a break!"

At these words, Imbali remembered her mother; how she had been the best at soothing her mind.

As Lucy mumbled about Jenkins and his future prospects in the eyes of Mr Hertworth, Imbali was contemplating whether Lucy would appreciate her mother's method.

Whenever Imbali needed a distraction from the reality of the improprieties taking place in their hut, her mother would resort to narrating stories to her.

"What do you say I tell you of a lovely tale to take your mind off of things?" offered Imbali.

"A tale?! Like a fairytale, you mean? How is that supposed to be of any use to me at present?!" retorted Lucy.

"It may not do much, but I was thinking of a tale of a good-hearted girl, who just like you, when she thought all hope was gone, found the best of fortunes." As expected, Lucy's curiosity was piqued by this introduction.

"Long, long ago, a great chief ruled the lands of our forefathers," Imbali then began.

"What is a chief, my dear?" Lucy interrupted.

"He is a bit like a king; you know, like the kings and queens you have back in England."

"Oh yes, we are familiar with those!" Lucy smirked. "Please forgive me, carry on, my dear."

"As I was saying, this king, one day, sadly became blinded while at war with one of his rivals. Doctors from far and wide tried to cure him, but none of them could restore the king's sight. Tricksters and false magicians offered him remedies too, but none of them worked; and these impostors would run off with the blind king's gold filling their pockets.

"As time went by, the king began to despair of ever finding someone who could offer him a remedy. But one day, a humble looking man presented himself to the king and said to him: 'If your majesty could capture the only king more powerful than you, and bring him here to your palace, you will see again.'

"'Which king can possibly be more powerful than me?'

"'The king of the seas, the Great Whale, Sire, is more powerful than you!' the man responded.

"'Capture the Great Whale? No one could do such a thing,' the king replied.

"'What about the princess, your daughter?'

"'She is but a girl!'

"'But, you see, Sire, this whale responds only to maidens, and not just any maiden; she must be of pure heart and noble blood. Who better than your own daughter, my king? Besides, the whole kingdom knows her to be a clever girl; catching a whale would be nothing to her.'

"'My daughter, but of course! Indeed! Send for her at once, said the king to his servant. And pay this good honest man handsomely.'

"The king had become so blinded by his own misfortune, he would stop at nothing to regain his weakened power. The princess liked to help everyone, and as her own father demanded her assistance, she agreed at once to his plan. She chose three of the most valiant king's soldiers to accompany her, and together they set sail at sea…"

Imbali would have carried on with her fairy-tale, however, as the tale progressed, she began to feel the peaceful breathing of Lucy's chest under her own bosom.

Lucy had at last found some comfort in a much-needed sleep.

The bed was too small to accommodate them both; Lucy's generous body could barely be contained on such a small bed all on her own, let alone if Imbali remained on it too.

She then decided to slip out of Lucy's embrace, with care as not to wake her. The bed creaked a little as she moved, but Lucy only stirred and shifted into the warm spot Imbali left behind, resuming her steady breathing.

Once free, Imbali looked around the room, her gaze landing on a soft, folded blanket at the bottom of her bed. She unwrapped it and made a small nest for herself on the floor beside the bed, settling down for the night. It was far from comfortable, but she found a strange contentment in being close to Lucy, hearing her soft breathing from above.

At last it appeared this long day would come to an end in such a manner; with Lucy on Imbali's bed, and Imbali on the floor. However, the peace Imbali presumed she had managed to secure was soon interrupted by the very woman who had earlier ordered Lucy to hold her tongue.

"You can lie on her bed," the woman remarked, "she doesn't seem to mind your sweat!"

"I thank you, but I am fine here," Imbali responded. Imbali turned her back on her, but even so, she could feel the imposing gaze of the woman hovering above her.

Imbali then decided to turn back and face her.

"You did not finish your story," the woman said abruptly.

"Oh… I did not realise I was loud enough for you to hear it," Imbali countered, apologetically.

"Your voice was not loud; I could not help but listen… what happens to the princess next?" and then after a very brief pause, she added, "please…"

Imbali cast a bewildered glance around their quarters, scarcely able to believe the strange turn her evening had taken. Her gaze then drifted back to the woman who, having abandoned her perch on the top bunk, now sat cross-legged on the floor beside her, wearing an expression full of attentive anticipation.

Deciding, after a few cautious looks, that this unexpected listener was indeed in earnest, Imbali resumed her story. She spoke softly, her voice weaving more of the tale of the kind-hearted princess who, despite her many misfortunes, eventually found the most beautiful of happy endings.

22.

The next morning, Lucy was the first to awaken. To her utter surprise, she found Imbali lying on the ground and another woman resting right beside her, on the same floor.

She was eager to know what had happened between the two, but she could not bring herself to wake either of them. She considered waiting until they woke on their own, yet her anxiety over Jenkins' state of affairs would not keep her in the room for much longer.

She had just walked out of the room when she bumped into none other than the man himself, who was hastening towards her cabin.

"There you are! I was afraid I would have to wake you both up by force!"

He offered Lucy a tender smile before passing her, and then without much regard for any of the other inhabitants, he walked inside the cabin, looking for Imbali. He located her as she had just awakened, "My girl, you have no idea what a lifesaver you have been to me!" he exclaimed even before he got to her. "It took me… I don't even remember how many days to try to make sense of those numbers, and still, I couldn't do it!

"How did you do it?! I thought it might have been your luck when you put the papers back in the ledgers, but the shipmaster is sure it wasn't!"

At the mention of the shipmaster, he recollected what he had come for, "In fact, don't bother explaining it to me, make haste girl, he is waiting for you to explain it to him too!" Jenkins could scarcely contain his excitement.

Imbali, on the other hand, appeared rather startled by Jenkins' enthusiasm, and worse than her, Lucy was totally at a loss regarding the man she had despaired about all night.

Jenkins would have gladly grabbed Imbali by the hand if that meant speeding up her walk to the accounting room. It seemed to him she was seriously determined to bring his patience to its limit, as the more he hurried her, the more she kept dragging her feet.

"What is the matter, girl? Is there anything you require at this particular moment?"

"No, Sir, nothing is the matter," and after a short pause in which she managed to gather her strengths, she added, "I was simply contemplating how Lucy fared... you see, Sir, she was worried all night long."

"Of course! Of course, Lucy should hear it too. Why didn't I think of that?" He looked back and gestured to Lucy to follow them.

To see Jenkins motioning to her was indeed a big relief to Lucy. She hurriedly caught up with them, and accosting Imbali she enquired, "He hasn't said a word to me... I cannot understand why he hasn't said a word to me! Can you make sense of it?" and then, with her thoughts taking a gloomier turn, she added, "do you think him gravely angry with me?!"

There was sincere concern on Lucy's part, however, Lily could not but find the situation quite entertaining. "Come now, Miss Lucy; I am sure the reality of the situation is not as bad as you imagine it to be! Even I could not really make much sense of what he said to me. So, the best we can do for the time being is to follow him, and I am sure we shall very soon find out what has affected him in such a manner."

Having Lucy walking alongside her felt much better than walking alone to whomever Jenkins intended for her to give an explanation to.

By the time they reached the cabin where the shipmaster was waiting for them, Imbali had long managed to distract Lucy's mind from Jenkins and his odd behaviour. As they finally entered the room, the tête-à-tête the two women were having with each other seemed quite lively in its nature.

*

Inside the cabin, the shipmaster was having his own conversation with Mr Hertworth. Mr Evans was a meticulous shipmaster. Whenever chance presented itself, he liked to show off the order he eagerly strived to achieve in his records.

But he was also an honest man, and though he liked to ingratiate himself in the eyes of his superiors, he would not take credit for an effort he knew was not his.

The ledgers which Jenkins brought to him yesterday had, until then, a rather annoying incongruence with the numbers. Strangely, some of the numbers in relation to purchases he had made during one of their previous stops did not tally with the finances he knew to be accurate.

Yesterday was the second time he had requested them in order for him to have a look at one particular entry once again. Shortly after he received the books from Jenkins, he could easily ascertain a few of the papers which had come loose from the ledgers had been placed in a different order from where he last had them.

Somebody had reordered these papers, and now all the numbers and calculations tallied perfectly.

"So, you see, Sir," the shipmaster was saying, "No matter which angle I looked at the calculations from, they just would not make sense. As you can imagine I was quite pleased with Jenkins as I assumed that he had reordered the papers, so now the additions were all making sense. But then what he said really caught me by surprise! He says it was not him to have done that! Can you guess who, Sir?" and not waiting for much of an answer he happily carried on, "apparently it was the negro you came aboard with, Sir! Can you believe it? A woman did the maths! And to make the idea even more shocking, a negro woman!"

Edmund had, until the last few sentences, shown but the faintest interest to Mr Evans, appearing mostly unengaged with the report being narrated to him.

At the mention of the negro, however, Mr Hertworth was a different man.

"How do you mean? She did what?!" Edmund could not hide his surprise.

"Exactly my point, Sir! I was as surprised as you are! How on earth would she know how to figure out such calculations?" The shipmaster was very pleased to see his employer finally engaged with him. He then proceeded to take the particular papers out from the ledgers. "As you can see here, Sir, these additions are not easy to do. I will be honest with you, Sir, I would not be able to do them without my pen and paper with me, but according to Jenkins, it only took her but mere moments to make the numbers tally; all in her head!"

*

When Jenkins, Lucy and Imbali entered the accounting room, they could not immediately recognise the man the shipmaster was eagerly conversing with.

"There you are, Jenkins! I was just informing Mr Hertworth whom we are indebted to for solving our mishap with the ledgers." The shipmaster said these words to Jenkins; but it was Imbali he was looking at suspiciously. His, however, were not the only pair of eyes looking at her.

When they walked in, Imbali's face was emanating such a radiant smile.

If anyone had paid enough attention to Imbali since she came on board, they would have noticed such a smile was quite rare for her usual sombre expressions.

Edmund had last seen her after her recovery from the feverish night in his cabin, however, he had many-a-time recollected details about her in his mind.

When her eyes locked with his, the radiant smile died out, but already, it was a new addition to his recollections of her.

Edmund was not the kind of man to be easily impressed by the gentler sex. He could certainly boast of having seen and experienced them all. However, all the women who had managed to secure any inkling of interest from him had only been of the white kind.

Never in his entire experience had he presumed he could possibly give a second thought to a woman whose shade of skin differed from his.

He could not pinpoint the exact moment when notions associated to this negro started penetrating his mind in the manner in which they currently were.

The realisation that he was thinking of her much more often than he deemed appropriate came to him when he was all alone in his library; that same cabin where he first accused her of jeopardising the safety of his precious books.

He was in the library simply because he had already spent a good part of the night trying to force himself to sleep, hoping to find some solace in reading.

Since that feverish night, he had been unable to find much comfort in his own bed, as every time he laid on it, he could not help but remember her; the most vivid memory being that of their two bodies intertwined. These recollections of her were starting to become quite uncomfortable for his own moral integrity.

However, the most striking presence of hers in his mind was that of her eyes. In the few glances they had shared there was a strange intensity, and it captivated him.

There was something in the manner she used her eyes which made them quite unique in their purpose. He was still unable to pinpoint what it was exactly, but whatever talent her eyes possessed, it was strong enough to radiate her entire face. And her face was indeed very different from any negro he had ever come across.

But then it occurred to him, when had he ever considered a negro's appearance to be of any significance?

Initially, he tried to persuade himself to find a logical explanation for the dangerous trail of his thoughts; perhaps he must have been away from civilisation for far too long. Thank heavens he was returning home.

And, he assumed, once he laid eyes on the women of his kind, these odd thoughts involving this negro would long be out of his mind.

This positive, mental reassurance however did not last very long, as shortly after he came to this conclusion, he then realised his ship was rather well stocked in women of his kind. But none of them had managed to secure as much space in his mind as this negro had done.

Inside the cabin, both Mr Evans and Jenkins had been conversing freely about what appeared to be Imbali's numerical capabilities.

Edmund appreciated he was expected to make a remark or two, or perhaps even join the shipmaster in acknowledging what Imbali had done.

However, though Edmund's mind was inclined to address her, he did not.

He felt rather annoyed with her.

She had not done anything to cause his annoyance at present, but rather, it was what she was doing in his mind which agitated him.

And so, he simply carried on staring at her, while yearning for her to look up at him once more. But the more he wished for one more glance from her, the angrier he felt. This contrarious mood was noticed by the shipmaster.

"Are you feeling uncomfortable, Sir?" whispered the shipmaster, moving closer to his employer.

A sudden idea occurred to the attentive employee; perhaps he had gotten himself quite carried away with the happy findings of his ledgers. Perhaps he did not need to involve Mr Hertworth with such frugal matters; and more importantly, with lowly people such as the negro standing before them. Perhaps he had utterly misread this nobleman; he had honestly thought Mr Hertworth quite different from the rest.

Did he not rescue this negro himself? Was he not the one to bring her aboard this ship to protect her from whatever malice was afflicted to her? And lastly, did he not just order him to have a bed installed in a cabin of white women for this negro?

Putting his own considerations aside, Mr Evans proceeded to explain himself, "I wanted to inform you of how we managed to rectify the miscalculation I told you about. I beg your pardon, Sir, I did not think–"

However, his words were left hanging, as Mr Hertworth simply walked speedily out of the cabin, without offering a word to anyone present.

23.

Mary, for this was the name of Imbali's eager listener, would not stop praising Imbali and her storytelling. The tale of the princess and the great whale was, by early afternoon, the talk of the upper deck, and by evening of this very same day, Mary had gathered a growing assembly inside their sleeping quarters.

This assembly had come together to request what Imbali had so freely offered the evening before. She felt slightly hesitant at first, as never before had she found herself in a situation like this. But she soon yielded to the pleas of her unexpected listeners.

At first, the modest space inside the cabin was comfortable enough to accommodate the women, but as the night progressed, Jenkins, accompanied by a small company of men, had come to join the gathering too.

By the time Mr Evans had gotten wind of this new occurrence and came to the women's quarters himself, each pair of eyes was eagerly fixated on Imbali. As he joined them, the narration had reached the very point where the princess, at last, was about to enter the belly of the whale.

*

"'Who will come with me?' The princess asked of the three valiant men at her service. As she spoke, the mighty whale began to close its mouth, and she saw the fear in their eyes rising, gathering, swirling like an all-encompassing sandstorm. She knew then, in the depth of her heart, that none of them would follow her into the belly of the whale.

"'None of them can accompany you, my princess,' said the same man who had put our princess on this path. 'The king of the seas has granted permission to you alone.'

"And the princess despaired. She wanted nothing but to restore her father's eyesight, to cure his ailment, and bring him happiness. But she was just a girl, one girl, facing a challenge so enormous even the bravest soldiers of the kingdom were afraid to face it.

"'What am I to do?' she thought it in her mind, and she spoke it to the winds, and the man heard her, and he replied: 'You shall not need to conquer it by force, my princess. He has granted you permission; all that is required of you is to find the compass trapped inside the belly of the beast.'

"'A compass?! How is a sea compass going to help heal my father?!'

"'But with this compass in your possession, you will command all the seas; surely then it will be a simple matter to command the whale to heal your father–'"

"–This fellow isn't up to any good, is he?" Jenkins interjected. Others in the crowd concurred, and Imbali smiled.

"Well, yes, he is not," she obliged. "In fact, he is a terrible trickster who will stop at nothing to send our poor princess into the belly of a whale to do his bidding."

"Why can't he just get it himself?!" someone else asked.

"We'll get to that. But for now, our princess is facing the biggest quest of her life. Now, she was no stranger to courage; and bravery was not foreign to her. But faced with the depth of darkness behind those monstrous jaws, she hesitated. Anyone would hesitate, to be fair. One whale could sink this

158

entire ship with a single blow; it can lift us clear out of the water! Its tongue alone is the weight of an elephant, let alone its entire body. Anyone would be scared; faced with such a mighty creature.

"But the trickster would not allow her to waver from this path. He had come so close. He had found someone of noble heart and blood to retrieve this compass that meant the world to him, but the story of the trickster and the compass will be revealed in time; just not here; where his biggest challenge was convincing the princess to face her own paralysing fear."

Someone from the audience asked again, "but why can't he just get it himself?"

"Well, this is why; he was not noble, and he knew it. He knew that the king of the seas would never grant him permission to enter. And it is this fact that he used to convince the princess to do what he never could.

"'He has given you permission.' The trickster reminded; 'he will not harm you.'

"With more words of encouragement, the princess steeled herself and climbed into the canoe set to take her to the mouth of the beast. With one last look at the boat she would leave behind, she held on to the reed oars and started rowing. Each time the oar sliced the water, she felt as though her own strength was growing. Left side, right side, left side, right side, on she went, determination in her heart, and prayer on her lips.

"But then the King of the Seas opened his mouth once more, water cascaded like a waterfall, drenching her and rocking the canoe violently, back and forth, side to side. She tried to hold on to something, anything, but she felt herself fly, felt herself fall, and even as darkness engulfed her, courage did not fail her.

"She landed on something soft. And after gathering her strength, steeled herself once more and began walking into the dim and putrid depths of the whale's stomach.

"After what felt like hours of navigating the dark and unpleasant place, she finally came across a tower of objects, and right there, amongst them, she caught sight of a small, unassuming compass, just as the trickster had described. She reached for it, but as her hand closed around the brass chain, a voice echoed from the shadows.

"'Who goes there?' it called, startling the princess. 'Has the whale swallowed you too?'

"At first, the voice filled her with fear, but she soon regained her composure and spoke firmly. 'Who are you, and what is your purpose here?'

"Upon hearing a maiden voice, the man changed his tone, 'if you help me, I will see to it that you are richly rewarded.'

"The princess glanced around and discerned the faint figure of the man in the murky darkness. 'I have no need of your rewards,' she said. 'And by the look of things, I cannot imagine what you might offer that would be of value to me!'"

As Imbali's narration proceeded, Mr Evans could see how her listeners grew increasingly absorbed. As for him, he could hear no more of it. Promptly, he headed to his master's cabin.

"I beg your pardon, Sir," the shipmaster said, interrupting Mr Hertworth and his companion's leisurely evening. "Please allow me to say that I do not personally have anything against her," he continued, introducing the subject of his visit, "she does seem quite amiable when compared to the rest of her kind; however, I believe it my duty to bring to your attention a matter which my morals will not allow me to be silent about."

"I suppose you are referring to what is occurring in the women's quarters?" Edmund remarked.

"Well, yes, Mr Hertworth," he blurted, surprised at hearing his employer so promptly aware of it. "I mean to say… we are all expected to believe in the stories of our holy book, are we not?"

"If you do not approve of it, then why did you allow them to gather in the first place?" William interjected.

"I shouldn't have! Quite right, Sir! But the women did seem to find leisure with her, and some of the men too; and God knows how many of them can do with a bit of distraction.

"As I said, I don't mind the girl; she does seem quite innocuous to do any harm to anyone, but I could not help become quite perturbed by the nature of the tale; it does seem to me a bit too unchristian for our ways, Sir."

"What would you have us do?" William probed, allowing himself the liberty of speaking on behalf of Edmund.

"Nothing, Sir, there is nothing I cannot take care of myself! But I am simply unsure whether I should allow this evening to carry on, or if I should–"

"–You should do nothing," Edmund said.

"What do you mean nothing!" William exclaimed. "You have brought a pagan in our midst! What other profanities are we to find out about her?!

"Let me go up to her, and I will politely question her beliefs and come to a common ground with her," he then offered. "We both know her to be one of the smart ones, surely she will understand what we deem is acceptable and what is not."

But much to the confusion of both Mr Evans and William, Mr Hertworth offered no reply.

William's frustration with his friend's apparent indifference to the events unfolding on his ship deepened with each passing moment. Alas, unable to contain his irritation any longer, he rose abruptly from his seat and motioned for Mr Evans to follow. Together, they made their way towards the women's quarters.

Mr Evans could not fail to notice the belligerence all over Mr Bormer's countenance. He began to regret involving him, though indirectly.

"I can speak to her myself, Sir," he said, attempting to ease the tension, "no need to burden yourself with such trivialities."

"It is too late for that now!" William retorted sharply. "You should not have brought her doings to our attention if you thought yourself capable of dealing with her!"

"Quite right, Sir," Mr Evans conceded. "But I know she means no harm. Indeed, I did not appreciate her meddling with what is, in my understanding, the story of a prophet of God; but I was just thinking, how many of our men are truly familiar with our Bible? Not many, I am sure; so, in the end, no harm done after all."

But William would not be dissuaded from confronting the negro himself.

"Enough of this spectacle!" he commanded, his voice cutting through the murmurs of the assembly still gathered around Imbali. "Everyone, disperse at once!"

As the crowd began to obey William's command, Imbali too came into the corridor, and as William located his target, Imbali felt his sharp eyes upon her.

She became trapped in his stare. An imperceptible tremor ran through her, her composure slipping as memories of that dreadful experience at the Von Hisen's flooded her mind once again.

She distinctly recalled having seen him in the company of one of the men who were in the summer house. As the memory grew clearer, she realised it was on the very same occasion she saw Mr Hertworth for the first time too; and as her thoughts turned to Mr Hertworth, she noticed, in the distance, the very man himself making his way toward them.

She forced herself to regain composure, just in time to hear the rest of the exchange taking place between Mr Jenkins and this gentleman.

"I mean no disrespect, Sir, but she did nothing wrong! We insisted she tells it to us. So, if you must be angry at someone, let your anger upon all of us, not her!"

"Who do you think you are to allow yourself to speak to me like this!" William could not believe his ears. "I can have you dismissed! Do you really wish to lose your job for someone like her?!"

Mr Hertworth did not speak a word as he joined them, instead he made a brief, commanding gesture to Mr Evans, who immediately set about dispersing the remaining assembly.

As the crowd left, William turned to address Edmund.

"We cannot allow her to desecrate amongst us! You must do something!"

"But, Sir, I was just telling Mr Bormer, she is not at fault here...," Jenkins began, but before he could continue, Mr Hertworth interrupted.

"It appears there are some who find your storytelling somewhat discomforting; perhaps you care to explain yourself," he addressed Imbali directly.

"As far as I understand, there are some others who have been fascinated by your tales. You may be in possession of your own unique way of narrating fables; however, even I could not fail to notice their familiarity. Where did you get such a tale from?"

"It was narrated to me by my mother," Imbali replied. She had remained silent as Mr Bormer spoke to her and about her; but now, Mr Hertworth was addressing her directly.

"I am not sure who narrated it to her in particular; but I know the elders in our village are familiar with it too," she added, raising her chin to meet his gaze.

"Do your people have a different version of our scriptures?"

"I cannot say, Sir," she said, "but even if we did, none of our elders can read; so perhaps their stories may have simply been passed down to them, just like my mother passed them down to me."

"I see...," he said. "And... can you read?"

"I can, Sir."

"And write too?"

She offered a faint nod this time.

"Very well…," he remarked thoughtfully, "I think we can put your talents to better use elsewhere; I hear some of your own people would rather not have you in the kitchen with them, is that not so?"

"It was just a very small misunderstanding, Sir. All is well now."

"I do not doubt it; but–"

"–Sir, I would rather stay where I am," she interjected.

"And you will find I would rather have you elsewhere!" he exclaimed.

Dear goodness! What was he saying?!

He was striving to appear as uninterested as he could bring himself to be, but what if she understood all he wanted was to have her back in his bed.

He could not believe he had been presented with an opportunity to have her all to himself once again. "I remember you are quite familiar with my library, are you not?"

Again, she chose not to answer his question, lowering her gaze to the ground rather than meeting his eyes. Taking her silence as permission to proceed, he continued, "There is something in there I believe you can assist me with, and if you care to follow me there now, I will instruct you on what it is I need of you."

The conflict taking place within Edmund was truly surprising to himself.

What was the need to drag this negro down to his library with him?

How could he behave in such an ambiguous manner around his men?! When had he ever publicly solicited the company of a woman, no matter how insignificant the woman may appear to be?

And since he recognised her to be so insignificant, why were thoughts of her the only object to have disturbed his senses for many days now!

He had certainly been able, for all his four-and-twenty years of life, to embody the moral character he strived to abide by.

His reason had been the compass of his moral conduct.

He would not be a man overcome by his carnal passions. Until a few days ago, he regarded such feelings perditions to be left to the common man.

He did indeed possess many passions, but his passions had, until now, solemnly been of a much different nature from what he was experiencing at that particular moment.

Edmund truly believed in the physical and mental superiority of the Englishman above all. And indeed, men such as him could certainly not afford themselves the liberty or frugality which may be aroused by a weakness in his judgement. Passions of the flesh may very well lead a man to perdition, if such a man allowed them to overcome his mind.

So, then, how to rationally explain the perplexity of his feelings of late, and may God forgive him, the foolish reactions his body had been inclining towards.

However, no matter how inexplicable his current situation was to him, he fully acknowledged to himself that something about this negro had slowly, but quite steadily, taken hold of his mind and his senses.

"Edmund! What do you think you are doing?!" William demanded, rousing Edmund from his thoughts "Are you rewarding her, instead of punishing her for the deviation she has been causing amongst the crew!?"

Edmund returned his friend's gaze with a mocking smile, "I believe by engaging her in the library, where I can keep my eyes on her, she won't have much time to deviate the crew, will she now?"

"A negro in the midst of your books?! You don't like it even when I go near your books!" William countered. "And now you are telling me she has been there before?!"

"I did mistakenly venture in there once," Imbali interjected defensively, "but I assure you, I have not set foot in it since that day."

"Who gave you permission to address me?!" William said to Imbali.

"She is not talking to you, is she?" Edmund replied in Imbali's defence. "Leave her be!"

William turned to Edmund, his face a mask of utter shock. He wished to counter the reprimand, but upon second thought he decided against engaging with Edmund. He directed one last glance at Imbali, before he walked away.

Edmund began addressing her once again. "So, will you care to follow me?" he probed. "I am asking you to come with me as I truly require assistance, which at this moment I believe only you can provide me with. You said you can read…?"

"Yes… but I fail to see how such information can be of any value to you."

"Well," he then said, "while in your hometown, I became intrigued by a manuscript which looked too good for me to pass on it, so I quickly purchased it without fully inspecting it. Too late I realised I had been hasty, as once we set sail, I noticed many of the entries in the latter part of the book had not been translated into English, and they are still written in what I believe to be your native language. Therefore, I have no choice but to ask you to please be kind enough to my curiosity and help me enjoy the rest of the entries in my purchase."

"Can you not do it once you are in England?" she asked.

"Well… I really doubt I would be able to find anyone who can speak your language and at the same time be fluent with mine."

To be fair, Imbali considered, she did owe this master her current safety as well as wellbeing. She had already spent quite a few sleepless nights tormenting herself about how she would ever be able to repay him for the large amount of money she saw him deposit in Von Hisen's hands in order to secure her release. If a simple translation was what he claimed to require from her, then perhaps she could indeed grant him this service.

Perhaps she really ought not to be unfair to a man, who from the first moment she laid eyes on, had demonstrated nothing but magnanimity towards her and everyone around him. Everyone on board seemed to have a general good opinion of him, and if she was to go by Mr Jenkins and Lucy's accounts, he should be considered quite the best amongst his kind.

But how could she now begin to reconsider all she had known about masters such as him? Could it be possible for a master of such rank and power to truly embody what a gentleman of his race ought to be? Had she not learnt that being all alone with one of them was a situation to avoid. And with such experience, how could she now allow herself to think of this particular master differently from all the other ones she had come across before him? Besides, he may have been the one to rescue her from the summer house, but she did see him in the company of one of them.

She made up her mind, but before her lips could convey the refusal he could easily discern in her eyes, Edmund intercepted her.

"Believe me when I tell you, my morals, and quite honestly my tastes too, are rather impeccable in their nature, as such you will find you have nothing to fear from my end. I assure you my expectations of you are nothing remotely close to what those men may have wished from you," he lied.

"How can you expect me to think differently of you when I saw you back at the house with one of them! And I am quite certain the other gentleman was another of those men who came along with you!"

"I came to that house because I felt it my duty to pay a courtesy to a man who has been trading with my family for a long time," Edmund explained. "But I must have you know, I find what Fredrick did that night truly unpardonable, and as a result I immediately dissociated myself from him."

"What do you mean, 'dissociate yourself from him?'"

"Fredrick is no longer an associate of mine. He was supposed to be on this ship with the rest of us; but as you can see for yourself, he has been left behind."

Perhaps Edmund could not fully grasp what this simple revelation meant to her; however, though her lips remained sealed, her eyes had now acquired a whole new expression which was more than enough to convey to him what she would not with her words.

Was this particular master implying he had intentionally left one of his own behind because he loathed the way this acquaintance of his had behaved in regard to her?

She stood motionless, staring at him. To Edmund's satisfaction, she was willingly offering him the opportunity to fully immerse himself in her eyes.

Staring back at her, he suddenly recalled he was familiar with her eyes. The sketches of Von Hisen's second daughter had truly done justice to the various expressions Imbali was capable of conveying.

How could the daughter of a despicable man such as Von Hisen manage to secure such a treat from Imbali? He could not dwell much on this consideration as, after he knew not how long, Edmund had to rouse himself from the timeless encounter of their eyes.

He realised she must have already spoken to him.

"...if you could show me this new book of yours," he heard her say as his attention moved away from her eyes.

"It may very well be that you have overestimated my abilities, however, I will endeavour my best to please your request, Sir."

As she spoke, she waited for him to take the lead. He stepped forward, and she followed.

When they reached the stairs, Mr Hertworth gestured for her to go first, and he would have followed right behind, but he felt a hand hold him back. It appeared William had one final remark to make, but this time he intended it solely for Edmund's ears.

"I do not recognise you any longer… If I did not know you better, I may be inclined to presume you as interested as Freddie was."

24.

"What do you make of it?" he asked, as Imbali remained quietly engaged in her inspection. "As far as I understand, it could be a collection of poems, or so the first few pages indicate."

"I am not very familiar with this content, Sir…," she said at last. "I really do not think I can give such words their due justice."

"What sort of words are they?"

"I do not believe these entries to be poems, Sir" she offered, but she appeared unsure. "I think this manuscript could be more of a journal… I cannot tell."

"But you do understand the words, do you not?"

"Yes Sir, I do, but–"

"–You will do," he interjected more firmly than he had intended.

As he thus spoke, she looked up from the manuscript. She'd kept herself beside the door, and only now noticed the presence of a desk and chairs, two chairs to be precise; she could not recall these details the last time she had been there. There had been no furniture in this cabin other than rows upon rows of shelves stacked up with what she presumed to be a precious collection from all of his travels.

"Even if I was to try… I do not need to stay here to do this, Sir," she pointed out. "If you would not mind handing over the copy to me, I would rather leave this cabin for your use, and I can deliver it to Mr Jenkins once it is finished."

"I have little use for this cabin at present," he replied. "And I do wish for you to take your time and be at your comfort while you partake in this task, which has become quite valuable to me."

He gestured toward the neatly arranged writing tools on the desk, and said, "while you are here, you will have access to whatever materials you might need."

"What about you, Sir?"

He paused for a moment, before responding, "if privacy is what you prefer, then I shall leave this cabin entirely to your use, madam."

"You cannot address me as madam,"

"How do you suppose I address you then?"

"I have provided you with my birth name, Sir; you are more than welcome to use it... if you must." As she spoke, she marched into the cabin, ready to begin her new task. He understood her meaning.

"I gather you wish me to leave. But you shan't need to commence tonight, it is quite late already; you may begin tomorrow morning."

"But I cannot come in the morning, Sir."

"Why not?"

"I will be in the kitchen in the morning, Sir."

"You do not need to concern yourself with my kitchen anymore."

"I wish to continue as per our initial arrangements all the same, Sir."

"What arrangements?!"

"You allowed me to come on board with the understanding I will be working in the kitchen; and I do wish to carry on doing so."

"But I have now provided you with new work," he countered.

"I can do both, Sir," she insisted. She appeared resolute, and he understood her insistence on this matter had no end in sight.

"Very well, as you wish," he conceded at last.

*

An unanticipated routine began forming for Imabli on the ship. She would spend her day occupied in the kitchen, and each evening, she would go to Mr Hertworth's library to translate a page or two of the manuscript before retiring for the night in the women's private quarters.

She concluded that Mr Hertworth had granted the full use of the library to her, as she had not seen him since he left her with the manuscript.

But on the third day of this new routine, as she worked her pen, a knock on the door startled her. It was him.

"Please forgive me for the intrusion, I did not mean to startle you," he said. "I won't be long; I only came to get a new book for the night."

She paused in her task and appeared as if she was weighing the credibility of his words carefully; and alas, to his satisfaction, though she said nothing to him, she resumed the meticulous task she had been absorbed in before his sudden intrusion.

He walked in and proceeded to the shelves. It did not take him long to find the book he was looking for, though in truth, a book was not the only reason he had come.

He watched her, and even from his distance, he could not fail to notice the contentment with which she applied herself to her task.

He did not mean to linger long, but on his way out he decided to speak to her, "Are you enjoying it?"

172

Her pen stopped moving; and she looked up at him.

"I will not lie, Sir; I am enjoying it," she said most sincerely.

"I told you, you would be up to the task," he offered with a smile.

He walked closer to the desk, appearing intent to look at her work, his eyes skimming over several lines she had written.

She allowed the inspection for a few moments, before she signalled she wished to resume her task.

He understood and receded from the desk. He was almost out of the door when she spoke once again.

"As I suspected, Sir, this is a journal, written a good while back. I am still not too sure if the content will be all the same as I continue, but I think it must have belonged to a sailor."

He was surprised to hear her addressing him out of her own accord.

"What makes you assume the manuscript belonged to a sailor? The cover does look quite refined for something like this to belong to a simple sailor."

"Maybe these entries were not written by the sailor himself," she speculated. "I have heard some of these narrations before, I suppose you may consider them similar to songs; they are sad in nature, more like a plight of a man lost at sea, yearning for his loved ones...," she explained. "The elders in our village would sing it to us when we were children."

"Who taught you how to read?"

He received no answer to this enquiry.

"Forgive me, if my curiosity may appear out of line to you," he continued as she looked away from him, resuming her task. "I am simply trying to understand you better. It is obvious to me you have been educated to very high standards by somebody, and I am merely trying to solve the mystery of where all your talents come from. I mean the way you express yourself alone is something I have not heard since I left the genteel society back in England!

It is obvious you are indeed quite capable with your mind too. First, I see you reading poetry," he said gesturing at the shelves, "and it was not simple poetry you were enjoying that night, but one of the finest of its kind.

"Then you work out some providential numbers with the ledgers, which according to my men, was quite a puzzling headache even for them.

And to top it all, you manage to bring delight to so many amongst the crew, men and women alike."

"You are quite mistaken, Sir, I did not do anything with those books, apart from handing them back to Mr Jenkins the way I thought he was carrying them himself. So, if you think some credit is due, then such credit should go entirely to Mr Jenkins," she remarked.

She then turned back to her task, leaving Mr Hertworth with no further excuse to remain in her company.

25.

Two days went by, and with just over a week to their arrival back in England, time became of essence to Mr Hertworth. He grew more conscious Imbali may not be able to complete the entire manuscript, and as such he insisted he required more of her time in the library.

Upon the insistence of Mr Evans this time, Imbali found herself capitulating to Mr Hertworth's wish. She spent less and less of her time in the kitchen, and more of it in Mr Hertworth's library.

Her presence in his library was no longer an evening occurrence, but an affair which took several hours of her daytime too. In keeping with her new routine, one afternoon, she arrived at the library much earlier than Mr Hertworth could have anticipated. As she opened the door, it was her turn to startle him. She considered whether she ought to leave and return a little later, but as she pondered so, he found whatever he had been searching for on the shelves. He pulled out a small book and looked at her, "Do you remember this?"

She glanced at the book and recognized it immediately.

"After you dropped it that night, I began to read it again," he said. "Are you familiar with other works of his?"

"Why would you ask, Sir?"

"Well, I am convinced this man cannot be as much of a heretic as our Church would like us to believe," he replied.

"I would not presume to know, Sir," as she spoke, she decided to step into the cabin and sit on her usual chair.

Edmund read aloud to her: "'The whole world is summed up in the human being. The devil is not a monster waiting to trap us, but rather he is a voice inside. Look for your devil in yourself, not in others. Don't forget that the one who knows his devil, knows his God,'" he paused and looked again at her, "I really cannot see what is so heretical about this?"

"If I may, Sir; I think a person's heresy should not be imposed based on one's understanding, or... convictions in his own faith." She looked up at him, seeking his reaction.

He appeared surprised, "I must say I find myself in agreement with you." He then approached her with more daring than usual and noticed her fingers lingering over the paper she had been working on.

"Would you allow me to show you a passage from the book?" he asked. "I wish for more of your thoughts on what he says next."

"I know what he says next, Sir, you do not need to take the trouble to show it to me."

"Oh? Please, enlighten me," he smiled.

"In his next passage he talks about one's ego."

"Goodness; you are quite right, again!" he noted with a curious look.

He kept his polite distance, but carried on reading to her, "'every breath is a chance to be reborn spiritually. But to be reborn into a new life, you have to die before dying,' I believe this is where he is talking about suppressing one's ego; am I right?"

He saw her faintly nod her head.

"But how are we to do that?" he asked. "I mean, how would you do it?"

"I think the path we choose to take can be quite subjective, but I can only suppose, in suppressing the ego, one must take all else into account."

He looked confused, "I do not quite follow you."

"What I mean to say, Sir, is surely one must contemplate the consequences of taking any step if what will come is undesirable according to, for example, our society's measure of consequences, even if the outcome is desirable to the one taking the step."

"He says all of this in that one sentence?!" he chuckled, unable to contain his surprise.

She smiled at him in return; a genuine smile meant only for him.

Edmund at last decided to try his luck. He would not leave the cabin this time, as she most likely expected him to; instead, he took a seat in the second chair, directly across from her. He could sense her assessing his every move, but she said nothing to him, and quietly resumed her work.

He remained silent for a while, but as he realised she would soon be leaving for the night, he found himself addressing her once again.

"You know, you are yet to tell me which patron educated you almost as if he intended you for one of those high societies in Europe."

She stopped writing and looked directly at him, "Why do you assume I must have had a patron educating me?"

"Please do not misunderstand me; I do not mean to imply any evil doing on your part," he offered defensively. "All I am asking is how you managed to become this remarkably clever, considering... ehm, I suppose, considering the limitations you must have had."

"Again, Sir, you still insist upon your assumptions! You mean to say, because of the colour of my skin, I cannot be as learned as any of the fancy ladies in your circle?"

"Come now, Imbali," he then said, deciding to address her with the same familiarity she occupied in his mind. "I expect you to know me well enough to understand what I am asking you; you simply intend to tease and embarrass me further." As he spoke, his eyes implored her to have mercy on his curiosity.

She paused for a moment, taken aback by his friendly use of her name. But her surprise quickly faded away, as when she spoke next, she did not sound contrary to him.

"Very well, if you must know, it was Miss Von Hisen's doing."

"You must be joking!" he exclaimed. "You mean to tell me that the same arrogant, pompous, younger version of her father, is the same person who extended such a magnanimity towards you and instructed you in all that you have become?!"

"Though I must say you are being quite unfair to Miss Johanna, it is not her to whom I owe my gratitude. I mean to say the younger daughter, Miss Clara Von Hisen."

Imbali surprised herself at her own defence of Johanna, however she simply could not allow him to speak ill of Clara's sister.

"You don't say! Pray, do tell me more," Edmund's curiosity had been piqued even further.

"There is really not much to tell; Miss Clara is quite different from the rest of her family. I believe she possesses a kind and generous heart." At this remark, Imbali was interrupted by a rather inelegant smirk from Edmund.

"I certainly cannot boast to have seen much of her big heart, but I can definitely tell you that no member of such a family has given me the slightest inclination at consideration for anyone except for themselves."

"Clara does not agree with their ways!" Imbali insisted. "You only met her once; therefore, how can you claim to do good justice to her character?"

Edmund did not offer much of an answer to her, but he seemed to concede to her observation.

"It all happened quite long ago," she then rejoined. "One day, she saw me sneaking into their study to have a look at the book their tutor had just finished instructing her and her sister with. I was much younger then, as was she in fact; we are talking about a good five or six years back, we both did not really think much of the consequences," she continued, appearing lost in some distant thoughts. "One thing led to the other and before long, after every lesson of theirs, Clara would find a way to me and teach me everything she had just been taught."

"Were there any consequences?" Edmund could not help but enquire. "Was something done to you because of Miss Von Hisen instructing you?"

Imbali's gaze moved away from him, and her attention appeared to be completely back on the manuscript.

"Please forgive me, Imbali; I do not want you to think me inconsiderate towards Miss Von Hisen, but I simply could not help but wonder, considering all that I have witnessed for myself. Tell me," he insisted, "has anything else ever been done to you prior to that occasion?"

In spite of their growing closeness, Edmund was acutely aware of how perilous it may be for him to close the distance between them. However, he found himself leaving his own seat and making his way to her.

"Mr Hertworth, you really do not need to trouble yourself over matters which are in the past," she said dismissively, rising from her own seat and making her way to the other side of the cabin. "I will forever be indebted to you, Mr Hertworth, much, much more than you can ever imagine; but I assure you, you do not need to trouble yourself on my account."

"I will not insist for tonight," he allowed, stopping by her chair. "But you must tell me more about her. I suppose as a recompense for her lessons, you allowed Miss Von Hisen to depict you in her drawings?"

"How do you know about the drawings?!"

"See, I was right!" he cried. "You appear to be quite mistaken in your good opinions of this Miss Von Hisen, I must tell you."

"But Miss Clara promised she would not show them to anyone!"

"You ought to know, not only was I shown several of them, but she seemed quite delighted to show them off to the other gentlemen who were with me!" He then braced himself to approach her, much closer than he had ever been to her in this room, and losing his gaze in the same eyes Miss Clara Von Hisen had beautifully depicted, he said, "I do not know her well enough to pass a verdict on her motives; however, one allowance I will give her; she may very well be the first Caucasian woman to have proved many scientists wrong about our intellectual superiority!"

"Caucasian? I have never heard of such a word."

"I see your favourite Miss Von Hisen has omitted some things from her education," he teased.

Imbali could no longer bring herself to defend Clara, and to Edmund's utter joy, she did not retreat from his nearness.

"Well, madam, there are some men of science who claim that our race is in possession of an intellectual superiority to which the Malayan or Ethiopian kind could never aspire to."

"Do they base this claim on scientific evidence or their own suppositions?"

"Well… I suppose the evidence is strongly on their side," he countered. But as he spoke, he did not sound as sure as he expected himself to be. "I mean, according to them, our appearance alone is an indication of how superior we have evolved within the human species..."

"And aren't these scientists caucasian themselves? And, if that is the case then I would say, one may be inclined to project their own superiority over others in order to find comfort in dehumanising an otherwise perfectly formed human being!"

"Upon my word!" he exclaimed, seriously taken aback by the spirit she was showing him. "I will not pass a verdict on what others may wish to claim as their own facts; but if you were to ask me, I can no longer agree with them, even if I wished it."

"Whyever not?"

"I must tell you, since meeting you, you have put me in such an advantageous position to ascertain that such a claim is indeed flawed. And I must add, you are indeed mistaken if you attribute your proficiency solemnly to Miss Clara's teaching.

"I can sincerely tell you, if we were back in England at this moment, I am positively sure you would certainly put to shame many of the young ladies who can claim to have been educated by the most prestigious tutors."

"You are being ridiculous now, Mr Hertworth!"

"I am in full earnest! You must believe me!"

"Well, in that case, I thank you for the compliment, Sir, but you truly overestimate my merits," she exclaimed merrily, her eyes sparkling with amusement. Her laughter radiated effortlessly, and he felt his composure waver beyond his stoic forbearance.

Promptly, he returned to his seat, and she too returned to hers.

26.

To Imbali and the rest of the crew, Mr Hertworth's visible contentment at having his latest purchase made available for his own understanding elevated the positive impression so many of his employees already had of him. However, to Edmund, the few hours he managed to secure in the pleasure of Imbali's company became quite indispensable for his daily functioning.

His days were mostly spent in solitude, and memories associated with Imbali took up most of his time and attention.

A simple look at his wardrobe would bring back the memory of that coat of his which had been blessed by being wrapped around her body. He would have much preferred if she had kept it on, instead of the new black, woollen frock she now wore whenever she came to him. He presumed her new attire to be from those he had instructed Jenkins to provide for her, alongside the bed she now slept in.

She troubled his nights too, as he simply could not get himself to rest peacefully on his own bed. Every time he laid on it, without fail, he would recollect her feverish, voluptuous body wrapped around his.

He could certainly see why men such as Fredrick would want to possess her.

However, unlike any of the men prior to him, Imbali had allowed Edmund glimpses of her truest beauty. This quality of hers, laced with a peculiar superiority of mind and character which emanated from within, made him certain such qualities were yet to be seen in any woman of her kind; she truly was a rare woman any man would want to behold.

He initially despised himself for such thoughts, however the more time he spent in her company, the less his own guilt became, as he realised his desire for her was not a mere carnal thirst, but rather an attraction his entire being was enveloped in.

"I see you are rather early this evening," Edmund noted as he came into the library.

It was early October, and the ship had been journeying for close to three weeks; in less than two days, they would be anchored at the port of Exeter, Edmund's home.

"I wish to finish early this evening–" she responded.

"–Why? You know you can take your time; you are not expected to be anywhere."

"Mr Evans expects everyone to be diligent with their duties, and I wish to be of service to Miss Lucy in any way I can," she looked up, granting him a timid smile, before returning to the manuscript.

"What are you doing?" he asked, noticing her twiddle meticulously with the binding.

"I am trying to repair it before I am to return it to you."

"You are familiar with such things too?"

"Well, we cannot all be fortunate to have our own library, can we?!" she jested. "I had to make do with whatever nature had to offer in order for me to repair the few books which were in my possession."

"And what is it you are using?"

"It's a paste made from fish skin," she said, presenting it to him. "It is very common in our village; it can be slightly tricky to make I suppose, but once you get it right, it is the best mixture to give new life to anything, especially a book; at least that was the case for me!"

"You mean to tell me; you made this glue yourself?"

"It is not as difficult as you may think, Mr Hertworth."

She treated him with the familiarity they had come to have between themselves, but she appeared resolute in keeping her mind on the repair of the book.

"I did not expect you to finish so soon," he confessed. Eager to assess a reaction from her, he then added. "I honestly thought I may be given an excuse to keep you engaged all to myself a little longer."

"Mr Evans has been more than generous with his concessions to me, but I am in full earnest to perform my duty alongside everyone else. But have no fear, I have completed all the pages. Of course, I cannot claim to have done justice to the original; but I have endeavoured to satisfy you to the best of my capabilities all the same," she concluded, presenting the completed manuscript to him, alongside his original copy.

He took them from her hand, and a slip of paper fell out of the manuscript.

As he picked it up, he read the words before him:

> It is the opposite,
> The opposite of how the night breaks into dawn, and the sun rises without any fight,
> It is the opposite,
> The opposite of how the wind travels unbroken throughout the passage of time,
> It is the opposite,
> The opposite of how the phases of the moon are aligned with the days that fly effortlessly by,
> It is the opposite,
> It is a battle fought with menace entirely blind,
> It is being broken without any pieces, inside the confines of a fragmented mind,

It is unaligned with any wants made for a prolonged
and beautifully dreamed life,
Until at last, predestined souls are brought by.

"These words are not from this manuscript," he said slowly, once his eyes had gone over the lines several times. "Where do they come from?"

"I beg your pardon, Sir! It is nothing worth your consideration," she appeared mortified, and she rushed to retrieve the slip of paper from him.

She had jotted down the words racing through her mind the night before, supposing not much harm could come to his remaining stock of paper. But how silly of her to forget to retrieve the evidence of her misdoing.

"You are quite wrong, Imbali! I believe this is indeed something worth my consideration!" He then read the words aloud to her again. "May I enquire who has inspired such words from you? Because I can only suppose these words to be yours... are they not?!" he probed.

"I really do not know what came over me!" she countered, sounding rather startled by her own actions. "Please, Mr Hertworth, be kind to my mortification and return the slip back to me and let's forget all about it!"

Edmund did not return the slip to her, instead with the words still in his possession, he began to walk about the cabin.

Imbali may not have intended those words for his attention, but they were starting to acquire a noteworthy meaning to a man who had been growing dangerously engrossed with her.

He began to consider whether he ought to come clear with his wishes. Persuading her to oblige him may not be as challenging as he had initially considered, he thought. She might, willingly, accept an offer from him after all.

He had persuaded himself his gradual, infuriating attachment to this woman was merely physical, and if only she would allow him to possess her body, he would certainly be rid of her from his mind. Surely, his admiration for the other extraordinary qualities he had come to discover in her would simply fade away in time, as he would soon mingle back into his regular society, and his dear mother would ensure to provide him with the best, brightest bride his station in life expected him to settle down with.

He looked at her and decided to press a little further, "What made you write this?"

"I-I…," she began hesitantly, "I must have become so absorbed in all this reading, a-and I must have simply allowed my silly mind to get carried away."

"Have you written anything else like this?"

"I would not dream of wasting more of your papers, Mr Hertworth!" she cried. "I assure you this is the only one I have taken the liberty of using–"

"–Come now, Imbali!" he interjected. "When did you begin to consider me miserly? You surely ought to know me better than this!"

"You are indeed anything but that, Mr Hertworth!" she responded quickly, though her voice faltered with embarrassment. "I only meant that I understand how precious paper is, especially when one is at sea for so long…," her expression was marked by deep shame, and her unease with the current situation was too plain for him to ignore. He could not do it at this moment, and most certainly not now while she was being this thoughtful towards him, he decided.

He returned to his seat and composed himself, "You must write more; and once we arrive in England, I will personally escort you to have them published. Once my mother becomes aware of your work, she would love to show you off to all her acquaintances."

"Your mother…? You cannot be serious, Mr Hertworth! What would your mother want to do with me?!" She smiled at him, her unease slowly fading away.

"Indeed, I am serious!" he countered. "My mother will be delighted with you! I am sure you will become an excellent addition to her society! I can easily picture her adding her own touch to the performance of your writings at her social gatherings, and it will not be long before the whole of the English nobility in Exeter will be familiar with them!"

"I thank you for the thought, Mr Hertworth, but that will not be necessary."

"Whyever not?"

"Because I will not be staying in England for long."

"May I enquire about your reason for not wanting to stay?"

"Well... I suppose there is nothing for me worth staying in England," though she offered these words, her eyes appeared less affirmative. "Do not misunderstand me, Mr Hertworth," she continued, noticing the sudden frown on his face. "I will not lie to you and claim I will not forever cherish this trip as the most marvellous adventure life could possibly offer to someone in my situation. Indeed, I have a lot to be grateful for," she paused for a moment.

"You may quite possibly be right in my misjudgement of Miss Clara's motives towards me; I did consider her truthful… I suppose I believed her kindness to be sincere, but I harbour no resentment towards her; and would you like to know why?"

He remained silent, but nodded to her, and at his nod, she continued, "because here on your ship I have had the fortune of meeting Lucy! Lucy considers me her equal! Can you imagine such a thing?! Not only does she see past my skin, she also makes me feel appreciated; she truly seems to value my companionship! And I know I am not wrong about her!

"You know, I can honestly say Lucy, and dare I add, Mr Jenkins too, are quite possibly two of the most kind-hearted souls I could ever dream of meeting!"

"Your feelings towards these two individuals are indeed noteworthy, but please forgive me if I may sound presumptuous… but I thought you had grown in your regards towards me too."

"You are the master, Mr Hertworth!" she exclaimed. "A very good one… but a master, nonetheless."

"So... can I safely assume you think favourably of me too?" he probed, smiling at her.

"Think favourably of you?! We are not permitted to have an opinion on the masters."

"I am no master of yours, Imbali; I wish to know what you think of me."

"You may not consider yourself a master to me, Mr Hertworth, but your situation in life has made you so; and as such, I would not permit my tongue to utter any sentiments about you, whether in praise or criticism," she paused to glance at him.

He offered no reaction.

"But…" she then added thoughtfully, "one consideration I must give." Her voice softened, as her gaze came to meet with his. "I do not think I could ever find enough words to express my eternal gratitude for... not only for what you have done for me back then… with master Von Hisen; but for everything since. You have given me more than I ever thought possible.

None of your men, and even the women on board, would have welcomed me with the respect they have shown to me had it not been for you. And above all, you have done it all without ever demanding any favours in return!"

She gazed at him directly, expecting a response from him, but several moments passed before he managed to gather himself enough to respond. "Isn't this worth staying for...?"

"I am no fool, Mr Hertworth; such privilege was never meant to last. We are about to arrive at your home, and life will move along for each of us."

"But you have nowhere to go! Come with me, and I will be more than happy to keep you under my protection," he offered. "In fact, my plans could work quite well for you too!

I can no longer defer my duty to the family; and, as I am my father's heir, I shall take a wife. Understandably, as a newly married man I suppose I will not be sailing off anytime in the nearest future; but once I am able to discharge myself, I intend to set sail again, and I will take you along with me."

"You are very kind, Mr Hertworth," she said with a warm smile, "but we must go our separate ways. My mother wished for us to build a new life together in the New World, and though she is no longer with me; I intend to carry on further than England, once I am able to secure enough monies to pay for the passage."

As she mentioned her mother, her hand went to her neck.

"What troubles you?" he asked, though he understood very well what was amiss.

"Nothing, I… have just realised I lost something quite valuable to me."

"What is it?"

"My mother's pendant, Sir; you in fact, you were the one to return it to me, but I seem to have lost it again."

"I can have the ship searched for it."

"Oh no, Sir; that will not be necessary. I believe I must have dropped it in the… cabin, the women's quarters, I mean."

She was being sincere, but he was not. He no longer felt at ease for their conversation to remain upon her mother and the pendant.

"What sort of life do you intend to build in the New World?" he then asked more abruptly than intended.

"I… uhm… I cannot tell you," she confessed, as a new embarrassment wrote itself over her face.

"You must tell me!" he insisted.

"You may laugh at me, but I seek matrimony," she said at last. Her words had come out so softly he was not too sure he heard her correctly.

"You seek marriage?!"

"I do… not the kind of matrimony your women can aspire to of course, but a marriage is a marriage nonetheless."

"You mean to tell me you intend to sail all the way to the other side of the world only to find a man to marry you?!

"If that is your intent, believe me that may not be necessary! There are many African men who have found their way to England too. I grant you may be limited in your options around Exeter; but you will have plenty to choose from if you were to go to London, for example."

"Do not tease me so, Mr Hertworth! I am in earnest!" she retorted. "I certainly cannot claim to know much of the big world out there, as well as you may do, but from the little I read, I believe the man I seek cannot be found in England."

"What sort of man must he be then?"

"I do not care much for his situation, as I would presume it to be quite as limited as mine, but I wish him to be a free minded man... A negro exposed to the struggles mankind likes to inflict upon one another; such a man, I dare to hope, should possess a depth of understanding and compassion which might lead him to accept me as I am, with my failings and flaws, so that I may in turn grow to accept my own self."

"Why could you not find a man to accept you before we met?"

"I could never dream of finding such a marriage while I was in my own village… who would want to marry someone like me?"

"You don't say; pray, enlighten me! What may possibly be wrong with you?!"

"I am a bastard, Mr Hertworth! I am living proof of my mother's grave sins!"

27.

The ship had at last reached its destination. The port they were approaching was further inward of the main coast in Exeter.

Vessels the size of Odyssea would not normally be permitted to dock in this part of the cove, but the Hertworth's influence expanded to such limitless indulgences that the ship did not need prior approval from the local marine to approach this idyllic part of England.

As Imbali watched the noose of the ship being anchored to the port, she began to fear she may not see Mr Hertworth one last time. She had left him behind in the library, shortly after her shameful confession two nights before.

To be fair to him, she then considered, she could not fault him for not seeking her; he had been very busy after all.

For the past two days he had been engaged with his obligations to his employees.

Every single member of the crew had already been summoned by him, and everyone she heard from had talked about nothing else but the master's generosity in the remunerations they had received.

In her guarded heart, she would fondly remember Mr Edmund Hertworth as the man who managed to restore her faith in the male sex. She had grown to regard his familiarity towards her with the highest gratitude. He was an exceptional man in possession of one of the most benevolent hearts; a quality she had believed impossible to find in a gentleman of his race and position.

She indeed had no means of ever repaying all the kindness he had bestowed upon her. But, perhaps, if she managed to find employment in the first week of her arrival, and she diligently abided to her meticulous calculations of twenty shillings per week, then within the next six months she could have enough to purchase her passage to the new continent and may very well be left with enough to purchase some paper of her own. She wished to compose as many poems as her brain would allow, bind them together and find a way to present a manuscript of her own to him. Though it would be nothing compared to what he had done for her, she hoped it would express some of the depths of her gratitude.

"If you please Imbali, Mr Hertworth is calling for you," Jenkins startled her from the thoughts of the master who had not forgotten her after all.

*

"Thank you, Mr Hertworth, for seeing me," she started as she entered the study he had been using to conduct his business. "I began to fear we would part ways without saying goodbye," she addressed him with a familiarity which she, herself, felt quite out of place as she spoke the words.

He had his back to her, appearing intensely engrossed in the view outside.

She waited for him to address her.

When he turned, the eyes which met hers bore such a penetrating gaze she could not help but wonder if he may be in some sort of physical distress. His reddened eyes looked through her rather than at her, and there was something distinctly disquieting about his entire countenance.

She stepped back.

"Mr Hertworth... you wished to see me?"

"Yes, I did; do come in," he said at last. He made his way to his desk with a little less grace than she knew him to command, and retrieving a pouch from one of the drawers, he presented it to her.

"I thank you, Mr Hertworth, but I must remind you, you owe me no payment."

"You cannot have missed how everyone who has laboured on my ship has been compensated in the same way," he remarked with a flat tone.

"I have not missed it; everyone is praising your generosity. But as you may recall, I cannot accept it."

"Whyever not?"

"Before I embarked upon your ship, you and I agreed my labour would serve as payment for my passage to England."

"Your labour...?" he sounded surprised. "Very well, I will not insist on this," he watched her for a moment before speaking again. "I recall you intend to carry on to the New World, is this still on your mind?"

"Yes, Mr Hertworth. I have a mind to venture further, to the Americas," she did not know why, but her response was timid.

"Unless you came on board with wealth I am not aware of, I believe such a journey is quite out of your reach."

What caused such a perplexing transformation in him? she could not help but wonder. However, no matter how altered a manner he chose to address her, Imbali decided she would not desist from the usual fairness their previous encounters had been conducted with. She may never see him again after all.

"I intend to seek employment here in England, Sir; and I have calculated that on a monthly salary as a maid, or any likewise profession, I should have enough to pay for passage by next spring."

"What do you mean by 'any likewise profession'?!"

Did she not see, in front of her was a man ready to grant her any wish she desired, as long as she did not leave his sight? He had spent the past two nights dreaming of her, and the past two days drinking himself to oblivion in order not to run to her and command her to stay with him.

"Do you have any idea of what you are insinuating by asking for 'any likewise profession'?! What if you were to encounter the same behaviour which is so despicable to you?!"

"An honourable maid is what I hope to be while in England, Sir!"

She could not help the prickle in her words; but what was the man thinking; calling her to him just to make such insinuations.

She found herself locking eyes with him. The usual liveliness was now overtaken by something different; an intensity she was yet to see in any of the previous looks he directed towards her.

"Stay with me…," he whispered into her ear. At last, he could no longer keep hold of the strain he had put upon himself.

The same man who had never given her cause for alarm, had now ventured to accost her through such an alarming proximity, there was no space between them.

"Mr Hertworth... w-what are you doing?!" she stammered, her voice faltering as her legs trembled in response.

And then quite suddenly, he sealed her lips with a kiss.

"What have you done to me?" he spoke softly, but his voice was laced with urgency. "I have tried to get you out of my head! You cannot imagine what agony I have endured by your side, desiring you in the most primitive way a man can want a woman… you have my remedy, I am imploring you to put an end to my misery!"

This unexpected proximity, the whispers and his deep, dark eyes penetrating hers was all her mind needed to regain its lucidity.

Not only was she awakened from her current stupor, but her brain was at last able to piece together that mysterious dream she thought she had on the night she was trembling on Lucy's bed. However, she now vividly recalled, it was not Lucy's bed, it was his!

She pushed him backwards, enraged.

"It was not a dream! You took me to your bed! And you took these same liberties upon me! You have no idea how many times I would look into your eyes and torment myself; wondering how my mind could allow me to think of you in such a way, doing… well, you know what you did!"

"Oh please!" he scoffed at her attempt at rebuke, "you seemed very pleased with my attentions!"

"I was unconscious! I had no idea where I was or who you were!"

"Oh, is that so?! Had I been somebody else you would not have stopped me?! Well, perhaps your head was out of it, but I assure you, your body was fully responsive!"

"It could not be! I would never approve of such things!"

"You said I was your angel come to rescue you; and you loved every part of it!"

Edmund was too far gone in his woes to contemplate the effect his words were having on her, until something in her gaze shifted, freezing him mid-thought.

"Was this your plan all along then?" she then asked. "Is this the reason why you paid him so handsomely?"

"I beg your pardon?! How can you suppose so?!" he was astonished at her supposition. "You must admit you have your own faults!"

"What faults do I have in all this?!"

"You led me on! Your writing led me to believe my attention would not be unwelcome to you!"

"How so?!"

"How else did you expect me to interpret those words!"

"What words?!"

"Your poem!" he reminded her. "I don't suppose you go around every day talking about opposite souls coming together, do you? You dedicated those words to me!"

She looked at him, incredulous.

"Am I not the one who inspired them?" he pressed further.

"I certainly did not think of you in any way you may have imagined! I thought of you as my saviour... I thought of you as the friend I could never dream of having; but I would never presume your person to be equal to me! I simply meant to express my gratitude to you!"

"Your gratitude is not what I want!"

"I believed in your assurances! I willingly opened myself up to you because I believed your kindness to stem from a place of genuine friendship!"

"Friendship you say?!" he derided her, "how can you suppose me a friend to you? You and I cannot be friends!"

A suffocating silence fell between them, in which their eyes spoke many things.

"I fully comprehend your meaning, Sir...," Imbali said at last. "I should have never permitted myself to suppose so. It was gravely wrong of me, and for that I wholeheartedly apologise."

She moved towards the door, eager to put enough distance between herself and the painful humiliation his words had subjected her to.

Edmund watched Imbali walk away, his frustration only growing in intensity. She had misunderstood his intentions, and explaining himself felt futile now.

"Since you refuse any payment from me," he called after her, "I must insist that you come to work at Hertworth Manor."

She paused but did not look back at him. Her voice, when it came, was steady but distant. "Thank you, Sir, but I cannot follow you."

"You have nowhere else to go."

"Lucy says I can find work with her."

"Excellent," he countered, "as my estate is precisely where Lucy will be working."

Her breath hitched and she finally turned her head towards him, as though considering a response, but before she could respond, he strode past her.

Unsure of what else to do, Imbali found herself trailing him.

*

On the upper deck of the ship, Edmund spotted Jenkins and Lucy deep in conversation.

"I see you are both still here," he said as he approached them.

Lucy turned quickly, startled by his sudden appearance, "I'm sorry, Sir. We didn't mean to linger. I was just waiting for Imbali to finish with you, and Jack– I mean, Mr Jenkins, was keeping me company."

"You are welcome to linger as long as you like," Edmund replied. "In fact, you'll both be coming to work at Hertworth Manor."

"We are?!" Lucy exclaimed.

"Yes, you are," he confirmed. "Jenkins must have neglected to inform you, but both of you are to carry on your diligent work with me at the Estate."

Jenkins and Lucy exchanged thrilled glances, clearly delighted by this unexpected offer. But Imbali stepped forward, her expression resolute as she addressed Mr Hertworth.

"I thank you, Sir, for looking out for my welfare thus far, but please understand that any further involvement from you will be most unwelcome." She then turned to Lucy, attempting to dissuade her from accepting the offer. However, Lucy remained unshaken in her excitement.

Lucy pulled Imbali aside, "You don't need to worry, my dear," she said cheerfully. "Being employed by a family such as his can be nothing but an honour for us! I can already imagine how comfortable our stay will be. And if the mistress of Hertworth Manor has a quarter of Mr Hertworth's kindness, then I am sure we can count ourselves the luckiest out of the girls leaving this ship today."

"Lucy," Imbali whispered. "You cannot forget the rumours! Surely you remember what some of the other women insinuated about... his considerations toward me. And if I was to follow him to his property, I would only be adding credibility to their gossip!"

"Come, my dear, do not fret over those envious rumour mongers! They all wish they had half of your brains, or even a hint of your talents!"

Imbali hesitated, recognizing Lucy's determination.

"I would never ask you to give up a good opportunity for yourself," she said at last, "but I must ask you to at least provide me with the addresses of the people I could call upon for work."

"Nonsense!" Lucy cried. "We won't part ways! I'm sure Mr Hertworth wouldn't have made such an offer if he thought it inopportune."

Imbali could certainly not disclose any details concerning her latest encounter with Mr Hertworth to Lucy, and no matter how strenuously she insisted, Lucy seemed to have forgotten all the places she had enumerated as possible places of employment.

In the end, Imbali disembarked from the Odyssea alongside Lucy and Jenkins, her apprehension masked by a calm far from what she felt.

28.

The news of Mr Edmund Hertworth's return must have spread rather quickly, as a growing crowd of locals gathered to greet him as he and his company walked by the coast.

To Imbali's relief, though the number was minimal, there were others like her in the crowd and as such, not many people noticed her alongside Mr Hertworth.

As for those who briefly looked her way, they appeared to be led by the simple curiosity of seeing Mr Hertworth making his way home accompanied by a poor-looking assembly of servants.

With many sailors returning home at last, a considerable number of happy girls were roaming provocatively by the coastline. Their presence did not appear to perturb Edmund much, but as more of them came on to him unabashedly, he directed a few glances their way.

These glances did not fail to be noticed by some of his peers who happened to be taking their morning strolls by the seaside.

Most of these gentlemen were either strolling alone, or in the company of other likewise gentlemen. There were also a few observers who happened to be enjoying their walk with their own female companions.

One of these females was the esteemed Dowager Lady Glenith, at the arm of her eldest son, who had just succeeded his father as Lord Glenith.

"I have often remarked to his mother how all this faffing about in the world was sure to lead to this kind of perdition," she began. The large parasol she was using to shade herself from the bright sun of the day did not provide her with an ample view of the scene, but she saw more than enough for speculation.

"These Hertworths can parade their immense wealth all they want; but as I have always observed, the lowliness of one's birth is always bound to be reflected in their behaviour! You would not allow such filth to accost you in such a way, would you, my dear boy?"

"Of course not, Mother," replied the obliging son.

"Can you believe her insolence when she tried to imply that you, out of all people, have been scampering about from one village to another in search of loose skirts!"

"I am not surprised she would say such a thing," he replied. "These upstarts will stop at nothing to convince themselves their blood is equal to ours."

"But she always ridiculed my warnings and would insist this son of hers was indeed above such lowly insinuations, and I should better attend to the misdoings going on in my own home," the mother eagerly continued. "God is indeed merciful to us, my son! I cannot wait to see her face when I tell her exactly what her beloved son got up to as soon as he arrived, instead of paying his respects to his family!

"But then, the fault is not entirely with him, I must add. If a mother truly loved her children, as much as I do of course, she would indeed not permit such liberal ways to corrupt his character."

The dowager Lady Glenith had many other disapproving remarks to make about her friend's first-born son, and her own son knew any type of response was currently not required of him, therefore, paying particular attention to his mother's conversation was not a necessity.

Though he would not partake in his mother's gossip, Lord Glenith's focus was on Mr Hertworth too. He was eagerly engaged in discerning if any of the aforementioned girls would succeed in securing Edmund Hertworth's attention.

Based on his count, he had listed at least five brunettes and several blondes vying for it, but none of them appeared to interest him much. Strangely, however, Edmund seemed to have given a particularly interesting look to a negro amongst such stock.

This indeed felt like a glorious day for Lord Glenith! He now felt incredibly glad to have given in to his mother and come out on this stroll. He too felt his own gratification at watching the righteous Edmund Hertworth partaking in the mundane pleasures he would usually scorn other men for. To be the eyewitness of such a fall was indeed worth his mother's insufferable rattling.

To their utter dissatisfaction however, instead of engaging with what was on offer, both mother and son saw Edmund make his way to Hertworth Manor with nothing but a trio of servants trailing behind him.

*

"The house is not too far from here, it is less than a mile away," Edmund informed, addressing Mr Jenkins, "we could easily arrive on foot, but I think a carriage might be better for this occasion."

He then sent Jenkins to call for one, and as the carriage arrived, Lucy and Imbali were helped inside. Jenkins supposed Mr Hertworth may ride along with him, but to his surprise, his employer went and sat inside with the two women.

The carriage rode along the narrow roads of the village of Soulgate while Edmund stared at Imbali. She, on the other hand, ensured to keep her eyes diligently locked to the ground.

As he looked at her, he could not help but reproach himself for his moment of weakness. He had never been inclined to such things, but as those ladies of the line came to offer their services, for the first time in his life; he wavered. A negro amongst them had made him look at her twice; but upon the second glance, he could not possibly bring himself to consider her even closely relatable to the object of his current desire.

29.

The carriage made its way along the coast, following a rugged path that wound by the seaside. As they finally came to a stop, the rocks vanished from sight, and the sea, which had previously appeared an ordinary shade of pale blue, now shone with such clarity you could see the far off shore unfurling beneath the water's surface.

From their viewpoint, it was quite difficult for the newcomers to evaluate how far this side of the property extended, as the coast itself was in its entirety part of the Hertworth Estate.

Hertworth Manor did indeed reflect all the splendid grandeur a family in possession of such wealth should occupy. There was nothing equal to it in size and splendour in the whole county.

The house itself was situated on the upper hills, further back from the coast. The grounds had been ingeniously levelled to hold the expansive and striking stone structure, but despite its fortress-like appearance, there was nothing inelegant about it. Dark, brick walls tastefully gave way to many large windows – a much more recent addition to the building.

They were required to walk uphill for a good while before they could reach the entrance to the manor.

Nature had particularly favoured this part of the coast; the long, paved pathway to the house was tastefully surrounded by a variety of trees and other species of greenery quite different in their size and nature.

Imbali could see nothing artificial about the views which surrounded them. Though it was evidently clear that great attention to detail was preserved in the maintenance of this part of the property, many of the taller trees had been purposely left to grow unattended to add an exquisite, dishevelled appearance to this extensive garden, thus accentuating the natural beauty the manor was surrounded by.

Edmund escorted Imbali and her two other companions into a modest looking parlour, before he proceeded further into the house.

He greeted his father first, before he went into the tearoom where he supposed his mother to be.

Suffice it to say, when Lady Hertworth saw her beloved son walk toward her, she was in raptures of joy. She could not refrain from admiring him and kept alternating between how much more handsome he had become to how fastidiously darker his complexion looked. Soon after, his younger brother came along to rejoice his return.

While the Hertworths were thus engaged, quite unexpectedly, the butler announced the arrival of Lady Glenith and her son.

"My dear Edmund, I see you have returned at last," Lady Glenith said, offering her hand.

"Yes, milady, it is good to be home!" Edmund obliged, most cordially.

"No more scampering about I hope," the lady proceeded.

"No, Ma'am, I believe I am back for good."

After greeting the rest of the company in like fashion, mother and son were offered a seat with the company.

"My dear Priscilla," Lady Glenith addressed her friend, "please do not presume my visit inopportune; I am sure you must have a lot you wish to share with your son."

"I must say I am quite surprised by your sudden call," Lady Hertworth replied, "I wonder if I should begin to suspect my own staff passing news from my home to you!"

"You are quite mistaken, my dear, the truth is quite simple, rather. I was on my usual morning stroll, with my dear boy of course, when we happened to see Edmund by the port as he arrived. It was quite a while ago; I expected him to be with you much earlier. He did seem to me quite taken by... uhm, I suppose some distractions, but I am glad to see I was wrong.

"You know, Edmund," the lady then continued, turning to him, "your mother has not talked about anything but your intention of finally settling down! I really should not be telling you this, as this is indeed quite unfair to the poor young ladies, but I must tell you!" she paused for a moment, "you have no idea how many girls in our town and, in our nearest vicinity too, are eager to be introduced to you!"

She appeared to expect some sort of acknowledgment from Edmund, but as she received none, she decided to continue on her own.

"I suppose they will have to do...," she then paused again, pondering upon her own mental considerations. "But I had also heard, and I must say from a very good source too, some very good families from far counties had considered the prospect too but, I suppose to some, wealth is not everything."

The refreshments arrived, and to the relief of everyone present, Lady Glenith became occupied assembling her plate with the cold meats, biscuits, and various fruits presented to her. Light conversation broke out around the room as the refreshments were served, but Edmund did not have any.

Neither was he fully present in the room either, Lady Glenith noticed. He stood apart, detached from the chatter unfolding around him. He had been standing since she arrived and kept himself beside the door, appearing eager to be elsewhere.

His distraction did not escape his mother's notice either. Observing his impatience, she then decided to steer the conversation toward a piece of news she hoped would unsettle her friend and curtail the unwanted visit.

"I see you do not know everything, my dear," Lady Hertworth began with a self-satisfied smile, "not only will my boy finally settle down, but he will also take his father's seat in Parliament!"

"Oh…? What wonderful news!" Lady Glenith exclaimed. "I must announce it to the world! This changes your prospects considerably!" she declared, looking at Edmund directly. With this bold declaration, the lady successfully captured the attention of everyone in the room, Edmund included.

"I fail to see how I am the one in need of better prospects," he said.

"You did seem a bit distracted when I began talking to you, Edmund dear! I did not mean to imply you needed to care for such things, my dear boy; I was referring more to the young ladies to whom you are to offer a prospective marriage," she retorted defensively. "Of course, you do possess many merits, my dear Edmund; any lady would indeed be very lucky to have you as a husband; but… in essence it is the life of a sailor you are offering; a very rich one to be sure; but in all honesty I could not think of many honourable young ladies from my high circles who would be happy to settle for… well, that which is of no consequence any longer!" she said with a sigh. "Your post in Parliament will indeed change everything! Are we to have a ball, then?"

"I am no expert in such matters, ma'am," Edmund felt compelled to respond, "and therefore, I find I must leave you and my mother to discuss such details."

"I ask, as an idea has just come to my mind," she continued. "Arthur dear," she then turned to address her own son, "what do you make of our cousin, Lord Burrow's daughter, she will do very fine as a connection for our friends, would you not say so?"

"I would not know, Mother," the son obliged. "But, if I were Mr Hertworth, I would not want anyone to meddle in my choice of bride."

"Nonsense!" his mother countered, "this is the way of the world! And I think it our duty to offer our help in any way we can. I must tell you, Lord Burrow is an earl, my dear!" she addressed her friend once again, "and he has only this one daughter. I am no expert on such things I must admit, but it could very well be plausible for Edmund to inherit such a title once her father passes away. That is sure to be much more valuable than your baronetcy."

On hearing such a slight, Mr Edward Hertworth, Edmund's brother, could not hold his tongue any longer, "Forgive me if I am wrong, ma'am; your son is now a baron and so is our father. As far as I understand, we are equal."

This younger brother, two years his junior, resembled Edmund very much. He too possessed the dark eyes and hair Lady Hertworth's boys inherited from their father, and just like Edmund, Edward took great pride in the family position in their society. Though his father's title and wealth may never come to him, he simply could not allow this lady to discredit their name or standing.

"Upon my word! I see your education may still need some polishing!" she countered, annoyed at the comment. "I am sorry to say, my boy, but you seem to be quite ignorant on some subtle differences. Your family may possess the same title as us in the eyes of the Crown, but everyone knows the difference between one acquired with new wealth and one possessed by one's birthright."

She was most irritated at the discourtesy Edward had shown to their standing in society, and as such, decided to leave shortly after.

As his mother's guests were finally taking their leave, Edmund excused himself from the tearoom and made his way back to the parlour.

His mother followed him soon after. It seemed he had anticipated her arrival, for as soon as she entered, he promptly began introducing the three people he had brought along with him.

Imbali could certainly not fault the proud looking woman for the evident disdain her countenance displayed at such an unconventional breach of their etiquettes. Having her beloved son taking the ridiculous trouble of personally introducing such lowly personnel so shortly after he had returned must be something she was yet to experience.

"Edmund, dear, you will never change, will you?" she began with a sigh. "Please do not tell me this is the reason you were so agitated around our guests," she added, rolling her eyes with a mixture of exasperation and amusement. "Always scampering about from one salvation to the other! Where will you tell me you found these now?"

She was not really interested in the answer however, as she immediately continued, "but you really do not need to trouble yourself with these inconsequential details; I will have Mr Newby escort them to the servants' quarters, and thereafter I am sure he can find something for each of them to be employed with."

It would turn out Lady Hertworth was truly at her best with this generous offer. As Imbali would later come to know, no person had ever been offered anything, let alone employment within her property, unless she herself had carefully scrutinised such a person.

"Come, my dear, let us return to the tearoom," she solicited, eager to have her son all to herself.

However, the lady found herself stopped short at proceeding with this suggestion as her son surprised her.

"I thank you, Mother, for your offer, but I would like to have Jenkins and Lucy at my personal service, and this girl here," he added, turning his attention towards Imbali, "will be looking after the library situated on my floor."

As he spoke, an uncomfortable silence filled the parlour.

"You wish to have a negro in that fancy book room of yours?" Lady Glenith exclaimed, breaking the silence.

"Upon my word, my dear! You are still here?" Lady Hertworth cried, startled to hear her friend still lingering around her house.

"I wished to enjoy the coast from this side of your property on my way out, and I happened to overhear you talking. I certainly did not mean to pry on your private matters!" she explained defensively.

As she spoke, she inspected the trio of servants, but Imbali in particular.

"I suppose it is quite nice to have one's own son so attentive to domestic affairs, but I must caution against this. They can be useful at times, yes," she said, waving her hand dismissively. "Why, I once had one in my service who could carry several barrels of water all on her own, a task which would normally leave two of my strongest servants struggling. Quite extraordinary strength! I was quite pleased to have her, I admit. But upon my word; I do not mind confessing I had been so wrong in my judgment! A thief of the worst kind, she was!

"I later discovered she was the culprit who would ransack the stockings from our stores! And filthy creatures, I must add," she wrinkled her nose, and reached out to Imbali as though to punctuate her point.

"Do not touch her," Edmund commanded sharply, pulling Imbali back before Lady Glenith's hand could reach her.

The lady withdrew, her hand freezing mid-air. "Oh! I-I didn't mean any harm." She appeared taken aback by Edmund's sudden intervention, but she recovered quickly enough to press on a little further, "I would not want to contaminate myself

209

with their filth of course, but you must understand, Edmund dear, they are rife with lice and all other sorts!"

"I find myself in agreement with Lady Glenith," Lady Hertworth intervened at last. "I, too, know them to be most unreliable my dear Edmund; and it is such a menace to tame them!" she paused to look at the trio once more. "To be quite frank I do feel rather weary about all of them; I think you better dismiss them all," Lady Hertworth concluded.

"This is my wish, mother," Edmund responded firmly. "And I trust you to ensure they are made to feel as comfortable as possible in their new roles."

Lady Hertworth's lips tightened; her irritation barely concealed. She so wished there were no witnesses to these exchanges, however despite the unwanted audience, she could not resist countering her son, "I truly cannot fathom how a negro could be of any use with books!"

Lord Glenith, for his part, though he did not say a word, had been quite intent at analysing the spectacle before him.

Was it his imagination, or did Edmund Hertworth seem particularly attentive to this negro? This did not appear to be the same negro he had looked at with particular interest earlier at the port, but something about the way Edmund looked at her gave him pause.

Lord Glenith would certainly not risk being caught staring at any female in front of his mother, but could it be this was the object which might finally crack Edmund's flawless reputation? If so, he decided, the fallout would be worth his partake.

"Since Mr Hertworth himself can vouch for this negro," he started, "then I do not mind being charitable and offer her work with us. I am sure Mama can easily find some chores for her in the pigsty or even the kitchens; is that not so?" he solicited, directing a tacit message to his mother.

Imbali's gaze finally rose from the cobblestone floor she had been staring at throughout this whole exchange. She looked up at the person who seemed to have been providentially sent to provide her a way out of her impasse with Mr Hertworth. She would have earnestly accepted this offer of employment by this English nobleman; however, before she could formulate any words of acceptance, Mr Hertworth interjected.

"Such charity will not be necessary today, Lord Glenith; she already has work here at Hertworth Manor, and now if you would excuse me, I must see to my business."

In the next moment, intentionally ignoring his mother's astonishment, he turned to speak to Imbali directly. "Now, if you would please follow me, I would like to show you to your post."

But Imbali appeared resolute in holding herself motionless, intensely hoping for the ground to open up and swallow her alive. So, Mr Hertworth, quite unceremoniously, took her by the arm. As he did so, a very intrigued lady and a disappointed son were left to witness Mr Edmund Hertworth escorting a negro inside the house.

30.

It took Edmund two flights of stairs to reach the library. Hertworth Manor had two libraries; the main library was situated on the ground floor, filled with grand books his predecessors had been quite keen to assemble. Yet, despite its grandeur, Edmund had confessed to Imbali during one of their leisurely conversations, these books felt rather cold and unloved to him.

Upon returning from Oxford, he had longed for a space of his own, filled with books he chose for himself; and as consequence of this wish, his mother commissioned for a private library to be set adjacent to his sleeping chambers. In time, both Edmund and the content in this new library grew wiser together.

"You said to me you did not believe me capable of securing any respectable work on my own, but now you have just ruined the opportunity of my securing one," she reprimanded him, once they were alone.

"You already have work."

"I do not want the kind of work you are offering me. And if you would allow me, I have a mind to go back and accept that gentleman's offer."

"You have no idea what you are asking for!" he cried. "Do you have any idea how much of a swine Glenith is?!"

"Is he?!" she countered mockingly. "I do not know the gentleman; but you... are you very different from what you are accusing that gentleman?! Tell me, Mr Hertworth, what is it you truly want from me?!"

"I do not know! And not knowing it is what is driving me insane! All I know is that I have been unable to think about anything but you, almost since the first moment I met you!"

"You must not realise what you are saying, Sir! The man I know you to be is too noble for this... and I must beg you to put an end to this conversation immediately."

"I do understand what I am saying very well! You are the one who needs to understand me!" His gaze burned with intensity, silently communicating what his words could not.

"Is this what you want?" she said suddenly, gesturing hesitantly to her body. "You can have it all! I willingly grant it to you! I suppose you can rightfully make a claim to it considering how much you paid for it."

She began fumbling with the buttons of her gown. Her mission however was proving to be a rather difficult task, as her stoic attire was sealed together by tiny fastenings at the back.

Edmund, for his part, found himself caught off guard, unsure how to process this sudden turn in their interaction. Was Imbali herself suggesting putting an end to the maddening desire he had been feeling for her? And if she was, could he go ahead and take her up on this offer, which, after all, was the only thing he had craved for a long while?

Indeed, this preposition could work to her advantage too.

Not only would he gladly allow her to depart from him afterwards, but he would personally ensure to provide her with all the comfort she could want during her passage to the New World on board one of the Hertworth ships regularly sailing to the Americas.

While he was thus absorbed in his own considerations, she had turned her back to him, her voice trembling as she asked him to unfasten the buttons she could not reach. Her face was now hidden from him, leaving him unable to discern her emotions. His gaze, however, was drawn to the bare skin her efforts had exposed.

She braced herself for the inevitable touch, but as he came upon her, instead of his hands, she felt the warmth of his lips near her ear, his voice soft as he murmured, "not like this."

The sight of her bare back, the curve of her figure, had a total adverse effect on his spirits.

She felt the tips of his fingers graze her skin at last, but he was not using them to remove the rest of the buttons; instead, he was slowly undoing the hard task she had just undertaken.

All the tears Imbali had been holding back were now free. She crouched into the furthest corner of this precious room, and she thus remained until she no longer had any tears left.

Edmund was the first to break the silence.

"I fully comprehend we may have started on the wrong footing here in England... but my attachment to you is such, I fear I may have lost my sense of honour..."

"Do not speak of attachment to me, Mr Hertworth! What you demand of me is not attachment! At least the others before you had decency to name it what it is!

"You may choose to view yourself superior to them, Mr Hertworth, but I can tell you; you are no different from the rest of them!"

"You are being unfair to me, Imbali..."

"Am I?!" she countered. "You may not have put shackles and chains all over me; but believe me, this situation between us is no different!"

"All I am trying to offer you is my protection!"

"Pray tell, whom do you suppose I may be in need of protection from? Look around you Mr Hertworth! I see nobody but you here! Can you protect me from yourself?!"

"I cannot fail to understand how my behaviour must make me appear in your eyes at present, but you cannot in all honesty expect me to believe our time together did not signify anything to you. You truly cannot expect me to believe you have not been able to understand my... well, I do not know exactly what it is I feel for you, but certainly you could not have missed my strong regard for you."

"You cannot forget what I am, Sir! You may have grown to consider me superior to any other African person you may have encountered in your life, but I assure you, whatever considerations you think you have for me are nothing but a fleeting lapse of your judgement; which must have been provoked from the unfortunate closeness our time together must have inevitably aroused in your idle mind.

"But your idle days are now behind you," she then continued, raising herself from her corner. "You will have plenty of company to entertain and stimulate you and... I am sure you will forget me in no time." There was a solemnness in her tone, but the sadness depicted in her eyes was such, Edmund could not bring himself to contradict her words. And so, he quietly allowed her to proceed with whatever her heart wished to say.

"Let me ask you this," Imbali continued. "Had I not been who I am, would you have made such a proposition to me?"

"I fail to comprehend the meaning of your question."

"Had I not been a negro, would you have denigrated me to such an undignified consideration and asked my body of me?"

"Imbali, you must know you are not bestowing your full justice upon me at this moment! You must allow some fairness to the regard you must have sensed from me during our time together. You ought to know how I have come to admire and cherish all you have shared with me. It is indeed not only your body I most ardently desire, but–"

"–But nothing else!" she interrupted him. "There certainly cannot be anything else a man such as yourself could possibly want from someone like me! You irrationally talk of your regard to me at this particular moment, but in the nearest future, you will be addressing your potential future wife, and to her alone you ought to be talking of your regard!"

"I must marry! And upon God, you cannot expect me to marry you?!" he exclaimed.

"I will never in my life have such a presumption, nor have I ever wished to marry outside of the expectations compelled upon me, if ever a possibility of marriage presented itself. My only intent is to remind you how ridiculous it is of you to talk of such notions to me. And if you insist on keeping me here with you, what you solicit from me will certainly make you no different from everyone who made claims before you."

A heavy silence fell between them, and though Edmund wished to contradict her further, the words would not come.

But at last, he spoke again, his voice void of any emotions, "It appears we will not come to an agreement on this matter, but perhaps there may be a solution which could satisfy us both."

He looked around the room, "these books you see here are in dire need of care, and I can think of no one more suited to the task than you. Work here, under my protection, and I will personally ensure your passage to the Americas once your work is done."

Her brow furrowed in suspicion, "How do you expect me to remain under your direct employment considering our evident discord?"

"I won't be here," he said simply. "As you rightly recalled, I am to marry soon enough; and for such scope I must take care of some business out of town. You have made your position very clear to me; and just now with your words you have claimed some type of familiarity with my character. I appeal to this knowledge, and you have my word there will be no repetition of what I have regrettably made you endure."

There was regret in his expression, Imbali could not fail to notice it. And her heart could not do him the discredit of questioning the solemnity of his promise to her, no matter the recent uncomfortable turn of events she was still reeling from.

"Even so, I cannot accept such a generous offer from you," she then decided to respond. "As I was made to understand, I would need to work for over six months to secure the monies needed to pay for the passage. This room with all its content will not require more than a few weeks of my labour."

"Time is of no consequence, considering the delicate attention these books will require from you."

"But that will not be a fair transaction, and I have no intention of accepting any charity from you!" she insisted.

"It is not charity I am offering you. You require means to earn your passage to your next destination, and I require someone whom I believe competent enough to restore my collection to its previous glory. I may not be as versed as you are in such things, but I can tell you, do not let your eyes deceive you. Your work here will indeed consume the majority of the six months you have allocated to yourself."

With no further objections to make to Imbali, Edmund took his leave, and she was at last left all alone to contemplate upon her new surroundings.

31.

"Edmund... what is happening?!"

As Edmund opened the door of his library, he was met with the bewildered eyes of Lady Hertworth.

"Nothing you need to concern yourself with, Mother," he responded, eager to distance both himself and his mother from his library.

"Edmund, dear, why would you drag such... a person into your own library?!" his mother queried, unable to contain her astonishment. "Especially in front of such spectators! You know what sort of gossip Lady Glenith is!"

"I am sorry for causing you upset mother, but I would prefer if you would leave this matter to me," he countered.

"I suppose I have no choice but to... for now," the mother conceded. "Oh, what an odious woman she is!" she then continued, returning her attention upon Lady Glenith as they re-entered the tearoom. "I am sure she is out and about discrediting our family's name to everyone she will lay her eyes upon. But I must say, I really ought not to blame her mercilessly this time! This is all Edmund's fault!"

"Upon my word, Mother!" exclaimed Edward. "My ears must be deceiving me indeed! Did I just hear you find a fault in our impeccable Edmund?!"

"I believe she did," Edmund remarked, coming to embrace his younger brother. "Have no fear, brother, you have my full permission to rejoice in knowing that for once, you are not the one to have brought an infamous scandal upon our esteemed name! Also, I really liked what you said to Lady Glenith; if only our mother would do the same at least once!" Edmund teased.

Lord Hertworth had come to join the family in the tearoom, but he would not partake in the merriments of his two sons.

"When you came to greet me, you failed to mention you came along with dependents of your own this time?" His father queried.

"I did not think it necessary for me to mention it to you, Father," Edmund responded.

"It is rather an unpleasant commotion you are stirring; if one is to go by your mother's words," the father continued.

"Upon my word, Lord Hertworth! How can you remain so calm?! You talk as if I have been the only person who has witnessed Edmund's odd behaviour!"

"Mother, I must first be allowed to express how sorry I am that our long-awaited reunion did not come about in the cheerful manner in which I had hoped. But you must consider how valuable those books are to me!"

"Books?! What do books have to do with the spectacle you have exposed our family to?!" the mother remarked. "You have never given me cause to regret my trust in your impeccable conduct until this moment; but now how do you expect my poor, feeble heart to endure the absurdity you have brought along with you?!"

"I am in full earnest, Mother! I cannot fault anyone but myself for the poor state my library has become of course; however, as I have several times explained to you, some of those manuscripts cannot cope with such proximity to the sea, and as such they require a specific kind of attention," he appeared most pedagogical in his explanation.

"There is absolutely nothing wrong with all you have been piling up there. And therefore, you simply cannot expect me to agree with you this time," the mother cut him short. "Let us assume I find such trivialities plausible," she then continued, "even so, how can you expect any of us to believe that she... a negro you say, will be able to provide your books the valuable upkeep you claim they require?! What can she have to do with such things?!"

"Mother, since I can remember, you have always bestowed your reliance upon my judgement, and I must ask you to continue to do so. She may not look the part, but I can tell you I consider myself lucky to have encountered the precise person who can provide the best care to what you know to be indeed valuable to me," Edmund said as obligingly as he could.

"Let us not quarrel any longer, Mother. I am happy to be home, and as you happily divulged to your *dearest* friend, I am here to oblige you in all your wishes; when am I to leave for London?"

"Yes, indeed! I quite forgot! It is about time you relieve your father of his obligations! Our family seat has been vacant for far too long, if you ask me! Oh, I am so happy!" she cried out in full joy. "Now it will be my turn over her! I cannot wait to see her face when you become a Lord, with your father still alive!"

"I thank you, my dear, for your kind consideration to my life," the father chuckled.

"Do not be ridiculous, Lord Hertworth! You know very well I wish for nothing but your good health and long life; but you know, she was insinuating a prospect of matrimony with Edmund could not be comparable to a marriage with her own son! She says our family may be very rich, but we owe our status to a *profession*! And Edmund would only be offering his future wife the life of a sailor!"

"We heard mother," Edmund countered. "But have you considered that by indulging her opinions you may only lend more credibility to her claims?"

The family erupted in laughter at Lady Hertworth's expense, and, finding herself the target of their mirth, she then decided to steer the conversation in a different direction.

"I quite forgot you are to leave so soon, again!" she remarked melancholically, "but I will not be sad this time. While you are gone, I should engage myself with the preparations for your homecoming ball, and who knows, we might be able to announce your engagement as soon as you return!

"You know, Edmund dear, I already know of several girls who cannot wait to be introduced to you; I suppose an afternoon tea before the ball should quite take care of it, what do you say to that?"

"Not so hasty please, Mother, I do not know how long I may be required to be in London; how about you defer your plans until my return?"

"Nonsense! Your father was not required to be in London for more than a week altogether when he took the same post!"

"But you see mother, I am expecting a higher scrutiny than the one imparted upon father. Indeed, we cannot expect Parliament to take my travels as lightly as they may have taken my father's, considering the tumultuous times the Empire is going through," he hoped his father would not disagree with his observation.

"Very well...," the mother conceded, "I suppose you men understand these matters better than I do."

"Come, my dear," the father intervened at last. "Our son understands his responsibilities much better than you suppose him to. He will not disappoint in whatever he may endeavour to take upon himself... is that not so, Edmund?"

"Yes, Father," Edmund obliged, as his father's glare communicated much more than any word Lord Hertworth chose not to say at present.

The relief Edmund felt in having his mother succumb to his persuasion was very short lived, however.

As Edmund was about to dismiss himself from the tearoom, a certain inkling seemed to have roused Lady Hertworth's initial fastidiousness.

"I will not, under any circumstance, however, have that revolting negro in my house! I am sure we can find you someone more suited to look after your books!"

"It must be her mother!" Edmund countered, his earlier exasperation returning to him. "However, if you insist upon being rid of her that will be most unfortunate for our plans."

"How so?"

"If you do not keep her here, none of your wishes will come into fruition, as I will feel compelled to take to the sea again to personally return her home."

32.

Mr Hertworth proved true to his word. The following day he departed for some destination unknown to her, and as the days progressed, Imbali grew to regard his remarkable library as a blissful sanctuary.

She may have been quite versed at applying her fish-skin glue, however some of the precious books in this room appeared so damaged, bonding pages to the spines was not the only care and attention required from her. She would often spend several hours bent over a single book, minutely transcribing words which would have otherwise been lost. She did not mind it at all however, as her current labour was indeed a welcome distraction from the recurring thoughts of the man who had presented this opportunity to her.

As Mr Hertworth was no longer around to make any advances towards her, she began to ponder more about him.

He may have deceived her with his friendship, but she too was at fault, she acknowledged. She should have known better. She had done nothing to discourage Mr Hertworth's kind attention towards her on his ship.

If anything, she had solicited them! Craved them, and without realising it, she happily ran back for more every single time, on her own accord!

With this realisation in mind, Imbali grew to consider him less guilty, and though she would never permit herself to suppose a real emotional attachment from such a man, her heart could not deny her mind the pleasure of savouring the acknowledgement he had singled her out, no matter where those attentions stemmed from.

Other than an occasional stare or two, the Hertworth household steered clear from her. Imbali had been informed that her meal times were scheduled twice; and she would descend to the kitchens and eat alongside the rest of the servants.

Many of the servants were evidently keen to stay away from her too, but Lucy's affability towards her had not altered, and she would often tell Imbali the many anecdotes and gossip surrounding the Hertworth family.

"You know, it is not him you need to fear, my dear," Lucy was saying to her one evening.

"I understand his recent proposition to you could make you consider him less gentlemanlike; however I must warn you to stay away from his mother! She loathes you!"

"I can understand her reasons, and I may even justify her for having such feelings; but if she despises me so, then why is she permitting my residence in her house still?" Imbali could not help but enquire.

"Because she must, if she wants to keep her son here in England!"

"Whatever do you mean?!"

"It's the truth my dear! I heard he threatened to sail off again to Africa with you in tow if she dared to come near you, let alone cause you harm!"

Imbali could not believe her ears, "But what of his obligations to his family?!"

"Well, I hear he is still intent on settling down; but he forced his mother to cancel the ball she intended to have upon his return. But even so, I tell you, she seems resolute at having him married off any day now!"

"How? He has not been around much.... has he?"

"You are quite right, my dear. He keeps himself in London, much longer than he ought, I hear. I don't quite understand what his London obligations are, but she expects him to return soon, and when he does, apparently, she has laid out a list of grand young ladies to parade under his nose! But I tell you, he will not care for any of them!

"You know my dear, it may very well be wrong of me to put such ideas in your head, but I honestly believe it is you he thinks of."

"Do not let anyone hear you utter such ridiculous ideas, Lucy. God forbid Lady Hertworth hears you speaking so, and decides to direct her ire towards you!" Imbali cautioned, before leaving the kitchens to Lucy and returning to the solace of her refuge.

*

Just as Lucy would relate to Imbali the family gossips, many of the servants also came to know of the tales which brought Mr Edmund Hertworth and this negro together from Lucy. Inevitably, the account of how her son had rescued the negro upstairs found its way into the ears of Lady Hertworth too.

If she was to go by such accounts, she could not find much to reproach her son for. Such rumours would indeed highlight the noble and generous nature of her Edmund, as such, she had been very prompt in encouraging her staff to divulge the same account far and wide.

However, to her disappointment, her friend would not allow her to bask in this contentment.

"A new rumour of very concerning nature reached my ears just last night and I immediately felt it incumbent upon me, as your friend, to warn you," exclaimed Lady Glenith as soon as she stepped foot in the entrance hall of Hertworth Manor, her son trailing behind her.

"My dear, you are indeed all kindness to me and my children, but I can only suppose this gossip is nothing but evil wishes upon our impeccable name," remarked Lady Hertworth, conveying a most contrarious tone to her voice.

"I fully agree with you my dearest, but they now claim that not only has Edmund impregnated the negro, but that you, my dear, have decided to aid him in this profanity by consenting to postpone his homecoming ball until the birth – which is expected to be this Spring – in order for you to conceal the birth of a mulatto!"

"Upon my word! How preposterous! How can anyone in their right mind possibly consider such a blasphemous notion! Did you not think that if that negro was to be in an interesting state, as the rumours claim, you, most certainly would have been the first to notice it when you first encountered her!"

"Upon my word, you certainly give me less credit than I deserve. I would never assume such misgivings from your son, and therefore what reason could I have had to observe the stomach of such an insignificant creature!" replied Lady Glenith in her own defence. "Is that not right, my dear boy?" she then solicited from her son.

Lord Glenith had kept himself leisurely engaged with a newspaper he picked up from the tea table right beside him, but upon his mother's solicitation he felt obligated to offer his opinion. "I think Lady Hertworth must be right in her observation, Mama. I am positive your discerning eyes could not have missed it, if such gossip was to be true; besides," he then decided to add, "I can personally vouch Edmund would never involve himself with such lowly behaviour as the rumours have been implying."

These words were positively received by the intended ears.

"But you were right beside me when he passionately dragged her back into the house with him!" his mother interjected. "What is there to misunderstand?!"

"I honestly think you could very well be mistaken, Mama; I really did not see anything too extraordinary with Edmund's conduct," the son countered. "If I may," he then continued, addressing Lady Hertworth once again, "if she is causing such a headache for your family, then perhaps it may be better if we relieve you of her, and take the negro with us."

"I will not consent to have such filth around my house," his mother interjected. "I think each lady better deal with her own mess!" Lady Glenith concluded, before deciding she had caused enough discomfort to her friend for today.

33.

"What did she do to my son?!" Lady Priscilla Hertworth's wail echoed through the grand hall as soon as her friend was out of the door. "She must be a witch! I have heard of the likes of her who go around trapping innocent men like my poor boy!

"Call for the doctor at once!" she commanded, and Mr Newby obliged her order immediately.

The lady then stormed to her son's library.

"A learned negro then, are you?!" Lady Hertworth sneered, her voice filled with disdain as she approached Imbali. In the next moment, before Imbali could react, she felt a violent tug on her gown as Lady Hertworth's hand seized her with ruthless force, dragging her down from the ladder she was standing on.

The book Imbali had been holding fell from her grasp, but Lady Hertworth seized it and wielded it as if it were evidence of some great crime. Her other hand shot to Imbali's hair, pulling her head as she forced their eyes to meet.

"Where did my son find you? What did you feed to him to put him under your spell? Your abhorrent tricks may have worked on other stupid men, but I assure you, my son is far above any presumptuous deceit you may have ensnared him with!"

"I have done nothing to your son!" Imbali cried defensively, as she strenuously attempted to free her head from the lady's hold.

"They say my son has impregnated you! Did you spread such calumnious rumours about him, or did you have your friends do it on your behalf?!"

"I have not spread anything–"

"–So, you mean they are not rumours, but fact?!" the lady interrupted, releasing Imbali abruptly. "How dare you insinuate any wrongdoing on his account?! You may have lured him with your tricks, but I will not permit my son's name to be tarnished because of you! I will rescue him from your clutches!"

Lady Hertworth's voice dropped to a cold, calculated tone, "Newby can find a ship ready to leave for wherever in Africa you came from. Newby will also personally ensure you board the ship under his supervision. I have never lowered myself to enter into such dealings with the likes of you, but I suppose the occasion warrants it; so, if you speak to no one on the way, he will even ensure you are recompensed for your silence!"

Imbali's heart pounded, but she straightened her shoulders as she responded to the lady, "The only place I will be boarding another ship for will be the Americas! If you are so anxious to be rid of me, then my suggestion to you is to board me on the next ship going in that direction."

There she had said it!

"Oh, I see what sort of trickster you are! I did consider it would take me much longer to unmask you, but you have made my task rather easy! Money is what you have been trying to scrape out of him!" Lady Hertworth retorted with a big sigh of relief.

Imbali, at this stage of her life, still possessed the high spirits and bravery her young age of nine-and-ten could command, and therefore, she really could not dwell much upon what this lady thought of her character and principles.

"Believe what you will," she then felt compelled to add. "I followed your son to England so that I may find work and earn enough money in order for me to pay for the passage myself; but both you and your son seem determined at not allowing me to do so!"

"I can very well imagine the kind of work the likes of you hope to find here on our shores! But you, I suppose, must have understood the significance of my son's reputation! The moment you leave this house, to find your so-called work, you want to go around defaming his name by associating him with your filth!"

The lady then realised she had touched the hair of this negro and looked horrified at her own hands. Who better to wipe the filth off than the negro herself? She then ventured to bestow not one, but two blows on either side of Imbali's face.

"Newby, where is this doctor?! And you," she snapped, seizing Imbali by the arm this time, "come with me!"

Several servants appeared out of nowhere to her ladyship's aid and Imbali found her body forcefully constrained on a rather large couch placed right in the middle of the room.

The doctor appeared moments later.

"Let us see for ourselves if Edmund has truly contaminated himself with such lowly indulgences," she commanded.

*

Imbali struggled violently as servants held her down, her screams piercing the air. She had been in similar situations to this in her past, and she had been able to free herself out of it, but unfortunately for her, the doctor was resolute at obliging Lady Hertworth's commission to him.

As Imbali struggled and screamed with all her might, she sensed her mouth being covered with a foul-smelling cloth which made her feel drowsy; and in the next moment she felt her mind clouded by a total emptiness.

With the negro lying unconscious right under his nose, the doctor was now at his leisure to conduct the undertaking he had been summoned for.

Lady Hertworth did not need to wait long for the doctorly verdict.

"Not only is she not with child, milady, but no man has ever penetrated her."

The lady could not mask her surprise at hearing the negro was a virgin; however, she would not dwell much of her energy on such an immaterial detail. The full reassurance that her son had not contaminated himself with the filth which was currently pestering her house was all her motherly heart needed at that moment to find some peace.

*

Lady Hertworth's ire was so intense, most of the inhabitants of the Manor heard of her interaction with the negro, and it was not long before Mr Jenkins heard it too.

Mr Jenkins was no anarchist by nature, and he certainly would not shy away from giving deference where it was due; however, he had come to develop a fierce personal loyalty to the lady's elder son.

"I beg your pardon, milady," he began, stepping cautiously into the library just as Imbali stirred, regaining her senses, "but I'm sure your son would not approve of you mistreating her like this."

Lady Hertworth turned on him, "Upon my word! This is indeed too much impertinence!" she cried. "I really do not know what my son sees in you either, but I will certainly not allow any more of such disregard in my house!" She then spun toward her butler and commanded, "Newby, remove him from my sight at once!"

34.

Several days had passed since the day the negro had unceremoniously run out of Hertworth Manor.

"I am very glad to be rid of that arrogant good-for-nothing man too. But what of the maid who came with them? What was her name?" Lady Hertworth was enquiring from her butler on the day Edmund was expected to return from London.

Though she would not plainly vocalise her apprehension, Lady Hertworth's mind was contemplating whether she ought to rejoice in being rid of the negro, or dread what Edmund may do when he returned and found his entrustment not at the manor.

"Lucy, milady, Lucy was her name," replied Mr Newby.

"Well, you could make enquires from her on the negro's whereabouts! Did you not say she seems rather eager to give out information when solicited?"

"I am afraid that will not be possible, milady; she left along with them, on that very same day."

"Did she? Good riddance, I tell you! We certainly have no need for servants of questionable morals around here!"

"But... I have been keeping an eye on them," the diligent butler then informed her.

"Oh, have you…? Very good, Newby! And pray tell me, what have they been up to?"

"Nothing of consequence; I personally ensured nobody will take them on, and–"

"–all the same Newby! That negro is still an inconvenience to us!" the lady interjected. "We must prevent Edmund from finding her ever again. I cannot risk Edmund growing contrary to me!"

"What would you have me do, milady?"

"Find her before he does and be rid of her once and for all!"

"I am not sure I comprehend your meaning my lady…?" the butler said, his brow furrowing in evident confusion at his mistress's suggestion.

"Do not be absurd, Newby! She may be of no consequence, but I certainly cannot expect you to become a murderer, can I?!

"What I mean to say is, find her immediately and ship her away to somewhere Edmund is sure to never hear of her again!"

*

Out in the openness of Exeter, Jenkins had been exerting himself in providing for the two women under his care.

Fortunately for him, money was not a problem for the time being, as the remuneration he received for his services while at sea was more than enough to keep them going for a good while.

Lucy and Imbali for their part had been actively looking for employment too, but all the wealthy families who had advertised for servants seemed distinctly decided against them.

The seventh day of their departure from Hertworth Manor was the day Jenkins was expecting Mr Hertworth to return to Exeter. He did not mean to plead for himself to his former employer, however, his conscience would not allow him to rest until Mr Hertworth would personally discharge him of the obligation he had imparted upon him before the man's departure to London.

He informed Lucy of his intentions first thing in the morning and subsequently rode to the inn in which he predicted Mr Hertworth would need to stop before proceeding to Hertworth Manor.

Jenkins did not need to wait long before Mr Hertworth's arrival became known in the inn; several men seemed to have waited a good while to have an audience with the future Sir Hertworth.

The crowd around the nobleman was such that it took Edmund quite a while to finally notice Jenkins wave at him from afar.

"Why are you here? I specifically told you to never leave her alone!"

"I tried, Sir! You told me to not leave her alone with your mother, and I didn't Sir; but I failed."

"What do you mean you failed?!"

"Your mother didn't really bother much with her initially," Jenkins began to recall. "But then one afternoon, that Lord Glenith you warned me about came along with his pompous mother. I do not know what upset your mother so much, but shortly after they left, your mother... well, I am sorry to say but your mother was not very nice to Imbali, so I decided to intervene, but then her ladyship got very angry and sent me out of the house."

"What happened to Imbali? Where is she now?!"

"I left her with Lucy by the port."

"Lucy has been dismissed too?!"

"No, Sir, but when Lucy heard I had been dismissed, she decided to leave along with me and Imbali. I don't really know what your mother did to her, but the three of us have been together since then."

"Didn't you try to ask her what happened to her?"

"Of course we did, Sir! Lucy more than I, Sir, but she won't say a word about it!"

Edmund rose to make his way to the port, but it appeared Jenkins was still not done.

"Sir, I hope you won't take offence, but me and Lucy can't return to work for your mother. Can I ask, Sir, once she is safely back in your hands, would you be able to provide me and Lucy for some sort of reference... nobody will give us any work, and... you see Sir, I really intend to marry Lucy."

"You will not need references,"

"But I do, Sir, nobody is willing to take us!"

"The both of you will remain under my personal patronage, and whenever you are ready to set the date, you shall have your wedding! Now, Jenkins, hurry, take me to her."

Once they arrived at the location Jenkins had claimed to have left the two women, neither Imbali nor Lucy were to be seen.

"You should not have let them out of your sight!" Edmund reprimanded.

"I don't understand, Sir, Lucy guaranteed they would wait here until I was to return to them!"

"Where could they be then?" enquired Edmund, an exasperation growing inside him.

Jenkins saw no harm in a superior's reproach, but he too was feeling his own apprehension, and therefore it was not long before each man was blaming the other for their current loss.

They searched exhaustively in this part of the coast; and just as Edmund began to consider returning to the Manor and put a larger search party together, they managed to catch sight of one of the missing women.

"I really don't understand what got into her, Sir." Lucy cried coming upon them. "We were peacefully waiting for Jack – I mean, Mr Jenkins, to return from fetching you; but shortly after he was gone, without saying much to me, she left too. I did not think much of it at the beginning, but after a while, when she did not return, I became worried, and so I went looking for her, but I still haven't had any luck."

"She must have said something to you before she left?" Edmund probed.

"Well, Sir, I don't think she knew you were to return today," Lucy said.

"What is that supposed to mean? I need you to tell me exactly what she said to you!"

"She just asked me where exactly Mr Jenkins had gone off to, and I told her he had gone to meet you on the road."

"What did she say after that?"

"She did not say much after that, Sir...," at this point Lucy needed to pause, evidently in search of how to best narrate the following events. "What she did next is what got me a bit worried and then made me go looking for her."

"Then pray tell, what exactly did she do?" asked Edmund more calmly this time, relieved his enquiries were finally taking the right direction.

"Well, you see Sir, Imbali doesn't give out much of what goes on in her head, and I didn't think much of her prolonged silence, even though I kept on chattering away.

"But then, and mind you, quite unexpectedly, she just hugged me! She then said she would never forget me, and to pass her best regards to Mr Jenkins too, and then she just left!

"I was quite emotional after her cuddle, Sir; you see, I quite like her too. But too late I realised she was saying goodbye for good, and as I did, I ran after her, but I still haven't found her, Sir!"

"Did she have any monies on her?"

"I don't know, Sir...," Lucy hesitantly replied. "But I honestly don't think she had any."

"What makes you think so?"

"I am sure she wouldn't have allowed Mr Jenkins to take care of her expenses the past few days had she any monies on her... I believe she is not the type of girl who would easily accept charity from anyone."

This last remark of Lucy offered a much-needed comfort to Edmund's distress.

Lucy then diligently guided Mr Hertworth and Jenkins to all the locations she had already searched for Imbali herself.

"I think it may be more efficient to proceed with our search by splitting up," observed Edmund, "and we shall agree to converge again at this same meeting point by sunset, with or without her."

He then sent Jenkins and Lucy searching towards the southern, inner parts of the village, and he proceeded further around the western part of the coast. The northern and eastern parts of the village had already been exhaustively searched for several hours.

This period of absence away from Imbali and Hertworth Manor had indeed granted him with ample room to fully comprehend where his irrational, agitated heart had found its rest.

Edmund was returning home fully resigned to his plight. He had missed her, quite terribly in fact. Regardless of how he had come where he was at with Imbali, he longed for her, in her fullness, in spite of what troubles this longing may bring to him and more importantly to her.

He did not understand when, or how she had managed to conquer his soul.

Perhaps it was the manner in which her eyes implored him, when he first saw her surrounded by those human jackals ready to devour her. Or maybe it was during that sunrise on that vast field surrounded by idyllic floral replicas of her; or quite possibly it could have happened while her feverish body held on tightly to his, the first night Jenkins brought her to him.

But of one reality he was quite certain now; how thoughtless he had been in implying he yearned for her in the same primitive manner which other men may have led her to believe. Carnal gratification had now become quite secondary in his attachment to her.

However, as the future Sir Hertworth, Edmund could not disregard the obligations pinned upon him. Therefore, however unreasonable his heart may decide to be; his logic would still not be persuaded from the duties he owed to his name. And all that would be compromised; were he to allow himself the gratification his spirits were calling to.

And with this internal struggle still raging within him, Edmund had returned home.

35.

As the sun dipped lower over the restless waves, casting fiery reflections across the agitated waters before him, Edmund's unease deepened. With each passing moment, a growing fear that he might fail to find Imbali fuelled his relentless pace.

So consumed was Edmund by his spiralling thoughts, he failed to notice the unusual commotion unfolding just beyond his view.

A small crowd had gathered around a young woman, whom Edmund could not recollect noticing before. And this young woman had placed herself right in between Mr Newby and none other than Imbali!

"I do not know who you work for, but I will not allow you to cause her any harm!" this young woman was saying to Mr Newby. "Your superiors can come themselves if they wish to retrieve her from my protection!"

"You have no idea whose affairs you are meddling with!" Newby retorted. "Give her to me this instance!"

"I will not! Nor will I be intimidated by the likes of you who think they can go around mistreating people simply because you presume them to be lesser beings than you!" The young woman retorted back to Newby.

"I thank you, Madam, for your intercession," Edmund said, stepping forward. "I am this man's superior," he continued, his eyes wandering between Newby and Imbali.

"It appears you are familiar with her, Sir," started the young lady, noticing the manner in which the nobleman was intently staring at the negro crouched behind her. "Of course, I can in no way suppose to involve myself in your private matters, but I cannot help feeling obliged to inform you that she has indeed been of great assistance to me. In fact, had it not been for her, a sprained ankle would not be the only injury I would have to contend with at the moment, as I am sure I would have quite probably broken a few of my bones too.

"And I certainly could not allow this man here to mistreat her in the manner in which I saw him intent upon the moment he laid eyes on her!"

She really ought to mind her own business, the young woman considered. Perhaps this negro was one of his servants, and maybe she had vexed her superiors in some way; however, she could not help feeling compelled to explain the situation to the unmistakable nobleman standing in front of her, and a very fine one too, she thought.

She had been around this part of the country for several weeks now and was sure she had noticed all the titled men of the local nobility during the Sunday congregations; however, she had failed to notice this one.

"How has she assisted you?" Edmund asked.

"Well, it was quite silly of me, but while I was taking my usual walk by the coast, I could not help noticing those lovely lilies still standing tall on this cliff. You can imagine my surprise to see such flowers in such proximity to the sea, especially with summer decidedly behind us," the young woman explained. "I started climbing to the top of the cliff to observe them better, but then my foot slipped, and had she not been close by to hear my pleas and catch me, only God knows what could have happened to me!"

"I am truly obliged to you, madam, and if you would be kind enough to provide me with your name and the details of where you are staying, I shall ensure to have our doctor check on you," Edmund offered.

"My name is Marianne Blaby, Sir, and I am staying with my aunt and uncle at Ridgeway Cottage, but please do not trouble yourself on my account, nothing grave is the matter with me. However, I would be very grateful if you were to send me news of how she fares," the young woman said, while directing a supporting smile in the direction of the negro.

"Are you hurt?" Edmund then enquired, turning his attention to Imbali.

Imbali remained silent however.

"I do not think she is very much hurt, my lord, I think she may simply be in shock," offered Marianne, assuming Imbali may require her assistance further.

Edmund's domineering glance was such, this young lady could not be faulted for feeling obliged to plead for whatever wrongdoing Imbali must have committed; and her thoughtful objectives did not go unnoticed by Edmund.

But before she could venture another intervention of hers, the nobleman addressed her directly once again, "You are very kind, Madam; you must be quite right, but I think we have usurped enough of your time already."

He turned to Mr Newby to command, "you no longer need to trouble yourself with her, I will take it from here; but you can, on the other hand, escort Miss Blaby to her destination immediately, and ensure to have our doctor call upon her as soon as she reaches home."

"Come with me," he then said, turning his attention to Imbali, "Jenkins will soon be here with my carriage."

He watched the young woman walk away and as soon as he supposed it safe to begin his reprimands, he began, "I trusted you would honour our agreement! Instead, here you are endangering your life so recklessly! Why did you leave?! Answer me," he commanded, as her lips remained sealed.

"Very well, you can keep your mouth shut for as long as you like; but we are returning to the house this instant!" he continued, proceeding to escort Imbali into his carriage himself.

"I am not going anywhere with you," Imbali countered at last. She meant to say it for the attention of Edmund's ears only, however Miss Blaby appeared to have heard their altercation.

"I beg your pardon, Sir; I do not mean to pry on your personal affairs, but I cannot help but feel compelled to offer my assistance to her a little longer," Miss Blaby said addressing Edmund directly. "I really cannot help but blame myself for her current misery!"

She then turned to face Imbali, "I should not be riding in a carriage all alone with strangers, unaccompanied… you can understand that, can you not? Would you be kind to me a little longer and help me out once more?" She then looked over at Newby, and drawing Imbali closer, she added softly, "I would hate to be escorted home by that brute when I could go with you."

Edmund looked at Imbali, but she gave him no inkling as to what her wishes or considerations may be in regard to the situation at hand. But at last, Imbali looked up at Miss Blaby, and to Edmund's surprise, followed the woman into his carriage.

*

"Look at this state of yours!" Miss Blaby began soon after they had each taken their place. "Poor you! You must have ripped it while you climbed up to save me," she remarked upon closer scrutiny of Imbali's gown. "Do you have any other gown you can call your own? Sadly, people like you do not normally possess much, do they?" she observed, directing her attention to Edmund once again.

How she wished for this gentleman to finally introduce himself!

"I thank you for bringing it to my attention, Madam;" Edmund responded, "she will have as many gowns as she requires."

"If you would permit me, I have plenty of my own, Sir. I will gladly spare one or two for her," Miss Blaby offered, and turning to Imbali, she addressed her directly, "would you like that?"

"I thank you, Miss, but I am in no need of any gowns," Imbali responded.

Shortly after this exchange, the carriage arrived at Miss Blaby's address, and as Marianne was about to take her leave, her wish came to fruition.

"I am Edmund, of Hertworth Manor, pleased to make your acquaintance. I am forever in your debt, Madam."

"I did not do much, Sir."

"I beg to differ, Madam, you persuaded her where I could not," Edmund interjected. "You seem to have a certain way which works with her."

Marianne blushed at such an unexpected compliment, "I-I thank you Sir… I am indeed much obliged to you, Sir, for escorting me home."

She looked up at him, wishing for the gentleman to express a little more of his thoughts to her, but he simply offered her a quick bow, before she was left with nothing else to do but wonder at the oddity of the situation she had found herself in.

36.

"Is it true what that woman said back at the cliffs?! Did you really risk your neck for her?!" Edmund began as soon as he returned to the carriage.

"Pray tell me, is my neck any safer with you?!" she countered.

"What is that supposed to mean now?"

"Nothing which should be of consequence to you; but I cannot and will not return to that house!"

"Whyever not?! Jenkins tells me something has made you run out of the house; why was Newby after you? Has any harm come to you while I was away?" He placed himself in the same seat Miss Blaby had vacated. "I must know Imbali... tell me who has upset you?" his commanding tone gave way to a more gentle address.

"Here, take this," he offered, placing his coat around her shoulders. "That woman is right you know, your attire is beyond hope. First thing tomorrow morning, I will take you into town and buy you new dresses."

"Stay away from me!" she ordered, refusing his aid. "I do not need your coat, nor anything else from you!"

"Stop being obstinate! I know you do not possess much, and this gown of yours is now hopeless!"

"I am more than capable of mending it!"

"Stop being stubborn and take my coat! You cannot leave the carriage in such a state!"

"Maybe you should have considered this predicament before you started all of this!" she spat at him. "Mr Hertworth," she then continued, struggling to tame her frustration. "I have come to realise you will not afford me any independence, but I must ask... what is it you truly expect from me?!"

"I mean you must understand how this situation you have put me in, or rather you have put us in, is something I am truly struggling to comprehend," she paused for a brief moment, appearing intent at measuring her next words quite carefully. "You have, more than once in fact, made your...demands quite clear, and I willingly offered to accommodate your wishes; but even that won't do for you! What more can you possibly want to do with me?!"

As she spoke, the carriage approached the familiar sight of Hertworth Manor.

"I really do not think right now is a good time to be having this discussion," Edmund remarked, his voice low but firm. "We will not have this conversation here with all these spectators watching you," he said, as he noticed the considerable number of onlookers who were furtively staring towards his carriage.

"Oh really?! So, you suppose people are not talking about us already?"

"That should be of no consequence to you! As soon as you are feeling composed again, we shall discuss our future prospects."

"What future prospects?! Do you realise how ridiculous this entire situation is?! How can you possibly expect people like me to have any dreams of future prospects?"

"I will not be insensitive to your concerns; and therefore, I will not attempt to deny the difficulty my actions may cause for you at present; however, it cannot be helped," he countered.

"I am indeed captivated by you, and you cannot fail to see it is not only this I desire," his gaze swept over her, his meaning unmistakable. "But I must have you understand that I am impartial to everything about you!"

He inched closer still, the space between them shrinking to nothing. He cupped her face gently in his hand, his thumb brushing over her lips, "I gave you my word I would not touch you... but I so feared I would never see you again!"

Imbali did not withdraw from his touch; her eyes rose to meet his, no longer evading the earnest fervour of his scrutiny. Then he released her and moved back, just enough to meet her eyes.

"Look at me and swear upon your mother you are totally averse to me. Swear you are averse to me, to my words, to my touch... and to everything else you must know I feel for you! If you can do such a thing, I promise you, regardless of my wishes, I will let you go."

"You truly seem determined to see no reason in the reality around us, Mr Hertworth. Women like me are not granted the privilege of having partiality of feelings; I have never known what such notions entailed and I certainly cannot allow myself the inclination of considering them now!"

Her words struck him deeply, but not as deeply as the pain he had caught in her eyes before she turned away from him. Edmund had heard her resolute denials before, but never before had he witnessed the sorrow her own words seemed to stir within her.

She avoided answering his question directly, but he did not need her words. Her eyes, lovely yet full of turmoil, gave him all the confirmation he sought.

"Did my mother do anything to you during my absence?" he then solicited, eager to have her open up to him. "I now realise how wrong it was of me to have left you at the mercy of my family so hastily!"

"You cannot fault your mother, Mr Hertworth."

"I know I certainly can! Newby would not have come after you had my mother not solicited him to do so!"

"I do not blame your mother, nor anyone else; the fault is entirely mine."

"What fault?"

"I was the reckless one to let my guard down! I allowed my stupid head to fall prey to the deception you have been instilling in it! Too late I have come to realise what a simpleton I have been to not see you are by far the worst of your kind!"

Edmund took hold of Imbali's hand, "I know you do not find me as repulsive as you would like me to believe," he continued, looking at her with an expression Imbali was yet to witness in the eyes of any of the men who had previously tried to approach her as she allowed Edmund to do.

Edmund felt her shiver at his touch, "What is the matter? Are you unwell?"

"I am well..."

"Then what has perturbed you so?" he probed, holding her gaze.

"I-I…I was simply wondering if this is how it all started for my mother too," she replied. As she made this confession to him, her eyes remained fixed upon the tender way in which he caressed her hands.

"Imbali, I will not, of course, venture to pass a judgement on whatever choices your mother must have felt compelled to make in her life; but how can you possibly find my feelings for you remotely comparable to anything your mother must have experienced?"

"I always wondered if I would one day find myself sharing her fate...," she continued, as her eyes appeared lost in some distant memory.

"For how long will you continue to fail to acknowledge what you must know are nothing but sincere feelings which I have grown to feel for you; and I will not allow anyone, including you, to claim otherwise!"

247

"Perhaps those men had professed the same feelings to her...," Imbali went on, still absorbed in her pensive state.

"That cannot be! Because unlike any of them, I love you!"

*

The scene Lady Hertworth stumbled upon was indeed the last straw for her already strained nerves.

She had expected her dearest son to arrive from London hours earlier and had been pacing by the windows when she caught sight of his carriage. As Newby was nowhere to be seen, she decided to come down and welcome her son herself.

The last words Edmund had uttered to the negro had been stated with such vehemence, he might as well have professed his love in public. She was certain many of the servants had heard it too.

"Edmund!" She cried out, rushing to open the door of the carriage, "you seriously could not have brought yourself so low! I could never imagine you, out of all people, capable of such madness!"

"Mother! This is not a conversation to be had with you at this particular moment."

Edmund found himself startled and he immediately let go of Imbali's hand, "I must ask you to return to the house. I will come to you and discuss your dealings with her later," he added.

He then came out of the carriage and would have aided Imbali in doing the same, had not his mother interrupted him.

"I will not leave you under her spell any longer! You must come away from her immediately!"

"You gave me your word you would cause her no harm!"

"What would you have me do?! I believed her to be expecting a deformed bastard from you!" the mother responded defensively. "I could not have such profanity tarnish our name

248

or damage your reputation! I did what I had to, for your own sake!"

"You did what?!" Edmund exclaimed, incredulous. "And pray tell me, which latest gossip of yours has made you suppose she may be expecting my child?"

"That is no longer of any consequence. Thank God it is not too late! You are too conscientious for this nonsense, Edmund! I beg you to let her go before she tricks you into a full loss of your wits!"

"What have you done to her...?!" Edmund probed further.

"Is this all you care about, still?! How can you suppose I have caused her any harm? Is that the lie she has been feeding you?!"

"She has told me nothing, mother! It is you who has just confessed it to me!"

"You cannot imagine how much restraint I had to impose upon myself in order for me to bear her presence around my house! And I did it purely to keep my word to you!

"Besides, it is not just gossip any longer! Your father has just told me of several men who approached him directly; and they too are questioning if indeed you are still in possession of your full reasoning!"

"Mother, do not involve Father in this," Edmund interjected.

"But I must, Edmund! She has bewitched you with her arts! And I have underestimated her! I heard what she compelled you to profess to her just now! How could you make such a declaration to her?!"

"Do what you must, Mother! But you ought to know what you heard is true; and I cannot part from her!"

37.

A solemn meeting had been called at Hertworth Manor, following Edmund's disastrous confession of love to Imbali.

This meeting had been called by none other than Lord Hertworth himself.

"She is a fraudster!" Lady Hertworth burst as soon as her husband welcomed Imbali into the drawing room, "one of the worst kinds I tell you, I wish for no more mercy for her! I want this witch arrested now!"

Against the wishes of his own wife, Lord Hertworth had deemed it necessary to summon Imbali too.

Shortly after being in his presence, Imbali could not help but consider Edmund had not just inherited his father's physical features, but also his fair nature. Unlike his wife, Edmund's father did not seem inclined to be intensely prejudiced against her.

He ignored his wife's remark, and his commanding presence was such, when he spoke next, his voice carried a solemnity that even Lady Hertworth could do nothing but second him with her silence.

"In spite of what Lady Hertworth may think of your involvement in my son's lack of judgement, I have come to conclude you cannot be entirely at fault for my son's reckless folly," he said directly to Imbali. But as he spoke, the silence which dominated the room became interrupted by Lady Hertworth's disagreement once again.

"Upon my word, Lord Hertworth, what do you expect her to say?!

"All she wants is to ensnare my boy for her own scheming! She said she wants to take our son away to the Americas! Edward was there; he heard it too! Tell them boy!"

"Forgive me, Mama, but I would not be too sure about what she expressed to you exactly that day...," Edward offered defensively as he felt his brother's accusatory gaze preying on him.

"That is quite enough from us," Lord Hertworth said with a gesture of his hand. "Now," he then continued, addressing Imbali again, "my son has informed me he felt it incumbent upon himself to rescue you from your birthplace, and therefore I will not ask you if you would be interested in returning there. However, as I am sure you can understand, it is no longer feasible for you to sojourn within the house."

Lord Hertworth proceeded to respectfully enumerate to Imbali how he had considered alternative employments with many other respectable families, however his wife was keenly averse to this suggestion, as the lady could not risk more contamination upon her son's reputation by allowing the gossips to travel alongside this negro.

By the end of the council, Lord Hertworth's excellent conciliatory abilities proved a success, as mother and son at last came to a hard, contentious consensus.

Lady Hertworth had capitulated to her son's hard-fought compromise. She would allow Imbali to continue her employment for the Hertworth family, as long as her laborious duties kept her as far away as possible from the residential house. In turn, Edmund had consented to never seek out or speak to the negro again; and more importantly, he would actively apply himself to choose amongst any of the suitable brides his mother would present to him.

*

For the next several weeks, a new order gradually became the norm in the house.

Many young ladies from prominent families would be invited to have tea with the family. Sometimes, these invitees would appear voluntarily too, as Lady Hertworth's hunt for a bride had become common knowledge, not only amongst the local nobility, but in the bordering counties too.

Tea parties were not the only gatherings taking place in the house. Balls and intimate dinners would also be extended whenever Lady Hertworth sensed the slightest favourable disposition in her son towards any of the young ladies competing for his consideration.

The new arrangements suited Imbali quite well.

Though she was not made of a strong physical constitution, the time she spent working on the Hertworth's fields was providing her with many reasons to be content with her current situation.

Many of the other labourers seemed unbothered by her presence, and to her relief, nobody outside of the house seemed privy to how she had come to work with them.

While Imbali spent most of the day on the fields, evenings were purely her own. She spent them quite blissfully by a wild and remote part of the coast, where the locals rarely ventured into.

It was during one of these walks Imbali had the pleasure of another encounter with Miss Marianne Blaby.

"You cannot imagine how pleased I am to see you again!" Miss Blaby started as soon as she caught sight of Imbali in the distance.

"Do you know how many times I have been tempted to approach Mr Hertworth in church to ask him of you?!" she proceeded after bestowing Imbali a surprising, unexpected embrace. "I mean, I ought to find a reason to talk to him!" Miss Blaby explained, "I could not address him directly, as we were yet to be officially introduced to one another.

"You know, I must confess I was quite annoyed at our polite society! Since the moment I found out who he was, I had been tempted to call on him, instead of spending several days waiting for him to call on me!

"But then you would not believe what happened just this morning! He remembered me! And then he asked to be properly introduced to my aunt and I! Can you imagine the mighty future Lord Hertworth publicly asking to be introduced to me!" Miss Blaby did not require much of a response from Imbali, so, after a short reflective pause, she leisurely rejoined, "You know, I could not stop praising the Lord for the sudden change in our plans! You see, I was to return home last week; but then father was solicited by the county bishop to offer his services in a different parish; Mama was so inconvenienced by the move!

"And since Papa would be unable to journey all the way down here to return me home, Mama thought it best for me to extend my stay here until father would be done with his new commission in the new parish."

"You must miss your family, I am sure..."

"Well, of course I do... but then I should consider, I would never have had the great pleasure of having Mr Hertworth speak to me had I returned home!" Miss Blaby countered. "As I was saying, just this morning, he asked to be introduced to me, and he then asked me if the doctor had come to check on the injuries he thought I may have sustained on the day we met.

"You know he seemed particularly impressed by my charitable recollection of you! And I then said to him, how could I not be grateful for the heroic, selfless act you undertook!

"I will not claim to fully know what he thought of me, but I think he really thought well of me when I told him I really could not care two straws that you are negro!"

"I-I thank you Madam...," Imbali felt compelled to respond.

"He seemed intended to take his leave, but then he turned around and approached me much closer than I would have thought it appropriate. He then said that he indeed thought me very virtuous for my kindness towards you, and he then recommended I look for you around this part of the coast and I could personally express my gratitude to you.

"You know, I thought very ill of him the first time we met! He appeared quite cross with you, and I assumed him to be the usual capricious type these titled noblemen tend to be! But you cannot imagine how fondly everyone speaks of him!

"He was not cross with you, was he?" enquired Miss Blaby, eager to understand the man further.

"No, Madam, as you heard, Mr Hertworth is all kindness," Imbali replied.

"You do not need to address me so formally!

"Oh, dear me! I do not remember your name! He told me this morning... but in all honesty, it sounded very complicated to me," she said, quite apologetically.

"My name is Imbali, Madam."

"I am very certain I will not remember even if you were to tell me several times! And I told you not to call me 'madam'! I am certainly nothing like any of those titled ladies Mr Hertworth is constantly surrounded by.

"Let's settle, you will call me Marianne and you will allow me to choose an easier name for me to remember you with?" Miss Blaby appeared quite pleased with her idea. "Does your name mean anything in English?"

"It does...," Imbali obliged, recollecting her first encounter with Edmund, "It means flower."

"Oh, yes! You are quite right! He did say so himself this morning in church! He was too kind to my struggle trying to remember your name, so he told me your name meant flower in your mother tongue... but upon my word!" Marianne suddenly let out. "Do you remember the wildflowers I was trying to grab before I slipped, and you caught me that day?!"

"I do..."

"They were lilies! They were wild lilies which I had never seen before! This is indeed providential!

"I do not mean to imply that you are wild, my dear, but I must confess I never expected to meet a pleasant negro such as yourself! My dear, let your name be Lily! What do you say? Do you like it?"

"I do like it...," offered Imbali.

"Very well then, Lily you shall be from this day forth!"

The two young women spent a considerable time conversing about whichever topic Marianne was happy to share with Imbali; though most of the remarks involved Marianne's monologues about Mr Hertworth.

Only after what Marianne declared to be several hours, she finally felt it was time for her to return to her aunt.

38.

Winter had long descended upon them. Imbali's labour on the fields had significantly lessened, and while many of her work fellows were now busy undertaking chores across other parts of the Estate, none of the stewards seemed to expect her to undertake much else.

She had seen nothing of Edmund since her dismissal from the house.

True to his word, he oversaw the union between Mr Jenkins and Lucy. Imbali did not witness the wedding herself, but the new Mrs Jenkins came to find her and shared the happy news with her. As Lucy showed off her wedding band, she also shared news of Edmund.

Lucy told her, despite all the favourable conditions, none of the esteemed young ladies aspiring to consort with the next Lord Hertworth were yet to succeed in satisfying his requirements, whatever they were.

Other than the occasional meetings with her friend, Imbali spent much of her time quite alone during the day, and in the evenings, she would take a walk around the wilderness by the seaside where not many of the locals would venture.

Occasionally, she came close enough to the Manor, and on several occasions saw him from afar. Edmund appeared to be most at his leisure, surrounded by so many beauties. He danced quite a lot, Imbali considered, surely it would not be long before he would forget all about her.

But then one evening, as she took her usual walk, she became startled by none other than the shadow of the man relentlessly in her thoughts.

"You cannot imagine how much I have missed you…" Edmund began, stepping close enough to caress her. "I can think of nothing but you…"

Her body stood timelessly pressed against his and he held her in one of the most tender embraces a man could bestow upon a woman.

She too had missed him. This was the simple truth she could no longer deny.

Her mind would still firmly oppose the senseless bond Edmund had dangerously weaved between them, however the truth was, she had been unable to remain impartial to his declaration of love to her.

And this evening, as she felt his touch, none of her rational resolutions could come to her aid; her senses seemed quite eager to receive the advances she had vehemently abhorred until this man appeared in her life.

"What of your ball…? You cannot be here, Edmund; your father forbade you...," she attempted to remind him – and herself. She was struggling to keep any cohesion in her own mind, let alone in her speech; and too late she realised she had addressed him with the same familiarity she regarded him in her heart.

"I see I am finally no longer Mr Hertworth to you!" he remarked, unable to stop himself from gloating in yet more proof of her reciprocal feelings. "My name has never sounded this good before!" He whispered.

Imbali was no longer capable of commanding her own body; she became lost in the novelty of the sensations she allowed Edmund to evoke in her entire being with his delicate caresses.

Initially, Edmund appeared satisfied with these innocuous touches; however, as the moments went by, the tenderness of his embrace morphed into something more primitive. He began laying his demands upon her once again. His dark stare penetrated hers, and at last, her eyes consented.

He unfastened her gown and gently eased her body onto the sand, "I love you, Imbali… Do not worry, very soon, we will not meet outside like this; I will bring you back to the house, right beside me."

If only he kept his mouth shut!

He was unsure of what he had said or done to rouse her from her imminent submission, however, Imbali quite suddenly freed herself from his hold.

"Let us be clear on one thing, Mr Hertworth!" she began, refastening her garment.

"What happened to you addressing me with my given name?" he interjected.

"I have come to terms with what needs to happen between us, Mr Hertworth," she rejoined, emphasising his formal name. "However, I must beg you not to consider me bound to you."

"Whatever do you mean 'not bound to me'?"

"What I mean to say is once you are done with me, this is not to be repeated again!" she explained. "Your father will ensure to compensate me for my labour, and I will be able to discharge myself of my debt to you."

"Why do you insist upon wanting to leave?!" he asked, feeling the old exasperation returning to him.

"This is not about my wants, but rather what needs to happen."

"And what is it that needs to happen, pray tell."

"I-I… will submit my body to you this one time… and one time only." As she spoke her eyes no longer met his.

"And after?! What will you do after I have had you?" he demanded, the gentleness with which he had been addressing her no longer there.

"Mr Hertworth, I must ask you not to make this much more difficult than it needs to be, please!"

"Difficult?!" he cried. "You can lie to yourself all you want, but it is very obvious you want me as much as I do! You may be ashamed of your feelings for me, but in doing so you are unjustly punishing yourself too! Do you think it was easy for me to relent to you?" he continued, his voice rising with more intensity than he had intended. "But unlike you, I did not allow my fears to dictate against what I believe to be fair and just!"

"Pray tell me, what is fair and just about all this?" she countered, gesturing to the wilderness around them. "I will not fault you for not understanding my motives, Mr Hertworth; but I will not be able to bear the mortification of being around you after I have consented to behave in a way I cannot help but find despicable in its nature!"

"Then tell me this; why did you not avail yourself of the perfect opportunity my father gave you to finally be rid of this mortification?!"

His inquisitive eyes were met with silence.

"You could have revealed to my father your desire to proceed further into the New World, however you purposely chose to give it all up! Why did you not tell him?!" he insisted, ignoring the hurt he was evidently causing her. "You did not shy away from disclosing it to my mother! I know you understood him to be fairly predisposed towards your plight; however, you intentionally chose to miss the one opportunity you had to be rid of me!

"Why did you stay silent?!"

She did not answer.

"For God's sake Imbali, confess it to me!"

"What is it you want me to confess?"

"Tell me you love me as much as I do!"

"It is not possible for me to love you, Mr Hertworth!"

"Please do not presume I do not appreciate the difficulty you must have endured in declaring such strong feelings to me, but women like me cannot afford the privilege of corresponding such emotions!"

A tense silence lingered between them. She drew a deep, steadying breath before she spoke again, "This proposal is all I have to give; and I chose to stay behind to willingly grant it to you."

She finally stared back at him, almost as if eager to confirm the veracity of her words.

It was his turn to keep his silence, but at long last he spoke, "Do you honestly wish to tell me you mean to equal what I have confessed to you with such a proposal?!"

"Mr Hertworth, I did not mean to offend you... I simply–"

"–I understand your position quite clearly," he interrupted. "I have kept you away too long, I must urge you to return to your quarters immediately." With those words, he turned away, appearing eager to dismiss her.

*

Unbeknownst to Imbali, Edmund's attention was caught by a shadow and a movement in the darkness. He did not know how long the intruder had been there, but someone had just witnessed their interaction. As he dismissed her, he made his way in the direction he believed the intruder had followed.

For some time, he searched on his own, but at last he decided to make enquiries from the man he had placed to watch over Imbali.

"Did you see anyone passing by this way?" he asked Mr Jenkins.

"No, Sir, you are the only person who has been around here tonight," Mr Jenkins obliged. "Other than the other Miss, but you said it is all right for Imbali to talk to her."

39.

Miss Blaby's path by the coast would not have been adequately lit for a leisurely walk had not the distant lights radiating from Hertworth Manor been so bright. So bright, in fact, she could easily catch glimpses of the occurrences inside the house.

The entertainment taking place in Hertworth Manor had become such a public affair Marianne too had become engrossed in the latest gossip involving all the titled contenders aspiring to consort with the future Lord Hertworth. And if such rumours were anything to go by, a certain Miss Burrow had recently been declared one of the favourites to very soon become Mrs Edmund Hertworth.

This Miss Burrow had been seen in Mr Hertworth's company much more often than any of the other noble young ladies, and rumour had it that Mr Hertworth himself had declared to his mother he had found her much to his liking.

From her distance, Marianne could not help but fantasise over what she knew may never be for a girl of her relatively poor status in society.

But while her thoughts were thus absorbed, she found herself face to face with the future Lord Hertworth himself.

"Good evening, Miss Blaby," Edmund obliged.

"G-good evening to you, Mr Hertworth," she countered once she overcame her initial surprise at finding him so far away from the enjoyment taking place inside his house.

"I see you have taken up my recommendation after all...," Edmund continued.

"Which recommendation, Sir?"

"I am talking about your recent encounter with Imbali."

"Pray who... Oh, you must be referring to my encounter with Lily!" she then recollected.

Edmund's brow furrowed slightly, his expression tinged with confusion, but he chose to remain silent and let her speak further.

"Forgive me, of course you do not understand! You see, all day I was trying to recollect the name you provided me during our conversation in church, and as I happened upon her during one of my walks, when she repeated her name, I realised I would never be able to keep it in mind!

"And at that precise moment, I felt I simply ought to find another name for her."

"Why 'Lily' out of all the names you could have come up with?" enquired Edmund, appearing quite absorbed in his own mind. He himself could have not come up with a better, more appropriate name had he ever intended to do so! "And did she give you leave to refer to her with such a name...?" Edmund proceeded, trying to appear as disinterested as possible.

"Oh yes, Sir, she did... or rather, now that I come to think of it, I am quite unsure... she does not say much, does she?"

Decorum required Marianne to wait for Mr Hertworth to formulate a reply, however she suddenly remarked, "You must forgive my curiosity, Mr Hertworth, but I really cannot refrain from enquiring about her evident superiority in every way. I have not met many people like her, however, even I can tell, in spite of my limited experience with her kind, she must be by far much more polished than any of the negros to have ever walked around us!"

For the first time, Edmund noticed, really noticed, Miss Marianne Blaby.

She appeared as a genteel, agreeable-looking girl. Though she was rather pleasing to the eye, she certainly lacked the superior refinery typical of all the ladies who had been exhibiting themselves to him. However, where she lacked in class, it was certainly compensated by her apparent benevolent and vivacious spirit.

Edmund was aware of his societal expectations towards Miss Blaby. He really ought to bring their conversation to an end. No harm would possibly come to him; but if a young and unmarried woman such as her was to be seen all alone with a man such as him, he knew the damage to her reputation would be grave indeed.

However, he could not dismiss her.

To have someone speak favourably of Imbali was a gratification he could not easily let go of.

And so, Edmund and Marianne carried on conversing for a little longer, and both parties seemed quite pleased to keep Imbali as their main topic of conversation.

Edmund eagerly informed Miss Blaby of how Imbali had procured her secular education, and he even ventured to inform her of how he had rescued her from that ominous fate the night he freed her from Von Hisen.

"I can only imagine what a sorry spectacle she must have been! But, forgive me, Mr Hertworth; I still fail to understand how her plights have become your concerns? I mean, sadly she is not the first negro to experience such an unfortunate violence upon her, and she certainly will not be the last!"

"You are indeed quite right, Miss Blaby, but I had to hold myself responsible because of the part a compatriot of mine played in the violence she experienced that night. As you can understand, because of his actions, I found myself obliged to bring her along with me, knowing what would happen to her if I left her behind."

"I supposed she worked with the rest of the servants in the house, but I believe that not to be the case... right?" Marianne probed further.

"Unfortunately, you are quite right, Madam. She proved herself to be a good investment for me! Quite early on, I discovered her excellent skills with books, but unfortunately, my mother would not have her near any of our libraries."

"I understand your predicament, Mr Hertworth; though I would never presume to find myself contrary to Lady Hertworth, I must confess to you, if I was to be the lady of my own home, I would not really mind what colour he or she may be, as long as the person is diligently taking charge of their obligations."

Miss Blaby was truly pleased with her daring assertion, as she could easily see the positive impression her remark had made upon Mr Hertworth.

"Miss Blaby, I can do nothing but commend your fairness towards the lesser amongst us," Edmund obliged. He seemed poised to extend his praise of her further, but a sudden movement in the distance caught his attention. His expression shifted, his thoughts clearly drawn elsewhere.

"Madam, please excuse me," he said hurriedly. Marianne barely caught his parting words before he turned and strode off.

*

This evening, the sea was particularly serene, and the entire coast felt quieter than usual. Imbali had not taken heed of Edmund's command, instead, she remained where he had left her.

She meant no offence with her proposal to him, and as such she wished to explain herself better, if only he would return to her.

As her mind remained on Edmund, she suddenly felt a pair of hands drawing her towards the edge of a nearby cliff.

Had Edmund at last come to avail himself of her? She considered, as the man tenaciously pressed on with his demands upon her body.

The advances being imposed upon her possessed such an intensity, she could not help but wonder how cross she must have made him feel with her preposition.

Never before had Edmund embraced her in such a way.

However, she would not back down from her offer to him; and if Edmund chose not to be gentle with her, she only had herself to blame.

She then sensed his hands struggle to unfasten her garment.

"If you would let go of my a-arms I can a-assist you with removing it," she suggested.

"Here is a good girl! You are indeed full of surprises! I was certainly not expecting you to be this docile! He must have trained you well!" a stranger's voice slithered into her ears.

This man was not Edmund!

"You are not him!"

Imbali then began a fervent struggle against the man.

"Why are you fretting all of a sudden? I will not hurt you!" The man insisted, strengthening his grip. "Do not make me force you! I saw what a good girl you can be when you want it!"

As her body was slammed against the rocks, the man must have presumed her secure enough for him to focus on her attire once again. However, this motion was all Imbali needed to find the vigour to turn around and push him off her. As he stumbled backward, he tore the front of her gown open.

The sight of his accomplishment injected more vigour into his determination. But such determination did not last very long, as before he could attempt another step towards his prey, he found himself pulled back from Imbali and wrestled to the ground.

It took Marianne a good while to catch up to Mr Hertworth. Visibility around the coast was poor; however, the little she could see was enough for her to come to her own conclusion about what had just occurred.

She found Mr Hertworth delivering blow after blow upon another noble looking man; and close by, cuddled up under one of the rocks, there was Lily in one of the poorest states a man could bring a woman to.

"Mr Hertworth, you will kill the man!" Miss Blaby yelled, while at the same time trying to get him away from his victim.

As Marianne's efforts managed to get through to Mr Hertworth, Lord Glenith secured enough distance from Edmund.

"You will regret this Hertworth!" he started. "She asked for it! She offered herself to me!" he yelled, glaring at Imbali with all the disgust he could convey. "You know nothing of her; and here you are blindly venting all your anger upon me! Why are you not asking her? Ask her how she herself could not wait to undress for me!"

Mr Hertworth would have thrown himself at Lord Glenith with much more vehemence had Mr Jenkins not arrived to prevent any further harm.

"You will not ask her, will you? Very well, let's see if she will deny it while I am in her presence!" he turned his miserable face in Imbali's direction.

"Do not look at her!" Edmund yelled back. "If I ever see your eyes look towards her, I swear to God, I will pry them out of your sorry face! Jenkins, take her away!"

"But, Sir, I cannot leave you in this state!" Jenkins countered.

Marianne then decided to intervene once again, "Come, my dear; I am sorry I cannot offer you much else at present, but you must allow me to wrap this shawl around you."

Imbali did nothing but stare up at Marianne.

"Lily... do you hear me?"

Imbali could not be certain how long Miss Blaby had been addressing her, but at last, she permitted Miss Blaby to cover her dreadful state, and she also allowed the lady to guide her to wherever they were going.

40.

Several hours had passed and the sun had begun to rise on the horizon of Soulgate.

Miss Blaby had offered to provide refuge to Imbali, and Edmund could do nothing but accept the providential offer.

"Lucy is with her at the house too," Jenkins informed his employer. "Miss Blaby's relatives did not seem too inconvenienced by Imbali's intrusion. When I left the house, she was finally settled in and about to sleep."

"Why did you leave your watch?" Edmund reproached. "How could you allow Glenith to get close to her! Had I not clearly instructed you not to let your eyes off her? I am holding you personally responsible for what has happened!"

"I accept the blame, Sir, but I am sorry to say, Sir… I left my watch because she was in your company."

Jenkins was right, Edmund recollected. He had found himself caught up in his chatter with Miss Blaby so much so he had dismissed from his mind the sighting of what must have been Glenith himself.

*

Inside the Manor, Edmund paced the parlour restlessly as he waited for his mother to come out of the room where Lord Glenith had been escorted to. The doctor had been called to provide his best assistance to the man's injuries.

Lady Hertworth seemed to have managed to come to a compromise with the man, as Lord Glenith had at last been dissuaded from reporting Edmund's offence to the authorities, or anyone else as matter of fact.

"I will not reason with you any further on this topic, Edmund" Lady Hertworth began as she joined him in the parlour.

She assumed him sensible enough to know he ought to offer his apologies to Lord Glenith and make amends; before the latest rumours reached far and wide.

"Mother, I will bring her to the house," Edmund informed her.

"You will do no such thing! For as long as I am the lady of this house, that abomination will not step foot through these doors!"

"Mother, I am not asking for your permission, I am simply informing you. I will no longer compromise on her safety by allowing her to be out of my sight!"

"Edmund, dearest, I do not understand how she has managed to trick you so, but we are very close to announcing your engagement to Miss Burrow, and I must do for you what you no longer seem capable of doing for yourself."

"Mother, I must have you know the only reason I have consented to court Miss Burrow is because she has consented to offer residency to Imbali once she becomes my wife."

"Edmund! You cannot expect an honourable young lady to consent to such ridiculous obscenity!"

"Mother, I am a gentleman; and as such I will honour my wedding vows in accordance with my principles, however, if Miss Burrow has any doubts in regard to the credibility of my morals, then she is better off keeping her father's name!"

"If you were to bring that negro into this house, you certainly cannot fault anyone, let alone Miss Burrow, for questioning what your true intentions may be!" remarked Lady Hertworth, wary of pushing Edmund to feel any animosity towards Miss Burrow. She could not allow Edmund's irrational obsession to compromise all she had been working to achieve for several weeks.

"This is not about Miss Burrow! It is about your inability to see how she has blinded you with her fake pretence of good virtue! You have heard Lord Glenith! The negro offered herself to him."

"Mother, you know nothing of her virtue!"

"On the contrary, Edmund, I know enough of the hatred her kind feel towards us! I can tell you they are all the same, with no exception! And I can guarantee you she will stop at nothing until she has ruined you in any way possible!"

"You can choose to believe Glenith all you want, mother, but unlike you, I know what I saw."

"You only saw what she wanted you to see!" she countered. "Were you present when she gladly led him on? You did not see her eagerly partaking in all that occurred between them! She even offered to undress herself for him, Edmund! What more do you need to hear?!"

"He is lying!"

"No, he is not! She has been lying to you all along, Edmund!" Insisted Lady Hertworth. "Unlike you, I can plainly see her trickery. If she meant no evil to you, why did she not acquiescence her virtue to you long ago?! Explain to me why she was still virgin when Glenith possessed her?!"

"Mother, Glenith did not possess anything! I prevented it! And I now must ask you, mother, do not speak of what you know nothing about."

"You prevented nothing, Edmund! How else would I know such information?! Not only has he possessed her, but she freely granted to him all she has been denying you all along!"

271

41.

As he left his mother's presence, Edmund took the direction to Miss Blaby's residence. Upon arrival however, he found himself unable to face Imbali. He wandered around near the cottage, his thoughts in tumult.

No matter how hard he tried, he simply could not bring himself to disregard the torment his mother's revelations had caused to his spirits. Edmund could have indeed expected his mother, or anyone in his circle, to come up with any sort of slanderous accusation, however even he could not deny the possible legitimacy of his mother's last words. There was no way for any of them to be aware of Imbali's virtue.

He considered he ought to hold Glenith accountable for his state of distress, however he could not. His torment was not related to Glenith's actions.

For months, he had made his intentions plain to her.

He had grown to understand her character to such an intimacy, he understood the meaning behind her resistance to him. He appreciated her internal struggles; in fact, he had grown to love her even more because of them!

And as he understood her, she came to understand him best. Or so he thought… Was it all pretence?

How could she have allowed Glenith to spoil all he had built for them?

Why Glenith, out of all the men she could have given herself to?! Perhaps his mother had been right all along?

Perhaps women like Imbali were incapable of appreciating anything but what men like Glenith offered them.

It really seemed he had done it all wrong!

Now that he was to think of it, she too had tried to convince him of the emotional inhibitions of her people many times. It really seemed people like her were not capable of appreciating anything but the force men ought to impose upon them!

At last, Edmund could no longer keep himself away from one more obligation towards himself; she owed him an explanation at the very least.

"Miss Blaby, I will never know how to return the favour I have imposed upon you and your relations," started Edmund, shortly after being shown to the living room.

"You do not need to thank me for anything, I would have indeed felt obligated to assist you, even if you had not probed me to do so," remarked Miss Blaby.

"It is very good of you to call upon us," she continued, intently staring at the dressings wrapped around both of Edmund's hands. "You must forgive me, Mr Hertworth, but I was gravely concerned for you... and had you not called upon us, I had a mind of coming myself to check on you."

There was such a spontaneous sensitivity in her comment, Mr Hertworth could not help but direct a generous smile towards her.

"You are very kind, Miss Blaby. I assure you, all is well with me. What you see here on my hands is simply my mother at her best with her attentive considerations towards me."

"I cannot agree with you, my lord, and I will confess I am very glad to hear your mother has paid attention to you where you would not. You have no idea how afraid I was when I saw the state you brought that man to," she continued. "Of course,

I will not pretend with you and claim he did not deserve what you gave him, as I truly believe no woman should have to endure such impositions, be her negro or not! But I was afraid of the consequences you may have to endure."

"How is she faring?" Edmund at last brought himself to ask.

"Quite well... I mean, well enough considering the circumstances. The woman you have sent with your man has been very attentive towards her.

"Mr Hertworth, I must confess how truly inspired I am by your compassion, and should you require me to, I am prepared to house Lily with me, if the circumstances require it."

"I thank you, Miss Blaby, but that should not be necessary. If I may impose on your kindness for one more day, I will send for the doctor to examine her first thing in the morning."

"I really do not think you need to bother the doctor, Mr Hertworth; other than a few bruises and scratches, there is nothing else wrong with her."

"I do not doubt your judgement. Nevertheless, I will still need to ensure no consequences have arisen from... well let's say, the unfortunate situation we have had to witness," remarked Edmund.

Miss Blaby appeared quite lost at this last remark of Mr Hertworth. And Edmund could not help but reproach himself for allowing his own rage towards Imbali to cloud his sensitivity towards a young lady's innocence.

"Please forgive me for my unpardonable offence, Madam."

"You are quite mistaken, Sir, you did not offend me in any way. I was simply surprised at your allusion–"

"–That is of no consequence any longer, Miss Blaby," he interrupted. "May I ask you to escort me to her? I would like to personally inform her what is to occur next, as her stay with us is no longer unattainable."

"I fully comprehend your scruples... but may I ask what you intend to do with her?"

"That is yet to be decided. I would still like to take her explanation into account before I make a final decision regarding her circumstances."

"Very well," Miss Blaby concluded, before proceeding to escort him to the room where Imbali was staying.

This room, though modest, was neat and tidy. The furnishing may have been quite bare, and the faded patterns on the walls showed it could very well do with fresh redecorating, however, despite its simplicity, the room appeared comfortable.

As Edmund stepped inside, his eyes immediately settled on Imbali, who was comfortably seated on the room's sole chair. Lucy was fast asleep on the single bed in the corner of the room.

"Why are you not on the bed?" he asked abruptly.

"I assure you, Mr Hertworth, Lily is very well taken care of," Miss Blaby intervened, unable to allow him to assume otherwise.

"Of course, Madam, I will not dare to question your capable hospitality. I was simply surprised to see her sitting up, instead of resting," he responded, as his eyes remained firm on Imbali.

"Mrs Jenkins has been watching over me all night while I lay asleep, Mr Hertworth," Imbali felt compelled to inform them.

"How are you feeling," Miss Blaby asked Lily.

"I thank you... I am well."

"I see my gown fits you quite well," Marianne then noted, alluding to the new attire Imbali was wearing. "I did not think it would," she teased.

Silence fell around the room; Marianne had inadvertently caused an air of awkwardness to engulf them.

"You see, Mr Hertworth, I really could not allow her to keep that miserable gown on, considering... well considering all that had happened to it..."

"You are very attentive indeed, Madam. And now, may I usurp upon your consideration a little longer and ask you to please excuse us for a brief moment?" Edmund at last demanded.

"Of course, how silly of me! You must have plenty to discuss with your servant," and Marianne hurriedly made her way out of the room.

*

As the host's receding footsteps could no longer be heard, a total silence fell all around them.

Imbali was the first to speak, "Is your hand in pain…?" she began, "I hope you did not injure the other party too severely," her gaze lingered on Edmund's bandages. She intended to enquire if his altercation with another lord had caused him any issues with the authorities, however something in Edmund's expression made her decide against speaking any further.

"I see you have finally decided to reveal where your considerations have been lying all along," he said. "But please, I beg you, you must not worry about your lover, he is doing quite well! I guess even my punches could not be good enough to hold you two away from one another!" Edmund scorned. "I must compliment you on one of the most amazing performances you could have staged.

"Bravo! Indeed, my heartfelt compliments for your acts!" He carried on. "But I will no longer allow you to make a fool out of me!"

As she began to comprehend the meaning of his accusations, her expression acquired a most petrified look.

"Do not, ever again, waste your time looking at me like that!" The distance Edmund maintained between them only added more severity to the tone he addressed her with. "It seems only I was left to finally understand what your intentions have always been. How could I have failed to see you for who you truly are?!

"When did you design such a scheme against me? Answer me!" he yelled.

"I do not understand what I am supposed to answer…"

"You do not understand me, you say? Very well, I will speak a language you understand!

"Did you or did you not offer yourself to him?!" his eyes were desperately imploring her to contradict him.

But she was not contradicting him.

"Can you deny you offered to take your filthy gown off for him?"

Though her lips remained sealed, her emotions should have conveyed to him much more than any words could do; however, Edmund seemed insistent on his blindness.

"Speak, woman!"

"I cannot deny it," her lips finally uttered.

"And you have no defence for yourself, I see!" he concluded for her. "When did you begin to fancy him? You owe me this clarification at the very least."

At last, Edmund's inquisition roused Lucy from her sleep.

"I beg your pardon, my lord, I didn't hear you coming in!" She exclaimed, jumping out of the bed.

"Please, Lucy, do not worry yourself, return to your sleep," interjected Imbali reassuringly as she moved towards Lucy.

"Who are you to decide what is to happen?" Edmund countered, cutting across her.

She looked up at him, and as she did so, he noticed the state of her face.

He could see a few bruises scattered from her temple all the way down to her chin. But out of all of them, one bruise in particular caught his attention the most.

The cut was situated on the left side of her upper lip. It did not appear to be too deep, but something about it was calling

Edmund to her lips. He instinctively let go of her arms and took hold of her face to better inspect it.

"Has anyone put anything on this?"

"There was no need," she replied coldly. She then disentangled her face from his hold.

"I guess you only allow other men's hands to touch you, not mine... am I right?" He reluctantly let go of her. "You know, I cannot help but wonder how talkative you must have been around him! He claims you were eagerly aiding him and could not wait for him to have you! Why did you choose him? You drove me insane, and you knew it; but not once you thought of having pity on me!"

"If I may, Sir...," Lucy ventured in her attempt to aid her friend.

"Mrs Jenkins, I must ask you to stay out of this! I would not want to offend you, so out with you," commanded Edmund, showing Lucy to the door.

"Sir, please allow me to stay," Lucy pleaded.

"I said, out, now!

"Pray tell me, was this your scheming or Glenith's?" he continued, as soon as Lucy had sealed the door behind her.

"You know what, do what you do best, do not speak; I do not want to hear anything else from you. You will leave England as soon as that may be possible! I will not allow Glenith to enjoy you at my expenses! You wanted to go to the Americas, and so you shall!" He then continued with a newfound vehemence, "Go and find your free man! I would rather have a negro have you than Glenith!"

Though her eyes were still looking in his direction, the sadness had vanished; instead, she had brought back the distant expression she used to look at him with during the early days of their acquaintance.

"Let me guess... you want to stay now, do you?!" He grabbed her by the arm, "I will not allow you to hide behind your walls this time! Talk to me!"

"No, Sir, I don't want to stay, but I have not worked long enough to earn the monies you would spend on securing a passage for me," she said, while trying to free her arm from his hold.

"Then consider it a payment for the services you have provided to Glenith! I suspect you do not have much to take with you," he rejoined, looking at her from head to toe.

To Edmund, Imbali's figure had never seemed to require the adornment a beautiful gown could add to a woman; but now, he could not stop himself from admitting how Miss Blaby's simple gown marvellously accentuated Imbali's curves.

"Prepare yourself," he said, locking eyes with her once again, "I will have Jenkins provide you with your usual attire." He then brazenly stared at her figure once more and then added, "I really doubt Miss Blaby would want to wear this gown again, but you will return it to her all the same!

"I will personally ensure you are embarked on the next ship to your beloved destination!" He then proceeded towards the exit and slammed the door behind him.

42.

Lady Hertworth's diligence towards her son's wellbeing was finally paying off.

Upon his return to the house, Edmund informed her he had dismissed the negro from their lives for good.

"My appointment in Parliament will soon be concluded, Mother, as such I will not be needed in England for a while. I will speak to father and ask him to allow me to take the next commission at sea, instead of Edward."

"You certainly cannot do this any longer, Edmund dear. Your father is ready to hand over his duties to you, and I have already started making all the arrangements for your betrothal to Miss Burrow."

"You have done what?!" he cried. "When did I give you leave to make such arrangements for me?"

"I know you have not said anything to me yet, but we all expected it, considering how you have been courting her!" the mother responded defensively.

"Courting her?! When have you seen me courting anyone? Pray tell, when has exchanging a few words with a lady become equivalent to an official courting?"

"Come my dear, this is how these matters of the heart have always been conducted! Your father and I are not the only ones happy with your and Miss Burrow's understanding; her family too will eagerly approve of your betrothal! Such an alliance will indeed suit both families very well."

"I really do not see how our family would benefit from connecting with them. If anything, Lord Burrow's finances will be greatly uplifted by making an alliance with us! Please do not tell me you have been persuaded to believe otherwise."

"Of course, I understand they will benefit too, but you ought to see what an advantage the connection will bring to our family name."

"How so…?"

Well...," she then began, "I know how your father, and you too in fact, do not give much credit to such reports, but they still call us the 'genteel nobles', and therefore, I must say I am indeed quite rejoiced at the prospect of you marrying into a real aristocratic family such as the Burrows. You may even become an earl one day!"

"Nobody in their right mind cares about such trivial details in this day and age, Mother!" he replied, exasperated. "And if Miss Burrow believes she is doing me a favour by connecting her valuable name with us, please let her spare herself the inconvenience!"

"Edmund, you indeed do Miss Burrow a grave injustice! She has never said a word about it!" replied his mother defensively. "But you need not worry about such things at this particular moment; you can leave this matter to me," she added, eager to prevent her son from developing any prejudice which could jeopardise his possible marriage with the girl in question.

"For now, let us simply rejoice in finally being rid of that odious negro!" she exclaimed. "I can see your spirits are still quite upset by the ordeal. Go and rest my boy. I will make sure you are not to be disturbed for the rest of the day," she solicited, watching her dearest child walk away to his upper chambers.

She could not remember seeing such misery depicted on Edmund's adult face before. Though only momentarily, she did feel a slight sense of guilt for the part she had played in her son's current state of emotions, however she would not fault herself for securing her son's safety out of that negro's tentacles.

*

"You have a visitor, milady," the butler informed Lady Hertworth as soon as Edmund was out of sight.

"I am in such a state, I really cannot bring myself to see anyone today, Newby."

"I beg your pardon, milady, but this visitor insists upon seeing you."

"Who is he?" enquired Lady Hertworth, surprised at the insistence.

"Lord Glenith, milady."

"What else does he want now? I thought he claimed his injuries to be utterly severe! I wonder where he found the strength to walk all the way here!" she exclaimed. "Very well; show him to the library, I will be there soon."

"I beg your pardon, milady, may I suggest I show him to the saloon, as there you may be more comfortable to receive him?"

"Thank you for your suggestion, Newby, but I can expect my meeting with him to be slightly uncomfortable even for me, therefore I would prefer to host him where I can keep him away from people's ears."

*

"I will not consider myself satisfied until you have handed that negro over to me," Lord Glenith began, as soon as Lady

Hertworth seated herself in front of him. "Dead or alive... that is quite inconsequential at this point!" he added.

"My dear Lord Glenith, you really do not need to exert yourself on such a trivial matter; she is no longer a problem to us!

"Once again, I must thank you for all the assistance you have provided in securing Edmund's wellbeing, but we can now safely put this incident behind us!"

"What has happened to her?"

"She is leaving our shores for good! Not sure where to, but we are finally getting rid of her!"

"This is not what you and I had agreed, Lady Hertworth! You promised me I could have her!"

"And I kept my word! I did give her to you! You have known of her whereabouts for a good while, and I constantly ensured to keep people away from that part of the coast! So, I certainly cannot allow you to blame me for the unfortunate altercation you encountered with Edmund. Perhaps you should have gotten to it earlier!"

"I tried, several times in fact; but your son's watchman has been quite an annoyance to my task!" Glenith complained. "Just so you know, milady, you have been misinformed," he then continued, taking their conversation to a new direction, "you assured me she was untouched!"

"And so she was, my dear Lord Glenith!"

"No, she was not! It was very obvious your son had delighted himself with her plenty of times before!"

"You are indeed wrong! I heard the proof of it from a most reliable source; and I can guarantee no man, including my son, has approached her."

"You cannot be sure of what your son has been doing with her!"

"I can indeed! I have personally been watching every step he has taken around her!"

"Well, you clearly have not been watching as carefully as you ought to! Last night she was expecting your son to come to her! In fact, not only was she expecting him, it was him she was offering herself to! The familiarity which she addressed him with indicated so."

"No, she would not! Edmund gave me his word, he would not dare approach her, otherwise our deal would be off!"

"Well, Madam, I am not too sure about the terms of your deal with your son, but last night had she not believed me to be him, she would not have allowed me to come near her, let alone permit me to lay a finger on her! She is quite strong I must say..."

"Oh well, my dear Sir, let us look to the future now. You have been of good service to this family! I knew my son would want nothing to do with her once you had her."

"Lady Hertworth... unfortunately," he hesitated, "I did not have her; your son took her away from me before I could make such a claim."

"I am truly disappointed, Lord Glenith! What more could I have done for you! This is beyond foolish!" exclaimed the lady, unable to contain her dissatisfaction at the man's incompetency. "What is done is done," she then remarked, "the negro will be sent off, and it will not be long before Edmund capitulates to marrying Lord Burrow's daughter.

"All I need you to do for now is keep yourself away from Edmund until we officially announce the betrothal. After the engagement, there will be no harm in making Miss Burrow's connections to your family known to Edmund too. Surely, Edmund will not keep quarrelling with someone who, after all, will become related to him by marriage. I am quite positive, by then, he may even come to value the services you provided to him."

"As you know, Madam, Lord Burrow has personally entrusted his daughter to my care. And with such duty invested upon me, I will need to reassure him the future Lord Hertworth is fully recovered from his obscene impartiality towards such lowly inclinations, if he is to consent to this union."

"Come, my dear Lord Glenith, as I recall, my son is not alone in such impartiality!" retorted Lady Hertworth, unable to allow the man to walk away discrediting her son without any consideration to his own faults.

*

"May I be of any assistance to you, Mr Hertworth?" exclaimed Mr Newby, startling Edmund from his position.

Contrary to Lady Hertworth's belief, her dear son had not retired to his room after all. And his last-minute decision to retreat into his father's library meant that he overheard all that was exchanged between his mother and Glenith.

43.

"Mr Hertworth, what a surprise!" exclaimed Miss Blaby. Not expecting to see him at her door again so soon.

"I beg your pardon, Madam, for such imposition... uhm, you see, Madam, there is something I need to discuss with you... and I really cannot wait until the morning to do so."

"Oh... I hope nothing is the matter with you, my lord?!" she enquired, worryingly. "Please, let me show you to our tearoom."

"All is well with me, Madam, thank you for your enquiries," he hesitated, and remaining where he was, continued, "I fully understand how this evening may not be the best moment for such a conversation, but I can no longer restrain myself from confessing my serious intentions towards you.

"In spite of appearing hasty, Miss Blaby, and indeed I would not fault you for thinking me so, I must avail myself of this opportunity and ask if you would do me the honour of consenting to be my wife."

As Edmund finished his proposal, it took Marianne quite a while to comprehend its meaning.

"Am I correct in understanding you wish to marry me, Mr Hertworth?" She could, understandably, not believe her own ears.

Just this afternoon, after Mr Hertworth had left their little cottage, her aunt reported the latest gossip involving a certain illustrious Miss Burrow who was eagerly awaiting Mr Hertworth's imminent marriage proposal. And now the same Mr Hertworth was proposing marriage to her instead!

"Of course, I cannot expect you to give me a definite answer at this particular moment. I can wait... perhaps you will need to discuss the matter with your family. You can take all the time you require, Madam."

Not once, since Edmund had walked away from the conversation between his mother and Glenith, did he stop to consider the possible consequences of the scheme which occurred to his infuriated mind. But he was rational enough to comprehend the significance of proposing to a Miss Marianne Blaby; and because he understood the implications such a proposal would have upon his mother, he felt more inclined to proceed with it – though his true motives lay with someone else entirely.

He had been a total ass! And to make amends, he would do whatever was necessary to never put her in such a situation again.

"Miss Blaby, are you alright? Shall I call for assistance?" Edmund had to enquire, as Miss Blaby's pallor was starting to look quite worrisome.

"Mr Hertworth, I must ask... why me?"

Edmund could do nothing but admire this woman's direct ways.

He was yet to seriously consider how this decision of his would transform her life as she knew it; however, at the moment he was too engrossed in making decisions with another in mind. "As I said, Miss Blaby, I have come to develop such a regard for you," he responded, wanting to offer her as much sincerity as he could, considering the limitations at hand.

"You must think me a simpleton Mr Hertworth; but I think I have understood you well enough," she cut him short.

"I am quite at a loss here, Madam. I had no intention of offending you, and if for whatever reason you decide to reject my proposal, I will not hold any grudge against you."

"You misunderstand me, Mr Hertworth. All I am saying is I do not want you to pity me!"

"Why would I need to pity an honourable woman such as yourself?"

"Because from the first moment of our acquaintance I have done nothing but make a fool of myself in front of you! And I do not want you to feel obliged to propose to me simply because I have shamelessly exposed my feelings to you!"

"If I went around proposing to women simply because a woman appears to have any inclination of the heart towards me, I can assure you I would have long been married, Madam!"

"Then why did you choose me, when you could indeed have anyone! In fact, Miss Burrow is waiting for your proposal as we speak!"

"This is precisely the reason!"

"I do not understand your meaning, Mr Hertworth."

"None of the other ladies have ever shown to possess the genuine candour you possess. And this is the one quality I truly admire in you!"

"I thank you, Mr Hertworth, for your kind words; however, I have always believed a person required much stronger feelings than this, in order for a man to relent in taking such an important decision."

"You are talking of love, I presume, Madam."

"Well, Sir..., my feelings for you have been abundantly clear for a while, but you..."

"Miss Blaby, I must interrupt you here. I urge you to consider the difference in emotions between our two sexes.

"You may indeed declare yourself to be in love, but what is it you truly love above me? The answer to this question lies entirely with you; but what I can tell you is I do not define love as a prerogative for matrimony.

"Indeed, the vivacity of your temperament, and your kind predisposition to the less fortunate is what has truly elevated you amongst the rest in my eyes.

"Can these considerations be enough for you to consent to be my wife?"

"Yes! Of course, I consent to be your wife, Mr Hertworth!" Marianne exclaimed with joy. Edmund paused for a moment and blessed her acceptance with a gracious smile.

"Miss Blaby, while we are on this topic," he then rejoined, relieved to have been able to secure the first part of his retaliatory plan, "my mother, the current Lady Hertworth, may try to cause a few issues to prevent such a marriage."

Understandably, Marianne's countenance took a radical turn, and an evident gloominess overtook her glowing expressions. She wished to hear more of what he thought of her, or at least he could have expressed more towards her acceptance of his proposal, but here he was turning their conversation to his mother.

"You do not need to be saddened by such inconsequential details Miss Blaby. Unfortunately, my mother likes to ascribe herself to the old ways of our society, but as your future husband, I will not allow anyone, including my own mother to be a cause of any offence to you.

"What do you say we leave first thing on the morrow to finalise our union?"

"Oh... Mr Hertworth, are you suggesting an elopement?! I have read several accounts of such things but never have I imagined myself eloping to Scotland!"

"That will not be necessary, Miss Blaby; a simple trip to London will have to suffice."

"Uhm... I must confess to you; I always wished for my father to conduct my wedding... but I have no doubt you know what is best."

"I shall write to your father first thing," he obliged. "And once we have secured his approval, I suppose we can have this matter finalised within a week at most."

"Mr Hertworth… I must ask; will you be content to be so far away from your family and all your acquaintances? I mean, a man such as yourself cannot be satisfied with such simple arrangements."

"As long as you are content with the arrangements, then I cannot ask for anything more. I have never considered such details to be quite consequential Miss Blaby, you can rest assured. You can leave my family to me."

"Will you not tell them of your intention to marry me?"

"Once our marriage has taken place, we will return to Soulgate, and I will then introduce you to Hertworth Manor as Mrs Marianne Hertworth. After such an introduction, there will not be much my mother or anyone else can do about it."

"My goodness! Mrs Hertworth! How will I ever get used to the sound of it!

"Oh, Mr Hertworth, this is indeed too much happiness for me! I do not deserve it!

"Wait... did you say first thing tomorrow morning? But, how would that work?" she then remarked.

Noise coming from the parlour roused her from her current state of happiness. "I think my aunt has finally returned from her errands. If you would excuse me, Mr Hertworth, I would like to share the news with her."

"Of course, Miss Blaby, I understand you must have a lot you need to discuss with your relatives."

"Oh, indeed I do, Sir; but I wonder," she then considered, turning back to him. "What will happen with Lily in our absence?"

"You seem quite settled in your renaming of her, I see!" Edmund remarked, while offering Marianne one of the most cheerful expressions she was yet to witness on his face. "We shall have to impose on your relations a little longer, Madam. She must wait here for our return."

"I thought you had decided she would be sailing off to the Americas; Lily herself has informed me so."

"You are quite right, but that was before you and I had come to our understanding, Miss Blaby."

"I am quite unable to follow you, Sir, what does she have to do with our *understanding*?"

"It is quite simple! Remember how I told you I hold myself personally responsible for her wellbeing?" he asked, though he did not require her to answer. "And, as I have no female relations, looking after her has proven to be quite a challenge for me. However, since you have consented to become my wife, I do not think we need to fear for her wellbeing... do we?"

"You see," he then continued, "as the future Lady Hertworth, you will have the authority to choose any person of your liking as your closest companion... and if I am not mistaken, you truly value Lily's companionship, do you not?"

"Of course, I do! And now I value her more than ever!"

"That is settled then!"

"So, you mean to say, your mother will no longer object to her presence in the manor?"

"She may at first, but, just as I will ensure my mother will not bother with you at all, in the same way, I am positive you will find the power to overcome my mother's resistance towards your protectee."

"Very well, Sir; let us assume your mother will cease her hostilities towards her... but you must consider… I mean to say, does she meet the requirements to be presented as my companion once I join your society?"

"To be quite honest, she will not need to fit anywhere! Besides, our society will be eager to welcome you as the future Lady Hertworth, and if such a lady is pleased with the company she surrounds herself with, then they will have nothing to do but to accept it."

"Oh, Mr Hertworth, you are truly an angel! I simply cannot believe your goodness!

"What have I done to deserve a man such as yourself?!"

"Please, Madam, I am truly not as angelic as you think," Edmund replied modestly. "I simply consider it my responsibility to ensure the wellbeing of everyone under my care. And now that I have found you, I am relieved to entrust this particular responsibility to you."

"Yes, Sir," she said eagerly, "you can entrust her with me."

Edmund offered a brief nod, seeming to have little else to add.

"May I invite you to dine with us this evening, Mr Hertworth?" Marianne then asked, eager to keep her husband-to-be by her side a little longer.

"You are too kind, Madam," he replied graciously, "but I must decline. As you can imagine, there are several arrangements I need to attend to before our departure tomorrow morning."

"Oh, of course!" Marianne said, suddenly flustered. "I suppose I should make haste with my own preparations. Will Lily be left here all alone?"

"She will not be alone," he said. "And if your relatives would not mind hosting her a little longer, I have made arrangements with Mr and Mrs Jenkins."

"Oh... I rather thought you might bring Mrs Jenkins along with us on the journey."

"But Mrs Jenkins is greatly needed here, given the unfortunate events that our poor girl has endured," Edmund explained. Then, after a thoughtful pause, he added, "However, you are more than welcome to invite your aunt or whomever else you wish to accompany us tomorrow. Will that arrangement be satisfactory to you, Madam?"

Marianne offered a polite nod, "is there anything troubling your mind, Sir?" she then solicited. She could not miss the manner in which Edmund's attention was no longer upon her, but rather he appeared as if he wished to be elsewhere.

"Nothing, Madam," he obliged, rousing himself from his thoughts. "I was simply contemplating how her presence must impose upon your relations."

"She has been no imposition, I assure you, Sir! Besides, Mr and Mrs Jenkins have been nothing but most attentive not only to her, but our entire household too!"

"That is all very well, but I wish to discuss such arrangements with Mr Langton all the same; besides, as your nearest relation I ought to seek his permission after all."

*

Marianne's uncle had been in the quietness of his study, but quite suddenly he found himself startled by his niece bursting into the room.

"I will never know how to thank you enough for allowing me to stay with you all these months!" rejoiced Marianne, venturing around her uncles table to embrace him.

"What has taken over you?!"

"Nothing is wrong with me Uncle, but... Mr Hertworth is here, Uncle, and he wishes to have an audience with you."

"What sort of audience can he wish to have with me...?"

"Have my poor eyes mistaken me, or has Mr Hertworth come to our house again?" enquired the aunt, coming into her husband's study.

"Oh, my dearest aunt! I will never be able to thank you enough for calling me to you!" Marianne cried, turning to her aunt and throwing her arms around the elderly woman.

"Indeed, that man was Mr Hertworth; but you will never guess what he came for!"

"I assume he must have come to see his negro again, is that not so?"

Marianne then let go of her aunt and turning to both her relations she said, "I am grateful to you both for allowing me to keep Mr Hertworth's negro here with us... I must tell you, she too deserves my gratitude."

"Whatever for?! Why would you ever need to be grateful to somebody like her!"

"Come, my dear aunt, stop with your nonsense! Had it not been for my providential encounter with her, Mr Hertworth would have never even noticed me, let alone propose to me!"

"Mr Hertworth proposed what to you? I beg you my dear stop talking in riddles and come out with it at once!" said the aunt, struggling to keep up with Marianne's words.

"What did you say to him?" the uncle intervened.

"What could I have said, Uncle? Of course, I have accepted his offer!"

"I see..."

"I am terribly sorry, Uncle; was I supposed to come to you before accepting him?"

"No, that is of no consequence, I am not your father after all. You did right, I can only suppose; I am simply concerned at this sudden turn of events.

"I must say to you it is quite uncommon for people like them to notice people like us... and I cannot help but wonder how you have managed to secure the attention of the heir of one of the most prominent families in the whole region."

"Mr Langton, I am gravely offended by your insinuation," interjected the aunt. "You may not be able to appreciate it, but my dearest Marianne indeed possesses the famous beauty all the females in our family have always been known for!"

"You misunderstand me, my dear, our Marianne's beauty is not in question here, but..." Mr Langton seemed to be struggling within his own mind, but at last he settled on concluding, "It will all settle itself in the end, send the boy in."

*

As Marianne led Edmund to her uncle, she then hastened to Lily.

"You will not believe what has just happened to me! I intended to make a full speech out of this, but my mind seems completely unable to think rationally; but thank you, thank you, thank you, a thousand times thank you for being by that cliff that afternoon!" Marianne said to Lily, bending over to hold Lily's hands in hers.

"You do not need to thank me for anything, Miss Blaby–"

"–But indeed, I do, Lily!" interrupted Marianne. "Had it not been for you, Mr Hertworth and I would never have become acquainted! And I would not be on the verge of becoming his wife!

"My goodness; I still cannot believe it! I am so afraid I will soon wake up and find all this to be nothing but a beautiful dream!

"Lily, dear, you can keep this dress if you like. I think it suits you quite well."

"I-I thank you, M-madam," Lily responded at last. She rose from the chair and walked to the opposite side of the room. She stood there for a while, facing the wall. "I will be leaving it behind… I am sure I will not require anything this fancy in the new continent."

"New continent?! What are you talking about?!"

"Oh, my poor head! I forgot to inform you he has changed his mind about you travelling to that part of the world. Instead, you will stay here!"

Lily faced Marianne. The drastic turn of countenance on Lily's face was so intense Marianne could not help but become concerned. "You do not need to be afraid any longer! Mr Hertworth has personally entrusted your safety to me!

"I of course understand your concerns; both Mr Hertworth and Lucy have informed me of your previous unfortunate experiences, even prior to the unfortunate encounter you had the other night; but you have no reason to be afraid any longer!

"Once I become Mrs Edmund Hertworth, I will take you to live with me at the Manor, and I am sure that odious man will think twice before accosting you again!"

"Miss Blaby, you do not understand; this is not what I am concerned about."

"What are you concerned about then?"

"I am truly grateful for your kindness towards me… but all I can tell you is I cannot go back to that house."

"Are you afraid of his mother? I will confess I am quite afraid of her too; but Mr Hertworth says he will ensure to keep her away from me, just as I will ensure to keep you safe!"

"If I am permitted to leave, nobody will be obliged to do anything for me!"

"Indeed, Lily, I am yet to see you so passionate about anything like I am seeing you this passionate about leaving England! It is not so bad here; especially if one is fortunate to have a patron like Mr Hertworth."

"Miss Blaby, I am indeed obliged to you, but I must urge you to reconsider; please!"

"Is there anything in particular you are eager to get to?"

"No, there is nothing I am eager to get to, but–"

"–That is settled then! You will come to live with us! Imagine how romantic it will all be!" remarked Marianne, as her mind speculated about the new life awaiting her as the future mistress of Hertworth Manor.

"Please, Lily, stop insisting," Marianne continued, cutting off another attempt by Lily to object. "There's so much I need to prepare for our departure tomorrow, and frankly, I could use some help.

"I hold his judgement in the highest regard; and he is positive you will do very well as my own personal companion once I take my role as Mrs Hertworth. And I, of course, can do nothing but agree with him! And quite truly, Lily, I do like you! You are so different from all I have ever read about the likes of you! Having you around feels like a lovely breath of fresh air!"

*

Meanwhile, the meeting between Marianne's uncle and Edmund was reaching a close. By the end of it, Mr Langton appeared quite pleased with the manner in which the eldest of the Hertworth boys had conducted the polite formalities expected in such cases. At the door, as Mr Langton offered his hand to Edmund, it appeared the young man had a little more to say. "I wish to thank you for hosting such an unexpected guest—"

"—No matter boy, we are to be related soon enough," Mr Langton interjected. "Besides, your man has compensated me quite amply, as you, I am sure, are aware. My niece informs me she is to leave our shores quite soon, is she?"

"No, Sir, she will no longer leave," Edmund responded, "I have informed Miss Blaby of what is to occur. But if you would allow it, I wish to speak to your guest personally and inform her of the new arrangements."

*

Mr Langton personally led his soon-to-be relation to the room at the back of the house. Marianne had recently vacated it, and as they came in, Mr Langton saw Mrs Jenkins beside the negro. With his presence not required, he excused himself.

"Why did you not tell me the truth about what happened that night?" Edmund demanded, the moment after Mr Langton shut the door behind him.

He then looked towards Mrs Jenkins, who immediately understood his meaning, and quietly left the room too.

Though startled by his sudden arrival, Imbali merely turned her gaze away, retreating into the safe silence she so often held around him.

"You misled me into believing Glenith's words against yours," he continued. "You could have confided in me when I came to you; why did you not tell me?!"

"There was nothing to tell," she responded at last.

"There certainly was! For God's sake! What did you expect me to believe?!" he accused.

"I came to you to get answers from you; I–"

"–No, you did not!" she surprisingly interrupted him. "You came to throw your own conclusions at me!"

"You are perfectly right; but I was in a terrible state, Imbali! I behaved like a total ass! I was furious at you; I was insanely jealous you could have chosen another man over me!"

"This is ridiculous, Mr Hertworth! What do you think you are doing in this room with me, while your betrothed is right beside us! You cannot mean to deceive her, do you?!"

"Yes, this is insane; you are totally right about this too! But I cannot get out of it! You can condemn me all you wish, but I am no longer capable of returning from this path, and I will do anything I deem necessary to keep you with me!"

"At the expense of an innocent woman?"

"She has agreed to it!"

"She has agreed to marrying you because she believes in you! Wait a moment...," she then paused. "I do not think I have fully understood what you mean. You said you will do anything necessary to keep me with you... what do you envisage to do with me exactly?!

"Surely even you cannot fail to see how irrational this is. Truly, Mr Hertworth, what do you expect to come out of this?" It was now her turn to interrogate him.

"I do not know where this will lead us, but I can no longer allow you to roam out there in the open and risk anything else ever happening to you again!"

"Why did you choose her?"

"Because I know she will do you no harm."

"But she will be harmed!"

"What do you suggest I do…?" His whisper startled her, she did not realise he had been moving closer. "You may strive to resist my devotion to you, but she would love to be in your place right now."

"That is because you misled her about your true motives!"

"I have not been able to stop thinking about the injury I saw on your lips... I should have prevented him from approaching you," he continued, appearing disinterested in everything but her lips. "Considering all I know, I should have known Glenith stood no chance against you... but I should have taken better care of you! Do you think you could find it in you to forgive my unpardonable behaviour?"

"Mr Hertworth, you do not need my forgiveness–"

"–But I do!" he pleaded. "Right now, I require nothing more from you!"

"Why are you doing this to her?"

"I told you already, I am doing this for you!"

"She believes you to be sincere in your regard for her!"

"But I have been sincere with her! I told her my reasons for marrying her and she agreed to them!"

"I have no idea what you told her, Mr Hertworth, but I know for sure no woman in her right mind would accept to be condemned to this sort of deceit!"

"How about you start being sincere with me for once?! When will you stop pretending with me!"

"How can you accuse me so?! I offered you all I have to offer!"

"You insulted me by offering your flesh to me!"

"What more can I give you?!"

"I do desire you, Imbali, that I cannot deny; much more intensely than anything I have ever desired in my life! But I have come to crave more from you. Your body will have no value to me while I know your heart is not pleased with what I am offering you in return!

"Do you honestly suppose your offer would have pleased what I have grown to feel for you? How can you still fail to see I need your whole being to open up to me?!"

"You are on your way to your nuptials with Miss Blaby as we speak!" She inched away from him, "there cannot be a way out of this! And know that if you insist upon keeping me with you while you are married to another, whatever intentions you may have towards me will be equal to all the others who tried to cage me in before you!"

"For God's sake, Imbali, it is you I want to spend the rest of my life with! You marry me and let us forget all about Miss Blaby and everyone else along with her!"

"You cannot be serious!" she cried out in full astonishment. "Look at me, Mr Hertworth! Your people call me a negro!" she presented her skin to him, "and you are an English gentleman! Such a fairy tale has never existed, and it will certainly not start with me!"

"All I am asking of you is to give me hope!"

"How can I give you any hope when it is decidedly impossible for me to have any! So please, do not ever speak of such nonsense to me!"

"Very well! Have it your way; but know that you have left me with no other choice!" Edmund turned on his heels and left the room before she could make another remark against him.

44.

In the afternoon of the fifth day since their departure, Mr and the new Mrs Edmund Hertworth returned to Ridgeway Cottage to release Marianne's relatives of the duty of housing Imbali.

Mrs Edmund Hertworth would have eagerly remained in the village a little longer in order to introduce her husband to whomever she laid her eyes on, but Edmund's priorities must preside over hers.

Mr Jenkins' meticulous watch over Imbali could now come to a close. In this regard, his final instruction had been to escort Mrs Hertworth's new lady-in-waiting to the carriage that would transport them to Hertworth Manor.

As Edmund's carriage arrived at the Manor, Lady Hertworth rushed to meet her son, "Edmund! I searched everywhere for you! Where have you been? You left without saying a word to anyone! I thought you may have gone to send the negro away yourself; but no-one at the port could give us any information of your whereabouts." His mother was unable to notice anyone except for the beloved son who had returned safely back to her.

"As you can see, I have returned," Edmund responded coldly. "Mother, there is someone I would like to introduce to you and the rest of the family," Edmund stated as he solicited

Mrs Hertworth to descend from the carriage and take her place beside him.

"What is she still doing here?!" exclaimed Lady Hertworth. Her eyes had gone past Marianne and became fixated upon Imbali.

"Mother, you seem to leave me no choice but to introduce you to my wife right here, whilst we stand at the door."

"I want to know why she is still here?!" Lady Hertworth continued, her tone possessing much more vehemence than the first time.

"Mrs Hertworth, please accept my apologies on behalf of my mother for this poor reception," Edmund offered, turning to his wife. "It appears I require a private consultation with my mother before I can announce you to everyone else.

"Mother, may I urge you to take this conversation somewhere more private?" he then said, turning to his mother, whilst the rest of the convoy was ordered to wait for him in their positions.

*

"You said you would send her away to the Americas! Why is that witch still with you?!" his mother yelled at him as soon as she and her son were alone in one of their more private saloons.

"She is not going anywhere, Mother! You, and everyone you like to surround yourself with, will bear that in mind!"

"I do not understand you anymore! You must be out of your mind, Edmund!"

"Mother, I know all about your scheming with Glenith!"

"W-what are you talking about?!" the mother stuttered defensively. "I have no idea what scheming you could be referring to."

"Please, do not bother denying any of it! I heard you both the night Glenith came to claim Imbali from you. For now, you can rest assured I am the only one who is aware of all you have been plotting.

"I also ensured you no longer need to resort to other families to elevate the ranks of the name which seems undignified to you."

"Edmund, your marriage to Miss Burrow has nothing to do with Lord Glenith!"

"That is no longer of consequence, Mother! Had you not been so fixated on her when we arrived, you would have noticed the woman I was trying to introduce you to."

"So, you mean to tell me my ears have heard you correctly?!"

"Yes, Mother they have! I have procured myself a wife! That woman outside is Mrs Marianne Hertworth! And," he rejoined, after a solemn pause, "if, for whatever reason, accidental or otherwise, she is to ever find out why you are so averse to Imbali, then you mark my word, I will not hesitate to let father know of all you have schemed with Glenith."

"Let it be known! I will no longer submit to your empty threats, Edmund!"

"These are not empty threats! I will inform father, and we both know father will not be very pleased to hear his own wife scheming against his family name!"

"You can threaten me all you like, but if you think I will stand idle and watch you walk towards your perdition, then you certainly underestimated me.

"Who is this wife of yours?! Only a nobody would ever agree to marry you without your family's consent! You may be angry with me; but how could you deprive your father and your brother the right of attending your nuptials! How will you explain yourself to your father?!

"You must nullify this marriage immediately! I will not allow you to sink our name with you!"

"Mother, I must ask you to refrain from insulting my wife."

"Your wife you say! Pray tell, when did you have the time to find her? All you have been preoccupied with is running after the skirts of that odious negro the moment you landed back in England!"

"Mother! You will cease to insult her too! I will have you know ,from this moment forth, not only will she live in the manor with us, but she will be engaged as my wife's personal companion!"

"I see! Now I fully understand you! You really have thought of everything!

"So, this woman must be the fool you plucked out of nowhere! And you think she will idly sit back and watch your pursuit of that negro!"

"Marianne is a very honourable woman who has consented to be my wife in spite of knowing how difficult it may be for her to deal with such a mother-in-law!" Edmund responded in kind.

"I have never seen this Marianne in our circles; where did you find her? Who is her family?"

"I know all that is needed to know about her. And I am quite content with who she is and where she comes from."

*

As mother and son were busy with their heated exchange, Edmund's younger brother felt it his duty to welcome the newcomer into the Manor.

"So, you are the long-awaited Mrs Edmund Hertworth! I could scarcely believe my ears when I heard!" exclaimed Mr Edward Hertworth as he came outside to personally inspect the subject which had stirred so much gossip inside the house since Edmund's arrival. "Our greatest Edmund Hertworth at it again! But this time, I must say, I cannot find myself in disagreement with this latest trophy of his!" he remarked, while offering a most obsequious welcome to Marianne. "But come, sister, you must allow me to make amends for Edmund's negligence! I really wonder what could have been so urgent to take him away from you as soon as you arrived!" His eyes shifted towards the carriage in which Imbali had been striving to make herself as invisible as possible.

"I thank you, Sir, but I am quite content to wait for my husband to accompany me inside," responded Marianne timidly.

"You are family now! I no longer want to hear you addressing me so formally, sister. I have your permission to call you sister, do I not?" he enquired, though his expressions appeared not to require her approval.

*

It did not take long for Mr Edward Hertworth to penetrate Marianne's initial resistance towards him; and it was not long before she found herself escorted inside the house whilst the rest of the convoy were ordered to stay put where Mr Hertworth had left them.

Subsequently, Edward proceeded to personally introduce Marianne to the entire household of Hertworth Manor, and once such introductions came to an end, he refused to hand Marianne over to Mr Newby.

"Mr Newby and I are acquainted, Mr Hertworth...," Marianne solicited.

"Are you now?! That is very curious indeed! You must tell me all about it! But this tale can wait until another day," he said, before proceeding to address Newby directly.

"I thank you, Newby, but if I am not mistaken my new sister is quite happy with my company, are you not sister?"

"Yes, I am, thank you, Mr Hertworth," responded Marianne.

"This will not do, sister!

"How many more times will I need to remind you to drop the formalities between us?"

"I beg your pardon... Edward, I will endeavour to remember it," she obliged.

"This is much better! Now, sister, would you like me to show you the rest of your new home?"

"Thank you, Edward, but I would rather wait for my husband," Marianne insisted.

"Very well... I see I have no choice but to hand you over to him!" he conceded.

*

"And here, my dearest sister, is where I knew we would find him!" Edward remarked as the sound of familiar voices could be heard from afar.

"This room here is where the egregious son and his loving mother usually come to whenever they have something to hide from the rest of us," he whispered to her as they were becoming privy to the conversation between Edmund and Lady Hertworth.

"Edward, should we not make ourselves known...?"

"I see you are one of the righteous types!" observed Edward, before proceeding to make their presence known.

"I see your surprises will never cease, brother!" Edward teased as they entered the room. "You deceived us really well this time, Edmund! But then to be fair, I cannot blame you for hiding such a lovely woman from me!"

"Nice to see you too, Edward," Edmund responded coldly. And turning his attention to Marianne, he said, "I thought you would still be outside with everyone else."

"I was, but then your brother came..."

"Come, Edmund! You certainly would not have me leave my lovely sister-in-law all alone outside, only with the company of the servants!" interjected Edward.

"Very well, mother and I do not have much else to say to each other anyways," Edmund concluded, proceeding to escort his wife out of the saloon.

*

"Mr Hertworth, I did not mean to disobey you; but your brother insisted so much... and I did not think anything would come out of me being admitted into the house," Marianne explained hurriedly, rushing to match his pace to the front of the house.

"Mrs Hertworth, I appreciate your explanation, and I know how difficult Edward can be; however, I thought I had made myself abundantly clear to you!"

"I am sorry to have displeased you so, Sir..."

"I am not displeased with you, Mrs Hertworth, but you too cannot have missed how adverse my mother is to... well, as you say, Miss Lily! And whenever I am not around, it is quite necessary for you to ensure her wellbeing," Edmund said as his temper softened towards his wife once again.

"Mr Hertworth... uhm... I did not intend to prey on your conversation with your mother; but I happened to overhear..."

"How much did you hear?" Edmund enquired.

"Not much, Sir, I assure you! Your voices could be heard from afar; and by the time your brother brought me to that part of the house, I think your conversation was coming to a close. But I could not help overhearing your favourable praises towards myself and my family. And for that I am truly grateful to you, Mr Hertworth!" said Marianne, pleased to see her husband looking at her quite favourably, once more.

"You know, Mr Hertworth, though you had explained to me quite clearly before, I think I have just understood the true nature of your mother's animosity towards Lily."

"How so...?"

"You see, though I cannot fault your mother for being quite averse to our union, I do not think she is particularly averse to me per se. I think she has simply become contrary to anything or anyone you tend to give your protection to," Marianne explained. "But I will strive to turn her heart around... just as I have done with yours."

"I am sure you will, Mrs Hertworth... believe me, if I did not believe you capable of doing so, I would not have brought you in the midst of such animosity!"

45.

As a consequence of his marriage to Marianne, Edmund became the head of the family. His commission as the new Lord Hertworth was passed in Parliament and Edmund's father was at last permitted to retire.

The new Lady Edmund Hertworth comfortably settled as the mistress of Hertworth Manor, and with a new order in place, the Manor witnessed a drastic change in personnel. Lord Hertworth proclaimed Mr and Mrs Jenkins as the official butler and housekeeper, while Mr Newby was relegated to remain at the personal disposal of the retired Lady Arthur Hertworth.

Imbali, too, had a new place within the household, officially serving as Marianne's lady-in-waiting.

Though the senior Lord Hertworth had not expressed much in regard to his eldest son's choice of bride, or other conducts as a matter of fact, his wife would not stop soliciting his intervention against their son; especially when it came to the matter of Edmund's obstinate refusal to dismiss the negro.

"Does he really suppose by getting rid of all the old servants he will be able to placate the damage he has caused to our name?!" Lady Priscilla burst to her husband as he peacefully tried to retire for the night. "Have you realised he has located her in the room right next to his?!"

"My dearest, if I am not mistaken, Miss Lily's room is adjacent to Mrs Hertworth's, not Edmund's," corrected the husband.

"Upon my word, Arthur, not you too! How can you be this tolerant towards their collective nonsense?!

"This is the result of all those liberal ideas you have put in his head, I tell you! And I see you intend to do nothing about him! However, unlike you, I will not watch my son stoop lower and lower by the day!

"Have you not heard? We are to have a ball too! He wants to show her off to the world!"

"Priscilla, dearest, you are agitating yourself for nothing. All will be well in the end, you will see."

"Pray tell me; how?! And that senseless wife of his! How can she be so oblivious to what is occurring right under her nose?!"

"Because nothing is occurring under her nose! I know Edmund to be an honourable man, and he will conduct himself as honour requires of him!

"And furthermore, my dearest, you indeed ought to be quite pleased with this wife of his!" teased the husband.

"How can you expect me to be so?! What else is to be expected from the daughter of a clergyman!"

"That is indeed a very honourable profession, as far as I am concerned."

"Her father is a man of profession, I tell you!" repeated the wife, exasperated.

"Pray tell me, would you rather have Edmund married to the African woman, instead of the daughter of an honourable Englishman?"

The impact of this last statement caused exactly the reaction he had expected from his wife. Her astonishment was such, she was rendered incapable of formulating any coherent reply, and so he continued, "Therefore, I urge you to stop meddling with Edmund and leave it to him to sort out his own affairs. He has already done half of what his duty requires of him, and in time he will comply with the rest."

"I see tonight you are indeed intent on vexing me in every possible way!" the wife cried out. "How can you even suggest our son could possibly marry such a person! A negro?!"

"Because, had he chosen to ignore his obligations, I tell you nothing could have prevented him from taking the African to the altar, instead of this woman you seem determined to despise!"

"That surely must be against the law!"

"You are quite mistaken, my dear, I tell you. There is nothing in our English laws preventing Edmund from marrying whomsoever he chooses; and, if I were you, I would stop pestering him beyond his limitations. Instead, you could begin to show some appreciation towards the strain he must have imposed on himself by returning to this house with a respectable Englishwoman!"

"Then why is he keeping the negro here?"

"Leave him be, Priscilla! Did we not agree to trust his judgement the moment we entrusted him with his first ship? And I intend to keep doing so, regardless of how you, or I, may feel about his current conduct!"

*

Imbali appeared rather uncomfortable in her role as Marianne's companion. She preferred to spend most of her time in the solitude of Edmund's library, away from Marianne's company. However, Marianne disliked her companion spending so much of her time away from her; in fact, Lily seemed to have become quite indispensable to her.

"I knew I would find you in here! You have been cooped up in this dusty place long enough for today," Marianne said, coming upon her.

"You have no obligation to these books anymore! You do understand your duty is purely to me now. Come into the garden and read to me, Lily! Edmund is nowhere to be seen; and I really cannot think of what to do with my time!"

Marianne then shifted her gaze from the books and looked at Lily directly, "Lily dear, has he passed by here before he took off? I have not seen him for the entire day!"

"No, Marianne; I have not seen anyone...," Lily answered quietly.

"Oh, poor you!" Marianne then exclaimed. "You must be terrified of the Lady Mother. I can hardly blame you for wanting to hide away from her! Of course, I am quite relieved to find her more favourably disposed towards me," Marianne sighed before she continued. "But there are times I find myself still struggling to come to terms with how horribly mean she can be to you!"

Lily offered Marianne a reassuring smile, "Her disposition towards you cannot in any way compare to how she may choose to treat me, Marianne; not only are you her equal, but you are the new Lady Hertworth after all."

"I suppose you are right...," Marianne reflected on this for a moment. "Lily dear... what do you suppose he sees when he looks at me?" She enquired rather suddenly, as her gaze appeared lost in some mental consideration of hers. "To tell you the truth, I fear he may consider me rather ordinary looking. I will not fool myself of course; I know I am no reputable beauty; and name was certainly not in my favour! As such, I really wonder what extraordinary charity I could have bestowed to deserve such a distinction from him!"

"You are too modest with yourself," obliged Lily. "I have seen my fair share of female beauty, and I do think you very pretty."

Marianne laughed, "I hope you are not offering your opinion of my merits based on the likes of you; but I must say, you on the other hand, are not displeasing to the eye at all!

You may be negro, but I would certainly not mind possessing some of your charms myself!"

"I thank you for praising me so, Marianne, but in truth I do not think a woman's worth should be defined solely upon her physical charms...," Lily felt compelled to confess. "In fact, if I may be permitted the speculation, I would suppose your own husband too may have been more impressed by the beautiful courage you have shown since the first moment he met you."

"You are too kind, my dearest Lily," Marianne said, quite pleased with the compliment.

"I have been meaning to ask you; have you ever had a man in your life? You could very well have a family of your own one day; in fact, I do give you leave to choose whomever you please from around the estate!

"Of course, I cannot claim to be a matchmaker for people like you, but I have noticed there are several men whom I suppose you could mate with!"

"I... uhm... I-I do not know; I have not considered it," Lily responded at last, momentarily confused by the offer presented to her. A sudden knock on the door, however, brought this conversation to a close.

As Edmund entered the room, Marianne was the first to acknowledge him. His wife ran to him to demonstrate her longing for him, and she appeared completely untroubled to have Lily witness such demonstrations of affection.

However, as the wife was profusely engrossed with her husband, Edmund's eyes were captivated by the woman who would not face him.

He then detached himself from his wife and came nearer to her.

"I see you have finished mending another one," he commented, looking at the book she held. "But this glue of yours does not seem to be in agreement with your fingers."

"It is nothing that a little water and salt cannot take care of, milord," Lily interjected; and as she spoke, she distanced herself from him.

Edmund then turned his attention to his wife, "The weather has turned at last; I believe it is about time you have your ball."

"A ball?! My goodness! I have so yearned for a ball in this house!"

"I am to leave again, but I shan't be gone for long, a week altogether I expect. You can set any date of your choosing for the week after my return. Would this provide you both with enough time for your preparations?"

"Oh, Edmund! I have been ready for this occasion! In fact, I even have the perfect gown for it! But," she then continued, turning her attention to Lily, "we must have one made for you! But that should not be a problem; it is nothing that a quick trip to the modiste cannot take care of," she said reassuringly.

"I-I do not need to be at your ball, Marianne...," Lily found the strength to object.

"Do not be silly! You are to be my companion in the eyes of our society!" Marianne reprimanded, "this is my moment of truth, and I need you right beside me!" she exclaimed, as her gaze sought Edmund's approval.

"If you so wish it," Lily capitulated. "But I do not need anything else purchased for me. I can simply wear one of the many dresses you have already provided me with."

"Come, Lily dear, I cannot in all honesty have you attend my coming out ball dressed in your usual grey!"

"I cannot but agree with you Lady Hertworth," Edmund intervened. "Let it be a bright gown," he suggested. "But whatever the colour, it should be nothing too revealing of course. I really cannot understand why you women need to reveal so much of your attributes these days–"

"–But Edmund, that is what fashion dictates these days." Marianne interjected.

"I suggest we leave such fashion to the French then," he responded sharply.

With nothing else to say in the company of his wife and her companion, he appeared ready to leave, but Marianne held him back.

"Where are you going this time, Edmund dear, and when are you to leave?"

"I am to go to London," he informed her. "Mother already knows of your ball, but she also knows you ought to take charge of the preparations yourself... with your companion's assistance of course; you are the new lady of the house after all."

"I shall...," Marianne responded obligingly. "But what of the Lady Mother?"

"My parents will be leaving for the country before your ball; we cannot have two ladies presiding over the estate at the same time, can we?"

*

Later that night, Marianne decided to venture into her husband's room for the first time since her arrival at the Manor.

"I hope I am not imposing...." she began, as her trembling hands closed the door behind her.

"Milady! I was not expecting you to come into my room," Edmund countered, surprised to see her coming to him.

"I did not mean to startle you, but I wished to speak with you..." she said timidly. "You will be departing to London again…"

"Yes, I am," he probed, as she appeared to struggle with collecting her thoughts. "Do you foresee any issues arising during my absence?"

"No, of course not; b-but... I-I thought I ought to come to you this evening so that perhaps you... I mean, we could finally consummate our marriage," she let out at last.

315

"Milady, it is getting rather late, and as you know, I will need to be on the road in a few hours," he said dismissively.

"Is there something the matter with me?! Am I not pleasing enough for you?"

"You are being quite ridiculous! You know very well what a beautiful woman you are! Do you not hear Edward and everyone else talk of how much they envy me for the wife I have secured for myself?"

"I do not need everyone else to think so! I need you to think so of me, Edmund!"

"But I do think you a very beautiful woman!"

"Then why do you not come to me?! Why are we yet to have our wedding night?!" rejoined Marianne, as tears started to flow from her eyes.

"I really do not think it proper for a wife to question her husband on how and when he intends to avail himself of his marital obligations."

"Obligations?! Is that what being with me is to you?!"

"I do not mean to say you are an obligation, Lady Hertworth! You are my wife," he corrected himself.

"Do you realise I am only your wife by name! You are yet to make me your wife in the full sense of the word!

"You have forced me to relent my pride, my dignity, and everything else I ought to feel! I have put them all aside and came to you tonight with the hope you would finally have me like a husband ought to have his wife!"

"It is getting rather late; tonight cannot be that night."

"I wait for you every night, Edmund! I have been waiting for you to come to me since the first night of our wedding!"

"You certainly could have not expected me to come to you while we stayed in London, in such a precarious way?!"

"What about every other night after that?!"

"This is quite enough, milady; let me fetch you somebody to escort you back to your room."

"Look at us! You will not even address me with my name! Why am I still Lady Hertworth to you? When will you address me as a husband ought to address his wife?!

"Am I ever going to be permitted to address you as my heart pleases?!"

"You shall have it your way, *Marianne*! You can address me as you wish, as shall I; but now I must ask you to return to your room!" and in saying so, he proceeded to open the door of his room for his wife to depart from it herself.

46.

The senior Lord Hertworth, accompanied by the lady mother, decided to depart from the estate the morning after Edmund had taken his leave.

Marianne obsequiously paid her respects to the leaving couple. She attempted to offer a curtsy to her father-in-law, but the man helped her out of her discomfort by embracing her.

She then turned to face the mother, and as she attempted to offer a similar gesture, she was met with a rather pointed question, "Are you with child yet?"

"Uhm... no, not yet," Marianne answered, stepping backwards.

"You've been married long enough," the lady remarked with an insinuating glance.

"Though I suppose you may never be with child at this rate!" she scorned. "Well, I hear you wish to take your companion to the modiste, is that so?"

"I-I ought to, I supposed," Marianne responded defensively. "It is Edmund's wish… and mine," she added, "to see her dressed as best as she may possibly look on my debut."

"You have better things to do than waste your time dressing her up, you silly girl!" the lady concluded, before deciding to relent to her husband's calls to follow him into the carriage.

Lily had witnessed the interaction between Marianne and the Lady Mother, and as such, renewed her refusal to take a trip to the modiste. Marianne did not care to insist this time, as she had more pressing matters occupying her mind.

She had the running of the house all to herself at last.

*

Edmund's return from his trip was delayed beyond what he had originally anticipated. He was expected to return a week after his departure, but seven days had passed and still no sign of him. But Marianne was sure of her husband's return, and as the evening of the ball approached, her conviction came true as Edmund arrived in the early hours on the very morning of the much-anticipated ball.

The Manor buzzed with excitement, as did Marianne.

"There you are! I've been searching everywhere for you," Marianne exclaimed as she came to find Lily near the servants' quarters. "Why are you not up in your room?" she asked, her tone a mix of curiosity and mild reproach. "Have you heard the news!? Well, I really doubt you may have heard," she continued, her excitement spilling over, "Edmund is back at last!"

Marianne then noticed Imbali's appearance, "My goodness, your hair! Is it just my illusion or is your hair quite drenched?! Have you just taken a bath in there... with the servants?!

"You really did not need to! You know you could have come to avail yourself of the bath in my room! How many times have I offered it to you?!"

A hint of annoyance marked Marianne's tone, "You really ought to put some of your obstinacy aside, Lily, and listen to me when I tell you something which is purely for your own good!"

"Forgive me, Marianne, I simply did not see the need to impose upon you when I can easily avail myself through other means."

"And by other means you mean to say an escapade into the servants' quarters?" Marianne shot back. "Well, never mind that! Come with me now! Let me get you dried off." Marianne's voice grew more urgent. "If we wait any longer, and Edmund finds you like this, who knows what he might say!"

Lily wished to be in her own room to avail herself of her own means, but Marianne insisted on keeping Lily with her. "You can use my things, Lily dear; in fact, you can take whatever you use with you once you are done with them," Marianne presented not only a hairbrush, but a comb too.

Lily looked at the offer presented to her, but she would not take them.

"I will only ruin them for you Marianne," she countered, and with that she simply took her usual cap out of the pocket of her dress and placed it back on her head.

Lily then looked up to Marianne and as their eyes met, Marianne took a deep breath and spoke. "Lily… Edmund and I have yet to consummate our marriage.

"You know, Lily, I never wished to disclose this information to anyone… I have indeed been too ashamed of it," Marianne pressed on, her voice overtaken by despair. "I know very well he loves me, otherwise, whyever would he choose to marry me, right...? But I sometimes fear… there might be something keeping him away from my bed. Something else, some kind of futile distraction." She met Lily's eyes, searching for some form of reassurance. "You have known him longer than I have; surely, if there were another woman, someone noteworthy, you'd have noticed, would you not?"

"I...," Lily stuttered, and when it was no longer possible for her to keep her silence, she said, "I-I did not notice anyone around him."

"It must be true if you say so yourself!" rejoiced Marianne. "Dearest Lily, you must help me!"

"How can I possibly help you, Marianne?"

"Well... I know I am not the only one to value your friendship; Edmund too, values it, quite highly in fact... and so perhaps you may say a word or two to convince him to finally make me his lawful wife!" Marianne pleaded, tears now starting to fall.

"I understand you may not comprehend my apprehension; you may never have a child of your own, but I would gladly raise my child to truly see you only second to me!" Marianne's sobs intensified with every word.

"How am I to do my duty as the lady of this house if he will not come to me! Lily, you must understand, I will never be able to secure any authority in this house, and protect you, if I do not conceive the future heir!"

*

As the evening approached, and once Marianne was certain everything had been taken care of, she became determined to appear her most radiant. Though several servants were at her disposal, it was Lily's approval she sought most as she prepared for the ball. When she felt ready to descend for the evening, she ventured to pay attention to how Lily prepared herself.

"I am very sorry I was not allowed to procure you with a dress of your own, but I must say this dress does suit you quite well," Marianne remarked, her eyes appraising her companion's appearance. "I grant you a brighter colour may have helped brighten your dark complexion a bit; Edmund was right after all! I now wish I had not consented to you wearing black… but still, I must say it agrees quite well with your proportions. I admit the fit around your bosom may not be as concealed as I would have liked; but dare I say, your figure is not much different from mine!"

"I thank you, Marianne... I will wash it and return it first thing tomorrow morning."

"You mustn't, my dearest! I insist you keep it!"

*

Marianne was every bit the vision of radiance she wished to be.

She wore a majestic red gown which draped her figure with noble elegance; an exquisite set of diamonds added a brilliant sparkle to her ensemble.

As she descended into the ballroom, a surge of satisfaction washed over her as she noticed the admiring glances of her guests, all of them drawn to her beauty.

Lily followed behind her, her presence more subdued, and yet her appearance attracted the attention of the only gentleman whose gaze Marianne could not capture.

Edmund made his way toward them, and as he neared the staircase, Lily's eyes met his. The intensity of his expression caused a cold shiver to run through her, and for a brief moment, she feared what might follow.

But her anxieties proved unfounded. Edmund did not approach her. Instead, he directed his attention to Marianne, his manner all charm and gallantry. He took his wife by the hand and led her to the centre of the ballroom, where they began the first dance of the evening, drawing the eyes of every guest in the room.

Several of the attendees appeared quite intrigued by Lily's presence amongst them, however.

As Marianne was busily engaged with her husband, Lily thought it best to keep herself by the back corners of the ballroom, further away from the scrutiny her presence was stirring.

She caught sight of Lady Glenith amongst the women scrutinising her, and as she saw the mother, Lily began to dread the presence of the son.

"I see you still do not fail to arouse interest wherever you go," a voice startled her from behind.

She turned; to her relief this man was not Lord Glenith.

"Mr William Bormer, at your service," the man offered most obligingly.

"Would you please do me the honour of dancing with me?" he then continued, "I do not recall your name, but I can assume you may recall mine... you and I have met before, do you remember me?"

"Y-yes... I do," Imbali felt compelled to respond, but with polite firmness she declined his invitation to dance.

"But I have news from your home."

Lily could not help but look at him with interest.

"Please, dance with me," he insisted.

"I am not here to dance, Sir," she countered.

"Quite right, you are here as the new Lady Hertworth's companion I hear..."

As Mr Bormer and Lily conversed, the buzz around Lady Glenith was getting louder and louder. Lady Glenith had not taken her eyes off of Lily, and she appeared to be feeding gossip to the crowd which had gathered around her.

"I remember," Mr Bormer continued, "you had the same effect on Edmund's ship... and back in your hometown too; you like to captivate attention, do you not?"

Lily gave him no acknowledgement. However, Mr Bormer appeared undeterred, "You may be interested to know, Miss Von Hisen no longer goes by such name. She has wedded," he casually remarked.

"Which of the Miss Von Hisen's...?"

"I see I have managed to arouse your interest at last!

323

"The first daughter, I believe Johanna was her name. She married a compatriot of ours, Mr Galloway. Fredrick Galloway. Do you remember the man?" he probed. "I ask because he was left behind by Edmund... because of you."

"I really cannot see how this may be connected with me," Imbali countered, keeping her expression as impassive as possible.

"I beg your pardon; I meant no offence of course, but even you cannot fail to see how Mr Galloway must have found himself in a most inconvenient predicament, if he bound himself to marriage so far away from home."

"–Thank you, Mr Bormer, for keeping my companion entertained," Marianne called out cheerfully as she approached, "I am afraid I need her."

"Of course, milady," William replied graciously. "I understand she is here as your companion. I must say, you are truly fortunate to have her in your service. She is quite remarkable."

"What a small world! Are you acquainted with my Lily?" Marianne asked with pleasant surprise. "My husband never mentioned it to me."

"Oh, yes, we are indeed acquainted, though not as well as I might have hoped!" William replied with a playful air. "On the ship, Edmund claimed her full attention; I scarcely had a chance."

Marianne's curiosity was piqued.

"Please, do not misunderstand me!" William quickly clarified, sensing her reaction. "I do not mean to imply any misgiving on your husband's part! Our Edmund is above such things, of course! But... as you may know, your Lily is a clever, resourceful one. Edmund greatly valued her intellect; their bond was purely academic, I assure you."

"Oh, yes, I am well aware of their connection," Marianne replied smoothly, her polite smile now edged with subtle coldness. "And now, if you'll excuse us, I must introduce her to some of our other guests."

As they walked away, Marianne's pleasant demeanour evaporated, "What an odious man!

"Did he upset you?" She then asked Lily, "Edmund suspected he might, and he sent me to intervene."

"No, nothing of consequence," Lily replied. "Marianne," she then ventured cautiously, "what he said about my interactions with his lordship on the ship–"

"–Do not be ridiculous, Lily dear," Marianne interrupted. "Do not rattle your brain over such nonsense! I, for my part, gave no value to any part of what he said! It is so obvious that man is nothing but jealous of Edmund!"

Marianne approached the gathering surrounding Lady Glenith with an air of confidence far from what she felt. But this was her moment, a chance to prove herself to Edmund, to demonstrate her wit and resolve in defending both her companion and her place as the mistress of the Manor.

"My dearest ladies, thank you all for gracing our humble home this evening," she began, inserting herself smoothly into the conversation. "Allow me to introduce my dear friend, Miss Lily. She is not from here, obviously, but–"

"–How can you address her as if she were our equal?!" interjected Lady Glenith in horror. "I am all astonishment; I must tell you!"

Marianne's composure remained unshaken, "I understand your reservations, Lady Glenith," she replied with a measured smile, "but I simply adore her, and to tell you the truth, I see her as nothing but my equal!"

Many of the ladies surrounding Lady Glenith exclaimed their disbelief.

"How can that be possible?!" one said. "How can Lady Hertworth condone such extravagance?" another continued.

"Perhaps she had no say in this matter," Lady Glenith offered. "Maybe… our new Lord Hertworth had his own designs in thrusting this negro upon you!"

"You are quite correct," Marianne answered, her tone sharp but composed. "My husband is indeed benevolent to those less fortunate than ourselves." Ignoring the insinuation, she continued, "and my Lily would have been beyond salvation had he not been in the right place at the right time to take her away from an entire horde of men intent at preying upon her virtue!"

"I had heard of Lord Hertworth's gallantry," Miss Burrow chimed in, "from the man himself in fact, but... I thought the receiver of his kindness to be someone more deserving!" Unable to refrain from displaying her evident disdain towards the negro, she continued. "While our Empire benefits greatly from Africa, I cannot imagine how one is to brace oneself around those beastly rebels who can barely presume themselves anything closely resembling the human race!"

She paused for a moment and offered a smile to Marianne, "I presume the event must have happened during one of his travels? We all know how much Lord Hertworth enjoys his adventures; all sorts of adventures, I imagine."

Marianne returned the smile, "Come now, Miss Burrow. *My* husband may have shared some of his adventures with you during your past, brief acquaintance, but from him I personally came to know they cannot all be as bad as you claim. My Lily, for one, is far from savage. Are all negros as wicked as Miss Burrow suggests?" she asked, turning to Lily.

"I… I cannot say, Marianne," Lily replied quietly, her voice trembling.

"My dear Lady Hertworth, you are indeed too good; why would you need her opinion on such matters?!" Miss Burrow interjected most scornfully. "Did you not say it yourself just now? What other evidence must you need? And

Lord Hertworth's gallantry is nothing but a testimony of our superiority over them!"

"How so…?" Marianne probed.

"Why, it's obvious!" Miss Burrow then exclaimed. "Lord Hertworth extended his aid, even when faced with the savagery of her own kind turning against one of their own! What clearer proof of our superiority could there be?"

"You are mistaken, Miss Burrow," Marianne said with deliberate calm. "It was not her own kind who sought to harm her, but our own countrymen."

A flicker of discomfort crossed Miss Burrow's face, "Oh, well, I see… but then again, surely a negro cannot be expected to appreciate female virtue as well as we do," Miss Burrow continued, recomposing herself. "Therefore, I still believe Lord Hertworth could have indeed spared himself the trouble! Besides… I cannot help but wonder what required her to be around our countrymen to begin with!"

Lily's restraint finally gave way. She decided to speak for herself; her voice low and yet firm enough to cut through the crowd.

"Perhaps Lord Hertworth would not have needed to intervene if your countrymen hadn't been preying on our land to begin with. And you spoke of our savagery," she continued, her gaze locked on to Miss Burrow, "if seeking salvation from an unhinged master is what is mistaken by some as beastly, then perhaps the one pillaged may simply be seeking freedom from an outside pillager, who himself may present his own savage disposition!"

"How dare you speak to me like that?!" Miss Burrow shrieked, her voice rising with indignation. "You may be accustomed to exploiting your masters' indulgent generosity, but I will not tolerate such insolence from the likes of you!"

The room fell into stunned silence, broken only when Miss Burrow, followed by several affronted guests, swept out of the manor in a flurry of indignation.

Lily, visibly shaken, turned to Marianne. "P-please Marianne, accept my apologies," she stammered. "I... I do not know what came over me. I never intended to offend your guests."

Marianne placed a calming hand on Lily's shoulder, "No harm done, my dear. It serves her right for poking her nose where it does not belong anymore."

As Marianne spoke, her gaze drifted toward Edmund. He stood at the edge of the gathering; his expression unreadable but his eyes this time were fixed upon her. In that moment, as their eyes met, Marianne felt a rush of triumph; everything had unfolded exactly as she had intended.

47.

Marianne's ball had finally drawn to a close. The grandeur of the evening faded into the night, but for Lily, peace eluded her. Long after the last guest had departed, she lay awake, the stillness of her room offering no respite from the unease clutching her heart.

She had made sure to lock her door securely, yet an oppressive apprehension cast long shadows over her thoughts. Edmund had not approached her during the whole evening, and yet she could feel his gaze upon every movement of hers.

"You were brilliant this evening," Edmund's presence startled her, and before she could react, he had seated himself right beside her. "I could not have been more proud of the way you stood up to them."

"How did you manage to get into the room?!"

"Did you truly think a mere lock can keep me from you?"

"You should not be here!" she cried, sitting up and pulling her shawl tightly around her shoulders.

"I miss your company," he confessed.

"This is dangerous; too dangerous!" she whispered fiercely. "You must leave at once before anyone sees you here."

"I stayed away from you all evening, do not ask me to stay away any longer!"

"Please," she begged, her voice trembling with fear and desperation. "Go to your wife. She must be waiting for you."

"What makes you suppose she is waiting for me?"

"Well, it is quite understandable since you are married," Imbali reminded him, unable to articulate her thoughts better.

"Why didn't you wear something bright tonight?" he then said, his eyes lingering over her as though her protests were inconsequential to him. "I would have wished for you to wear a yellow gown... but no matter. Come with me, I have something for you." His voice dropped to a near whisper as he extended a hand toward her.

However, Imbali appeared intent at not obliging him, so he allowed himself the permission to grab her hand, before soliciting further for her to follow him to the long mirror adorning the other side of her room.

As she stood by the mirror, he removed the shawl from her shoulders and in the next moment extracted a precious looking box from under his coat.

The room was poorly lit, but despite the darkness engulfing them, Imbali could not miss the brilliance of the stones adorning the piece of jewellery Edmund removed from its case.

"I would not have kept myself away from you this long, my love; but having this specifically made for you took much longer than I expected."

Imbali's eyes did not linger long enough on the necklace; instead, her stare fixed itself on Edmund.

"Milord... you cannot seriously expect me to accept such a thing from you! Go and give it to your wife instead!"

"I am not too sure you would want me to present this to her," he retorted, as his hands proceeded to place this piece of jewellery around her neck.

"I do not want it! Please leave my room this instant," she ordered, while her hands tried to keep him away from her.

"Look at it! This necklace can only be on your neck and no one else's!"

Contrary to her own will, Imbali found herself gazing into the mirror in front of her. It was immediately apparent Edmund had spared no cost in the commission of this brilliant piece.

But the precious stones did not retain much of her attention, as the moment her eyes caught sight of the pendant cascading from the centre of the necklace, tears started welling up in them.

Imbali could not be faulted for not noticing her mother's amulet. Edmund had specifically chosen yellow sapphires to be placed all around the chain, as their tones beautifully blended with the colour of the amulet which he knew to be so precious to her.

"My goodness! I thought I lost it forever! How did you find it?!" she cried, as she held tight to her mother's amulet.

"I had it with me all along... it fell right under my feet the first night you spent in my cabin."

"I thank you for returning my mother's trust to me; but I cannot accept this, nor anything else you ask of me," she said at last, removing the precious gift off her neck.

"Milord, you are a married man; and your lawful wife is right beside us waiting to have your child!"

"I will not disagree on who my lawful wife is; but I expect you to fully understand, my union with Marianne is nothing but a marriage of convenience! I presume you do not need me to remind you whom I wish to lay with!"

"Whatever role I might have resigned myself to occupy in your life vanished the moment you bound yourself to Marianne," she interjected.

"I admit, I should never have involved her in this mess! If only I did not act so hastily after... well after what happened that night! But it cannot be helped any longer."

"There is really no point in looking back at the past; you and Marianne are bound to one another, and she is hoping to build a future with you. You are certainly not helping anyone by dwelling much longer on... well this!" concluded Imbali, as her eyes descended upon the piece of jewellery she offered back to him.

"This necklace is proof of what you know very well too, Imbali. You belong to me!" He closed her hand around the necklace. "God is my witness," he murmured into her ears, "I only came to you with the intention of giving you back your mother's entrustment, but every time my eyes fall upon you; you blank my ability to reason," he started to approach her in his usual ways.

"Edmund, please stay away…"

"I cannot!"

"I-I…," she began, "in truth I cannot think when you come upon me in such a way!"

"Then let me in!" he pleaded, "let me be with you!" His voice was gentle, however Imbali could not help but recede from him until the wall behind her prevented her escape.

"T-the conditions are no longer as they once were," she stammered, forcing herself to speak. "You are now a married man, and you cannot expect me to betray Marianne's trust in such a way. I have strived to oblige you until this moment, but I cannot in good conscience carry on any longer."

"What is that supposed to mean?"

"Marianne has defended me in front of so many of her equals, knowing she may very well risk her own social condemnation! Edmund please, you must find it in yourself to finally let me go!"

"You are not to go anywhere!" he countered, his expression turning almost ominous. "And I suggest you better tell your conscience this; I give you my word; you leave me, and I will have no scruple in nullifying the marriage the next day!"

"You would not dare such a thing!"

"With you gone, I will have no need for her!"

"You cannot be this insensitive to her!"

"Go ahead then; try me!" Edmund countered, firing all the frustration he had been brewing inside of him. "You have not seen what I am prepared to dare for you!

"It appears even your mother's amulet is not good enough for you, is it?" he then remarked, as he snatched his precious gift out of her hand.

"You care so much of her upset, but in doing so you hurt me!

"You may insist upon your failure to value my feelings; but it has become quite impossible for me to be without you! Only you can now be my source of solace, not her! What must I do to persuade you to stay with me?"

"Give her a child!" she let out at last. "I give you my word; you will no longer hear me speak of leaving again if you would grant your wife the gift of the child she longs for."

End of Part Two

48.

Several weeks had passed since Marianne had become privy to Lily's past experiences and inner thoughts. Without any company, in the monotonous routine of her days, she would rise and proceed with her daily reading of Lily's diary until the late hours of the day.

Lily had recovered at last, so Marianne had heard from the servants.

The recovery should have come as a warning to return the journal where it belonged; but the events laid out in front of Marianne had become of such remarkable value to her, she simply could not bring herself to leave the manuscript alone.

"Is that my journal you are reading?" The sudden voice made Marianne jump, her hands trembling for a moment as she clutched the diary before quickly hiding it behind her.

She looked up to see Lily standing in the doorway, "What are you doing here?!"

"I knocked… several times; I-I came to see you...," Lily responded hesitantly.

"Have you now?! Tired of sharing my husband's bed, are you?"

From the depths of her heart, Lily wished she had seen wrong, but she knew it was her diary. "Marianne...h-how much of its contents have you read?" The trembling in her voice betrayed her rising fears.

"Enough to know what a despicable person you are! I trusted you with my life! Instead, you have been throwing yourself into his arms at every opportunity!"

"Marianne it is not as it seems–"

"–Not what it seems?!" Marianne spat. "Don't lie to me! Don't you dare! You lured him onto you, even though you knew I loved him from the first moment I saw him! You say so yourself right here!" She thrust the diary towards Lily.

"How I wish I had let Newby take you away that day! How I wish I had not protected you!"

"Please, Marianne, you must let me explain myself!" Lily implored, "you have to believe me; I didn't mean for any of this to happen–"

"–I selflessly defended you where everyone else would not; and this is how you choose to repay my kindness?! I have given you five years of my undying trust, my friendship, and yet you took everything from me!"

Lily opened her mouth, but no words would come, her lips trembled as her gaze dropped to the floor.

"So, it was you who sent him running to my bed that night, was it?!" Marianne then added mockingly, "I suppose I should thank you for having the power to manipulate my husband, should I not?!"

"I did not mean to manipulate him; I only wished to oblige you…," Lily protested, her voice shaking.

"Oblige me!?" Marianne exploded. "By making a fool out of me for all these years!?" She shot up from her chair, but the movement was sudden, too sudden, her face contorted with pain. A gasp tore from her lips as she held her stomach.

"What is it?!" Lily cried, lunging forward to steady her mistress.

Marianne's hands trembled over her womb; horror filled her eyes. "My child…!" She cried, "oh God... I feel the... pains, those same pains everywhere!"

"Marianne, please!" Lily pleaded, tightening her hold around her mistress. "You must let me take you to bed! Such distress must be dangerous for you both!"

Marianne wrenched herself free, "No! Leave me be! You did this to me!" she sobbed, stumbling away from her. But Marianne's agony only deepened. "Dear God, please do not castigate my poor child because of her sins!"

"Marianne, stop! Let me help you!" Lily hesitated only for another moment before deciding to defy Marianne's command. She caught her just as Marianne faltered again, guiding her toward the bed despite her protests.

"Summon Dr Bathia! At once!" Lily then shouted, her voice echoing through the halls.

*

With Bathia's arrival, Marianne dismissed Lily out of her sight.

The minutes stretched on, but at last, Dr Bathia's examinations were complete.

"Fear not, I could not perceive anything concerning, milady; the child has grown to a rather good proportion," he said.

"But what of the pains I felt!"

"I can only suppose you may have put too much strain upon yourself," the doctor continued reassuringly. "I do not suspect any worrying outcome for this child, thankfully." He hesitated for a moment. "As for your discomfort… it is my conviction it may very well be related to your delicate constitution, milady."

"And what, exactly, is that supposed to mean?!"

"It all remains to be seen, milady. But I must urge you to be cautious." He was measured in his response, and yet Marianne could not fail to perceive the gravity in his tone.

"In fact, the child may very well be with us sooner than I anticipated. But as far as your wellbeing, I should counsel Miss Lily on how best to look after you... where is she?"

"Why do you ask? She is no longer a patient of yours; why should she be of any interest to you still?!" Marianne exclaimed, her tone tinged with annoyance.

"Nothing of consequence to me," the doctor responded calmly. "I was simply surprised not to see her by your side; she seemed very eager to be beside you when I last saw her."

"I no longer require her presence," Marianne continued in the same tone.

At such words, a palpable discomfort settled over the doctor, "I see, milady... this is all the better I suppose. Then, now would be a good time to discuss a letter I have received with you," he said, pausing for a moment as if to gather his thoughts. "It was an unsettling letter to be quite frank... from my colleague, Dr Hashford."

Marianne's heart skipped a beat, but she immediately masked her reaction with a calm, almost dismissive tone, "Why would you think that to be of interest to me?"

"Because *he* was very interested in you!" Dr Bathia studied her for a long moment before he spoke again with a subtle, but telling tone. "Well, I supposed as a long supporter of your efforts, you would have been quite keen to share your happy news with Dr Hashford yourself–"

"–My husband forbade all communications with him," Marianne interjected. "And I am not one to transgress my husband's bidding."

"Aha... I see your predicament, milady," the doctor observed. "But, based on my own presumption of your closeness with him, I happened to inform him of your current state, and the hope you will soon succeed in delivering the long-awaited child.

"He then wrote back to me and was keenly interested in the child this time," Dr Bathia's gaze sharpened as he continued, "and in particular, in his own words, Dr Hashford alluded to an event... an occurrence, rather, that, in his estimation, may not be entirely without connection to your present state," he concluded, offering a small, almost imperceptible smirk.

A sudden chill ran through her.

Dr Bathia knew! He did not have to say it more explicitly. Yet, for reasons she could not quite grasp, he had chosen not to speak of it directly to her husband.

Her mind raced with fear, but she held her expression steady, "I do not comprehend what you mean to imply by disclosing to me your own correspondence with a man I told you my own husband does not approve of!"

"Oh, I think you do, milady... You aren't without faults yourself, are you?" Dr Bathia countered. "But you may be pleased to know I do not presume myself to be in a position to pass judgment upon anyone, both you and my other patient, I mean... I merely wish to ensure the health of both you and your child."

Marianne said nothing as she waited for his verdict on her own guilt.

"Following Dr Hashford's letter, I may have come to my own conclusions on your current success," the doctor continued. "I was always convinced you and his lordship were quite unmatched, but even with Dr Hashford's... *intervention* I must stress your constitution is not one of the strongest and for such purposes, I must solicit you refrain from anything which may be too upsetting to your spirits; and it would be a shame, wouldn't it, for unnecessary strain to arise and disturb the delicate balance your household has had so far?

"It would be most unfortunate, after all, if you were to suffer undue distress because of Miss Lily's return." Dr Bathia words were gentle but edged with unmistakable meaning. "Your wellbeing, as well as hers, I believe, lies quite within your capable hands, milady."

Marianne held his gaze for a moment, her lips parting as though she wished to speak, but instead, she nodded her head in the faintest of acknowledgments.

Dr Bathia rose, smoothing his coat with an air of finality. "Now then, I trust you will take care, milady, for your health, your peace, and the harmony of all concerned."

With that, he took his leave, leaving Marianne to ponder upon the unspoken condition for his silence.

*

As soon as Dr Bathia stepped out, Marianne hurried to the drawer where she kept Henry's letters. She needed to read them again, searching for any clue as to what he might do next.

His second missive had been more comprehensive than the hurried note he had sent to her before he left India.

In it, he begged her not to presume he had run away from his obligation towards her, instead, he had considered his stay in India no longer safe for *her* wellbeing.

There was not any remorse for what had taken place between them; instead, he ventured to castigate Edmund for never appreciating her, and unlike her husband, he believed himself capable of great affection towards her.

He then disclosed he had now settled somewhere the British authorities had little or close to no jurisdiction. He had secured a very good commission at some sort of prestigious medical institution, somewhere in the Ottoman lands, confirming the Pembrokes' intelligence. It was a temporary offer at present, he wrote, but he soon hoped he may be able to receive a more secure post as a scholar in some elite university.

He plainly solicited her to abandon her husband and join him. He claimed the land to be beautiful, much like their county back in England, with hills and mountains. He supposed she would like the place as much as he had grown to like it. He did acknowledge he may not offer much in terms of name to her, but he supposed himself to now be in provision of good means to ensure all the comfort Marianne's heart could desire.

Marianne had set the letter aside at the time, unanswered, but the memory of each word lingered pungently in her mind.

She then turned to the fresh envelope she had received only that morning. Upon reading it, she understood at once Henry must have sent her this missive after his communication with Dr Bathia.

There was not much of a repeat of his declaration of his love for her, and after reproaching her for not responding to his previous letter, most of the content was dedicated to enquiring about her interesting condition. By the end of the letter, he boldly declared this child to be his, and as such, he urged her to respond to him immediately and inform him of her decision regarding his offer.

She crumpled the letter and hurled it towards the fireplace, wishing she could erase her grave error as simply as she could destroy his letters.

She had come to dread the birth of her own child; she would have never imagined such a thing not so long ago.

Evidently, Bathia appeared to like Lily very much, she then considered. Had he not just used Lily's wellbeing as a leverage for his silence? What if one of these days he told Lily her not-so-well-concealed secret?

Surely, if Edmund was to know she had conceived this child through Henry, then she would have provided Edmund with the perfect reason to finally pursue his heart's content with Lily.

She could not risk such an occurrence, she decided at last, regardless of Bathia's implicit threat.

She ought to get rid of Lily at once. She would deal with the menace Henry had become afterwards.

49.

Down in the kitchens, Mrs Jenkins would not allow Lily the inconvenience of putting together a tray of fruits and cold meat for their mistress.

"This is not your duty, my dear," she said, taking the task into her own hands. "She has taken ill, has she?" Mrs Jenkins continued, "is she well enough to come down for dinner?"

"I left when I overheard Dr Bathia say there is nothing of concern, and I thought it best to come down and get a plate for her."

"Well... since she will not be coming down for dinner, it falls on you to dine with his lordship this evening. Go back up to your room; you must look your best, I tell you!"

"I will not be joining him for dinner," Lily countered, "tonight, or any other night!"

"But, my dear, you must! His lordship has been very categorical in his instructions to the whole staff!

"My goodness, you must not know!" Mrs Jenkins then added, "I will have you know his lordship and her ladyship have not dined together since the day you became ill! And this morning he personally came to me and ordered all your favourite meals to be prepared for today's dinner! He wished it to be quite grand, I tell you," Mrs Jenkins winked at her friend.

"Surely, you don't want him to suffer any longer, and you know he won't eat unless you sit beside him... regardless of her ladyship," Mrs Jenkins added with a smile.

"Oh, Mrs Jenkins, she knows everything!" Lily cried, allowing her tears to cascade down her cheeks.

"Oh dear! I see the source of your new trouble," said Mrs Jenkins, drawing nearer to console her friend. "Of course she knows; but did she say anything to you?"

"She does not need to say anything!" Lily cried. "It is all my fault! I foolishly kept a journal!"

"I know she is our mistress, and I do feel sorry for her; but I could tell she was up to no good cooped up in your room rummaging through your personal stuff all day long!

"But it is about time, if you ask me!

"It's not your fault if his lordship chose to remain steadfast in his attachment to you! And though it may not be very kind of me to say this, I think she has only herself to blame if she could not attach her own husband to herself! Heaven knows you have done all in your power to turn him her way!"

"Lucy, that is too unkind of you to say!"

"No, it's not! I only speak the truth! You have no fault in any of this, don't let her convince you otherwise! She knew the Lord's heart belonged to you, and instead of being open about such knowledge she pretended her oblivion and has been scheming all along!"

"You are mistaken, Lucy; surely, she would have said something to me if she did indeed know of it," Lily countered. "Indeed, I cannot fault her for despising me! My only regret is the manner in which she came to find out about us – about his lordship and I, I mean… How will I be able to face her the same way from now on?!"

"Come, my dear, you are too innocent for your own good," Mrs Jenkins countered. "I guarantee you she knew of the lord's feelings towards you from the first day; why else would she let us into her house?!" she chuckled, unable to withstand Lily's tears.

"But you have nothing to fear from her, I promise you! The last time I heard his lordship speak to her, he threatened to break off their marriage if she tries to be mean to you!"

"My God! He cannot be serious!" gasped Lily.

"Oh yes, he did say so indeed!"

"He sounded pretty serious when I heard him, and I suggest you stay clear of her, until his lordship is to enact what he supposes best for you," Mrs Jenkins rejoined, appearing very pleased with life.

"She is to have his heir! Surely that must signify more than anything else… No, Lucy, I am sure you must have misunderstood him!"

"Now, off with you!" Mrs Jenkins exclaimed, turning away with an air of feigned exasperation. "You are determined to make me say more than I ought, and I shall never hear the end of it if Mr Jenkins were to learn I let my tongue run away with me, as I am too often accused of doing!" And with that she ushered Lily out of the kitchens.

*

Once dismissed, Lily proceeded to the upper floor of the house, where she waited beside Marianne's chamber for the maid to appear with the tray Mrs Jenkins would not allow her to take.

She collected the tray when it came, and taking a deep breath, she made her way to Marianne. As she entered, she noticed letters scattered beside the hearth. She put the tray down on the dressing table and attempted to pick up the crumpled letters when Marianne ordered her to leave them be.

Lily hesitated before rising, turning slowly to face her mistress.

"They are letters from Henry," Marianne said coldly, lifting herself up against the headrest. "He's always loved me. Henry could have made me happy, but in spite of knowing his feelings for me, I chose Edmund; but you knew that too, didn't you?

"We both know what happened this afternoon was entirely your fault," she continued, not requiring Lily to respond to her.

"Marianne…," Lily's voice was unsteady but pleading. "It all happened before I met you… I-I tried to put an end to it, but–"

"–But he would not allow you to leave him, is that it?!" Marianne scoffed, her lips curling into a bitter smile.

"I wished to be of use to you, Marianne," Lily continued desperately. "I considered myself at fault towards you,"

Marianne let out a harsh laugh, "you still insist upon making a fool out of me!

"You know, your illness turned out to be a blessing for me after all! With you no longer a constant presence over me, I have managed to succeed, and soon enough I will birth Edmund's child!

"I suppose the Lady Mother must have been right all along; you may be a witch after all!"

Lily stood motionless; shame and mortification laid bare on her face.

Marianne stared at her with open contempt, her eyes narrowing with hatred before she spoke again, "You are lying to yourself if you believe what he feels for you to be anything worthwhile!

"It is simply your negro flesh he desires, like other men have done before him! And you know it very well! You purposefully denied him, kept him pining after you all these years, dangling yourself in front of him whenever you felt his constancy waver towards me!"

She paused, her gaze gathering all the disdain she could summon, "but you understood this very well; isn't this precisely the reason why you gave yourself to him in the end?! I suppose you weren't too ill for it, were you?"

Lily's gaze shot up to meet Marianne's, guilt flashing through her eyes, "Marianne, I-I am terribly sorry, Marianne... I have no excuse, I know; it was wrong of me! I wronged us both and I regretted it immediately, but fear not Marianne, it will never happen again!"

"Do not bother defending yourself! With my child on the way, you must have realised whatever charms you had on him would avail you of nothing!" Marianne scoffed. "The least you can do is spare me your impudent lies and be honest for once!

"Perhaps had you not been the negro that you are I might have even acquiesced to allow him his diversions with you, but never will I allow you to be his whore right under my nose!

"But, I must ask you... what do you expect he will do next? You seem sure he would have had no scruple in choosing you over me; but what of my child?!

"Worst still... Do you hope to get yourself impregnated?!

"Do you wish for my child, the heir to the family, to share the same blood as a pretentious, monstrous bastard? Will you condemn my innocent child to the same misery you have inflicted on me?!"

Lily kept her silence, her gaze evading Marianne's.

"You say you wished to oblige me... I read your claim; you wanted to leave him for my sake when I married him, isn't that so?" Marianne continued, less fervently this time. "Well, now is your opportunity to be true to your own words! Get away from us; and I am sure once you are gone, he will in time grow to value me as the mother of his child."

"Since you have read my words, then you must know I have tried, Marianne..."

"I do not care how you manage it, but you must! Thank God Bathia assures all is well with me and my child... for now; but God knows what else may go wrong..." Marianne's words acquired a solemn tone, "surely, you do not wish to have my child or I on your conscience, do you?!"

"You have said quite enough, Marianne; please do not jest with such things," Lily protested. "You shall not suffer, Marianne; and your child too shall not suffer…" her voice was barely above a whisper.

"Will you go, never to return?"

Lily said nothing, but the firm nod of her head was enough for Marianne. Then, with a dismissive glance, she ordered Lily to leave the room, and Lily could do nothing but oblige her.

But as she reached the door, she hesitated, lingering as though there was more to be said. Yet, Marianne, with her resolute air of finality, left no room for further words. Swallowing the agonising ache rising in her chest, Lily stepped into the corridor and softly closed the door behind her.

50.

Inside the study, Edmund had summoned Mr Jenkins. This evening, he expected to receive news of a matter of grave importance.

"Where is your man?" he asked sharply.

Moments later, Mr Jenkins escorted a young, flimsy looking man who appeared to be from the royal navy. As a result of his extremely tanned complexion, had the man not been dressed like a member of the royal militia and spoken like the common Englishman, one could not be faulted for assuming he was one of those Indian men who delighted in dressing in accordance with the current fashion of their colonisers.

"Good evening, officer," Edmund began, deciding to address the man first.

"It is certainly not a good evening, I tell you! You must have a word with your man!" whined the officer, rubbing his wrist.

"I would have done nothing to you had you come with me of your own free will!" interjected Jenkins.

"Coming to the house was not part of our agreement! We agreed to meet secretly; I've seen some of my superiors come in and out of this house; and now you've dragged me all the way here! Does he not trust you enough? You could have told him yourself!" countered the man defensively.

"Come now, officer, it is quite alright! No harm done!" Edmund stepped in.

"I certainly consider myself harmed, my lord! I did not agree to this! The least you can do is pay me more!"

"Be quick man, spill it out if you don't want me to report you to the authorities for espionage myself!" Edmund said, eager to put an end to this waste of his time.

"Fine, fine, no need to resort to such threats!" the man cried. "It was quite difficult to trace the man, to tell you the truth," he started, theatrically.

"May I take a seat...," and as he sat, he continued, "as you suspected, Dr Hashford met with a fair, rich-looking lady inside a coach, on the same night our coachman went missing."

"Go on...," solicited Edmund.

"According to the coachman, the encounter between the two was so passionate he could not help but take a peek, and that's when he saw it.

"He said when he recognised the woman as Lady Hertworth he looked away, but–"

"–How did he know the man to be Dr Hashford," Edmund interrupted.

"He had driven the man to the same house several times, and that's how he came to know of the doctor's name.

"And so the next morning, he went to the doctor's place and threatened to report the affair to the husband of the lady... which he knew to be you, milord," the man added with a smirk.

"Let me deal with him, Sir, he must be trying to take advantage of the situation!" Mr Jenkins intervened, coming to hold the man by the collar.

"Fine! No need to resort to such antics!" the officer countered defensively.

"As I was saying, the coachman wanted money from our doctor, and the doctor did give good monies for his silence.

But supposedly, our greedy guy went back and asked for more until he sucked our poor doctor dry, and that's when he closed his lease at his place and ran to those bloody infidels, as you know!

"And then with Dr Hashford gone, our coachman would not sit still, and that is when he came to our good man here," the officer continued, turning his gaze towards Jenkins. "But apparently, *he* sent him off threatening to have him arrested... and we do not have the best reputation for how we treat them Indians in our cells, do we? Our poor man got scared, and he was lying low until I found him!"

As the officer concluded his narration, he locked eyes with his lordship, waiting for something.

"If you have nothing else to add, you are free to go...," Edmund said coldly. "Mr Jenkins will see you are generously remunerated for your services," he concluded, dismissing the man.

*

Alone once more, Edmund sat behind his desk, attempting to determine his next course of action.

"You didn't come to see her... What could possibly be more pressing than what Marianne endured this afternoon?" Lily's voice cut through his thoughts, startling him. She had entered unannounced, but as soon as he saw her, he set his papers aside and rose to meet her.

Ignoring her reproach, he pulled her toward him, his fingers grazing the bare skin of her arms her stoic gown did not conceal.

"Do not look so grave," he teased, noting the seriousness of her expression. "I will not do anything to you if that is what you fear... at least for now," he added, a slow smile playing on his lips. "I only wish to inspect your full recovery; you would not mind Bathia carrying out an assessment of your health, would you?! I simply wish to carry out my own assessment too!"

His gaze swept over her, admiring the rest of her figure. Her body had regained its previous splendour. Her cheeks were once again marked by the delicate golden glow he so admired, and her sickly eyes sparkled with life once again. "You are truly a wonder, I must say," he murmured, lifting her chin for her to meet his gaze. "You know, I begin to fear my mother may have been right all along; you have indeed bewitched me with these lovely eyes of yours!

"I always assumed them to be black, but they are nothing of the sort."

"My eyes are nothing but ordinary black," she countered, looking away.

"You are mistaken," he retorted, turning her face back toward him. "They are the exact colour of the night sky! I do not know what depictions poets such as you may wish to attribute to such a colour, but as I look into them now, I see the night sky encompassed in them. The kind of night one wonders at while at sea; when the moon casts its full radiance upon the water, illuminating the stars around it… does that make sense to you?!" His voice had taken an almost reverent tone, as though he had momentarily lost himself in her eyes.

But Lily refused to be swayed by his reverie.

"This matter no longer concerns what may have been between us, milord," she said, her tone measured but not unkind. "We ought to focus on what we have become instead."

A small smile appeared on her lips, "soon enough Marianne will be delivering your child... Indeed, that is something quite joyous to look forward to, don't you think?" she continued, her tender smile growing on her face.

"You are so beautiful when you smile; I want to see this same smile every morning when I wake next to you.

"–No, please, do not alter it," he then pleaded, as the smile began to fade away. "Keep smiling at me, my love," he traced the curve of her lips with his fingers.

He lingered there, contemplating whether he ought to relent from his constraints and kiss her. "No…," he then murmured, almost as if speaking to himself. He would not avail himself of the opportunity, not yet. "Your smile will have to do for now," he added several moments later, recomposing himself.

A long pause settled between them before he finally spoke again, "It is rather late. You should return to your room...

"I shall speak with you tomorrow; there are some things… I–" he hesitated, "I am referring to when you were ill... there are certain events I must discuss with you, Imbali…"

"Edmund, what is it going to take for you to care for Marianne?!" she demanded, cutting through his thoughts.

He stared at her.

"Dear God! You are still thinking of her!" he cried, growing more incredulous at Lily's loyalty to Marianne.

"She is not well, Edmund! Bathia said so himself!" Lily insisted. "You have abandoned her! I see it… she is tormented by the very man she calls her husband!"

"Today of all days, I must beg you not to speak of Marianne to me!" he responded angrily.

"But I suppose I must direct my gratitude to Marianne all the same." He then added, "Mrs Jenkins tells me you would not have dinner with me, but here you are, come to me in all your might, out of your own will for her sake!

"But you do not need to care about her, she certainly has no care for you! She almost killed you; do you realise that?"

"My illness had absolutely nothing to do with her!" she countered, receding from him.

"She may not have poisoned you directly, but I do hold her responsible all the same! You wouldn't have been scampering into the foulness of that rathole had she not brought us all the way down here in the first place!

"Enough of her!" he cut in, as Lily appeared intent at contradicting him once again. "You do not know what Marianne has been up to! Believe me she deserves no more of your sacrifice!"

"Edmund… I wish for you to be good to her, Marianne should not be upset," she managed to say.

"What of your upset?! What of you and I?" he retorted. "But have no fear," he added immediately after. "I assure you, your Marianne will not suffer for long, if that is what you care about still!"

"How can she not suffer? You threatened to leave her, and I cannot allow it!"

"I have my reasons, Imbali!" he cried, "but that is of no consequence to you at present," he continued, resuming his composure. "Bathia supposes I ought to concede time to Marianne until the child arrives, and so I shall, but to tell you the truth, she can very well keep *her* child! That will only make my predicament much more agreeable than she can imagine!"

"Edmund, you are talking of your own child… the child you and the entire family have been waiting for all these years!"

"It was all in vain! It is you; it was always you who ought to mother my children, not any other woman!" he smiled at her. "Leave Marianne and her child to me," he came to reassure her, "you and I shall marry and that is the end of this conversation, as far as you are concerned."

He then reached for the door, opening it for her, and without another word, he guided her towards the hallway and waited for her to make her way up the staircase.

There was not much else she could say after having been dismissed in such a way, but on the staircase, she turned to look at him, desperate for one final glimpse, but his door had already closed behind him.

*

In the quiet stillness of her room, she sat at her dressing table, her hands trembling as she considered how to proceed.

She must have left her curtains open earlier on, as quite suddenly, a breeze called her to the window. She went to it and gazed at the moonlight pouring in from the world outside, losing herself in the allure of its beauty; her thoughts wandering back to a time before her present.

Only at the break of dawn, as the sun began to rise over the view before her, she returned to her dressing table, took a paper out of her stock, and dipped her pen into the inkwell.

*

"So, you are going at last," Marianne's voice cut through the air, startling Lily as she left through the back doors of the kitchen.

"M-Marianne!" Lily stammered. "It is wet here… besides you ought to be in bed."

"I saw you going to him; I guessed you must have gone to give him your farewell?"

Lily lowered her gaze, "He does not know... I am leaving him to you Marianne."

"Good," Marianne acknowledged. "But if your idea of an escape is to run to the New World, I suggest you abort it immediately. We both know that is the first place he will set sail for when he realises you have gone; and we both know he will search for you! So, if you truly mean to give him up, you must go to a place where he will never find a trace of you again!" She then paused for a moment before she rejoined, "since you are so obliging to me and my future child, then I will strive to help you; I think you should go to the Ottomans!" She proclaimed, appearing satisfied with her suggestion.

"Why would you want me to go there?!" Lily did not hide her surprise.

"Because it is the only place I am convinced Edmund will have no means to trace you! But despair not; unlike you, I will not be selfish.

"I could write to Dr Hashford and let him know to expect you; he is there as you know, and I could solicit his protection for you. I am sure you will have nothing lacking!

"But I must warn you," Marianne then added, as a sudden thought came to her mind, "Henry is no weakling! Do not suppose you can trick him like you have done with Edmund! I will recommend he finds you a suitable position once you are there. Do not dare suppose you can have more than that from him!"

"I know Dr Hashford to be a kind man, but I truly cannot expect him to inconvenience himself on my account; you do not need to write to him for me," Lily responded. "I will be fine, quite on my own Marianne, thank you."

"Very well, if you put it like that…" Marianne conceded. "I am glad to see you haven't taken much with you," she then remarked, inspecting Lily's small bag. "I can provide you with enough coins for you to acquire whatever you may require once you arrive at your destination."

"I thank you, but that will not be necessary."

"Oh…! Has my husband showered you with coins as well as jewellery?"

"I-I… have never accepted any of his offerings."

"What of that necklace you wrote about? I saw it in your trunk. It is quite a noticeable piece of jewellery I must say… I read how precious it is to you; something to do with your mother, was it?" Marianne paused for a moment, "I hope you have left it behind." She then continued, "I say so for your own safety, Lily dear. It is indeed quite unsafe for a single woman, especially a negro, to be carrying such a fine thing upon herself. God forbid; the authorities may even mistake you for a thief running away from her masters!"

"You can have it, Marianne," Lily responded as she tightened her grip on the bag and turned to face the horizon ahead of her.

She would not look back.

51.

In the house, Edmund was set to confront Marianne; but first, he knew he needed to speak with Imbali. She had not come down for breakfast, and after enquiries, Mrs Jenkins informed him Lily appeared fast asleep in her bed.

He thought it best to leave her to rest, but as the hours passed, he decided he ought to assess for himself how well she fared. Following their altercation from the previous night, Lily may not be in her best spirits after all.

As he entered her room, he was rather surprised to find the thick curtains still drawn, and the room engulfed in darkness.

He looked towards her bed; the little light which came in from the hallway reflected upon a shadow; she was peacefully tucked in under the blankets.

He could not bring himself to wake her up from sleep of course, but he thought her behaviour rather odd; Lily had always been an early riser.

Better leave her be a little longer, he decided.

He made his way back to the door, but as he passed by her dressing table, he noticed a sealed envelope addressed to him.

What could possibly be the meaning of this?

He turned to look at her, overtaken by an uneasy suspicion. Upon closer examination, he noticed an oddity he had not observed at first. He advanced towards the bed, drawing back the neatly arranged covers only to discover a mere assemblage of towels, artfully contrived to deceive.

A sense of dread began to overtake him as he hastened back to the dressing table and broke the seal of the waiting letter.

'My dear Edmund,

I watched the sun overshadow the moon, and I am reminded of when it all began; of the moment fate wove our paths together, binding my destiny to yours.

But just as the sun and the moon are forever destined to trace their own orbits, meeting only in fleeting, fated moments, so too must we follow the course set before us.

I have tried, God is my witness, how ardently I have tried to defy the currents, but love, when burdened by the weight of impossibility, ceases to be love at all. It becomes an anchor, dragging us into a sorrow too heavy to bear. You set me free once, but in my freedom you began to carry the shackles, as you became bound to my unseen chains, yearning for the very thing I cannot give in return.

The colour of my existence pales beside you; against it I am but ether, weightless and fading, while you burn so brightly, so assured of your place in the world.

I can hear you whispering in the shadows of my mind, reminding me of my promise. Yes, Edmund, I did promise you, but staying beside you has become a painful mistake I must now undo.

I have never had the courage to face the consequences of our love, even as it unfolded before me, but this sacrifice is not only for you, but for something greater than us both.

You are a man bound to your obligations, and now more than ever, you must hold to your obligations and become whole with Marianne. Let this child be, where you and I could not be, let the blessing of a life so precious take over you.

I wished to say goodbye, but I must depart in a single, solitary moment, like a tide in its quiet ensemble, retreating from your shores. But as I go, I leave with the hope that this child, this new life, will teach you to love with all the passion, all the tenderness I have known you to possess. That where I could not remain, another will find the warmth of your devotion.

I will remember you always,
Imbali.'

A long while passed, yet his eyes remained fixed on the words before him, reading them over and over as they blurred into one another.

"We were so close… How could you?!" he whispered; his voice hoarse with disbelief. "You promised me… You cannot have left me… You promised!" With a shuddering breath, he sank into the chair, the very same chair Lily must have sat when she penned those devastating words.

"Is there a problem, Sir?" Mr Jenkins came to enquire.

"She cannot have left me…," he said, stirring himself from his stupor as he looked up to meet the inquisitive gaze of his loyal servant.

In the next moment, a sudden urgency overtook him. Rising abruptly from his seat, he hurried into the hallway calling out for Mrs Jenkins.

In search of clues, a full inspection of Lily's room was the first course of action to be taken. But Mrs Jenkins declared not much to be amiss from it, and as such, she believed Miss Lily could not have gone far.

However, Edmund had the promptness to carry out his own inspection of Lily's trunk.

For years he had sought to shower Lily with all sorts of precious gifts, but she never accepted anything from him.

The one occasion she had been compassionate enough to retain any of his gifts was when he had presented her with the necklace embellishing her mother's amulet. He could clearly see it, amongst her other possessions, but with one important omission.

The chain, adorned with its brilliant stones, remained intact, but the amulet itself had been carefully removed, leaving only the chain behind.

He called out for Mr Jenkins, "Take men with you! Check the port!" His command echoed throughout the house.

*

Mr Jenkins had preceded his employer to the port, and by the time Edmund joined him, he had already concluded his own enquiries. He reported a total of four ships had left the harbour in the last 24 hours. A small commercial vessel going in the direction of eastern Africa, and the other three were all sailing in the direction of England, though one of them was directed to the port of Liverpool, instead of London.

"And one of the two ships headed to London is bound for the Americas thereafter, Sir; I believe she must have been on that one!" Jenkins concluded.

"How can you be so sure?" Edmund countered.

"Because it's one of your ships, Sir; I also found out a woman befitting Miss Lily's description was seen around the port, exactly in the vicinity of that ship, in the early morning hours."

"Do not simply suppose, Jenkins; you must have the records checked!" Edmund commanded. "What of the other one, headed to East Africa, is it?"

"Oh, no way she could have been on that one! It took no passengers on board, nothing but sheep and cattle, Sir!"

"Very well," Edmund conceded, "how long will it take to know for certain which one she was on?"

"A day altogether, Sir," Jenkins obliged. "Do not trouble yourself, Sir. I'll personally check the records and set sail on the next ship and bring her back to you myself; I'll drag her by her legs, if I must, Sir."

"You shan't leave without me!" Edmund commanded, as he turned on his heels and back into the carriage.

"But your duties, Sir... surely her ladyship's situation requires you to be near her," Jenkins attempted to reason. Then, as though struck by a sudden realisation, he gasped. "My God! What a fool I am!"

Edmund spun around, "what is it?!"

"I saw her…! I was returning from the port when I saw the two of them, Miss Lily and her ladyship that is, by the back door, earlier this morning!" Mr Jenkins began hurriedly. "At first my stupid head thought nothing of it, but now I remember Miss Lily had a bag with her! They were talking; now that I come to think of it, Sir, Miss Lily had a certain look on her face! I did not like it, Sir!"

"Her ladyship may have something to do with this, Sir," Mr Jenkins pressed on, no longer able to hold his thoughts to himself. "I know it is not my place, Sir, but… you have supposed her ladyship's child to be Hashford's for a long while; I must ask, why did you allow things to come this far?"

"Because I could not accuse Marianne of infidelity based on the mere words of a coachman!"

"But the coachman was sure in his claims!" Jenkins pressed.

"I needed evidence!" Edmund snapped, turning away from Jenkins.

"But in truth," he then rejoined, his tone softening as he spoke again, "I could not fault Marianne for seeking what I would not give her elsewhere… I found myself incapable of faulting an innocent child for the conduct of his mother, no matter how grave the mother's fault may turn out to be.

"I intended to allow myself the certainty… I wished to be sure; a resemblance, an inkling, anything that may allow me to ascertain the child's resemblance for myself," he explained, but as he did, his jaw began to tighten, and his expression darkened. "But if she has dared to send Imbali away from me, then she will only have herself to blame for the consequences!"

*

So overcome was he by his anger towards Marianne, he began calling for her as soon as he stepped back into the house. "You have come to the end of your road!"

He stormed up the staircase, his voice ringing through the halls as he called her name.

Reaching Marianne's chamber, he threw the doors open with a forceful swing and strode towards her, "I do not know what you have said or done to persuade her to do your bidding, but fear not, with or without her, you are to join your beloved immediately!"

Marianne kept her gaze on the untouched plate resting on her lap, forcing a composure she did not possess. "E-Edmund… I can understand you may not be in your best spirits at present, but surely you cannot reproach me for what *she* has done!"

She lifted her eyes, adopting an air of feigned concern, "I suppose she must have understood you have an obligation to me, and our child, of course–"

"–You knew you had it coming and you sent her away from me on purpose!" he interjected, "Isn't that so, Marianne?!"

Without waiting for a response, he thrust a letter before her, "Here, read this! Can you say you have nothing to do with this?!"

Marianne took Lily's letter from his hand, skimming through the lines. When she reached the end, she carefully folded the paper and gave it back to him, her expression unmoved.

"I still fail to see how I can have anything to do with her decision... even you know this is evidently her style; not a word in there belongs to me!"

"Is it, Marianne? I suppose this is not how you have been corresponding with your lover... am I right?!" A sardonic smile appeared on his lips as his eyes locked with hers.

"I hear Hashford is relentless in his correspondence with you," he continued.

Marianne stiffened.

"N-no... w-why would you imagine such a thing?" she stammered, her composure faltering.

"You mean to deny he has written to you?" he pressed on, "I suppose I must have a word with Jenkins since he seems to be providing me with the wrong sorts of intelligence."

"I... do not deny it, of course," she admitted. "But you must have also been notified that I did not engage with the correspondence; I do not correspond with him. I have not sent a word to him since you banished him from the house."

"I see," he scorned. "Some sinister speculations have reached my ears, Marianne." He continued, "but I would like to hear it directly from your mouth all the same."

"Edmund, I... what are you implying?"

"This child is not from me, is it Marianne?!"

Marianne became pale, her countenance shaken by the startlement Edmund's words had caused. "I-I cannot breathe...," she then stammered, her trembling hands clutching at the covers before she threw them aside.

She staggered to her feet, desperate to put distance between herself and Edmund's piercing stares, but as she walked backwards, her legs faltered, and Edmund was left to witness Marianne convulsing all over. Soon after, she fell to the ground.

Dismay overtook his mind as he stood there staring at her, lifelessly still.

But it did not take him long to realise what he ought to do. He lifted her in his arms and laid her motionless body back in her bed and immediately cried for aid from the rest of the household.

*

There was not much else for Edmund to do once Dr Bathia, alongside several maids, were all upon Marianne. He left the room only to notice his shirt stained with blood – blood from Marianne.

The dreadful wait to receive news, any news, proved to be rather unbearable for his nerves. He had several times attempted to grant himself access back into Marianne's chamber, only to be told nothing was certain in his wife's current state.

"Her ladyship has lost a considerable amount of blood... but the child is resilient, in fact, it appears determined to hold on to life," Dr Bathia said quite warmly to him.

"This is all my fault! I should have held my tongue!"

"I would not be quite so severe upon myself, my lord, if I were you;" the doctor offered.

"Is it not too soon for the child to be arriving?!"

"This is not about the child... I am afraid to say, incidents such as these are highly probable considering her ladyship's frail constitution. I am sorry, but this outcome was to be expected."

"Marianne is anything but frail I tell you! I find your suppositions preposterous," Edmund countered. "Surely, there must be something you can do for her!"

"Her ladyship may strike as positively robust in appearance; but sadly, her internal constitution is not as blessed as she is on the outside."

"What do you suggest I do?!"

"There is really not much any of us can do at present, milord... this is purely out of our hands.

"But you may go to her whenever you wish to do so. However, I can only presume a grave matter must have upset her ladyship, and as such, I must urge you to avoid any topic which may upset her serenity for the time being."

52.

Edmund could not bring himself to face Marianne; but Dr Bathia had remained a constant presence around her ladyship. On the third day of his stay, however, the doctor came to personally solicit for his lordship to visit Marianne's bedside.

He did not need to say much, as the exchange their eyes had was enough for Edmund to understand he could no longer delay this duty to Marianne.

A faint scent of lavender lingered in the air as Edmund stepped into the room, but it did little to mask the metallic tang of blood. A basin of reddened water sat on a small table nearby.

"How are you faring?" he said, approaching her.

Beside Marianne, two nurses were each absorbed in attending to her. One meticulously dabbed at her forehead, and the other was busy with a bloodstained cloth, which she rinsed in the basin on the table beside her.

Edmund, careful not to disturb them, took his place on the other side of the bed.

"I am sorry I did not offer a better consideration to your state, Marianne...," he sat beside her on the bed as she opened her eyes for him. "It may not mean much at present; I was angry with you, Marianne, but never once I wished for any harm to come to you or this child."

"I am quite familiar with the consequences of your anger, Edmund..." she responded, smiling at him. "I must admit it has not always brought adverse consequences to me. Had it not been for your anger towards Lily the night after Glenith tried to force himself upon her, you and I would have never married. I was very grateful for your rage that night, Edmund."

She hesitated for a moment before reaching for his hand, and he willingly offered it.

"I will not claim to know what would have been... but of one thing I am sure, Marianne; I have always considered myself indebted to you. Perhaps had I not involved you in my own... faults, I suppose you may have been in a much happier life; perhaps you and Hashford would have married and settled down and had a child whom you would not need to keep from his father."

"Edmund, please…," Marianne said, tightening her grip on his hand. "I will not be unfair to your intelligence. I admit, I did incur a brief moment of misjudgement, but whatever it was I shared with Henry did not signify anything to me." A visible sense of dread was overtaking her once more, "but I wished for my child to be none but yours!"

"Please, do not strain yourself, Marianne" he urged, as his eyes met the attentive scrutiny of one of the nurses. "All I wish for at this moment is for you to rally your strengths. When you are in good health once again, we will talk, only then Marianne, not now."

Silence fell between them, heavy as each became absorbed in their unspoken thoughts. At last, Marianne spoke again, her voice weak, but certain.

"I heard Henry claim to you that he has loved me…," she paused for a moment, seeking his gaze, "but I have come to realise what he wished to offer me is not what I have come to regard love to be. I have witnessed how a man ought to love a woman from you, Edmund. You have never wavered in your steadfast dedication to her; no matter what the world may have decided to put in your way.

"Henry has never looked at me the same way I have seen you look at her." She then continued, "I did envy her, that was an undeniable truth for a long time; but in time, as I grew more familiar with her, I understood it was not Lily per se I envied, but rather the feelings I know you both had for one another…" she paused for a brief moment, "she loves you in return...very much."

Edmund raised an interrogative brow.

"She has kept a diary for all these years. I read it... word for word, all that occurred between the two of you. I read an endless account of how she too reciprocated your attachment… it is in my trunk, Edmund," Marianne revealed. "I kept it from her, please return it to her for me."

"You will return it to her yourself, Marianne," he responded, though he sounded less sure than he wished to be.

"I was destined to be the villain of your story." Marianne then rejoined, "you and I both have our faults in our conduct towards her, but I more than you. Lily was too good to suppose anything beyond what I wished for her to see," she pressed on. "I have always known it, Edmund; I heard you that night at my uncle's house; how you felt about her… I befriended her, cared for her, I made her love me all because I wanted you; only she could make you be mine," she offered him a smile as she struggled to keep her eyes on him. "Edmund…I know I will not make it... you must make amends with her, for my sake too."

"Do not speak so Marianne, you are not dying! You will not die, isn't that so?" Edmund solicited, seeking reassurance from the nurse. He then turned back to Marianne, who had already closed her eyes again, evidently to find some respite from her painful distress.

"I sent her away…," Marianne spoke again, her eyes remained closed, and her words came out so softly he could barely hear her.

"I have done Lily wrong, grave wrong to you both… I-I don't know if she did… but I told her to go to Henry," she strenuously forced herself to continue. "You must give me hope, Edmund, God may not castigate me so severely if I know she will be with you…"

"Marianne, what do you mean you sent her to Henry? What–"

"–Please, Milord, her ladyship must preserve her strengths," the second nurse solicited, noticing a change in Marianne's state.

This same nurse then rushed to call for Bathia, and as the doctor came beside Marianne, Edmund was ushered back out of the room.

*

Marianne had been pushing relentlessly; for how long, she did not know. But as she began to feel her last spates of strength fading away, she heard the frail cry of her child filling up the room.

"She lives!" the doctor announced. "You did it, milady!" Bathia said to Marianne, while his nurses were engaged with the continuous flow of blood which appeared to have no end in sight.

The cry of the child grew in vigour, and Edmund returned to the room. For a moment he glanced at the child Bathia had ventured to put in his arms, before his eyes came to meet Marianne's.

"She shall be Lily…," Marianne murmured. "Promise me you will make Lily look after her, regardless of who has fathered her…"

"Marianne, it is done!" Edmund cried, "all you must do now is gather your strength! Your beautiful daughter will be waiting for you when you wake up!"

"Let Imbali hold my Lily…," Marianne whispered, before breathing her last.

53.

A commotion taking place downstairs stirred Edmund's attention away from Marianne.

He could not hear much, but he could clearly distinguish Jenkins' altercation with another familiar voice.

In the next moment, Henry himself burst into Marianne's room, "You did this to her!" Hashford yelled, throwing himself upon Marianne's lifeless body. "You sent her to her death!"

"Marianne... she... her body was not meant to endure this," Edmund said, his voice hollow, each word coming out as if he were speaking through a fog in his mind.

"You lie!" Hashford retaliated, "she was perfectly capable!"

"Bathia said so himself…," Edmund continued; his words were quiet, a fragile echo of the truth he himself clung to.

"Is her death what you wished to see for yourself?!" He then snapped, his trance giving way to the anger he had buried. "You failed to think of her when she needed you most! How do you suppose you could now appear in front of her?!"

"I came here to protect her from you!"

"Can you protect yourself, let alone Marianne, from me?!"

"I will not justify myself to you, Hertworth! Do what you must!"

"You may be surprised to hear me speak so," Edmund countered, "but I did not care much for your affront to me while Marianne was alive; had you been patient a little longer I would have brought her to you myself!"

"Spare me your condescension, Hertworth! You have never cared for anyone but yourself! You are the last person who can accuse me of wrongdoing!"

"You ought to know she died fully indifferent to you," Edmund said scornfully. "Had you truly cared for her the way a man ought to care for his woman, then you should have stayed behind and not allowed her to deal with your mess all on her own!"

"I have cared for nothing but Marianne! And this child is mine, Hertworth! Mine!"

Edmund did not react as Hashford expected him to, there was no outrage, just a cold, piercing stare at the man.

"Believe me when I tell you," Edmund leaned forward ever so slightly, "my strongest wish is for this child to be none but yours; it will then be my immense pleasure to settle more than one score with you!"

"Enough, you two!" Mrs Jenkins commanded, her sharp tone silencing the heated exchange between the two men. "Show the dead the respect owed to her; stop quarrelling over her like that!" Addressing his lordship directly, she then added, "we must take her out of this room and ensure an appropriate burial is set for her. Are we to bury her here, milord?"

Edmund turned to look at Marianne's still form, the reality of her death pressing down on him once more. Then, suddenly, a thought struck him. His eyes darted around the room.

"Where is the child?" he asked.

"Do not worry yourself, milord, the babe is well taken care of," Mrs Jenkins assured him.

"Please forgive me if I speak out of place," she then continued, "but was I right in understanding her ladyship had wished for this child to be named Lily? Did she wish for our Miss Lily to look after her child?"

"I do not know what she wished for!" Edmund snapped, exasperated. He turned away from the lifeless figure on the bed, running a hand through his dishevelled hair.

"Perhaps she trusted Miss Lily would know, my lord," Mrs Jenkins offered.

Edmund scoffed, his expression hardening. "She left us! Just as she always intended. And now, in death, Marianne thought it fit to place her trust in a woman who abandoned me without a second thought!"

From the other side of the bed, Henry, still kneeling, finally lifted his head, "Hertworth, I will not let you keep her body; you kept her from me in life, but in death, let me have her."

A sudden knock at the door interrupted them.

Mr Jenkins entered, his face looking very anxious, though he turned grave the moment he looked towards the bed.

"I am sorry to intrude like this, Sir, but I have just received news; news of Miss Lily… she has gone off to them bloody Ottomans too, Sir…"

Edmund's eyes darted to Henry, "has she been corresponding with him too?!"

"I never came across any of his letters addressed to her, Sir… they were always for her ladyship," Mr Jenkins took his hat off and pressed it to his chest. "I still do not know how Miss Lily managed it, Sir, but I don't think the doctor was involved.

"She boarded that vessel in the company of them animals instead of a regular ship with people, Sir; this is why we could not find any records of her in the books."

"But I thought you said that boat was heading somewhere else entirely!"

"And it did, but it is them Turks who own it, and I have just discovered she stayed on it until she was seen disembarking on their shores–"

"–You have the audacity to reproach me for my misdoings; when all along you have kept Miss Lily at your side for your own pleasure!" Henry cut in, his voice sharp with accusation.

"Careful, Hashford!" Edmund's eyes darkened. "I no longer hold Marianne accountable for what role she may have played in this scheme of yours, but you ought to know, I will kill you with my own two hands if I find out any harm has come to her through you!

"Tell me what you know! Marianne said she sent her to you!"

"I despise you, that is for sure; but I would never wish any harm upon Miss Lily, no matter how connected she may be to you!"

"Have you now decided to direct your attentions elsewhere, Hashford?!" Edmund's jaw tightened as he proceeded to close the distance between them.

Henry stood, meeting him eye to eye, "Believe what you will, Hertworth, but I am not your enemy in this." He drew a breath, his voice becoming more sombre. "It seems we are not so different after all... we both stand here as men who failed the women we wished to protect."

At these words, Edmund's shoulders loosened, the weight of what was said sinking in.

"You let your precious Miss Lily slip out of your hands, and I know you will try to find her...," Henry paused to look back at Marianne. "I am familiar with where she has gone off to, and I wish to take Marianne with me in the same direction."

"Bury her in foreign lands?!" Edmund countered, "you must be out of your mind!"

Henry's gaze did not waver from Marianne, "England holds no claim on me now... not without her." He drew in a slow, trembling breath. "Let me keep her body... and bury her beside me."

For a long, tense moment, both men studied one another in silence.

At last Edmund spoke, "Sorry, Hashford, but Marianne goes home with me. She is to rest according to the position she held while alive, amongst the family, in the Hertworth's burial grounds.

"And, I do not need your help in finding *her*." He then continued, "but you are quite welcome to come along and disembark at my stop in your Ottoman lands, before we head off to England."

Henry said nothing. He merely stepped back to his place beside the bed, his fingers grazing the fabric of Marianne's sleeve, slowly, reverently, as though committing the feel of it to memory.

Edmund for his part turned to address Mr Jenkins.

"Help Dr Hashford with all that is required... I am sure he would wish to do this much for Marianne."

Jenkins did not understand, "I am sorry, Sir... but what exactly am I to do?"

"Marianne's body will need to be appropriately prepared before her coffin is taken aboard with us," he clarified. "Once that is done, we leave at first light, on his course."

54.

On the fifth day of Marianne's passing, after nine months of being anchored on the shores of India, the Odysseus Britannica set sail once again.

Halfway through their journey north, Edmund stood on the top deck, gazing across the vastness of the ocean, so deep in thought he did not hear Mrs Jenkins approach.

"You are yet to settle on a name, milord," she said, as she placed the child in his arms.

Startled, he accepted the little bundle. As he looked at her, her eyes opened, and they sparkled at him.

It was rather difficult to discern for sure the tint, or rather the explosion of tints, in those innocent eyes. It appeared to him as if shades of winterly greys, surrounded by the warm hazel of solid oaks, had contested and then found their perfect synchrony in them.

"She resembles her mother in appearance, doesn't she?" Mrs Jenkins observed, rousing him from his own inspection.

At that moment, Henry appeared, walking towards them.

"Marianne wished for her name to be Lily," Edmund spoke solemnly, ensuring Hashford too would hear him.

"Very well, I am glad you approve of it too, my lord," Mrs Jenkins smiled, taking the child back in her arms.

"Was this Marianne's, or is it your wish, Hertworth?" Henry said, coming to take the little girl to himself.

"She is to remain with us... in spite of what others may think," Edmund continued, ignoring Henry's comment, and addressing Mrs Jenkins once again.

"You took Marianne from me; why should I allow you to keep her child?"

"Make no mistake, Hashford, nothing would please me more than to be rid of you for good...," Edmund countered. "But with Marianne's passing, I am no longer inclined to seek any settlement of scores with you. It is enough for me to know you will have your own conscience to battle with for the rest of your life!

"It is no secret I was not the most cordial to her in the days before she passed," Edmund continued, "I should have been more measured in my judgement of her shortcomings... but I could not. And for that I cannot help but blame myself! And because of this guilt of mine, this reason only, Hashford, I will raise your bastard as my own! If nothing else, I owe her this; to raise her child as she would have wished."

"Do not presume I need your charity, Hertworth! She may very well be yours too, and I have no wish to keep anything which may be remotely connected to you," he countered, sending another quick look at the child.

"Shame on you both!" Mrs Jenkins cried, taking the child back in her arms. "I am sorry to speak to you in such a way, milord, but this poor, faultless, child should not have to suffer, and I am sure if Miss Lily was here, she would not allow either of you to speak so!"

"It will be a consolation to know that Miss Lily, at least will do right by her then," Henry said.

*

The Ottoman authorities were quite swift in granting the Hertworth vessel unconditional permission to anchor at their harbour.

At first glance, the port seemed unremarkable when compared to all the other ports Edmund had de-anchored throughout his many travels, but the people gathered around it were of a rather interesting stock.

He had expected to find mostly Turks, but to his surprise, they were few in number. The harbour was lively with so many people from different nations who must have deemed it safe and indeed profitable to come here.

As the ship dropped the anchor, he braced himself for a long search, expecting to scour every corner for her; or even worse, to resort to Hashford's aid in finding her. Yet, it did not take long for his gaze to catch sight of her.

Amid the bustle, she had already begun making her way towards him. Her eyes met his even before his feet touched steadier grounds.

He would have run to her, but caution demanded he paced himself. And as he approached her, she then decided to keep herself at a distance; not very far from him, but far enough still.

"Why have you come?" she began.

Edmund could not believe his ears. Four entire weeks she had been away from him, and this is how she chose to welcome him?!

"It seems you were expecting me," he heard his own voice responding prickly to her.

"News of upcoming vessels travels rather fast around here," she responded.

He began to examine her.

She looked well.

She no longer wore her usual head cap. Instead, a gentle veil now concealed the thick waves of her hair.

The glow upon her cheeks had been rendered even more golden; the sun of these shores agreed rather well with her dark complexion.

The attire she wore concealed much of her silhouette, but Edmund could not fail to notice a rather interesting fullness her body seemed to have acquired. And this fullness only added to make her fastidiously appealing to him, even at that particular moment.

How did she manage to keep herself thus well kept, he then wondered. Had she found herself a new patronage amongst the locals?

"Why are you covered up in such a way?" he asked, taking a step closer.

"I am rather comfortable like this," she replied, stopping him.

"For God's sake, Imbali! I have chased after you across all the seas, enduring troubles you cannot imagine, and this is the grand welcome I get from you?!"

"I am sorry my reception is not what you may have expected it to be, but it cannot be helped."

"I see you have grown in confidence! I wonder where such confidence stems from, but it is of no consequence! Do you suppose this attitude of yours should suffice to be rid of me this time?!"

"Milord, you mustn't make this much harder than it already is! I am indeed very sorry for the troubles you must have had to endure on my behalf; but I wish you to know I have found my place in the world; I am content here."

"How have you been keeping yourself?"

"I have found myself an occupation."

"Are you mocking me?!"

"N-no, I am not," she responded hesitantly. "I have been teaching… children."

He looked into her eyes. They possessed a firm resolution he had yet to witness in any of her previous resistances.

He did not like it.

"You and I may have our history of bickering like this, but I assure you, this occasion does not in any way equal all the other occasions you have tried to push me away from you!" he said, as he came closer still.

"P-please don't come near me!" she protested. "Edmund, you cannot do this publicly!" she commanded, turning away from him.

"Your memory has been my only constant, torturous companion since the day you left! You cannot ask me to stay away from you!"

"This is all very wrong! I implored you to let me go! You were supposed to remain with Marianne, but here you are demonstrating an utter lack of consideration, and even worse, lack of judgment for where you are... where I intend to remain, I must add!"

"Marianne is dead!"

His words froze her in place and the ground seemed to shift beneath her feet.

The sounds of the harbour; the distant cries of gulls, the shouts of dockworkers and the rhythmic creak of mooring ropes all faded into a muffled hum. Her hand found the edge of a weathered crate stacked along the pier; her fingers curled tightly around the splintered wood.

She stared at him stunned; her lips parted, but no sound came.

"Marianne is no more...," Edmund softened.

Seconds stretched into what felt like an eternity before she managed to whisper, "No... I don't believe it... How-how can that be? When?!"

"In childbirth."

Her knees buckled, and she gripped the crate harder; the brine scented air sickening her; but she forced herself to focus, "The child... what of her child?"

"The child lives," Edmund's voice was subdued, "she named her after you… and entrusted her to your care."

Imbali blinked, the meaning of his words struggling to break through the confusion in her mind. She repeated numbly, as if testing the weight of it, "Entrusted… to me?"

Another long silence stretched between them, before she asked, "Why…, why to me? Where is she, the child?!" she then panicked.

"She is safe on the ship, with Mrs Jenkins… waiting for you."

Edmund's gaze darkened before he spoke again, "You may also like to know her child may very well be Hashford's; your precious Marianne was not as dedicated to her marriage as you believed her to be."

Lily's hand slipped from the crate. Slowly, she stumbled toward a nearby bench, the rough wood biting into her palm as she sank onto it.

For a long moment, she stared at the ground beneath her feet. The sudden chime of a ship's bell echoed across the port, finally rousing her from her thoughts. She turned to him.

"What of your dedication?!" her voice shook, accusing him. "You too had your shortcomings in your loyalty to her, and I collaborated with you in that!

"What if *we*, you and I, sent Marianne to an early death?!"

"You are being ridiculous! Marianne's death will always remain my deepest regret in all that has come to pass between you and I, Imbali," he countered. "But if you are to fault someone, then the fault is mine, mine only to bear; it has absolutely nothing to do with you!" He came to sit beside her.

"I, too, am at fault, Edmund! I should not have acquiesced to... to what took place between us!" she began to sob.

"I thought you had forgotten… or wished to forget!" he said, astonished. "I have despised myself every day since! You were unwell, I should have been stronger, more honourable...

I wished to speak of it to you afterwards, but then you came, and cared only for Marianne again–"

"–I recollect my conduct very well," she cut in, her voice trembling from her tears, "… every moment of it! *I* have committed a grave sin, and as always, for every sin, there is a price to be paid! But I ought to pay the price, not Marianne! I should be the one to suffer for it, not her!"

"You have done nothing to reproach yourself with," he moved towards her on the bench, wishing to console her. "Marianne's constitution could not withstand the pains of childbirth, Imbali, Bathia said so himself; her previous complications were also because of it."

"I am with child…" she then whispered, her voice so low he barely heard her. His eyes fell to her stomach, then back to her face, searching for confirmation.

"Say it again…," he pleaded.

"I carry our sin in me…"

"You have been carrying *my* child, and you intended to keep it a secret from me?!"

"What else would you have had me do?"

"You should have told me!"

"How was I to tell you?! I had no idea myself! I had no idea what was happening to me! It was only after several weeks I understood… I did not leave simply because Marianne wished it of me; I could not risk exposure; I was too afraid."

"Afraid of what?!"

"I remember how your mother reacted when she merely suspected I might be with child. 'A deformed bastard,' she called it!" Imbali reminded him, her hands instinctively cradling the life stirring within her. "If your own mother would think of it as a deformity, what would the rest of your society think?

"And… what of Marianne?! I cannot–"

"–am I correct in understanding you honestly supposed I would allow you to keep yourself and my child away from me?!" he interjected.

"I-I did… I do" her voice trembled. "Indeed, it will be the best outcome for everyone."

"When will you understand your place is right beside me?

"I love you, Imbali, you know very well I do. And today, right here, what you have given me is much more than I could possibly wish for from providence at this moment.

"You have offered me the best gift life could have offered to me, far more than I deserve!"

"B-but Edmund this child will be different... how will you be able to love him knowing everyone around you will despise him for what he is!"

He reached for her, his fingers meeting hers. "I will love him! You have no idea how much I believe myself capable of loving a child from you! And no one, not even my mother, will take away the happiness I feel knowing you, and only you, are to be the mother of my child. Of all our children," Edmund concluded.

End of Book One

Acknowledgments

I am very positive without my endlessly patient husband this book would likely never have reached completion. From reading my earliest drafts to offering me advice on the cover, and even tolerating my late-night typing, his support was constant and invaluable.

My wonderful daughter shared this journey with me from beginning to end, and my two boys, whose generous ideas and candid, often unsolicited, critiques kept me on my toes — thank you for being part of this adventure.

To my kind-hearted sister and to the rest of my family, I owe a debt of gratitude for the strength of your faith in me.

I am also very grateful to my editor, who became far more than just an editor, and to my special friend Aisha, whose wisdom and warmth guided me every step of the way.

Printed in Dunstable, United Kingdom